Taking
Jezebel

PATRICK KELLY

TABLE OF CONTENTS

ACKNOWLEDGMENT

Changes
Words and Music by David Bowie
© 1971 (Renewed 1999) EMI MUSIC PUBLISHING LTD., TINTORETTO
MUSIC and CHRYSALIS MUSIC LTD.
All Rights for EMI MUSIC PUBLISHING LTD. Controlled and Administered by
SCREEN GEMS-EMI MUSIC INC.
All Rights for TINTORETTO MUSIC Administered by RZO MUSIC
All Rights for CHRYSALIS MUSIC LTD. Administered by CHRYSALIS MUSIC
GROUP INC., A BMG CHRYSALIS COMPANY
All Rights Reserved   International Copyright Secured   Used by Permission
Reprinted by Permission of Hal Leonard Corporation

PART ONE: THE BEAUTIFUL SNAKE

The Scitalis is a snake whose skin shines with such variety of colors and symbols that, by these marks, it slows down any who glance upon it. It creeps across its terrain and cannot pursue its prey with speed, so instead it stupefies with its marvelous appearance. In this way, it can stun and capture its enemy.

—Isidore of Seville

In all chaos there is a cosmos, in all disorder a secret order.

—Carl Jung

CHAPTER I

A red truck tore at the pavement across I-10, barreling away at 94 miles per hour, moving out of Tucson and curving northwest, headed for the good ol' sun-shining Golden State of California. With nary a bump nor whistle—and barely a strain under its hood, despite the 180,000 miles of reckless freeway the pickup had already seen in its lifetime—it blazed along its course, a flaming flick of crimson shooting out across the night, almost floating above the dust its wheels kicked up, fighting forward in the trail of the beacon cast by its fluorescent floodlights.

If the terrain fought against the glimmer of rusted metal darting across its long-weathered length of gravel and sand, the driver didn't notice; he smoked his cigarette and bopped his head along to the crooning of David Bowie—*turn and face the strange! ch-ch-changes!*—oblivious to the faith and strain of his tireless machine, zoning to the music while he nibbled at a sweet bun, stripped from where it sat long-crusted to its cellophane wrapper, sugar-glued to the side of the instrument panel. He looked up, regarding himself in the rearview mirror: a harsh sweep of sweat-crusted ginger hair cutting across his sleepless blue-ringed eyes, covering up murky brown gems of restlessness. His left hand lay at rest atop the wheel, patting out the rhythm of the tune; his cigarette rested comfortably in the groove of his index and middle fingers.

The sweet bun was gone, devoured, and he flicked the remnants of his smoke out the window, watching in the rearview as it struck the pavement with a momentary orange flash. He lit another one and transferred it to his left hand, freeing the right to float over and find its way into a warm, comforting nest between the denim shorts and left thigh of his passenger. Plucking away at a hole in the fabric covering her lovely upper leg, he admired her downy waves, floating on the wind of the cab's cracked windows and mixing with shreds of the smoke his cigarette cast across her slumbering face. He wondered how long that spell of serenity would last.

As they bolted toward the Pacific, the bleakness of the midnight highway succumbed to the first signs of morning—the rolling hills of dirt and dust beginning to disappear. The orange cliffsides—mimicking the faces of wild men, whose whiskers were the stems and leaves of desert broom—dissolved away with the nighttime clouds, replaced by fresh-born rays of sun bouncing gold off the last smooth stretches of the plainlands. They sped past fading flickers of beargrass and cactus: reminders that they weren't home free, not quite yet.

Almost out of Arizona, the driver thought. *Wild Arizona. Wildly boring.*

They were almost to the real, urban wild of a proper city. Los Angeles, or close enough.

He traced the shape of his passenger's leg again, and felt the smoothness of her thigh, first emerging from the denim tunnel of her cutoff shorts, then dissolving into the crepiness of bare knee, a taut mass of tendon and bone. A flutter of something sweet and drowsy came over him, beginning in his *biscuits* (a word she used while scratching him in bed at night, it described that perfect union of ass cheek and hamstring—also known as the gluteal fold, it was so sweet when scratched, and remembering its name brought back memories sweeter still). The shudder worked its way farther up, toward his groin, where it settled into a solid erection.

"Quit frisking me, you little rapist. Watch the road." She'd bolted awake, glaring at him through the wild curtain of her hair. She moved his right hand off of her leg and mumbled under her breath, "Pig…"

His cheeks flushed with red, but he hid it well, taking a long drag of his cigarette, its ring of fire racing for the filter. The plume of smoke he exhaled rose to mask an embarrassed smirk.

"Sorry, Mare," he said. "I'm glad you're up. We're almost to the border."

"La de da!" She yawned.

"Come on…get the camera out."

Meredith obeyed, hefting her heavy purse up from the cluttered passenger side floor. Rifling through it with a fanfare of sighs, she retrieved and tossed their flipcam out onto the console between them. The threadbare LED display of the dashboard was just dimming in response to the sun, which freshly rose and cast its infant rays across their weary faces—hers far wearier than his.

"Thanks," he said, clicking the camera on and directing its lens toward Meredith. "Say hello, Mare. World, whoever's watching: this here's the most beautiful woman, *in the world*. And this—" He tilted the camera toward her denim-covered crotch again. "This is where our baby's hanging out. Hey, maybe you're watching this twenty years from now, kiddo—"

"Cut it out, Peter!" she interrupted, snatching the camera out of his hands. She clicked it off and threw it back into her purse. Puckering her lips while she parted her hair, she raked her nails through to the scalp, revealing a few inches of soil-dark roots peeking out from the bowels of her bleach-blond hair. She gathered the strands back into a bun and skewered them through with the quick stab of a pencil from the glove box and crossed her arms, slumped back into her seat, reflecting for a moment on their surroundings, watching as the highway they traversed regained some of its structural sensibilities—little vestiges of modernity creeping back onto the desolate roadside. A billboard on the right (**KOA Campgrounds, 3 miles— Just Past Arizona**), a parking lot full of semis flying by on the left (a flash of some scantily-clad lizard lot waltzing between rows of trucks, leopard-print skirt rising up her sides), more and more cars (kids in a minivan smooshing their faces against the windows). All those were indications that they'd made it through the long stretch of wild night—the dusty, lonesome terrain—and had entered back upon the real world, full of sound and tumult. As they passed under an overpass, Meredith fetched the flipcam from her bag again and directed its lens at Peter. She said, "World, son or daughter, whoever's watching this *pointless* video, here's the face of the pig I just caught fondling me in my sleep…"

"I said I'm *sorry*! What more do you want?" He paused to take another drag of his smoke, and turned the radio down. "Also, what a message to send our kid, Mare…" He gritted his teeth and resisted the temptation to scream at her, remembering the promise they'd made before they hit the road. "Hey, here comes the sign. Don't miss it, okay?"

"Yeah, o-*kay*." She rolled her eyes, whining, "I just wanted the world to know who you really are. Y'know, in case I end up dead at the bottom of a roadside dumpster or something." She smiled devilishly, stuck her tongue out, and panned the camera off to the right in a quick arc, just in time as the sign roared by:

WELCOME TO CALIFORNIA

ENTERING PACIFIC TIME

Beneath the words was an illustration, of three white flowers in full bloom, their petals curved against one another in sisterly affection. They looked soft, supple, yonic. The imagery brought back that familiar flutter to his biscuits and groin. He glanced at Meredith with a deviant's sly eyes, scanning her smooth thighs, tracing them up and past the gentle dome of her growing belly. Their eyes locked; she'd caught him. Instead of anger lurking there, alongside the restlessness, Meredith's blue eyes twinkled—as clear, as bright as the sky on the first day of spring, sprawled out for a picnic—with what Peter thought was love. Then she looked away, gazing back out her window, the sunrise haloed behind her mess of sleep-ruffled hair.

They'd crossed the terrain, she'd caught it on film, and now (again) she slumped far back into her chair, moving her hair to hide her face and cradling her still-small paunch. He imagined she was doing what she always did, lately—when they weren't fighting—thinking up names for Him or Her.

Janie? she'd say.

No, sounds too much like an old lady.

Janet? she'd ask.

Even worse!

"Hey, Mare. Earth to Mare! You okay?" He snapped his fingers beside her ear. "You zoned out there for a minute, mumbling to yourself."

"Thanks. I'm fine." She rolled her eyes again and withdrew, ready to continue in her reverie, granola bar wrapper peeled open, noshing on it with her head tilted back and cheeks taut.

Peter fumbled for another cigarette and watched her stretch her neck, folding her chin against the slope of her upper chest, ignoring him.

Outside, as full dawn approached, the ochre sand took on a sunny, saturated

5

hue. Peter admired the landscape he so often took for granted. He'd come to Arizona on a whim, to get away from the city, and had initially regarded its plateaus and badlands with high esteem; he was consistently shocked and inspired by the stern beauty of the desert, especially the way the sun dissolved at dusk and dawn, melting into the sand, their colors commingling, making it impossible to discern where one ended and one began.

"How much farther to the beach?" she asked.

"Just a couple hours. Hope you packed your white t-shirt."

A grin stretched across his face and he winked, a gesture she seemed not to appreciate; she rolled her eyes and readjusted the shaggy burqa of hair hiding her face so that only her mouth was visible. It was a full mouth, and was one of the things about Meredith that he'd first fallen in love with. Kissing them felt good, too, but he could settle on staring.

That tingle again.

She forced a grin of her own, crumbles of oat and flax peeking out through the fleshy curve of her mouth.

Despite the crumbs and the sleep-addled hair—or perhaps because of them— Peter thought she looked *pretty damn cute.*

"So," he said, drawing out the *Ooooooo,* a sure-fire sign that he was about to issue a pretty absurd proposal. "Are you up for sleeping on the beach again?"

She laughed, waiting for him to do the same. When he didn't, she said, "No, Peter, not really."

"Why not?"

"That was ages ago. And I'm pregnant, remember?"

"So?"

"Just, no. Let's find a hotel *near* the beach when we get there. Then *you* can sleep on the sand all you want." She arched her back, the fabric of her shirt straining against the growing weight of her breasts, hands reaching for the roof of the cabin. She tickled the pilled interior lining before she let her arms collapse back into the comfort of her lap. "We should have booked one before we left. Why didn't we do that? They have websites for that these days."

"I know. Sorry."

"When we get there, I need a nap. I'm still *so* goddamn tired." She rubbed at her eyes. "I shouldn't have taken all those sleeping pills."

He regarded her soundlessly, nodding, and tossed a fresh cigarette up to his mouth. It was the last of the pack and was coated in corn syrup from the residue of the sweet bun, but it would have to do. He lit it up and drew in a syrupy breath, filling his lungs and holding it there a while, hoping for a nicotine kick to carry him through the last stretch of their journey (and to nullify whatever close-call arguments they might still have left between them).

No use talking to her while she's so groggy, he thought. *For all I care, she can crawl back down that well of hers.* He chuckled.

She looked over at him with a single, raised *What's so funny?* eyebrow.

"Put that out, Peter. Now." She swatted the smoke away from her face with one hand and covered her mouth with the palm of her other, pinching shut her nostrils. Mumbling, she asked, "Don't you think you've had enough?" and made that signature gesture of hers—where she pointed with her chin; another thing he loved about her.

He looked down at the mound of butts, crumbled into a soggy mountain at the bottom of his soda cup. In went his just-lit smoke; it sizzled out.

Rest In Peace, Vices.

"Sorry," he said, with a noncommittal sigh, and watched her finally finish her snack. She licked her lips and fingers before she began a new search across their cramped quarters, rummaging about with deft focus, with the soaring, agile hands of a pianist, mid-concerto.

She groaned, huffed.

"Thirsty?" he asked, snickering as he offered her the soda cup.

"Not *that* thirsty, you jerk. You're just *so* good at annoying the shit out of me, Peter, you know that?" She finally found a bottle of water lodged in the abyss of her day bag. She dredged it out, took a swig, and turned to face away from him again, exposing the back of her sleepy head. The hair at the crown of her skull had been flattened by her nap; it had morphed to form a sloping plateau of yellow and ore, and it mirrored the glowing patina of gold outside—of the sunrise beaming 'round her head. "Not that it's very hard for you. It must come naturally."

Traffic was starting to pick up, along with her crotchety mood, and Peter wasn't much prepared for either. L.A. rush hour was hard enough to handle.

Harder still with a gut full of soda and sweet bun, not to mention a pregnant, angry wife in tow.

He distracted himself from the growing pressure of urine swelling against his bladder by picturing the relaxation he hoped awaited them:

a picturesque seashore, dotted with palm trees;

Meredith wearing the gift he'd ordered for her;

her face shadowed by the wide brim of a straw hat.

"We'll both feel better once we've checked into a hotel," he said. "We can finally unwind."

He patted her on the leg, but she slid his hand away.

"Nothing too expensive, but not a dump," she said. "If we have to question whether or not they have bed bugs, we *aren't* sleeping there."

The pastoral sound of gentle waves, he told himself, *flirting with the soles of our feet.*

"Whatever. You. Want."

"Are you even listening to me?" she asked.

"Sure I am, Mare! No bed bugs, not cheap, but not a dump, am-I-right?"

"Yeah, that's right." She smiled facetiously, a crude affront to the amnesty he'd granted, her teeth shining with rapacious ill will.

They were on separate wavelengths, though that was nothing new. Their communication had been lacking in courtesy for quite a while—as though they were screaming at each other from across the Pacific, on different continents, struggling to get their words all the way across the ocean of contrariety that separated them. And now Peter couldn't help feeling that he'd backed himself into another corner, though one not as dire as the prior night's, when they'd quarreled as they packed their bags into the truck, screaming *will this really last?* and *are we ready for this kind of responsibility?*.

The feeling that gnawed at him was not *just* because they'd been driving for hours without a piss stop; it was not *just* another sour morning moment, like all the rest they'd lately shared. This was more than Meredith yawning and stretching her claws. This was a creeping behemoth force that accrued in slow doses, building up like rust on old pipes, piling on since… Well, since all the trouble had started, even before she became pregnant.

That was a history he'd rather not revisit, so instead he withdrew.

Let her have her fits, he told himself. *I won't keep contributing. She can work it out herself.*

He drew inward, thinking back to simpler days with some fondness—to the days of his childhood. He was one of many siblings, raised two- and three-to-a-room. Their mother was loving, attentive, and beautiful. Their father was seldom around. Dad travelled for work, selling insurance, but that was fine by Peter; he loved his mother dearly, more than anyone else in the world. Every summer, they'd run around Prospect Park like Snow White and all her little dwarves, searching for the right hill upon which to set their daily outing: their board games, their blankets, their food. Once their wares had been distributed (he vying for the smoked sausage, but satisfied even with the cheese crackers), his mother would spread out, stomach-down across a red patchwork quilt with the spidery legs of her bikini top scattered limply beside her, splayed across the herringbone fabric like strands of spaghetti. There was never that harsh, permanent stripe of white across her middle back, bisecting her tanned skin; for her, it was smooth, tawny glow from shoulder to shoulder.

It was those summers which Peter missed most; the warmth of New York that made popsicles melt in his mouth. A damp, sleepy season, it was nothing like the dry, bone-crackling heat they got in Arizona from mid-May on through to September.

Back in the city, summer had always succumbed to fall and brought along pistachio-and-pumpkin pastries, steaming fresh from the oven. And fall always tipped itself over, abruptly swaying into the harsh, sometimes bitingly acidic wind and snow of winter nor'easters.

With Meredith, the progression of their relationship had been much like that: like shifting seasons. Imperceptibly, their laugher and love-making—their summer—had frozen into stoic resignation, bitter-sweet complacency, and later into cold, stern aversion.

Beside him in the truck, Meredith scratched at some invisible tic harassing her jawline. She parted her hair wider and gazed off into space as she said, "Let's just be quiet the rest of the drive. I want to imagine myself lounging along the coastline, just in case this trip's a flop and we end up swimming in the kiddie pool of a shitty motel, with water coming up to here—" She raised a flattened palm to her waistline

9

and added, "While wearing my *dry* white t-shirt, no less."

He looked over at her, crinkled up against the edge of her half of the truck with a pillow shoved beneath her, probably pretending the handle didn't hurt the way it had to be digging into her side, and he suddenly remembered one of his mother's favorite sayings. It was one she always brought up at certain key moments throughout his life—at the less-than-upstanding milestones of his adolescence.

After hiding his straight-D report card;

after tearing up a ticket he received for smoking outside the mall;

after faking her voice to call in sick to his first real job at the gas station just down the road from their house.

You can't run from your shit while it's still up your ass, Peter.

She never had the chance to use it in reference to his relationship with Meredith, but he felt pretty sure that their long-standing contention would qualify, by his mother's definition, as shit-lodged-up-his-ass. Deep up there, and he couldn't get it out no matter what he tried.

"Whatever you want," he repeated, but he thought, *you're the one still yapping.*

An ovular yellow stain drew his attention to the fabric covering of the passenger seat—a bit of some mustardly crust, stuck to the seat piping beside Mare's left leg. He scratched at it.

When his knuckles grazed her leg, she rustled against his touch. Combined with her blind gaze—staring at nothing—the gesture told him to leave her (the hell!) alone. He obeyed, letting her be—as she wished—to enjoy the last bit of rest before their trip, before their *Escape From Arizona*, was fully underway.

Even against the rising clutter of southern California traffic, amidst the whitewash of a brand new sun, bathed in the diffuse glow of her frizzy mane and decked out in her favorite, time-worn nightshirt (and those short shorts she so loved, reminiscent of a pubescent high schooler's getting-sent-to-the-principal's-office clothing—*bad*), and in spite of their differences, he thought she looked elegant, beautiful. For a moment, he forgot all that they'd been through, over the long, hard months of their quarrels. He disregarded all of that and focused on a simple, inward mantra (*No fighting, just be calm, No fighting, just be calm*) so he could stare at her, peaceably and with respect. So he could bask in the delight of her simple, charming countenance.

Maybe it's that glow *they always mention. The glow of our baby, growing inside her.*

He patted her leg again, and this time she did not rouse; she was asleep.

Westbound still, the truck blasted out the last few miles' stretch toward the coast, kicking up a stench of creosote and kerosene as it cut across California, burning through fuel and time as though both were infinite. The driver and his dozing passenger had sailed through the night—one in a blur of nicotine, the other dazed on over-the-counter dramamine, and both holding on to their momentary place of repose, a glimmering rest before a real release from their *Real Lives* back home. While they simmered and stretched their route from home to holiday (he in a state of rote focus, weaving through the growing congestion of cars; she in her shallow sleep, just now dreaming of clean sand and cool waters, and of a dull, glowing, white light quickly budding within her), they dragged along disquietude, smearing it across the highway behind them. Its monstrous limbs, puckered with dread, skittered along the gravel, leaving behind a palpable trail. The same beast's bowels sloshed around the bed of their truck like corpses cinched up in cadavers' pouches, scenting the air on their course with a deathly miasma so strong it cut clear across the arid mountains of their byway.

As Peter merged onto their exit in search of that shining, idyllic golden coast, another of Mom's expressions popped into his head.

He fully pictured her, God Rest Her Soul: post-church bun fastened high and tight at the top of her head, hose full of runs, hefting a boxed cake, home-baked. In that iconic Jean-Speak of hers, with a Brooklyn accent that cut to the core and let you know exactly when the time came to *listen up, buddy*, she'd said: *Sometimes you can't air out your dirty laundry, your skeleton closet. Sometimes you've just gotta destroy it.*

Obliterate it, he thought. *Purify it. Start from scratch.*

He added further to her adage, *Dip it in the Pacific. Yeah, maybe that'll do.*

CHAPTER II

Meredith opened her sleep-foggy eyes, just in the nick of time to watch as Peter emerged skipping from the front office of a salmon-colored motel, appropriately named The Peach Pacific, waving a set of rusted keys and grinning his stupid grin, with the front-gap she used to love but which somehow revolted her lately. She even thought she saw a bit of bread lodged there, between his chiclet-shaped incisors.

He approached her side of the car and pried at the handle with a cacophony of squeaks. The passenger side door exploded outward and a bag of sunflower seeds dislodged from the inside compartment, spilling little kernels all across the pavement of the lot. He bent to pick them up, frantically dropping each little bit back into his open palm like a cartoon character on speed. Once satisfied with the amount he'd retrieved, Peter stopped and turned to face her, still crouching to the ground.

"This place is perfect, Mare. We're only a skip to the shoreline." He'd almost finished his errand, a small pile of the little brown bits loaded up at the center of his palm.

"Good morning to you, too," she said.

Meredith looked past the bug-and-dust-crusted windshield and through the front window of the motel's lobby. Its gaudy interior was cluttered with clunky Asian ceramics (blue peacocks on chalk-white porcelain, copper coy swimming languidly along lacquer waterfalls) and weathered shag carpets long-flattened beneath a dusty, dingy fiberglass-and-plastic furniture set—a low white reception desk and matching pair of waiting chairs. Leaning across the check-in was the "concierge" Peter had mentioned: a milk-pale man in his later years, as evidenced by his slackened, parchment-thin skin. Hair, long overdue for a cut, hung in wiry gray tufts behind his cauliflower ears and from beneath his tattered baseball cap. He wore a bright orange vest, which provided a shock of contrast against the dark, wood-paneled walls of the dated waiting room. She could swear he was smiling at her from way over there, while one of his long-nailed index fingers screwdrived across the deep recess of his left inner ear.

"Great," she said. "Just fantastic. At least it's probably cheap."

"Super cheap. And look, we've got the whole place to ourselves." Peter made a dramatic flourish across the deserted parking lot—and clearly hadn't caught on to her sarcasm.

"Almost," she said, pointing with her chin toward a single black sedan parked in the farthest corner space. Worn flame decals were stamped across its sides.

Probably that creepy albino's car, she thought. *He looks like a flame-decal-driving kind of freak.*

She heaved herself out from the cab of the truck and hefted up her purse and day bag. As Peter bent down to retrieve the last of the spilt sunflower seeds, their room keys dangled from his back pocket. Meredith snatched them away and drooped toward the ugly motel, trekking up a flight of outdoor stairs coated in decades-old stained carpet. The keys hung from a cream-colored plastic hexagon emblazoned, laser-etched, with their suite number. Room 210.

Once inside, Meredith found their room's walls shared the same effervescent orange as the building's outer paint job. Cheap prints of generic coastlines and still-life photos of glossy fake-fruit baskets hung crookedly from the walls. The bedclothes: peach. The shower curtain: peach. The foot-flattened, still-damp floor mat around the molded, nauseatingly sulfurous toilet: peach, too.

They really went all out on the color palette in here, she thought, and dropped her bags onto a short table next to the room's front door (not peach, but flecked with nicks which the proprietors had failed to mask with a too-dark paint pen). She peeled back the window treatments (surprisingly, purple) and gazed out at an ambivalent scene.

A narrow road, across which stood a cluster of derelict condos; behind the condos, a slow-sloping, sleepy coastline, waves licking across the shore; a gray, muted sky as ominously still as it was peacefully soft, with not a lick of blue peeking through blankets of silver stratus clouds. In the far distance was the boardwalk— with a hulking ferris wheel, hovering dim and denuded, stilled by a very apparent lack of patrons.

And downstairs, right below her vantage point, was their truck, just as beastly and outdated as their new domain. Peter sat on the edge of the opened tailgate, cradling a duffel under one arm and staring across the road toward the sea. She squinted to make out what he was holding onto with his other hand. That mound of seeds was resting there, as imprecise and colorless as the muted landscape they'd (anticlimactically) come to. Even the barren desert from which they'd so longed to escape was richer in warmth than this overcast, sleepy scene. There was, however, something cataclysmic about the precise location of The Peach Pacific—at least, potentially so. For all its straightforward hokeyness, it was lodged somehow freakishly, clumsily, amidst the phlegmatic peace of a stretch of otherwise colorless beach. It certainly stood out.

She thought of other things. *Why am I still so tired?* and, still with a bit of guilt, *Why am I such a* fucking *putz?*

Meredith ripped off her shirt, slipped out of her shorts, and peeled back the covers from the first of two narrow little beds at the center of the room. She slipped into necessary rest, savoring the cold, starched caress provided by the bedding's fabric cocoon.

They'd come all this way, hoping to escape from their respective anxieties, and yet all she felt was a brooding combustion at the back of her throat, like bile battling for sweet release. The sense of estrangement she felt from Peter was like a coin sliced in two: each side was useless without the other, and without the blazing intervention of a piping hot tool, they could never reconcile their differences. The ache she felt was only enhanced by her surroundings. She already felt a longing to escape from that assault of peachiness. It was suffocating.

At least under the covers she could focus on herself for a moment—on her thoughts, on her strange situation. She could explore the real, concrete feelings of her changing body, of her slow-stretching stomach. Her skin felt more pliable than before, like putty that bends easily to the touch. It had taken on a thickness which was foreign to her—a durable but puffy, silken, pliant denseness, like she was growing an extra-protective layer of defense exclusively for the sake of her child. Altogether, it made her feel like an alien in her own skin, more than like a mother-to-be.

A dull ache pulsated above her gut and below her solar plexus. As she cradled herself in the bed, she imagined what the fetus smearing its way across her uterus might *just now* be doing inside her, and also pictured what it might look like when it came out of her in less than a year's time. The ache she felt caused her to reflect back in time, to the worst place, to a time of appreciable suffering, when she'd nearly drowned in pain. She remembered it clearly and still regarded it with fear.

it had started with a feeling of shock, a jolt of violent pain seizing across her spine, as every nerve distended and vein raised to the surface of her skin.

her head was guarded by the tautness of her own forearms, her flexed biceps; she cradled herself tightly, like a babe in utero; *in silent agony, she vomited until there was nothing left but fire clinging to the inside of her throat.*

that day, the worst day of her life, ended with a trickle of blood, a few clumps of imprecise meat, of ruddy tissue, and with the final bursting forth of an unmistakably anthropomorphic, phlegmy mass, dead-still as a lead ball.

its puffy eyes, open yet not seeing her, missing the light that was the heart of any animate being's living gaze; they were like black buttons sewn to the face of a doll.

Back then, she couldn't help wondering if she'd deserved that stillbirth, and still felt that way at times, wondering if it had served as a kind of penance, a sacrifice. Even more that that, it had felt like a punishment. Losing that first child had made her weak, or at least apparently so, and it had been an opportunity for her to reel Peter back in, to soften the hurt she'd caused in her disloyalties to him.

"Meredith…are you awake?"

Peter's voice roused her, muted behind the structure of the door leading outside, and was followed by the clatter of his knuckles.

She was up, stumbling to open the door for him, and then peeking blearily out through a sliver in the doorframe, just before his knuckles settled into a full-on, forceful knock. His closed fist hovered, suspended in mid-air as his eyes registered with concern. Slowly, his fingers unraveled from the accusatory gesture of his fist, softening as they reached out for a hold on her shoulder.

But she rebuffed his care in favor of the warm cave from which she'd crept. It was nice in there. Quiet, small, and soft. Like a womb.

"I'm awake," she said, "but I'm just going to lie back down. To rest a little."

He nodded his understanding and let her slip away, vanishing back under the starched sheets. She pulled up the quilted peach comforter and, as Peter laid his things down, she turned beneath the covers to face away from him.

She gripped at her bare torso, still feeling the memory of the first one, wishing after the new one's safe-guarding.

"It'll be okay," he said. He peeled the blanket back a tad and swept her hair out of her face. Moistness enveloped her mouth as his lips encircled hers; she felt the gap she still loved, free and clear of debris, her tongue sliding across that endearing dental chasm. Dry and creased, hard-worn fingers absorbed the trail of tears that had welled across the arcs of her cheeks.

He kissed her again, wordlessly. And again.

They lay there for a while, a mass of skin stretched across skin, their hair woven together in a static nest.

Meredith sat up and tumbled out of bed. She stumbled toward the kitchenette for a glass of water. It felt prickly going down her parched throat and had an acid taste which reminded her of spoiled milk. Behind her, she could feel Peter's gaze following her with care. She returned to her slumped mattress, to its solace.

Peter settled into the other bed and reached across the expanse between them with a pursed mouth and the gaze of a frightened puppy. With his legs hanging off the edge of his mattress, the room looked dwarfed, Lilliputian, and she imagined he must have felt that way, too: like an oafish, stumbling boor who didn't quite know how to act, or how to feel, or what to say.

She watched him watching her, and she memorized his smile. It was a closed smirk, a toothless ear-to-ear grin that seemed to plead for an admission, or for some kind of encouragement. It said: *We can do this.*

He strained to reach out for her hand and she accepted it.

"Let me rest," she said. "Please. We can go to the beach tomorrow."

He breathed heavily and sat up in bed—a giant on his teensy, pint-sized cot—yet he didn't let go of her hand.

"Okay," he said. "I'll be right here if you decide you want to talk." A nurturing tone cropped up there.

Just before Meredith fell back asleep—drifting back into the pained sensation of recollection—her hand slackened. Their fingers disentangled and fell to rest against their shabby bedsides. They both lay there, ensconced in their own places of shallow, uneasy rest.

CHAPTER III

Meredith saw the boardwalk, the ferris wheel. It glowed impossibly close at hand, shining brightly against the anterior window of the motel room, closer than the boardwalk could possibly be. Its gleaming lights shot crackled streaks across the domed television glass and sprayed the inner walls with blooms of hallucinatory shapes. A clamor of carnival sounds flooded the room—children screaming, parents chiding their children in staccato (Stop-Your-Shout-Ing-Son. Come-Back-Here-Right-Now. Don't-You-Dare-Touch-That). A medley of balloons popping, engines revving, gears screeching, gum chewing, teeth chattering, sweat dripping. A hairline fracture across the window blossomed into a fragmented Rorschach inkblot, forming the disembodied circle of a sliced up serpent, its severed head stretched taut, seeking solace in the pacifier of its own tail. Through the fractured glass, the ferris wheel—the snake—picked up speed as a continuum of rocking force that gained momentum, an eternal recurrence of the same repeated spasmodic pattern (Red seat, Blue seat, Green seat, Yellow seat, Red seat, Blue seat, Green seat, Yellow seat), its silhouette blurred against the fast-fogging window and mirroring the shattered Ouroboros pattern splintering across the window panes. Like the cut-up pieces of a loose jigsaw, the glass of the casement wobbled, ready to fall out against the growing pressure of the wheel, the malevolent spinning disk which continued to gain momentum. Wraith-like silhouettes billowed by from within their seats on the ride, within the home of their pastel cabs, still circling ad infinitum against her vision. Their revolution entranced her, like some magician's hellish hypnotism. The patrons' faces were obscured by the speed of their revolution on an axis that was, just then, flattened by some preternatural means, squashed out against the growing impetus of its ownmost infinite energy. Their cindery eyes, though in constant motion (along with their grayed, cadaverous bodies), bored into her conscience. The window shattered and, as the wheel tumbled onto its side, the front door was ripped off its hinges. The motel room was filled with a tempest wind.

Meredith shot up in bed, dripping with sweat, and clawed for bearings around her. She grounded herself in the small, ugly details of her surroundings: the boxy A/C unit groaning, dripping freon onto the carpet, below the very window she'd just seen shatter in her dream; and the glaring peachiness of all the rest (even in the dark, the profusion of peach throbbed at her from every angle). She inhaled, exhaled, and saw her own dulled reflection in the dome of the television glass atop the three-drawer dresser across the room. As she latched more tightly onto each of the concrete characteristics of her surroundings—feeling the starched, coarse fabric of the bedspreads, the dampness of her sweat-drenched thighs, the bitter taste of nightmarish sleep still coating her tongue—the last residues of the macabre, hypnagogic dream finally melted away.

Peter snored softly in the bed across from her, his lips curling gently upward with each exhalation. The slow tick of a turn signal and its flash of muted yellow dashed against the (still solid) window set in the far wall beside the (still intact) entryway.

Click. Click. Click. Pause. *Click. Click. Click.* Pause.

She got out of bed and made for the bathroom sink; leaning against the mini-fridge for support, she chugged a glass of water, wondering at the recurrence of its sour taste. She blamed her pregnancy, and her sleep-wearied senses.

The plodding tick and glow of the stranger's turn signal carried on just outside the hotel room, in the parking lot below.

She sat down at the low table beside the window, drifting into a moony state, and tried to make out the real ferris wheel some few-odd miles away along the darkened boardwalk. It floated in the distance—monolithic, dead, and dark above a multitude of condos and apartment buildings. A scattering of lights illuminated the misty midnight air like glowing diffuse fireflies—just a few insomniacs sitting wide awake, restless in their search for calm, skimming across the scant offerings of late-night television or the bottomless abyss of the internet.

She looked at the clock. 3:47 AM.

From where Meredith sat, the flame-emblazoned notchback was just visible at the far corner of the lot; it lay lifeless at the exact spot she'd seen it before. But closer to Room 210, just a few steps down the stained-carpet stairwell outside, was another car: it was a conspicuous flash of silver briefly illumined by its own fast-flashing right-turn signal (*Click. Click. Click.* Pause.). The vehicle was parked diagonally across two spots in the closest row of parking, not far from their truck. Its lowlights faced The Peach Pacific. Its turn signal announced its aberrant presence in the near-empty, ill-lit lot.

Two hunched figures, drowned in shadow, hefted up a third recumbent figure—most likely a man, as demonstrated by the gleaming bald spot of his exposed crown. They gripped a white tarp by its edges to suspend the bald man up in the air, but one of his arms flopped off to the side of the makeshift gurney, bouncing a few times in place before coming to rest, as still as air. His head rolled loosely around on his slack neck in a flaccid, naked, and altogether vulgar display while his limp body was hoisted away from what Meredith could only imagine must have been a horrendous murder scene.

The back of her throat clenched up. She felt a bit like a Peeping Teresa, yet she couldn't look away.

The two who were still living wore suits and their hair was slicked-back. One of them had leather driver's gloves on with holes cut out for his knuckles to poke through. A mustache made the taller man stand out as the alpha—that, combined with his stature and the gargantuan muscles bulging out of his too-tight jacket. The taller man also had a long scar—or perhaps a hairlip, it was difficult to say in the dim light—running up his palate like a tectonic rupture bisecting his face. He seemed to be comprised of angles: sharp cheekbones, a pointed jaw set with a cleft chin so pronounced you could sharpen a pencil in it. His biceps pushed out with the weight of their burden, the third man, and bulged against the arms of his suit jacket like meat packed in skin—like plump, bursting links of sausage.

The shorter man had richly tanned skin. He whistled a tune ("It's A Small World After All") across thin, unscarred lips. What fear the larger man produced by his menacing appearance, the short man made up for with an ultra-pervy countenance: licking his lips constantly while examining the insensate man, carrying on with his tune, snickering occasionally between bars.

The trunk of their car shot up and they dumped the bald man into its hollow recess, the dead weight of his body thudding audibly, like the sound of a ninety-pound free weight dropped onto carpet. The tall man slammed down the lid of their stopgap sepulcher and leaned back against the car with a sated sigh. He snatched a smoke from his vest pocket and lit it up, setting his face aglow with cindery warmth, which only served to accentuate his devilish aspect. The coal end of his smoke was just bright enough to illumine a set of narrow eyes that were as impish as the rest of him; they were altogether corrupt, yet somehow familiar to Meredith. They seemed red, but it was probably a trick of the light, or just the reflection of his cigarette on the moistness of his sclera.

Now that the bald man was deposited in their trunk, the two brutish, grunting suits slowed to catch their breath. They eased into a calm, freed of their burden. The short one bummed a smoke from the giant, revealing his own peepers: they were a muted, everyday brown, spaced evenly and about as deceptively normal as the rest of him. He had a slightly rounded gut and a pair of arms that looked simian, hanging low (almost to his knees), but not as ripped, not as imposing as his counterpart's.

Meredith's jaw tightened, the grooves of her top teeth grating against the casings of their perfect-partner bottom teeth, screwing shut. A dense moisture cloyed at the crook of her back. She felt an eerie air of acquaintance toward the short man, too. She squashed the sensation of déjà vu, focusing instead on dissecting the meaning of what she observed.

Assassins, she thought, almost chuckling in spite of the fear that choked her.

Secret Service? she wondered, seriously. *FBI? Local PD?*

No matter how she fiddled with the puzzle pieces, none of it made sense. They didn't have guns, not that she could see; and their car didn't have sirens mounted to its hood, though it could be an undercover unit. Still, for all the questions that remained unanswered, one resounding fact beat at her awareness: she was not meant to witness what she saw.

Meredith strained to hear a snatch of their conversation.

"Well, that's it. Job's done," the tall man said in a yokel accent.

"Yep," the short one responded. "You handled it just right back there, what with the spasming and the shouting. I'd never have thought to use my own sock like that. You're quick on your feet, John. No pun intended." Less bumpkin in his voice, more city slicker jejune. Meredith expected the opposite—that the big,

21

menacing one (whose name she now knew was John) would sound like an actor from a mobster film, and that the little one would sound like a shrimpy hick.

"Thanks, George," John said. "Now's the matter of a cleanup. Didja call it in?"

"Yeah. ETA's one half hour," George, the short man, said.

"A whole half hour? Well, ain't that just *fuck-all* great!" He gnawed at the rift in his upper lip, tracing the upward-pointing triangle of its shape with the tip of his tongue. "All right, the way I see it, we've got two options here. We can hang around and wait the half hour, stickin' out like sore thumbs to anyone passing us by, or we can hightail it and hope no one comes knocking on the stiff's front door. Whaddaya think, George?"

"Judging by the scarcity of cars here, I don't think option one's much worth wasting our time on, John. What do you reckon?" The last word, coming out of his gangster's mouth, sounded forced, almost sarcastic.

"I *reckon* so. But there's still the matter of *his* car to deal with—"

Meredith followed John's long-pointed index finger to roughly the region of the flame-decaled sedan, but her eyes kept returning to the suited men's car, to the sealed boot of their sedan. She couldn't help but envision the concierge—with his tuft of white hair and his cauliflower ears—dead and jammed into the depths of the trunk.

"There's that one, too—" George pointed to Peter and Meredith's flame-red pickup.

John only nodded, rubbing his mouth and chin, hiding whatever clues about his feelings might be concealed there. He scratched his head, threw his cigarette butt against the curb, and seemed to consider something for a long moment— staring down at the polished, glistening leather of his shoes. Perhaps it was just some abstruse clause, written into their undertaking, a thing they'd previously overlooked and which the truck had reminded him of. He reached down to pick up his cigarette butt, still glowing, and squashed the last of its flames against his own opened palm. He deposited the butt into his inner coat pocket and lightly tapped the outside of his jacket where it finally lay. Grabbing George by the shoulder, he ushered his colleague to the other side of their car. There, they turned away from Meredith's line of sight and huddled together, their too-tight black-jacketed backs twitching as their heads bobbed up and down in heated conversation. They turned back around and George glanced up toward her window, for just an instant, before he opened the driver side door of the shiny silver sedan (it was a 1970s Cadillac Seville with its original, well-preserved wire wheels) and disappeared.

John circled around to the passenger side door and paused, one hand gripping the handle while his other hand raked back through his grease-slicked hair. He turned toward the window of Room 210, too, behind which Meredith sat observing them observing her. He turned back away from her and gnawed, this time at his lower lip. In profile, his nose had a distinct shape: sloping outward from the brow ridge at an almost horizontal pace before it hooked abruptly downward, like a cliff dropping off toward his deformed lips far, far below, where the narrow, bony bridge of his nose was met by his two giant nostrils; they flared once, twice. And then he ducked into the blackness of the car, his gargantuan shape and thick voice now just a chilling memory, one carefully etched into the archives of Meredith's mind.

The right-turn signal stopped blinking as the car's engine growled into life. They pulled out of their presumptuous double-wide spot, curling around the almost-empty lot in a broad arc, and approached the narrow stretch of roadway that separated The Peach Pacific—that seminal slab of uncanny—from the rest of the banal coastline.

Once they turned and drove away, Meredith unclenched her jaws. Slowly, she loosened her elbows, too. She slid her hands away from her mouth, uncurled her spine—vertebrae by vertebrae—and unlocked her knees; she laid her head upon the table and rested her eyes, unsure what to make of what she'd just seen, unable to decipher whether it had been real or just an extension of her surreal dream. She willed away the pitch of listless wondering that tickled her from the base of her spine; she folded over upon herself, arms draped across the surface of the too-short table by the window.

Her thoughts segued loosely into an hour's worth of restless dreaming—of the pulpy mass, of what once had been life exiting her, splashing placental juice against her inner thighs on its way out; of knocking on her mother's door and watching as the lights sprung up in a curlicue from interior to anterior, finally illuminating the front door, inlaid with glass that had swans etched upon it, floating upon a lake. She recalled the look of her mother's face, glowing diffuse (and perhaps accusatorially) against the other side of that frosted surface as she said, "Who is it? Mare?" as though she'd expected that moment all along: the moment of her great iniquity and the end of all the excuses she'd made for herself—*It was just once, It was a mistake, It won't happen again.* It was the first of the nights she'd slept alone, on the sofas of family and friends, staring up at the sly blades of whichever ceiling fan swirled above her and wishing, willing it to kill her, to slice her open, thinking,

Come down on me. Crush me.

She dreamed, too, of the concierge's journey across the city, where she imagined him bolting along the 710, his stiffened body finally hefted out where it lay slumped inside its shoddy tarpaulin cocoon, and thrown into some landfill to rot. His cheeks billowed out with pus; his innards leaked from each and every orifice, attracting rodents and fowl, bottom feeders who gnashed and licked his corpse clean to the bone. She felt herself there, too; she felt her body being consumed alongside the victim of those suited men. She was full of pain and agony, yet she identified with those varmints, with the very predators who dined upon her corpse. Those leeching carnivores—the ones who'd *always* do what it took to keep living—she was one of them, too, whether or not she admitted it to herself.

Finally, she dreamed of herself, surrounded by naked men of all shapes and sizes—twenty or thirty of them, all huddled around and up against her, groping her bare flesh with warty fingers. A scrawny man with knobby knees launched himself onto her legs, pinning them beneath his bony weight; his nails dragged into her thighs. Hot breath rushed against her cheek as another man, one with a shaved head and a pierced nose, latched against her throat, hurtling her back and forth on the sticky, sweat-stained sheets they writhed upon. The loop encircling his septum swayed with the force of his collisions against her and into her. An old man—his naked throat distended with goiter, his forehead a dry and flaky mass, his ass cheeks curdled by the slow impact of gravity—choked her. She smelled his fetid armpits and his crumbling teeth.

Another version of herself watched it all happen. As though composed of air, some ethereal abstraction floated above the scene and yet felt all their scathing stabs as well. She lost some of the ether that held her spirit suspended there, and she sank down toward the orgiastic mass. As she descended, all the features of their shape, their scent, and their stomach-turning strokes, grew in sharpness. An acute needle, though inches thick, stabbed into her bowels with soaring sharpness. Their pricks pounded into her like rapiers, tearing her apart. By the time she'd fully fallen back into herself, she felt like half of a set of twin sisters, who'd once been conjoined but were now ripped apart, lying side-by-side and simultaneously defiled, each feeling their own pain plus that of their sister—a simultaneous, two-fold agony.

When the men sated their appetites, they disentangled themselves from her, receding into the walls like shadows drenched with light—there and then gone in a flash. She felt a sudden relief that was tinged with slow-bubbling concentration, as though she'd accomplished a great feat while still anticipating the efforts it might also take to transmute the pain she'd absorbed into an abreaction, the way a martyr can inexplicably flip her suffering into significance by some miracle of acuity, or by some arcane, otherworldly intervention. Though destroyed, she also felt purified, laid bare with nothing left to hide and no reasons left to fear.

CHAPTER IV

Peter woke up with a dry throat and made for the bathroom sink. The door was locked, the water running. He knocked.

"You okay?" he asked.

No answer.

He tried knocking again, but still no response. He leaned all of his body weight into the door and cupped his ear against its bumpy plywood; he shook at the handle and scratched against the door with his nails, not yet concerned—more annoyed than anything.

No fighting, he reminded himself.

"Meow," he said playfully. "Mare, let me in."

"I'm almost done," she responded, "just give me a minute." Her voice was muted by the door, the curtain, and the sound of the shower.

Typical, he thought, as he stripped down to his briefs, the elastic band tugging uncomfortably at his baby paunch of a stomach. He left on his slouched, stained tube socks, too. The sound of flowing water finally abated.

Peter closed his eyes and envisioned the day before them: forecasting a sunny, splashy, romantic afternoon of beachside recreation together.

Wishful thinking.

The door opened a crack and she looked out at him, her towel drip-dripping onto the uneven floor, pooling in the sloped linoleum; her soggy hair fanned out against her shoulders like the tendrils of a baby octopus, against deep-ocean sand, drawing its legs up and out into ever-tightening, circling spirals.

"Can I come in now?" he asked.

"Sure." She opened the door a few inches wider, clutching the front of her towel, her knuckles white and taut.

He slid past her and ran some sink water into a dusty glass. He dumped out the liquid and refilled it again with clear water that bubbled a bit before it settled in its home. Lifting it up to the light, he swirled it around and then brought it to his lips, downing every drop of the tepid, lukewarm fluid in a chin-lifted, quick-guzzling second. He refilled the glass, sipped again, and this time sloshed it around between his cheeks. When he spit the water back out, it was tinged a camel-brown.

Meredith watched him complete his morning-time ritual (his brows furrowed by the awful taste) as she hand-dried her hair with another bleach-white towel—tendrils unfurling further into flaxen tornadoes, grazing against the ivory cloud of her skin.

"The water here tastes kinda funny," he said, as he expelled a healthy heap of toothpaste onto his brush.

"So you noticed it, too. I thought it was just me."

"Nope, iis def-uh-rit-rey uh rittle bittah—" he said, through foaming suds. Bits dribbled past his lips, sloped across his chin, and splashed into the washbasin.

She turned away from him and moved back into the living and sleeping area, rifling through her luggage, obscured by the half-opened bathroom door. He launched it farther back, with a quick backward kick, so he could watch her getting dressed. She shook out a crisp white blouse; bits of fluff and dust launched off the plain, clean fabric and careened through the beaming morning light flitting through the window, swirling around her. He watched her scapulae bow out with her up-stretched arms and then disappear behind the shirt's silken form. His arms crossed in admiration—his toothbrush sticking out like a thermometer—while she brushed her hair. Lashings of water darted from each strand as she gripped her hair in clumps near her scalp, tearing away at teensy knots with a simple black comb.

"Why's it always have to be the bathroom?" Meredith asked.

"What?"

"In the morning, why do you always have to drink water from the bathroom sink? Even at home, you never drink from the kitchen faucet, and it's no different here. I just wondered, and I never asked before."

He thought about her question as he returned the toothbrush to its place alongside the sink, though he didn't answer her before completing the usual scraping of his inner thumb across the bristles, back and forth across its head, aerating the tool.

"I dunno," he said. "Why's it matter?"

"Touché." As she dragged a pair of white-and-purple-striped panties across her thighs and up the slight slant of her hips, he reached out for her. She flinched and swatted him away, spinning back on her heels. "Sorry," she said. "You scared me. I'm still not completely awake."

"I can see that." Her eyes looked puffy, encircled with a gray-green tinge.

"Nice. Just what every girl wants to hear in the morning."

"Emphasis on *pretty*, not tired." He chuckled, but she didn't reciprocate. "Meredith, can I ask you something?"

"Go ahead." She paused in her routine, lowering her compact mirror to resume eye contact, her lips contracted with annoyance.

"Are you okay? I mean, with everything. I'm getting worried about you. You've done nothing but sleep for the past full day."

"I'm fine, Peter." With her compact lifted back up, her eyes disappeared behind its pearlized green-and-white plastic cover. "I promise."

"All right, sorry."

"Stop apologizing. And if you really want to know, you're right. I didn't sleep well at all, even though it's *all I've been doing*—" She made air-quotes and continued, "I woke up with a headache and a sore neck, slumped against that table by the window."

He glanced where she indicated, at the dwarfed piece of furniture—a too-short table—and imagined her there, balled up uncomfortably.

"Want a massage?" he asked. "Maybe that'll help."

"It's not that. I'm not sore or anything, although I could *always* use a massage." She smiled at him. It was that beaming, bright simper that he loved so much—it was playful, sycophantic yet self-serving.

Finally, he thought. *A sign of some humanity.*

"Peter, do you ever have the feeling that you aren't really awake—like you're

28

still dreaming, even though you've already woken up? Even though you see and smell and feel the way you should when you're conscious, everything still feels like a dream…"

"Sure I have, baby. I hate that feeling."

"What do you do when you feel that way? How do you make yourself feel, well, *normal* again?"

"Hey, you're fine. What's normal anyway?" Peter shrugged.

Talk of dreams made him think back to their adventures in psychotherapy, which he'd been unequivocally unenthused about. They'd found their version of psychiatric help in a dowdy, old-fashioned, 70-something-year-old woman named Barbara, with gray hair that she still coiffed into a shellacked bob. At least Meredith had liked her.

Shreds of Barbara's psychobabble jumped into his head:

Mirror her feelings. Acknowledge her pain. Ask her if she wants help or if she just wants to vent.

"Yeah, I guess you're right," Meredith said. "I'm probably just stressed about the baby."

"Is there anything I can do?" he asked, and reached instinctually for her shoulders again. He wanted to massage them (she'd said it might help, after all), but she slouched him off and moved toward her suitcase, where she retrieved and pulled on the same tattered shorts she'd worn the day before: those ass-cupping denim cutoffs that always made his head swim.

"No. Anyway, it's not your fault," she said.

He wondered whether he should press the issue or deposit it alongside the others they'd agreed to leave behind them in Arizona.

What would Barbara say? he wondered.

He chose the latter and dropped it.

"All right," he said. "I'll get ready and we can head down to the beach. It's early, so maybe we can still beat the crowd."

She tightened up, her spine lengthening and lips pursing.

"And I almost forgot—" Peter reached into his duffel bag and brought out a long, flat rectangular box, wrapped by his own graceless hands in bright-pink paper and topped with a silver bow. He passed it over to her. "For you."

She opened the gift carefully, smiling cautiously, lifting back each haphazard fold of wrapping to reveal a generic brown cardboard gift-box. She separated the lid and peeled back a layer of lilac tissue paper covering up the gift. Pinching it by its shoulder straps, Meredith hoisted out the present, a one-piece swimsuit with an old-fashioned red-and-white candy-stripe pattern. It was dowdy and (charmingly) outdated, with a frill of swirling fabric sewn across the waistline to help hide her baby bump.

He imagined it floating around her body as she kneeled into the ocean.

"What do you think?" he asked.

Meredith avoided eye contact as she said, "It's cute, Peter. But I'd rather just read today, or write."

He subdued a flare of anger by reminding himself, in Barbara's voice, *Gotta make this work.*

"Still tired, huh?" he asked.

"Yeah, sorry. Like I said, *crazy* dreams. I just want a good, full day of rest. Hopefully I'll sleep better and wake up refreshed. We still have Sunday, and we can do whatever you want. Tomorrow."

"Whatever I want, huh?" He pinched her elbow and tried to pull her in closer, but she slipped away again.

"Within reason." She squinted and shook her head.

"Are you sure this isn't anything worth talking about?"

"I'm fine, really. The shower helped a bit, I think. It's just, I need some peace and quiet to sort out this feeling. Sorry…"

"It's fine," he said. "And now *I* can tell *you* to stop apologizing. We can drop it. Just remember, I'm here to listen if you need me to, and if it makes any difference, you know I'd rather be locked up in here with you." *Her very own knight in shining armor.*

"No, you go to the beach," she said. "Live it up, have fun, be happy. I want you to. I think it'll do us both some good. Let's have a bite of breakfast and then you're free to wander the coastline all day long."

She pulled on some socks and stretched her hair back into a blue scrunchee— it was big and bold and juvenile. Meredith always had the greatest sense of carelessness when it came to her appearance: she couldn't care less about fashion, yet she was somehow redolent with classical charm. Part of her appeal was in her approachability, her confidence—and in her doeish, innocent looks.

"If you say so," Peter said. "I wouldn't mind the sun."

She finished tying her hair back into a slick, still damp ponytail.

"Mare, do remember when we met?" he asked.

She nodded and said, "We were both eighteen, back then. It feels like so long ago."

"Yeah… I'd just moved into the dorms at UA, and my roommate invited me to my first college party. I don't think I ever told you, but I was *so* nervous about meeting college girls, and potentially ones older than I was. But you were there. Your friend Beth dragged you, right? You were wearing the same stupid scrunchee—the one you still have, the one you just put on. You haven't changed at all, Mare…"

Her back was still turned to him, and she listened to his reverie without interruption. A quiet moment passed before her deflated response:

"Let's get breakfast before you head out." She turned to face him, smiling, and poked at his half-naked torso. "You'd better get dressed. Don't you want to *beat the crowds?*"

Against the blood boiling in his cheeks, Peter forced himself to hear good-ol' Barbara's voice saying:

Remember, The Worst has already happened. Don't awfulize and catastrophize.

"Yes, ma'am," he said, more to Barbara in his head than to Meredith standing next to him. "Guess I'm skipping the shower."

"Save the water. You'll just get wet again at the beach."

"And when did *you* become Miss Oh-So-Environmental?" He stood at attention and saluted Meredith, playfully sticking out his tongue.

"The moment my pregnant belly started grumbling. Now let's figure out some food. I'm craving bacon and eggs."

"Now that's *not* so environmental," he said. When she raised an eyebrow at him, he elaborated, "Those animals, don't you know they die a cruel and painful death? Go veg, and stuff…" he trailed off, feeling a bit sanctimonious in spite of his joking nature. He was, himself, ever the loyal meat-eater.

"Then they won't mind much if we honor them with a tasty, funereal meal. In their honor." She licked her lips dramatically. "They'll live on within us, and within this guy or gal." She poked herself at the center of her belly.

"Now *that's* dark," he said, dragging his jeans up. He snapped a henley on and shoved his feet into some worn-out boots. "Let's go. We'll ask the old guy downstairs where's a good place to eat around here."

"I seriously doubt we have the same taste as *that* guy. He's, like, very *Addam's Family*, don't you think?" Meredith raised her arms perpendicular to the ground and dragged her feet robotically, lurching monstrously toward Peter across the carpeted motel room. She let out a guttural, creeping sound. "*Uuuuuuhhhhnnnnng.* We *must* find another bwain," she said.

"All right, Ms. Frankenstein, but now you've mixed up your tropes, so let's hit the road."

He heard Barbara (never Barb) in his head again:

If things are going well, roll with it. Don't question it.

Peter placed his hands against her shoulders once more. This time she didn't flinch. But, in his rejoicing at the change, he failed to notice the overcompensation she demonstrated—by her very willingness to play, and her forced sportiveness, which had started at the first mention of the concierge downstairs.

CHAPTER V

Outside, the morning had warmed some of the early dew off the sparse tufts of grass surrounding The Peach Pacific's barren, fruitless palm trees, sprinkled here and there as if to remind tourists that they were, in fact—despite whatever the hideous landscape said to the contrary—on the California coast. A light breeze stirred the whiskers budding on Peter's cheeks and blew into the shredded fabric of Meredith's holey shorts. It was spring at its end: damp and mealy, on the cusp of summer's induction, with growing moisture that would soon turn into blooms of fuchsia hollyhock and lavender lilac.

Their truck lay at rest where they'd left it. That, at least, was good.

But the lot stood emptier than before, missing one flame-decaled Datsun.

Meredith ignored the urge to go and examine the abandoned space as, together, she and Peter approached the doors leading to the front desk. Inside, she stopped to knock on the aged, giant ceramics filling the corners of the room and chuckled at the artist's poorly-rendered coy fish—grossly cartoonish—and elaborate peacocks whose tufts of feathers were dipped in unnatural pastels, and even some neons.

Peter struck the call bell with satisfaction and said, "I've always wanted to do that."

They waited half a minute before Peter slapped the bell again, this time more firmly.

Another long, silent pause followed the second ring; they looked toward one another for some inkling of hope, and then silently agreed: no one was in.

Meredith couldn't resist the urge to look back out the front windows and toward the farmost corner spot. It was as though her eyes were made of heavy, ferromagnetic metal, and the vacant space was a monumental magnet.

"Guess we're on our own," Peter said. "I think there was a Waffle House a few miles back, near the highway exit."

"Hell no! I am *not* going to any flapjack house," she said. The prospect of soggy pancakes and runny eggs was enough to destroy the spell the flame-decaled car's absence had cast over her, at least for the moment. "We're already staying in a shithole, Peter. I'm not *eating* in a shithole, too. Look, there's some menus over here."

Meredith scooped up a handful of leaflets and handed them over to Peter. His eyes lit up with excitement as he perused their dining options.

"What's your poison?" he asked. "Chinese? Italian? Classic American? You pick, Mare."

"Well, we do still want breakfast, right? Here, this one delivers." She picked out the flyer for a restaurant called *Garden Grill—American Fare.*

"Delivery works for me. Looks like the shower'll be blessed with my presence after all." He chuckled and looked to her for approval, a laugh, something; but she was distracted, no longer interested in the short-lived hijinks they'd been enjoying.

"Hello? Earth to Meredith. Anyone in there?"

"Sorry. Sounds perfect," she said, dully.

They ambled back outside and up the stairs to their room. As she read the menu aloud—"Two Egg Special; Flapjack Stack; Green Ham and Egg..."—she snuck as many glances as she could manage toward the corner spot, as if she half-expected the sudden reappearance of the concierge's missing car. "They have corned beef hash. I'll just have that."

"Hash?" he asked, almost shouting. "Thought you wanted bacon?"

"Well, I changed my mind, so what? What's wrong with hash?" She fumbled with the key, looking back over her shoulder. Her complexion was fading to the anemic white of a ghost.

"Nothing. It's just, usually you'd call it cat food." He grabbed the door key from her shaking hands, eyeing her with growing concern, and slid it easily into the lock. It clicked as it caught in the bolt, and caused her to jump. The door glided open. "Hey, what kind of *garden* do you think something like that grows in anyway?"

She laughed, halfheartedly, struggling through her panic to understand the joke.

"Get your shower," she said. "I'll call in the order."

"Yes, ma'am. But I didn't tell you what I want."

"The usual?"

He nodded. *Yes, the usual.*

After she called in their order, Meredith moved back to the window and sat down at the too-short table, both legs folded in toward her body (a posture she might not manage for much longer). She scanned the lot for any signs of the missing Datsun or the concierge, but they just weren't there.

She couldn't be sure, but down in the office, when she moved to grab the menus, she thought she'd seen a spattering of blood across the back side of the desk—little dried bits of red clinging to the back of the chair—but it might have just been ketchup, hot sauce, or whatever other red-colored condiment the gray-haired porter took with his scrambled eggs.

Go and check later, she told herself. *When Peter isn't here. Just to be sure…*

The sound of another of Peter's morning-time habits assaulted her: his off-key singing. It drew her back out of her moony, troubled state. Today the song was something she thought she knew, but she couldn't quite put her finger on its title. The familiarity she felt ate away at her, just as the countenance of the two burly men she'd seen—or *might* have seen—the night before had done the same. Hearing the song and recollection of the grease-haired men both caused a feeling of unease within her, a kind of fatal knowing whose basest meaning was eclipsed by her unreliable mood.

Deep, fugue-like sleep was the root of her problem. She was weary, tormented with guilt, and haunted by the memories of her misdeeds, yet all she could do was sleep. Those memories chased her still, because she hadn't told him all. He couldn't know it all, and yet she felt he *had* to know eventually; or else she might lose the baby again. Or worse, she might die in a pool of her own sweat, killed by the self-reproach that followed her, that ate away at her, so tender and acidic.

35

CHAPTER VI

In the shower, Peter let suds run across his face and fill his open mouth with a bitter taste that reminded him of their first night together: sipping Schnapps while The Cranberries played, making out as their friends puked into their own hands, laughing and thinking, *It's all uphill from here.*

He remembered the moistness of her pubis as his fingers slid into her and her mouth ripped open like a knife wound, in pleasure, wet and hot. That whole myth, about sleeping with someone on the first night, had proven to be just that—a myth. For the first time in his life, he didn't feel the need to play games; he was ready to settle down, to make Meredith feel good, every damn day. She'd given him a pretty good indication that her dreams matched his, too.

Since way back then, they'd aged together—less defined abs, less full hair. She was rounder, and still loved club sandwiches (she called them *a healthy lunch*); he was calmer, but still got riled up when he watched football on Sundays; she was smarter, but still guessed letters that had already been played on Wheel of Fortune, and shouted them out with credence; she had promised him forever at the altar, but was sometimes static cold when they made love.

Peter grew increasingly distressed by her detachment, but he still felt so much love for her, and still found her so beautiful that his jaw would sometimes stick shut while he watched her sleeping next to him, her mouth lolled open with a bearish snore; he would watch her wake up and swat him away, disentangling herself to obligingly make their breakfast; he watched her cooking, tasting their meal every step of the way.

He never thought to question her growing apathy, to bring it up as a concern. He simply assumed it was a phase—that every woman must grow disenchanted with her husband's charms at some point, and that in time she'd come around, and she'd remember the fierce joy they once felt together. If anything, he hoped that happiness would come back around increased, twofold.

Mostly, he'd been wrong.

He dried himself off, left the bathroom with still-wet hair, and plopped nude onto his bed. The moistness of his hair transferred to the peach pillow-covers. All that thoughtfulness, those recollections, sank into him deeper and faster than a fettered man sinks when thrown off a seaside cliff. It immersed him fully, in a heavy fever of concern.

"I think we should talk about it," he said, staring up at the popcorn ceiling. "Again."

Awfulizing. Catastrophizing. Inside his head, Barbara reproached him, but he didn't even care.

Meredith sighed. "There's nothing else to say." She was doodling in her sketchbook, at the table by the window. The book's violet cover obscured her lower face, and almost perfectly matched the purple drapes, creating an odd amorphous shape around the exposed sliver of her face. In her eyes, peeking out behind the veil of the notebook, he thought he saw a vindictive wince when she said, "It's the same thing over and over, Peter. I really don't want to talk about it anymore."

Her face disappeared fully behind the book.

"But maybe it'll help," he said. "Maybe we can still enjoy this weekend, if we just get it out of the way, get it over with. Out in the open."

She ignored him.

"Hell-*oooooo*?" he shouted. "Oh, that's really nice." He rolled out of bed and slid into a pair of swim trunks. "You know, we can't keep avoiding it forever."

"We aren't avoiding it. I told you all there is to tell. We've already *dealt* with it. Past tense, over and done." She dropped her arms into her lap, both hands holding onto the tome of her sketchbook with a death grip. "What do you want me to say? That I'm so, so sorry? I already said that, and so did you, but it doesn't mean anything if we keep on repeating it. It doesn't mean things are going to get any better, either. Or any easier. I'm *done* talking about it."

"Let's at least be optimistic, Mare." He tried to snatch away her sketchbook, but his fingers slipped off as though it had been greased.

"I told you, I just need time. And rest. Especially today." She set her pencil down; it rolled across the table and fell to the floor. He watched her watch this happen. They both stared at it resting on the shag-carpet floor, but neither of them moved to retrieve it.

"Is it the baby?" he asked.

She nodded after a pause.

The baby. Like magic (this time without words), that was his cue for empathy, and it worked every time.

He moved closer, stroked her hair between his fingertips and lifted up her chin. To him, she looked like an ethereal angel, an alien thing whose skin was all aglow, her face furrowed with all the savage elegance and frustration of *Judith Beheading Holofernes.*

"All right, Mare," he said. "I'll go to the beach, and I'll give you some space, and I'll let you rest. If that's really what you want, and what you *need.*"

She nodded, averting her gaze, and recommenced her doodling, as though he'd spontaneously evaporated at the last little inflection of the letter *T* in his enunciation of the word *want.*

Purify, he thought, and envisioned himself sprawled out on the sun-shining beach, less than an hour into his future.

Peter snatched a towel from its rack in the bathroom and paused to look at the vanity, with her products scattered across it—low-VOC hair spray and solid perfume that smelled so like her, like fig leaves and violets, subtle and green and warm; her bulky drugstore-bought electric toothbrush, its battery long-dead, though she still refused to throw it away and use one that took up less room on the counter; a vial of travel-sized shaving gel, made for men, though she was okay with that because it made her legs softer than the women's brands did; and a pile of hair ties, held together by a green version of her classic scrunchee.

"Eat your food before it gets too cold," she said, still doodling.

In fact, he'd forgotten all about the food. She lifted up a plastic delivery bag—

38

a giant smiley face with huge, bold, sans-serifed **THANK YOU ENJOY** printed beneath its beaming yellow head.

Two eggs, sunny-side up, and three slices of overcooked bacon, accompanied by runny grits. *The usual,* sort of. Three packets of butter encased with gold foil sat between his styrofoam plate and the plastic to-go container of his grits. He lifted back the lid and dropped in the butter; he watched it melt.

"Where's your food?" he asked.

"I ate it while you were in the shower."

"Oh. That was fast." He lifted a spoonful of the ground corn kernels to his mouth, sipping at it. The flavor was like watery sand. It was undercooked, coarse, and the butter hadn't melted fully. A clump of it lodged between the gap in his teeth. He licked it away and savored the waxy, oily tang of flavor. "How was your hash?"

"Fine."

He looked at her, scribbling away, and wondered just how she endured herself at times. She could be so painfully selfish, so childish.

"Are you mad at me, Mare?"

"No. Why do you ask?" Still scribbling.

"Because you haven't looked at me once in the past ten minutes."

"I can *hear* you just fine without *looking* at you."

"No, you're not mad at *me*. But you're definitely mad at yourself." He tossed away his empty, greasy containers.

She glanced up at him through the gap in the spiral-ring binding of her book. "You're wrong. I'm not mad at anyone." She set the book down across her lap, face-down, and bit her thumbnail, hard. "Or maybe I am mad—at you, not at me. I can't really explain how I feel…"

"Try to, at least," Peter said, licking the last traces of grease out from between his teeth.

She regarded his empty food containers. "You really wolfed it down."

"You're avoiding the subject, Meredith."

"No I'm not, *Peter.* I already told you. It's the same thing, over and over. I don't know what else to say."

He stopped to think for a moment, to clear his head, to drum up and sum up the situation.

Where's Barbara when you really need her?

He still recalled the very instant of Meredith's first admission, and still felt the sizzling pain of comprehension he had faced—just like facing it all over again (and again and again and again), as though it had happened yesterday and not so many months ago.

"I just want to know *why* you did it, and so many times. Can you at least tell me that?" His eyes burned as they welled with tears. Barbara would not have endorsed his behavior. "Would you have carried on forever, as though all was well, if I'd never found out on my own?"

She climbed out of her chair and tromped toward him. Her figure blotted out the sun and, haloed like that, she was no longer an angel; she was a monolith, grimacing down at him with menace as he dipped his hands vaguely through their luggage searching for sunblock.

"You know I can't answer that, Peter. I swear, you're like a little boy sometimes, all helpless and choked up. Eventually you're going to have to give up the charade and accept the facts. Things are going to be different. Always will be, in some ways. Forever."

"I know that." He swallowed what felt like a brick. It grated against the inside of his throat.

"If you really *do* forgive me, part of that means trusting that I'm dealing with this, too. And dealing with it for me is going to be a *lot* different than it's going to be for you. I deal with things quietly, privately. You know that, Peter."

"What do you have to deal with? Your own guilt?" That was wrong, and he immediately regretted saying it. He pictured Barbara sitting alongside them, writing in her shrink's notebook, and it helped him rein in his aggression.

"Not exactly," Meredith said. She forestalled the flow of conversation and pushed away his raised hand.

"So you aren't guilty, then? I mean, you don't *feel* that way?"

"I don't know about guilt. I know that I feel like shit, but I also know that I love you, even if I have a funny way of showing it." Her face tightened, like a vise screwed shut deep within her jowls. "I don't think you'll ever *really* get it, Peter. I wouldn't have done it if I didn't love you. I have that funny way of fucking up the things I care most about. I've always been like that, since before we met. I used to think you were the cure…"

"Guess you were wrong." Another needless stab, perhaps. He smoothed his wet towel nervously across his lap. He wanted to reach out to her, to touch her, but she was back up and at the table, behind her sketchbook again. Anyway, he'd found his sunblock and still needed to apply it. He did, smearing it generously across his bare chest and—to the best of his ability—over his shoulders, all the while pretending not to look at her for help, or for some trace of affection; she didn't offer either.

"All right," he said. "I'm going now, but I'll bring my phone with me, just in case you need me for anything. If you leave, don't go too far."

No goodbye, and she didn't even look up as he walked out the door.

Let her stew, he thought. *It'll do her some real good.*

Outside, his flip flops resounded against the perpetually rain-dampened carpet covering the stairs. He made his way past the motel's office, where a young couple suction-cupped their rounded palms across the double-door glass, their fat asses jutting out as they bent over, banging on its surface; they returned to their car empty-handed, and with no great answers. When they drove away, Peter walked over to where they'd stood—where Meredith and he had entered to look for breakfast recommendations only an hour before.

He tried the metal handle, tugging hard. No go.

Odd, he thought. *It wasn't locked before.*

Peter shrugged it off. He retrieved a pair of shades from the truck, locking the door before he slammed it shut and slid them on, making his way toward the narrow highway dividing the motel from the otherwise residential stretch of beach. There were nothing but condos, bungalows, and apartment buildings keeping him from gaining access to smooth sands and cool waters.

As he made his way south of the motel, the temperature fluctuated, settling on cool with a breeze. The wind peaked and its sturdiest gusts chilled the air, hardening his nipples into taut peaks. Much like the capricious, fluctuating mood of the morning, the weather coasted back and forth—between moderate and spine-tingling—for the duration of his few-miles stroll. Rain plodded in legato across his thighs and bare shoulders, persuading him to increase his pace along that increasingly crumbled stretch of sidewalk. He kept his eyes on the ferris wheel ahead, a titan sitting tall and gray in the distance. He skipped over cracks in the path, following the slopping sound of waves against the seashore. It sounded like the unhurried squelching of a lover's wet embrace. He envisioned Meredith's tensed thighs rising up and down—above the lap of another man—in tempo with the striking of the waves, and he fought back a rising, weepy ache.

Every few meters, he glanced down between the narrow stilts of raised cottages—little beach bungalows off to his right—and caught glimpses of an abandoned, sprawling coastline, darkened by the gunmetal clouds overhead. He wrapped a towel around his torso to warm himself up and stared at the ground; rows of rubbish passed by underfoot—cigarette, beer can, cigarette, cigarette, condom, cigarette, chip wrapper, apple core, cigarette.

The jarring disk of the ferris wheel grew in breadth above him, atop a dull exurban skyline.

Almost there.

When his knees started to ache, he quickened his pace. The lodgings to his right dropped off abruptly in favor of the first serene sand dune, dappled with hairy beachgrass shaken by gusts and smashed with travelers' footprints. He made his way over the sand, feet sinking in it, and dumped himself onto the boardwalk by way of a rickety wooden staircase, as worn through as a shipwreck, its beams knotted and gnarled. Back in the direction he'd come from, the motel stood out as a far-off peach brush stroke against a stark and blustery sky, a blushy stain against a blurry sepia canvas.

This wasn't the boardwalk he'd imagined; it was no bustling carnival, nothing like what he'd seen in photos. It wasn't flooded with the sound of laughter, nor the smell of hot dogs dripping at their stands. The delight of fluorescent bulbs flashing across marquees was absent. Instead, all of that was replaced by a mostly-vacant, half-abandoned, ramshackle swath of oddball storefronts, their windows backlit with neon, mounted with crumpled bills rolled up at their edges and browned with age:

WELCOME: OSCAR'S ODDITIES, OBSCURITIES, & ABERRATIONS;

THE MAJESTIC MARIAH SEES ALL;

DINAH'S ALL-YOU-CAN-EAT DONUTS: ONE FREE RIDE TICKET.

Peter walked past a bored teenager wearing a pinstripe uniform and white paper cap, playing with his cell phone behind the cover of a cotton candy stand. He passed a souvenir shop, closed, which advertised custom screen printing for tourists who didn't exist. The example they provided read,

I SURVIVED

THE CIRCULAR SERPENT

AND ALL I GOT WAS

THIS LOUSY T-SHIRT.

The place reminded him of a film, *Carnival of Souls*, except that he wasn't dead and he was also pretty sure the few people he saw weren't spirits. Unless spirits carried cell phones. The sense of abandonment that film captured, of deterioration and malevolence, was definitely there, though. And it gave the hairs on Peter's neck a micro-jolt of static so that they stood on end.

He made for the pier, which stuck out into the Pacific like the continent's own corroded protuberance. It seemed to bob in place alongside the ferris wheel, which stood on stilts and swayed in pace with its ligneous neighbor the pier. Both seemed to hang by their last fragile threads, ready to collapse at any moment. Along the way he spotted two young women holding hands. One had a mohawk, dyed blue, and a piercing shaped like a bone struck horizontally—and stiffly—through her nostrils. The other was morbidly obese and wore too-tight clothing, her love handles rolling over the sides of her dirty black jeans. When Peter passed by them, they glowered at him. The fat one raised her plump hand to expose her middle finger, and she grimaced like a feral cat, her fulvous teeth bared. He hurried along.

As he made his way farther out along the wharf, he ran his hands across the rope suspended along its edge. He let its coarseness grate against his palms and stopped halfway out, plopping into a seated position with his legs dangling over the edge of the construction, suspended ten feet above the billowing ocean below. Bits of salt water picked up in the sea breeze and sprayed against his calves. He stared up at the big, lifeless ring of the so-called Circular Serpent above him. It floated in place, and its little cabs swayed indistinctly. What looked like a girl in one of the lower compartments peered down at him, met his gaze, and matched his insouciance. It was only a doll.

While he swung his sandaled feet above the eddies, a stranger passed along the pier behind him, quiet as a breath.

Peter rose to leave—to find a less macabre stretch of beach—and he saw the newcomer. The man waltzed unhurriedly toward the far end of the pier with his back turned to Peter. He was wearing unremarkable gray track pants, which floated around his slim form, and a black hoodie pulled up over his head. The man approached the very tip of the walkway and turned sideways, revealing his profile: a fat lip, bulged and purple. His nose dribbled gouts of green fluid. The one eye that was visible looked swollen shut, its shape bloated, tumescent with bruising.

Peter walked toward the man and shouted, "Hey! Are you okay?"

The stranger's lower jaw unclenched and shot downward, releasing a flow of spittle that stained the boards between his sneakered feet. His mouth clicked back and forth, unhinged and shut with force, while his tongue rolled loosely around the repository of his mouth. When he turned to fully face Peter, the man released a guttural, grating, clicking sound—something akin to the noise of an electric can opener. His malformed face, now fully exposed, showed a neck swollen outward to meet the slope of his chin; there was no difference in width between the bulged shape of his face and throat. His lips were fleshed out by the bloating of his tongue, which lolled freely about its moistened home due to a shortage of teeth—and the ones that *were* present had browned and rotted, hollowed out with infection like the small cavities of a crow's wet, staring gaze. The skin of his lips crackled with a milky, pus-hardened casing between rows of open sores. His left cheek was pocked with small holes, like burning shrapnel had shredded out fresh, hot openings in his flesh, to reveal his shining gums and jagged, crushed molars. His left nostril was stamped closed by a thin overgrowth of some slick membrane. The right nostril hung open, receptive. There, tiny foramen interlaced together—writhing, stringy fibers deep inside of him, attached to the cartilage like parasitic worms. When the mangled orifice of his nose dilated with respiration, those white organic threads swelled, brimmed, and then shrank down again. His ears and brow were shrouded by his hoodie, smudged with effluent or worse, but those eyes—even in the shadow of his browned jersey—were crammed with blood and emotion, like the hate of a rabid wolf. The sockets of his eyes were tumefied by an overgrowth of fatty tissue, and puffy blood vessels framed his barbarous gaze like a throbbing, biotic purple trellis.

The man stank like fresh excrement smeared across the roadkill of a grubby vagrant. The stench radiated from him, and was growing stronger as the distance between them lessened. As the stranger took small, scuttling steps toward Peter, his hands—raised and writhing like so many French starlets in mid-croon—gained conviction, reaching for something to grab onto with fingers dancing like a violinist stuck in a mental loop on the Allegro section of Vivaldi's *L'inverno*.

As they latched across Peter's throat, he thought about

Meredith,

the baby,

their last conversation.

The necrotized skin of the man's cold fingers pared back with the ease of a ripe banana peel slipping off the fruit, his slick tendons and muscles exposed and contracting as they wrenched Peter up and off the ground.

Peter wandered backward and inward, to the time before his trip down the boardwalk, to where he imagined Meredith lying at rest, still seated with a pencil gliding leisurely across the pages of her sketchbook.

He tried to shut his eyes, to look away from the man's leprous face—exposed, his hood dropped back to reveal another necrotic slope of lesioned skin, and what was left of his brow. As Peter's breath caught behind the excruciating pressure of the man's stranglehold, the darkness behind his own eyelids increased in value toward absolute white, sliding across a scale of memories: coupled mid-coitus on the eve of their wedding; throwing dishes at one another across the dining room; driving across town and banging on her mother's door; the shape of Meredith's small hand and the sting of its smack across his cheek; the dampness of her whimpering face against his bare chest; photos of her young, teenage smile, teeth still imprisoned behind braces, and behind girlish, glittering pink lipgloss.

Bitter cold punctured through Peter's deadly daydream, grounding him back in the gravity of the danger he faced. Death's potential was close at hand, and the palpable fear generated by that sudden awareness—thanks in part to their tumble into the turbulent ocean—smacked him out of equanimity and into urgency, into survival mode. He told himself to *fight*.

Soggy and addled, Peter wriggled between the man's four rigid limbs. Their dead weight restricted his ability to fight back, but he managed to wrench his left leg out from its numbing fetter, and he kicked the man away.

The stranger sloshed violently in the water, spraying a foam of brown in his struggle, firing rockets of detritus around him in every direction. It looked as though he'd drown in his own hysteria, or choke on a flotsam of soda cans and beer bottles. A paroxysm of wailing erupted from the man's fractured mouth, and the living white strands enfolding his nasal cavity dropped down from their home in his cartilage and reattached themselves to his raddled cheek and upper lip. Little toothed suckers vacuumed to his flesh, lengthening his grimace, prying apart his face from the left commissure of his mouth to his earlobe. He looked like a venus fly trap, the shredded strands of his ripped-apart skin flapping like undulating cilia around his hemorrhaging face.

Peter took long strokes across the water, glancing behind him to see the man still spasming in place, beating against the tide, but sinking fast. Suddenly, as if giving into his fatality, the man's arms calmed. He sank, his blistered face angling upward as the rest of him was dragged down—cheeks disappearing, eyes (still opened) pooling with salt water, the tip of his nose vanishing. Those flaps of ripped, ravaged skin went last, their amorphous shapes of fat and meat dancing across the surface of the water before they were finally hauled down by the mobile, straggly, alien forms—those spaghetti-like, wormish, inscrutably living appendages which Peter had watched crack the man's face apart like a walnut, with ease.

Peter didn't look back again, not until he made it to the shore and collapsed—chest burning with saline sting, coughing and vomiting brine and bile along with that morning's eggs (the yellow shape of their gelish yolk spreading fast across the sand). He lay there like a dead man, his eyes wide open and filling with the light of the sun, impossibly bright for the leaden day he'd awakened to.

He held in every burning breath, exhaling to six counts as he checked himself for life—elongating his extremities, feeling across his limbs, checking that they were intact, looking for lacerations or stray objects embedded in his flesh. Fingers pleading at an astute, microscopic level for the wholeness of their macro being: mother arm, father leg, all attached, accounted for.

He laughed—maniacally, deeply—and vomited again.

I'm alive, he thought.

He dragged himself off the ground and scanned the beach for someone who might help. A glimpse of the teenage boy from the cotton candy stand; his best bet. His paper hat was gone—blown away in the surging breeze—and he held up his cell phone, directing its camera lens toward Peter. The boy's face held a mild countenance, eerily forbearing given the terrible circumstances, and his muted expression stayed the same as Peter lurched closer toward his spot on the boardwalk.

Peter crested a dune and clasped onto the handrails of the promenade's short entryway, lifting himself up onto his feet, atop the first planked step, and ascending each of the five remaining steps with a labor of agony more intense than any broken bone or torn ligament he'd endured before.

"Please help me," Peter said. His voice sounded foreign to his own ears, still ringing with waterlogged, shrieking peals.

The boy backed away from him, face ever stoical. The cell phone, lifted up, hid his mouth and any expression that may have also been hidden there.

"What happened?" the boy asked.

"I-I-I was…" A quick gasp of air. "Attacked. Please, call an ambulance." Peter pointed toward the water. "There's a man, out there. He might have drowned."

When the young man continued to back away, and continued to lift up his phone (even though Peter begged and begged, *help me help me help me please*), Peter realized the futility of his pleading.

"Please, call someone. You have a phone. For fuck's sake—" Peter toppled over the timber boards of the run-down boardwalk. When he looked up to see if the boy would finally take heed of his peril, there was a subtle change in the contours of the kid's otherwise insentient face. What had just been dead indifference—straight eyebrows above apathetic gray eyes—was now a gape of potent shock. The arc of the boy's orbital muscles told Peter that he should figure out the cause of this shift toward shock, and *quickly*.

In a flash, a stringy varmint tore open the leg of his swim trunks. It flailed blindly, waving the indistinct, slithering cylinder of its body back and forth through the air. Peter ripped it from the tattered fabric of his shorts. It thrashed more violently in his grip, grinding at the air with the minuscule, multi-toothed openings at both ends of its long, stringy body. Altogether, the creature was a few inches longer than his own inner palm, with a series of four plump rings encircling each end of its body. It twitched like rubber hosing suddenly blasted full of water, wriggling between Peter's fingers, craving release. It bit his index finger, hard. Peter loosened his grip around it, grasping the tip of his finger to stem the quick-budding crater of blood welling there and giving the creature a moment to escape.

A moment was all it needed.

It bounded across Peter's forearm, flipping over itself like a living, frantic helical spring, and embedded one of its heads into the crook of his arm. He felt it gnaw deep into the muscle of his inner elbow with a skewer of boundless, throbbing pain; it ate its way through him. He watched it disappear upward, inward, carving through the meat of his bicep.

Prostrated and screaming, Peter lay there, helpless while the creature found its way to the inside of his shoulder; it moved over his clavicle, eating through him like a hot, volcanic ember melting his insides. When it lurched across his spine, aiming for the brain, Peter's vision blurred.

The last thread of his awareness was a digging, resounding tap: like a continuous, throbbing bass shaking around inside his skull. He felt alone, but looked around and still saw the boy—somehow he'd sat there through it all, dumb and rigid, with his phone hoisted up like the last torch before eternal dark.

Vibrations. Peter's eardrums felt like they'd burst from the sound of it.

Heat. His whole body felt as though it was on fire. His skin must be crackling and curling in on itself, aflame.

Pain. He gritted his teeth together against it, felt them begin to crack underneath the pressure of his jaws. Every nerve was alight, tickled to their deepest roots with pain.

Before his vision completely left him, he heard a voice, coaxing him to give in, give up, and to let himself go. It told him, *Everything will be okay.* After that, all that was left to do was to rest, in perfect peace—just as they'd come (all the way from Arizona, straight to the apotheosis of tranquility, under sun and by sea) to do. Behind his eyes, his vision descended from a perfect value of white—from an ideal of purity—to a deeply bubbling and endless black.

CHAPTER VII

Meredith scratched her neck, at an insatiable itch, and smoothed out the wrinkled page of her sketchbook. She let her drawing hand flow—into the shape of an abstract, freeform horse, and then a dove, and then a beetle, all connected by the corkscrew of her pencil's path. Its leaden point suddenly cracked and rolled off the page. Instead of reaching for the sharpener, she grabbed another pencil from her kit and paused, her eyes closed tightly, imagining what a newborn puppy looked like. She let her inner eye lead the track of her drawing hand; when she opened her eyes again, expecting the image of a whimpering pup, the misanthropic face of a cur glared back at her instead. Its vapid, open-mouthed gaze choked out her inspiration. She slammed the book shut with a sigh.

Her mind wandered back to the dreams she'd had the night before: of the soaring, ceaselessly spinning ferris wheel and the mutant creatures riding it, staring down at her, staring into her. Their scrutiny toward her was fiendish, and goosebumps crawled across her skin as she recalled the look of their hollow eyes. She could still see them rotating through the air in their primary-colored cabs across the sky.

The feel of the mutilated men who had maimed her and raped her—who'd spread her open across those soiled sheets—was still fresh on her skin, like the grievous burns of an acid bath. She couldn't keep clear in her mind what was fever dream and what was reality because her mind vacillated anxiously between rational thought and a great fear mounting within her: a blind sensation that, somehow, all that she'd seen in her dreams had *really* occurred.

And she thought of Peter, too.

I love him, I hate him, I want to fucking kill him.

She sighed, with a breath whose weight was as heavy as those fetid, nude men had felt pressing down on top of her.

Seeking a distraction, she lifted up and stared at her ill-manicured hands. Little bits of crust were lodged beneath them. She picked at them using the thumbs of her opposite hand—right thumb sliding beneath left index, middle, ring, and pinky finger; left thumb scraping the grime beneath her right fingernails. A pile of dirt grew into a mound on the table.

She peeled back the curtain, half-expecting to see the return of that flaming black sedan, but nothing rested down there, except for their crookedly-parked F-150. She sipped at her coffee (cold now; she'd been lapping at it for hours) and curled her toes, thinking maybe about painting them pink, along with her newly-cleaned fingernails, but ultimately decided against it. Anyway, all she'd brought with her was an ugly shade of brown, a taupey hue duller than the landscape outside.

Hefting herself off the armchair, she scooped her way through their luggage for provisions and checked her pockets, too: their room keys, car keys, lip balm. Armed with these, and a bottle of water whose contents were wanting, Meredith headed for the far corner of the parking lot. As she neared the endmost spot, she glanced suspiciously around her.

No eavesdroppers. No tall, buff man in a suit to be seen. Not his shorter, anxious counterpart either. That was good.

Just. Fucking. Paranoid, she told herself.

But strewn across the pavement were shards of glass in disparate chunks—little sandblasted filaments along with a few blocks the size of her palm. Beneath a pile of the stuff were the beginnings of a pair of skid marks, which continued toward the turn-off, away from The Peach Pacific, and onto the two-lane beachside expressway. The tracks veered right, northbound, toward Los Angeles proper.

Little flashes of the night before crept back in on her, hauling up another dose of unease: the balding man dumped into the trunk of the Cadillac Seville, like a bona fide slab of dead meat; the searing gaze of the two men, leering up toward her sanctuary behind the faded violet window treatments; their cryptic conversation.

She decided to head back up to the room and await Peter's return. And she decided that, once he finally came back, they'd up and leave the place—for good, headed straight back to Arizona. Maybe the bargain of The Peach Pacific wasn't worth the risk involved in staying another night.

Back in the motel room, she stripped to her underwear and refilled her water bottle from the kitchenette's tap. She slurped it all down in a giant inebriate's swig—ignoring the searing bitterness of its flavor, like tinny, metallic plasma.

She ripped back the duvet of her plain little cot, lay down on top of the starched bedclothes and the flat peach sheets, and rested her eyes. In the quiet dark of the motel room, with a stomachful of splashing, sour water, she thought about her grievous past, about the misgivings and deeds she'd committed, which had so completely compromised the safety and security of their most intimate trust—and caused the rift between them; and damaged their relationship; and altered the trajectory of their lives together, forever. A splatter of pain shot across her innards (a rattling on her stomach lining, bristling across her intestines, leaping up her throat). She dismissed the pang to anxiety and, massaging the tip of her bulging belly, carried on fretting about the future.

Each time she had acted out, she remembered enjoying a feeling of primal instinct, of raw and unbridled energy, of basic sensation. It was as though she couldn't help but go to *him*, the other man—as if the pain she knew she caused (and was still causing) to her husband was trivial by comparison. It was all worthwhile: the incomparable gratification she felt with *him*.

She'd flown to him without question, every time he called. But the remorse soon followed. It sprang up, sometimes minutes after her infidelity—after the soaring outlaw climax was behind her. Still, she did it again and again, as if begging to get caught.

Will he ever forgive me? she wondered.

A slight pinch sprouted at the center of her belly as she remembered the feeling she'd experienced when Peter had found out. It was a sensation not of guilt, but one of hopelessness—of scraped-openness, of what a captured animal might feel when she eats her spoon-fed prey at the zoo, in front of many ogling onlookers.

I don't know what's wrong with me.

The motel room enfolded her—just a blur of peach and pain—as the pinch she experienced spread inside her like molten, glowing cinders.

Once she'd finally decided to fix it, to put an end to the affair, she knew that commitment to change would come with its own set of jagged, emotional shrapnel. She made herself as vulnerable as the flagellated Christ, and reveled in the powerlessness of her situation, letting Peter take control of things, likening the quiet pain she felt to some due and just punishment.

I wish he'd come home already.

She grabbed at her soft flesh, rubbing it in a clockwise motion to soothe the swelling ache, remembering how the power game had tipped and rolled back over to her side of the court. Each time she thought she'd made amends, as evidenced by Peter's propitiated smile—that dumb, gap-toothed grin—a feeling of nothingness engulfed her. She knew he'd forgiven her, at least partially, but his pardon meant an end to the private punishment she secretly adored. Without that pain, she no longer remembered the severity of her disloyalties. When she finally felt forgiveness from Peter, she found a feeling of void where there should have been one of warmth. Like Sisyphus, she was eternally damned to strive toward accomplishment, toward atonement, only to watch helplessly as her efforts crushed her and rolled out of sight.

If only he were here, I'd tell him I'm certain, ready, sorry. Come home, Peter.

The pain she felt burned through stomach ache and shot into downright agony, as though her stomach had been drained of its essential fluids and replaced by heavy sand—swapped faster than her mind could register the difference, though slowly enough to let her up off the bed and toward the restroom before she finally tumbled to the ground, reaching for the doorknob, struggling to maintain a grip between her sweat-damp palms.

She fell into the opened threshold and lifted up the toilet seat, just in the nick of time. A torrent of vomit hit the bowl, splashing across the rim. It mingled with the wastewater in swirling eddies of bile flecked with red. The brackish sputum evanesced down the toilet's drain. She lay her elbows down, struggling to keep herself propped off the ground, and fell sideways, coughing, grabbing for the faucet at the bathroom sink. On her knees, she turned the dial for cold and let the liquid trail across her lips, splashing it through her opened mouth and across her sullied face. It tasted like iron. She spit it back out, wheezing and huffing, spewing more of her insides across the shallow basin of the sink. Her forearms and wrists were dripping with the stuff, which was thicker than it should have been.

It clung to her skin in fibrous, snotty chunks, bobbing and unfurling down the lengths of her arms, swirling toward her elbows. The odor was foul, and growing worse; it caused her to vomit even more of the stuff.

Oozing with it, she lay down on her back and—foaming at the mouth—let the substance overtake her face in a slow-creeping fountain, cascading out of the crazed wellspring of her mouth.

She tore away at the sludge gooping from her and felt the worse for her efforts. It stuck to her hands like an impossibly thick, industrial fixative, binding her fingers together. The besmirched face that looked back at her in the mirror was more than enough to send her into shock.

Her lips were filmed over with what looked like thin, glaucous skin, blurring the blackness of her stretched and gaping mouth *(her heartbeat rising)* and dulling the sound of her screams. Her ears and nostrils let loose a trickle of rich blood, swirling across her neck and down her cleavage, staining her bra straps and dampening her chest *(her throat closing up)*. Her stomach undulated with spasms, like the ripple of a stone across a pond, the flesh visibly kneading and convulsing with wild life *(her eyes rolling back)*.

Meredith's fingers twitched across the linoleum. Her spine grew rigid and compressed. Her skull bashed the ground as her body seized and flailed. Through the worst of it, a soft voice cooed at her: *It's*—in Peter's voice—*going*—with the sharpness of a drill against her skull—*to be*—growing louder as a skewer bored into the front of her mind—*okay*.

All became white around her. The room filled with light. The glow suffusing every surface was accompanied by a thrumming din, like a fan droning overhead. Just as the intensity of the effulgence increased, the sound picked up speed, too. It seemed to threaten her, to warn of hazard.

Just as suddenly as the lightness had appeared, it dropped—like a quick descent to hell. Darkness pulled her from the vital peace of thrumming light toward bleak, devouring black; it swallowed her whole.

CHAPTER VIII

For the second time in a day, nightmares spit Meredith back up, sweat-drenched and gasping for air. She was alive and dripping with living, breathing, heart-pounding vitality, yet she couldn't help feeling like she was the victim of someone's bad, somnambulant practical joke.

She felt for the gentle slope of her belly and, instinctively, threw back the covers. Spreading open her legs, she felt around between them. The sheets were mostly dry, as were her girly bits, save for the fast-drying slickness of chilled perspiration between her thighs and floating around the shape of her body, like the chalk outline of a freshly marked corpse. The room lay intact with no signs of a struggle; no blood splatters or viscid bodily fluids were anywhere to be seen.

So it was, in fact, *just another goddamn dream…*

It took a second check to confirm the fact, but *yes,* there she was, alive and (seemingly) well. The terror had been so vivid; it had felt so real. Yet it had just been another nightmare, a vivid hallucination.

Where's Peter? she wondered. *When did I fall asleep?*

To Meredith, time had become twisted over the course of the afternoon—as skewed, as melted, as those clocks in certain Dalí paintings. She felt as though her skull had been cracked open with an ice pick.

She closed her eyes and thought back to the handful of yoga classes she'd sat through before (stretched through, hummed and breathed and did her best to *zen* her way through), to channel forth some kind of serenity. She pushed every molecule of breath from her lungs and gulped in a fresh, air conditioned swill of it, reminding herself that things were A-OK, and that—as Barbara would say—*the worst-already-happened*, that *it-can't-get-worse-than-this*.

When she opened her eyes again and saw her pallid reflection, gaping back at her from within the boudoir's single dressing mirror—mounted crookedly to the back of the bathroom door by two rickety wire hooks—she was reminded straightaway of her ownmost pathetic being. A mop of hair, slopped across her blood-drained, unnerved face; thin wrists and thighs too skinny for a woman who was expecting. She looked like a specter, her bone china skin disappearing into the anonymity of the white-washed walls around her.

Get it together, she inwardly commanded.

Standing up after the experience of dying in her dreams took an enormous dose of self-affirmation. She slipped off the bed—taking slow steps across the precipitous expanse of what had once seemed like a pocket-sized motel room—to throw on some clothes. She stilled her shaking fingers—physically manipulating them, slowing each digit's trembling one by one, pressing them against the flesh of her inner palms—and she managed to find a simple white t-shirt, which she slipped over her head. Next came the shorts, which had seen better days but—regardless of their grimy condition—still felt nice covering up her legs.

Welcome to the real world, in a too-short pair of ripped-up shorts.

Dressed and ready, she pushed back the last few strands of frizzy hair covering up her face, pulling them back into the aperture of Peter's favorite scrunchee, and dialed her husband's cell phone. She sat down at the table, waiting for the first ring.

Silence.

Three seconds stretched out, tautened across an anxiety she thought she'd already overcome—it was primed like a viper, screwed up before the attack.

No ring.

She tried again, this time with a new outlook—a toughened disposition: less anxiety, and more positivity. Still, she resigned herself to what she already knew would come.

No ring, just silence. Not even his voice mail.

From outside, the sound of conversation dissolved her stupor. She caught a faraway snippet, a snicker, and the happy sound of laughter.

A squat but toned woman was standing beside a tow truck. Her hair was slicked back into a five-inch ponytail; she wore grease-smeared overalls, from which her short, stumpy, big-calved legs jutted out. A man—your everyday, run-of-the-mill mechanic type—accompanied her and was laughing, too. They walked toward the far corner of the lot.

Save for Peter and Meredith's own dusty, dented pickup, there was only one vehicle they could have their sights set upon: the flaming, decaled sedan. The one that got away.

Yet sure enough, there it sat, in the selfsame spot.

The duo of archetypal grease monkeys clambered toward the spectral vehicle, their wrenches in tow. When the stubby woman slapped her own knee (at what must have been the other mechanic's best punchline of the day), Meredith wondered if this wasn't some new dream.

Buckled over herself—though not in the good sense—Meredith tried to fast-rewind through the experiences of the afternoon, to gather the constituent memories of her odyssey. So many small details were lodged there, as permanently as a scab whose aspect simply wouldn't go away—not fleetingly, like the details of some quotidian daydream, and not like waking up shocked, gasping at the straws of a nightmare for specifics. She remembered those particulars as vividly as a first kiss; she remembered them like the dull, painful memory of a broken bone.

Bits of shattered glass.

Tire tracks, expanding across the lot, veering out along the blacktop and away from The Peach Pacific, pointing toward the north.

The dead man, stretched across a tarpaulin tomb.

All that was there, gleaming at the front of her remembrance; yet also, antithetically, it seemed quite clear to Meredith that none of it had been real. The borderline between sleep and a waking, verisimilar experience closed in on her, like being trapped in a room with a spiked ceiling descending above her.

She stared down at her cell phone, clamped between her fingers, and prayed again, this time not knowing specifically to whom she pleaded.

Please bring him home, she thought. *I'm going crazy. Help me!*

But no one responded.

Outside, the odd couple backed their tow truck toward the front bumper of the car across the lot. They lowered a flatbed tilt-tray and effortlessly scooped up the clunker. As they secured the vehicle in place, Meredith propelled herself into slippers and burst out the front door. Full force from the first, she flew down the stairs and at them like a demented, blind, and blood-thirsty ghul. She didn't even feel her lips unclamp, teeth glinting as she screamed at them:

"What the fuck are you doing?"

Fear cropped up on the mechanics' faces, their lips drawn out in toothy O's, their eyes bulging. They all three stared at one another in silence for some long seconds—like two parts of a scalene love triangle, caught mid-liaison by the third jealous party—until the car let out a metallic peal, grating a foot from its home atop the tow truck. Its left rear wheel slipped from the safety of the truck's tilt-tray with a grinding scratch; the passenger window scraped against the side of the tow-truck before blasting into pieces across the lot.

They nearly lost their quarry, but the man shook himself from shock and rushed to struggle with a crank mechanism at the side of his rig; a motorized screech helped to straighten the car back out against its elevated flooring.

Meredith whined, repeating herself: "I said, what are you fucking *doing?*"

The girl-greaser visibly tightened—her back arching like a scared Halloween cat—and lifted her chin defiantly. The lady looked tough. She said, "Towing this car. Get outta here."

"It's not supposed to be there!" Meredith screamed, biting her lip, drawing blood; it pooled inside her mouth with a copper burn, dripping over the rim of her lip, staining her white leather slippers, disappearing into the cracks between her toes. She patted the outer edge of her mouth and rubbed her sullied hands across the front of her blouse.

"I don't think either of us are arguing there," the woman said. "S'why we're taking it, after all. Like you says, it's not supposed to be there." She pointed over her shoulder at the spot from which they'd lifted the car.

"I know—" Meredith said. "It's just, I mean, it was already taken."

"Oh." At a loss for words, the woman turned to her partner for guidance. He only shrugged. "Then I guess someone brought it back…"

"So then you don't need to tow it, do you?" Meredith wondered why she was so incensed by the situation, but recognized—at the back of her mind, with bubbling déjà vu—that keeping the car in its spot was somehow important.

"Not my problem, ma'am," the woman said. She turned on the heels of her worm-out sneakers to help the man settle their bounty and added, under her breath, "And not my decision to make, neither."

Meredith floundered for words, fighting off a touch of the jitters. She hesitated and underwent a *what-the-fuck-am-I-doing?* moment of embarrassment before she asked, "Well whose decision *was* it?"

The woman froze in place. Pink waves of rage floated into her hard-clenched neck and, as she turned to leer at Meredith from her place up on the truck, the anger climbed higher, tinting her cheeks a strident coral. "The goddam-President-of-the-fucking-United-States," she said, spit flying, hands clenched into a pair of chomping lobster's claws. "Who do you think? Motel Management makes these calls." She pointed toward the office of The Peach Pacific. "Take it up with them."

The *them* to whom the squat, fuming mechanic referred—by the trenchant point of her digit's line of fire—was nowhere to be seen. There was no one in the office, and if the *he* that she referred to meant the gray-haired concierge, well, he was already on his way up the coast with a course charted for cadaverville, also known as a landfill, or an incinerator.

"The manager's...*gone*. Long gone—I mean, he's gone away." Meredith resisted the urge to bite her already injured lip.

"Huh? Well, someone called us in. And while I'd be glad to gab away the day with you, I can't—we're paid by the hour." The woman's nostrils flared and lips furled into a tight-cinched, sphincteral lower-case *n*. "I also don't really give a flying squirrel *fuck* about whatever meltdown you're currently having, miss, so why don't you go back up to your room and take a goddamn Klonopin, Xanax, or whatever you prissy drugstore junkies are into these days."

This time, when the woman turned away, Meredith didn't try to reengage her in conversation. Instead, she turned and traipsed back toward the stairwell for the solace of her room, defeated. But before she'd fully withdrawn, her eye caught on something off to the left, just beyond their red pickup, like the momentary flicker of a bioluminescent bug flying close beside her face. Something flashed there, as vital and loud as the effervescent spritz of soda being opened after it's thrashed against a wall—yet camouflaged from her direct awareness, like a hidden picture puzzle. She scanned the landscape for some hint of what froze her in her tracks.

Behind her, the tow truck bleated out a mechanical cry as it strained with the weight of its new passenger. The sun blazed above her, melting her hairspray. Occasionally, cars flew by across the freeway, their purring sound just loud enough for her to catch above the racket of the tow truck.

She almost gave up, discrediting her hunch to more delusion but, in turning to mount the stairs, her eyes passed back over the double-door entrance to the motel's office. There it was: a simple, 8.5" x 11" home-made, inkjet-printed sign, taped up in the front window of The Peach Pacific. It said:

OPEN FOR BIZNESS.

CHAPTER IX

Meredith walked into the office—full of light shining through the all-glass enclosure of its foyer, glowing like a promise. But when she saw him, all the cheerfulness was sucked right out of the room.

She choked on her breath, nearly toppling over one of the giant peacock-painted ceramics. There he was: that freaky concierge, sitting behind his desk, his oafishness now rendered sinister (since, by all the logs of her memory bank, he shouldn't have been standing there at all). He should have been dead. Nevertheless, he *did* stand before her, with wiry tufts of his old hair sticking out from under a camouflage trucker's cap as he picked at waxy stalagmites deep inside the cave of his inner ear. He was just as she remembered him: translucent skin with tiny red capillaries running visibly through its surface; opaque irises the color of silty puddles; and narrow lips opening upon sharp, uneven teeth.

Since she hadn't spoken to him before, and since her only impressions of him had been based on his far-off countenance (and his presumed demise), she felt a forbidding emanation rise up in her gut, like acid working through her innards. She even watched for his breath, still doubting his real being. But there it was, a shallow inhalation. His chest rose and his distended gut pushed out against and over the silver, dual pistol buckle of his belt.

After a long pause, the silent exchange between them growing stranger every moment (now he was licking his lips, but not lustfully so; he genuinely looked as though he had the need to wet the dry skin surrounding his mouth, and even rubbed there with his brown, paisley hanky), she finally decided to break the silence.

"Are you okay?" she asked.

"Yeah," he said, and tucked his tired kerchief back away. "Everything okay with you, Miss Alexander?" It sounded more like, *Yuhp. Averythang okay witchew Miz Al-egg-zander?*

At the sound of her own last name, Meredith lurched, but she quickly realized he would have to know their name, assuming Peter had filled out some kind of form for the room.

"Yes, I'm fine," she lied, breathing a little easier. "I'm just a little…confused. And tired."

"You look a bit done in, yup." A compensatory pause occurred, during which his nostrils became the new focus of his spindly pinkie's excavations. He withdrew his finger from the cave of his nose and sniffed at it; he picked his bandana out from the front pocket of his brown-grounded plaid shirt and wiped his snot across it. "If yer tired—" pronounced *tarred*, "grab a cuppa Joe over there."

In the far corner, an old motel standard stood dusty with disuse: a white, worn Coffee-Mate machine sitting atop a tall serving buffet. Next to the machine were two black bananas, a stack of doilies, and some paper plates. And above the offering, placed high on the wood-paneled wall, another sign had been taped up. It said:

HELP YORSELF.

The pot she'd been invited to partake of was filled with a jet-black juice. Even from ten feet away, she could see it was very unlikely the "Joe" had been changed that week.

"No, thanks," she said, and thought, *I'm not that tired.*

'Suit yorself. Well, what can I do you for?"

Ask him. What's the worst he could say?

Having already lost interest in Meredith, the concierge drew out his desk chair and sat down to pursue some reading. She peeked over the counter, touching its cold laminate surface, and saw what he was looking at: a porno magazine.

The image of a dozen old, bare asses wiggled in her mind. Her resolve tipped and her thighs tightened. For a moment, she felt the need to run away.

The sound of distant sirens invaded her thoughts. She snapped out of the daydream as their yelping drew closer and turned to watch, squinting to make out the distant shape of them flying by. There were three or four, and they were in a hurry. They dashed past, southbound, frenetic blurs of crisis. Their clamor was another impetus; it helped her marshal together her wits. She turned to face the concierge.

"Were you here this morning?" she asked.

"No, I'm working the afternoon shift today—" *Aftynoon sheeft.* "That's one to seven."

"Who was working then?"

"When?" He folded up the dirty magazine and tossed it regrettably into a drawer.

"Early. Around seven this morning." She leaned anxiously across the desk.

"I'm not sure, ma'am. One of the other employees. Maybe it were Jimmy who're here then." His bushy eyebrows drew together. He scratched his chin.

"Jimmy. Is that his car they're towing?"

"No. Jimmy don't drive no car."

The concierge looked outside and gasped a little, drawing his gaze away from the tow truck, away from the decaled car, away from Meredith. He stared guiltily at the floor.

"What?" Meredith squatted to intercept his downward gaze.

"Nothin'—nothin' at all." Blood dashed for his cheeks; he wasn't a very good liar.

Outside, the two mechanics had paused at their task to watch the cops fly by and were just starting up again, sorting out the last details of their haul, filling out paperwork. From inside the office, it looked as though they were entertaining one another, laughing good-naturedly at some joke (perhaps at Meredith's expense), as carelessly as infant cousins humoring one another with dirty puns and playful jabs.

"Well then, is it your car, Mister... Uh, what's your name, sir?"

"Darrell." He smiled and thrust out a wrinkled, sun-spotted hand, but not before he brushed it across the fine orange polyethylene of his (completely unnecessary) safety vest. She shook his hand reluctantly, appreciating his hygiene-minded gesture but still very much doubting Darrell's cleanliness. Afterward, she brushed her own palms across the seat of her shorts.

"I'll take that as a no? You wouldn't be standing by and watching them tow it, would you?"

"Tha's right. Besides which, I don't got no car neither."

"They said you asked them to tow it."

"S'right. Well, not exactly. Boss ordered it. I just follow his command." He took his hat off and scratched his head, then lowered his paws to point at her in a declamatory gesture. "What's with all the questions, anyway?"

To her slack-jawed disbelief, when Darrell lifted off his hat, he unveiled a skull-full of the same wiry white tufts of hair that grew from the sides of his head. Where Meredith had expected a bald patch, an eagle's nest, there was instead a bounty of hair, not dissimilar to that which jutted out from the brim of his hunter's cap.

"Shit!" she screamed, and covered up her mouth. "Sorry."

"Ma'am, you look like you seen a ghost. Should I call over some of them cops what just flew by to check on you?"

"No, I'm sorry! Really, I'm fine." She walked over to stand beside the dying fruit. She forced herself to swallow some air, and opened her mouth to speak. "I'm just a little confused."

"Yup, so ya said. I think I should call someone. Head back to your room and I'll send 'em your way." He lifted up the handset of an old-time rotary. Its numbers clicked at his touch, rolling counterclockwise with a long sound that spelled out the number nine before two quick drags across a short set of ones.

She darted for the desk, reaching to peel the loudspeaker away from his warped ear. He opened his mouth to say *No*, but the pain of her vise-like grip on his hand stamped out a yell and let only a whimper escape. When he finally loosed himself from her grip, he shouted, "LET ME GO!"

Meredith slammed the phone down. "I'm sorry. I'm okay! You don't need to call anyone. I'm fine…"

"Shit, woman, you nearly ripped my hand off. That'll bruise f'sure." He rubbed his outer palm, scowling at her.

"I'll just leave you alone now…" She turned to walk away, but something kept her anchored to the spot, preventing her from leaving Darrell and The Peach

Pacific's office for the dark comfort of her motel room.

"Well, go on!" he shouted. "What is it? You fuckin' going or are you stayin'?"

"Look, I'm really sorry," she implored. "I didn't mean to hurt you. I'm just worried about my husband and, well, as you probably saw—I'm pregnant. My mind's been a little fuzzy lately, with the baby, and something's been eating at me from this dream I had. Maybe if I just lie down and forget about it, things'll go back to normal." She rambled on, more for her own sake than for this, as though verbalizing a wish might easily make it come true.

Darrell glanced briefly at her still-small belly and cracked his neck. "A dream? Dreams ain't nothing but your mind telling tricks on you. Don't let a dumb dream land you in the loony bin, Miss Alexander."

"You're right," she said, wretchedly. "You're absolutely right. It was just a dream. I keep telling myself that. I keep reminding myself, but I still feel crazy."

He replaced the cap on top of his head and, like magic, his creepiness melted into an endearing quality of commiseration, as if by their brief and heated interaction he'd been charged with the task of quieting her fears.

"What was the dream? What happened in it? Might help you feel better sharin' it with a stranger such as m'self."

She hesitated to tell him, warning him, "It's nuts."

"Try me," he reassured her, pulling a chair out from behind the desk for her. He pointed a command, *Sit!* and looked like a towering bushbaby, dark circles around his large orbs for eyes. Their blue was cerulean, which contrasted oddly with his otherwise grungy features: a hooked nose with wide-set nostrils; dry skin flaking in sheets; knobbed joints that made him look like someone's bedraggled old marionette.

"Don't take this the wrong way, Darrell—" she said it with a question mark, as if appealing for empathy in his name. "—but I kind of thought you were dead."

"Me? Dead?" He stepped back, curling his shoulders out and forward, his head floating down between them.

"Yes. Except, in the dream, you were balding."

"Balding?" He took off his hat again and raked his fingers through his coarse silver hair. "Not me. Blessed with a full head, thanks to momma."

"I see that. Anyway, in the dream, that was your car out there, and they already took it away."

"Why would they take my car away? I ain't even got no car, ma'am."

"I know that now. I guess they took it away because you were dead. Some tall, dark men—creepy, like in a mafioso kind of way—they were the ones who took you, and they ordered a cleanup. And then your car was gone in the morning."

Darrell paused to consider all this for some long, lean moments. The friction between them had come to a sharp, static point. She felt him withdraw inward, looking for a way to be done with her mess, to sever the odd link they'd formed.

"Look, like I said, I ain't got no car. That out there is *not* mine, ya hear?"

"Yes, you already said that." She stood up. "And not Jimmy's, either."

"That's correct, ma'am; not Jimmy's neither. And I'm clearly not dead. You can touch me if you wanna see for yerself."

The Herculean horn of the tow truck blared outside.

The two mechanics swung out from their corner of the lot, flaming sedan in tow, and honked their horn again. Darrell waved out at them, smiling, and pushed Meredith back down in her chair. The A/C clicked on overhead; they both looked up toward a grimy vent in the ceiling. Strips of dust waved down at them.

She looked back at Darrell, into his deep-set eyeballs, and wondered again if any of it was real. Everything felt so protracted: a charmingly redneck confidante, and the boiling feeling of things just out of reach, just beyond her control. If her mood were an elevator, it had just reached the bottom floor, the basement—no, the sub-basement. She was strapped for a solution, a way out, and locked in the shallow grave of her own paranoia, buried alive.

"Whose car was it?" she asked.

"A patron's."

She was as surprised by his usage of the word *patron* as she was by the fact that he told her so readily. A deeper wonder washed over her as she looked up toward the key rack, mounted and locked to the wall behind the desk, some four feet away. Rows of keys lined up in troops, inside of a glass-and-timber cage. A hand-written sign hung above it, as was so common 'round those parts. It said:

MANAGEMENT ONLY.

STAY OUT!

"A patron?" she asked. "I thought we were the only people staying in this shitty motel."

"Ma'am! You ever heard the expression *beauty's in the eye'a the beholder?* Besides that, *no*, you aren't. There was one more, 'til yesterday."

"Where is he now?"

"Gone. Skipped on his bill. Left his room all full of beer and stains, too, from what I heard."

Her eyes flicked back across the rows of keys locked up behind Darrell—dark slivers of old copper swaying slightly from wooden pegs, with plastic diamonds (laser-etched with room numbers) hanging from each by narrow wire rings.

She scanned them:

First row—all accounted for.

Second—all there, too.

Third row—one was gone. A gap between 208 and 212. That was theirs, Room 210. No surprise there.

And the fourth row—it was hard to see into its far corners from where she stood. Impossible to tell whether anything was missing. She wanted to stand up, to cross behind the desk, moving toward those dully glinting chunks of metal; she wanted to shatter the glass covering the keys so she could plainly see which room was still "in use," which was unavailable because of its stained carpets, because of the previous tenant's reckless abandonment. Her thoughts were interrupted by Darrell shouting.

"—and if he ever comes back, look out! That'll be the end of him, lemme tell you."

"Which room was he in?" Meredith asked.

He paused and looked back at the key rack. "Now why in the hell would I tell you *that?*" His hands were shelved against the sides of his wide waist, like an unfaltering guardian.

"I need to know!"

"No. You don't need to know nothing, Miss. Just go back to your room and chill out now, y'hear? Y'need to quit hypothasizin' and go to sleep, have a rest. I suggest you and your husband utilize our express checkout first thing tomorrow morning, 'cause I've had just about enough of your face for one lifetime. You're fuckin' mad, woman!"

Meredith jumped over the desk, head bowed like a kamikaze pilot on her final fatal journey, and pried at the seams of the key case, struggling for a handle on it, but it simply wouldn't budge. Darrell came at her from behind and, clasping a hand to each of her shoulders, threw her back from the wall. He positioned himself in front of the case, arms and legs spread wide.

"I said, get out!" He was screaming now, his fair skin brimming with vital, ruby-colored rage. "I can't help you no more'n I already did. The boss'll kill me."

Bos'll. Boss will, she thought, and pressed him further, hoping he would cave.

"He doesn't have to know," she implored, wringing her hands together, biting at her lip, like a transient with Tourette's or a junkie craving a fix.

"I'd like to help you, miss, I really would. But right now you need to calm down and get out. I'm telling you for the last time, leave!"

"Fine." She shoved a stack of papers off the desk as she passed by. Pages flicked through the air in all directions. As she neared the exit, she ripped down the **OPEN FOR BIZNESS** sign and threw it on the floor. She trampled it dramatically with one foot, stamping at it like a stubborn cigarette butt that wouldn't fizzle out, her ankle rotating with excessive theatricality.

Suddenly, she felt embarrassed. With her head bowed, she made a quick retreat from the office, like a punished puppy with its tail tucked between its legs. At the door, a last dash of hope compelled her to turn around once more. She looked back upon the mess she'd caused with mortification. The harsh fluorescent bulbs overhead beat off the heavy glaze of those towering, hokey pots. A taxidermic deer's head mocked her from its home on the wall; it hung (its tongue lolling out over one bucked bottom tooth) above a worn, maroon-and-blue floral print love seat, which Darrell had collapsed into, covering his face with his old, dry hands.

"Darrell—" She moved back toward him and touched him on the shoulder. He looked up at her, his mouth slightly parted. "I'm sorry."

"Shit," he started, rubbing at his lips. "You don't hafta apologize over and over again, Miss. Yer clearly worn thin." He peeked over the rim of his palms at her with scared eyes.

"I know, you're right. I just need to go lie down."

"You keep *sayin'* that, maybe it's time you actually go and *do* that." He shooed her on, with as much of a smile as he could muster.

She bent down to scoop up some of the mess she'd created.

"No," he said, shooing her again. "It's fine, I got this. You just go."

She turned again to walk away.

"Wait!" he stopped her. "403."

"Excuse me?"

"It's room number 403," he repeated. "Don't know why I'm tellin' you this. Don't go doing anything crazy or stupid, y'hear me? Besides, you ain't getting in there. I don't even have a key myself. The boss took it 'til the room's in op'rable condition."

She didn't turn back to thank him.

She was out of the office and up the stairs, past the second floor, and right on past the third, set on a fast track for the abandoned room— abandoned by a man whose name she didn't even know, whose car had been towed, and who may or may not have been balding.

CHAPTER X

Meredith stood outside Room 403, practically shuddering with apprehension, but the handle wouldn't move, not one fraction of an inch. She peeked through the window, hands cupped around her face to block out the glare of the sun. More cop cars blared by behind her, screeching down the highway—but a sense of wonder, of anticipation, kept her enrapt with the task of spying on the room. She could just see through the sheer purple window treatments; they cast a dreamy gauze of surrealism over the scene. The full-size mattress was upturned, flipped off its bed frame; it was leaning against the wall. The edges of the fitted sheet were hanging on by one corner. The bare mattress bottom was exposed to reveal a spatter of brownish stains from end to end. The tall dressing mirror was shattered at its center, smeared with a roadmap of cloudy red stains following the byways of cracks in the surface of the crushed glass, all converging at what had been the bulls-eye behind someone's closed fist. Next to the mirror, the television had also been beaten to a pulp.

At the center of the room, the carpet was mottled and stained. The spot had once been covered by the mattress, but was now visible through gaps between the wooden slats that replaced the cheap bed's box spring. A drawing was carved into the ground: a wide loop in red. The circular shape was divided into quintants by the five points of a star, each of them shooting through the boundaries of the ring circumscribing it. There were strange characters scrawled in and around it, but those were hard to see from Meredith's vantage point. It looked as though the design had been smudged haphazardly, like someone had aimed to destroy or distort its aspect, blurring it into the porous clumps of fabric comprising the floor's matted shag covering.

The head of the circle—to the left and right of the topmost point of the star— held two symbols, which jutted out like jagged streaks of lightning. These were crested by a set of smaller circles, set a few inches apart and connected together by a straight line, hovering over the total pattern of the drawing. In the center of the odd emblem, a mark that wasn't quite a letter had been drawn; it looked like an anvil, or a razor-blade.

Meredith felt a twinge of foreboding at the sight of the stamp—like cold corpse fingers tickling her spine—and an even deeper chill settled over her when she tried to decipher the cabalistic characters written in and above the circle. Although the symbol's meaning eluded her, it vibrated with wicked energy.

Suddenly, she remembered the men, John and George. She could still envision their slick, pomaded hair shining in the moonlight of yesternight, and pictured the body being dumped into their trunk, its limbs settling into the first stages of rigor mortis, crackling and not quite bending the way normal human arms and legs should bend.

Through the window, Meredith saw a sock, dirty and crinkled, sitting all by itself beside the overturned bed.

Some cleanup, she thought.

None of it made any sense. It felt as though the sequence of events had been finely diced and sprinkled around the landscape of her mind.

She turned away from the scene and let her body slide down against the window, carving a streak of clean along its dirt-coated surface. She snatched back her breath.

What's going on? she thought, cracking her neck. *We've got to get out of here.*

Jogging down the stairs, she tried Peter's cell again. No ring; no surprise.

Back inside Room 210 (with the comfort and familiarity of their possessions there to soothe her), she tried him again, but there was still no ring. Not even a click, nor a message that apologized and told her to *Try Again Later*. She flopped across Peter's bed, rubbing her belly, and felt a little calmer, but the scent of his unwashed hair disrupted her respite. Traces of him were smeared across the pillowcases, pulsating off the sheets.

Little reminders of him leapt out at her from unexpected places: a UA sweater with a drawing of two anthropomorphic wildcats spilled from Peter's bag and seemed to growl; his electric razor came to life, convulsing against the washroom sink; a pair of his socks slithered across the floor. She retrieved and lined up the items, running her hands across them like a witch doctor stroking her hoodoo talismans, draining them of energy, willing away the pain and mystery of their impossible animation. None of them stirred again. Satisfied, she heaved herself up and away from them and thought, *Pack.*

She threw all of their things, socks and swimsuits and whatever else she found, into whatever bags could fit them, forming a loose plan at the back of her mind as she tidied up the room, awaiting his return.

Another hour. No, half an hour, and if he doesn't come back by then, well, I'll just have to go and get him. Throw him in the truck if I have to, and drive away at full tilt. Just get the fuck away from this hellish place. No questions asked.

For as fast as she'd seen their vacation decelerate, from tolerable to deplorable, she wasn't ready to see how much shittier things would get if they she sat around waiting. She wanted to get back, to the incomparably comfortable quiet of Arizona.

Never thought I'd miss it.

Ready to go—with sunglasses set on the bridge of her nose and bags hanging off of both arms—Meredith drew together all of her willpower and opened up the front door, to permanently vacate The Peach Pacific. She glanced back for a moment, to check the room over, but decided nothing was worth another second's delay.

Just as the door was set to slam climactically behind her, Meredith spotted Peter coming down the road. A flash of hope soared within her. For a moment, she saw them back at home: happy, together, living their everyday, run-of-the-mill lives.

But as he drew closer, that feeling of hopefulness was drowned out by despair at the physical state of him. He wasn't wearing shoes and dragged his feet along the grit of the parking lot. A clicking sound, like the reverb of a thousand cicadas chirping up at her, slipped past the scarce margin of his injured mouth.

She dropped their bags and leaned over the second floor railing. As he ascended the stairs toward her, the sun began its westerly fall toward the start of evening. The eaves of the building cast sharp shadows over its coast-facing border and obscured Peter's face from her full view, but what she did see shook her. Though the strange clicking stopped as he drew nearer, it was replaced by the soundless suckling movement of his mouth as his jaw latched and unlatched, flapping open and closed with a scarcely audible smack that grew louder and louder.

Wide streaks of blood were dried across one of his forearms, streaking down from his inner elbow toward his wrist. A bevelled trail had been carved across that arm, starting at the bottom of it and moving up toward his shoulder. The thin skin covering his clavicles had ruptured and was the blazoned sanguine color of a freshly leathered hide, alternately puckered and peeling around the incline of his neck, where she could see a mass of tendon (or was it muscle) flexing and a thick vein undulating just below the surface.

"Peter? Peter!" There weren't words to describe the senselessness of the situation. She carried on shouting his name: "Peter! Peter! Peter!"

Of course, he didn't respond, but only continued traipsing ever so slowly closer, with the hollow-eyed gaze of a scarecrow. His breathing had the labored quality of a rabid dog, with no sign left of humanity; only the basest impulse of respiration remained—in with a rasp, out with a grunt.

Protecting her belly, Meredith withdrew for what she supposed was the relative safety of the interior room—relative compared to facing the beast her husband had become—but he caught her at the door and squeezed painfully at her shoulders, with hands that were impossibly strong. She got most of her body through the door and into the room, but Peter's hands were still locked tightly around her wrist, and his forearms were jutting through the cracked partition, bulging and distended. With her free hand, she slammed the door against his wrist.

His bones shattered against the force of her blow and poked out through the casing of his flesh, like bloody icicles. Still, he held on, and let loose that awful *click, click, click* as his mouth stamped open and shut.

Her fingers turned blue as she struggled to wrest herself from the fetter of his grip. She peeled back the door with her free hand, opening it wide and smashing it shut with all the force she could muster (blood vessels bursting in her eyes, filling her vision with red; teeth grinding and cracking with the force of her tight-clamped mouth).

Finally, his grip weakened.

She tugged the rest of her arm away from him and—pulsating, fraught—collapsed to the floor with a glutted gasp that became a laugh. She would have screamed, if only she had the energy. In an instant, she was rocketing up, shifting her weight forward, slamming the door shut before he could move through it.

The dissatisfying click of the lock slid home, but did little to calm her nerves.

Still, she made every effort to arrange herself, to quickly formulate some sort of plan, but—annoyingly—all she could think of were the gruesome zombie films Peter made her watch (where the pregnant woman gives birth to a mutant child, or the protagonist has to resort to murdering his evil, undead brother). Those films did little to compete with the real horror of whatever afflicted Peter; there was no pause option in real life, and no covering up her eyes at the scary parts.

Peter didn't so much bang *on* the door as he banged *into* it with the full weight of his body. He repeatedly smacked his quarterback's frame against the partition, all the while emitting that mournful ticking noise. The sound of it, like insects crying, sent fresh tingles through Meredith's core. He let out another banshee's wail, like a cow screaming as he's branded. This wasn't the Peter who'd left her earlier that morning, headed for the beach and a spot of quiet, away from his troubled wife. His gentle disposition had been replaced by some frenzied, feral spirit.

She peeked out from behind the curtains. In his fury, Peter had broken his nose; it caved in on itself, a mangled patch of split skin and protruding bone gushing blood onto his bare chest. Miraculously, he seemed unfazed by the damage he'd caused to himself. Whereas any normal man would be squirming in agony against the ground, Peter only doubled his resolve, picking up the pace of his constant crashing into the door. All that kept her beloved berserker from entering—and from bashing in her brains—was that inches-thick (and quickly-cracking) rectangle of wood. Its outline vibrated with each impact, threatening to implode.

THUMP, and the top hinge separated from the door.

THUMP, and the bottom hinge ripped out, too, splintering the paneled molding.

On the next impact, the door tore completely free of its housing, heaved from the cradle of the frame, and collided against the floor. Meredith protected her eyes from the chips of drywall flying through the air.

He was on her again in an instant, his skin eerily slick and cool. The strength of his grip had her screaming out in pain. They toppled onto the bed, Peter straddling her as she pushed his slavering, open mouth away from her neck with one hand, slapping against his back with the other. His breath against her cheek was moist and cloyingly sweet-smelling, earthy as peat moss. She dug her nails into the knobs of his spine and felt his skin peeling back like the thin outer film of a sliced onion. The sense of nausea that had itched at her now came crashing back, beginning in her stomach, where his knee squashed against the miniature life inside of her. She felt her baby wincing against the pressure of his shoves. Fear for its life activated a flood of adrenaline, bolting through her limbs, screaming a signal to *fight;* she seized beneath him and threw him aside like scraps of paper, rising to stand up on wobbling legs.

He fell off the bed toward the window, slamming his head against the edge of the table. A new spigot of blood rushed from the back of his head, yet his resolve didn't waver. He rose to his feet again and dashed back toward her, his tongue streaming with translucent sludge that dripped down the pitch of his chin. He leapt for her—eyes bulging wide, gouts of blood coating the room with an anarchic sprinkler's spray, rising and flinging from every surface of his body.

She dodged his tackle and circled around him, cradling her tummy with one hand as she scanned the room for some means of subduing him. She backed herself into the kitchenette and turned to dig frenziedly through the drawers, acutely aware that he could rip her apart in moments. Worried she might miss her chance, she settled upon a glass of water and threw it across the room. It smashed into his face, the glass shattering in a firework of crystal and gore.

He emitted a turgid howl. Meredith plugged her ears and watched as Peter rubbed his own skin to shreds, shucking it away like gauze, kneading it into balls of tender flesh. She threw another tumbler of sink water at him, but he swatted it away with ease, glowering at her, reclining onto his haunches as though prepping for a charge, kicking up some dirt.

Fuck, she thought. *I'm dead.*

As if to spite her fatalism, a flare of will rushed over Meredith—as though some divining force interjected with a reminder of her greater purpose, one she didn't yet know she served. Her outer palm settled blindly against a third-rate block of cutlery; it would do the trick. She didn't feel the handle sliding into her grip, and didn't anticipate the impetuous lunge she took toward him. She just moved, in an instinctual, physiological response to his threat against her. It took over, commanding her movement, steering her along on autopilot, toward what was—manifestly—the only way out.

With unfeeling resolve, she crushed him like a fly, swatting at the bulk of him, cutting through him with a knife that should have been too dull to peel an orange. It was like taking a routine drive, checking out just as the car's ignition roars to life and waking up to find she'd reached her final destination. She was completely disengaged from her plight, and let innate need—to protect her child, and herself—take over. To survive.

The knife glinted as she lifted it in self-defense, and it slid straight through the center of Peter's palm, skewering his hand and peeking half an inch out the other side. She withdrew the blade, feeling nothing but the vibration of blood circulating inside of her ears. The hole she ripped into him winked like a subtle orifice, its aperture quickly widening, spattering like thick, crude oil pouring out the top of a drill rig, coating Meredith, soaking her shirt and décolletage with sudden, mighty gouts.

She hefted up the blade again, lifting it high above her head, and brought it sailing down, where it cut easily through the side of Peter's face, ripping open his cheek. His mouth hung open to show a full set of teeth, jagged here and flattened there, as though they'd been eroded by a hundred years of sandblasting. He fell to the ground, gripping his face, wailing. She jumped toward him, landed astride him, and pinned him between her legs, thighs tight with the force of a lioness in battle.

Stabbing him in the face was easier than she could have guessed—the blade slid right in. With a few lashings, his head had been smoothly reduced to strips of hanging flesh and mashed muscle, pulpy shattered bones swimming below a set of unexpressive, cold-blooded eyes. In and out, up and down, she beat the fatal tip of her utensil into his throat, slicing open carotid and jugular alike to produce a violent arterial spray, blasting the room until she was enveloped in the red of him, dripping with it and encased equally by her own mindless fury.

Whatever remnants of humanity had lingered in Peter now twinkled out before her, like a bonfire's last surge. With a bravado of emotion, he dug his nails against the floor, spasming under her weight as he tried to skitter himself away; his life force ebbed, his eyes rolling up. Finally, fatally, he withered away, vibrating underneath her pudenda. The friction of his waning struggle caused a flicker there, like a match sparking. Then it died—as did he—and she returned to herself.

Budding with revulsion and faced plainly with the massacre she'd led, Meredith fell over, sliding in the wet, growing puddle of Peter's deep, terminal entrails.

"No! Jesus, Peter! Peter!"

She screamed and screamed, crying his name senselessly, pushing against his sides, hoping he would rouse. He did not. She kicked him, sobbing and stuttering, but gave up when his tongue flopped out, lolling from the gash she'd slit into the side of his face.

She cupped her mouth to hold back a rush of vomit, but ultimately couldn't stop its advance; it loosed itself from her belly, spraying out between her fingers.

He was dead, and that was unfortunate—no, it was *really fucked up*—but the unpropitious situation would only worsen the longer she sat there letting him rot. She realized she had to do something, other than sit gawking at his corpse. She stood up, tugging at his bare underarms, the hair there stringy, clotted together. His body was heavy with the dull, limp weight of death, but she managed to get him a foot away from the kitchen before his leg caught. It was stuck on the lip between rooms, a gap that separated the tile of the kitchen from the carpet of the sleeping area. The latter had been tack-stripped clumsily down, and she'd ripped it up with his leaden, dragging foot. She tugged and tugged, but his leg wouldn't budge.

Tears welled up and she flailed insensately across the floor. She lay there, stilling her breath until she thought she made out the sound of police sirens drawing near, climbing in octaves as they approached. Visualizing herself behind bars, she imaged what it would feel like giving birth—in prison—to a child she'd never see. It would live with her mother and go to church every Sunday, denied sweets and television after 9PM. She would agree with her mother, that it would be best if the child never met her killer mom, that jail wasn't the right environment for a child to be visiting. Maybe once he or she was older.

But the booming signal of the cop cars dissipated, leaving her alone to contend with her tortured thoughts.

She thought back on their worst moments, wondering perhaps if he'd been sick all along—schizophrenic, or a serial killer—but she knew him better than anyone did, and she couldn't come up with even the slightest indication of some hidden seeds of madness. His mother hadn't ended well in life—she died a young death, the details of which Peter never liked to discuss. But still, he would have mentioned something like this, something hereditary, which might put them at risk.

Like what? she wondered. *Depersonalization? Bipolar disorder? That was not some minor psychological setback. He was fucking ferocious, goddamn out of his mind.*

As much as, at first, it might have felt like Peter's attack had been a thing of fiction—like some soulless corpse creeping toward his wife with a fanfare of theatrics, accompanied by a soaring soundtrack—or a bad joke, it had all been very real. The burn of his blood in her eyes, and its burnished taste in her mouth, served as lingering reminders of that.

It doesn't matter anyway. He's gone.

Meredith paced the room for a solution to her problem but, when none came along, she found herself thinking of the men again—the suit-wearing tall and short men, John and George, to whom she'd felt so strangely connected. Perhaps they were to blame. Worse, maybe they worked for *him*.

No! she reassured herself. *Forget* him. *He's gone.*

She hardened at the thought of her affair, and shuddered to think it might have something to do with the way Peter had met his end. But she brushed the fear aside and resolved to drive away—to leave, without Peter, and to block out the pain of abandoning her duty as wife to him, as his widow.

Get out of here. Leave. That wasn't Peter—that was some kind of beast, a goddamn animal—

Unthinkably, Peter roused—just slightly, his bashed-in face gurgling with a hidden puff of air, a closing expiration. She hopped over to lift her bloodied knife from the hollow of his face and noticed, with relief, that Peter wasn't moving after all. She looked closer, just to be sure, squinting through the slow-bubbling viscera.

Something *was* moving. Something was moving *inside* of him.

Crouched low, Meredith gazed deeper into the crater of his head, almost tempted to stick a finger in. Before she could, an inhuman circle of jagged teeth emerged, with gnashing white denitcles that rotated hurriedly through the center of so much squashed meat, tearing through the mush of Peter, shredding him apart with the thousand tiny blades of its mouth, like an alien food processor dicing up its conquered ravin.

It jumped out, en route for her mouth, but missed its mark when she twisted away, smacking across the side of her head instead and attaching itself to the adipose cushion of her earlobe, tearing it immediately open with a cascade of fat and blood.

An explosion of pain ripped through Meredith as the thing ate away at the dense group of nerves inside that soft skin. It dangled there, thrashing about until she managed to grab a hold of its slimy, segmented body. It slipped between her fingers like tires on an oil spill, shooting up and out of her palms, landing in her hair, tangling itself up as it thrashed about, ripping clumps out by the root. Without a firm grip on the thing, the still-exposed end of it was free to prick her as it liked. It connected itself to the side of her neck, where it could freely feed on her. After it gorged itself on the remnants of her lower ear—its tube-like body distending outward as it peeled earlobe away from cheek—it continued to inch its way up the hard cartilage around the side of her ear, lurching toward her temple.

Meredith dug into its midsection with one hand, latching all five of her neatly-pointed nails through its outer membrane and loosing a brownish, stinking fluid which burned against her cuticles as it slid toward her palms. She yanked it away from her face, ignoring the smell of her own blistering skin. As it was dragged away, it reached for a last chunk of her flesh, catching her chin with one set of its needle-pointed teeth and dragging a chunk of her skin into thin strands, dangling from the helix of her upper ear. Its other orifice, abruptly torn from its job sorting through her hair, separated the derma of her neck from the muscle beneath; it held fast to her, peeling her open with ease, revealing the taut mass of sinew beneath, bursting her open from mandible to clavicle. Still, she succeeded in separating the thing, and aimed to throw it against the wall.

The beast discharged another dribble of chunky amber fluid from both of its mouths, as though rejecting some of its meal, and agonized in her palm. It stuck to her skin when she tried to pitch it, but (on what felt like the twentieth flick of her wrist) she finally displaced it, kicked it far across the room, and slid down the front of the fridge, catching her shuddering breath for a brief intermission.

Her repose ended abruptly when she saw that it was gliding nimbly back, floating toward the cuisine and toward her, moving across the carpet like a snake gliding across the surface of water. As it moved, its contours blended softly into the cream matting beneath it (the carpet and the thing were the same blushed, biotic ivory: the color of a newborn baby, corpulent and stretching). It clicked—just as Peter had before it—and quickly narrowed the gap, clambering for her.

She shouted inwardly, a reverb, a mantra, a rallying call:

Stand up! It's not over. Stand up!

A reflexive outburst of bile coasted up her throat and slipped over her chin. She brushed it away with the back of her hand, anosmic to its rotten stench, or perhaps just numbed to it—after all, her hand (along with the rest of her) was already coated with innumerable excretions: hers, its, and Peter's. She balanced at the edge of consciousness, wavering between the light of waking life and the beguiling hush of oblivion, fighting back more vomit and hidden tears, burying all of her emotion, save for rage.

Her cranial nerves were alight with searing pain, but still she strived to rise, to stand on her own two feet. As awareness coasted in and out of her, swimming atop waves of nausea—a chill, a slowing heart rate—the room began to wheel its way around her, her vision falling into dusky fog.

Stand up! She was almost shouting it aloud, bracing herself, wrenching herself up by the refrigerator's handle, its door flying open as she summoned all the quiet energy she had left within her for a parting hoorah, to go out swinging.

She lifted herself up only to fall again, slipping in the slick of the blood beneath her.

Not a foot away, the knife rested alongside Peter's corpse. She leaned over and hurriedly wrapped her fingers around it.

The wormy thing was weakened by its time spent exposed to the air, out in the open; it needed another warm head for its home. Its puckered mouths seemed to battle against the air as each end oozed more yellowish sputum. It trundled over Peter's corpse toward her, slowing with each labored inch it traversed.

With the knife lifted fearlessly above her, Meredith dug her heels into the ground, bent at the knees, and stabbed into the center of the thing; then she lifted up her scullery scythe and sliced down at it again. And again. She bisected it, cleaving it sloppily, bleedingly, into two fat chunks. Each segment drained out onto the kitchen tile, filling the cracks of the stained grout with an inky, bubbling broth. The two scant tubes of meat which had once made up its body now flattened against the floor, shriveling with a sizzle and releasing a miasma of foul effluent. Before her eyes, the wormy entity disappeared, with only the faintest impression of smoke—a puff that snaked through the air and dispersed itself, diffusing like cigarette smoke as it vanished forever, a phantom, an ethereal ghost she hoped she'd never lay eyes on again.

It's over, she thought.

Freed of terror's burden, she finally, fully stood up. She swabbed at the copious claret on her thighs and forearms using a dish rag, pulling her hair back into her scrunchee, and dug through Peter's pockets. By some miracle, she felt the cool metallic tip of what was surely the key to the truck. It had carried them to The Peach Pacific, and deposited Meredith and Peter into what was supposed to have been the place of their great, restive cure; to set them back on track, toward happiness, or at least a mitigation. A reprieve, a relief from their bickering—that's what they'd sought. Instead, they stumbled upon this creature, whose scant but deathly mien had separated them forever.

I fucking killed him, she thought, as though she could ever forget. She would now and always, forever more, have guilt—a concept she'd never fully let herself face—hanging over her head.

She squatted down to face him (although face wasn't the right word—not when he had so little left to regard) and kissed the most recognizable shred of his physiognomy that remained, his teeth; namely, his two front, gapped teeth. They were still there, in the pit of his flayed, smashed remains.

As she scooped up her bags, leaving his behind—hoping whoever found him might give him a proper goodbye; a funeral; a quiet, peaceful interment—she stopped at the ripped-open doorway to think. It was a gesture she hadn't had much time for in her scuffle, thinking. Thinking with a mind that was perhaps clearer than since they left for California (rendered so by the persistence of adrenaline, still bounding through her brain), she realized that whatever entered Peter might have also cached itself away somewhere deep inside of her. She thought back on the fevered dreams, the concierge, the ominous men named George and John, the car that had been there, that hadn't, and that had been there again.

Her child contorted inside of her with a clash that melted into warm support.

She reentered the room, and took the time to wipe the best part of the mess of blood from her face, staring at herself in the bathroom mirror for a spell, eyeing the peak of Peter's unmoving legs just visible in the corner of the glass.

Nestling her belly, she cleared the room for good.

CHAPTER XI

Meredith adjusted herself forward in the driver's seat, wiped herself once more with the sleeve of her shirt, and shifted the rearview mirror to her liking. Tires screeching, she pulled out from the lot of The Peach Pacific.

The concierge emerged from his place at the front desk. He glowered at her as she drove away, a pudgy aberration at the edge of her view, cupping his eyes against the glow of the setting sun.

Meredith rolled down the passenger side window and lifted up her hand, raising her middle finger in a final censurial message. She screamed, "Fuck You!"

She wasn't sure he deserved that. She wasn't sure of anything. Still, it felt good to scream, so she did it again; it was a bubbling, unintelligible howl.

Finally, away from the omnipresent doom of The Peach Pacific, she settled her restless rump and realized she needed to drive, and to go some*where*, to get to anywhere that wasn't where she was at present—to climb back up from hell, ring by ring, circle by circle.

Meredith cleared her mind of all the muck. For the first time since the start of their incredibly long weekend, she felt a surge of real happiness. It wasn't halcyon and was only fleeting, but it smacked her momentarily, pleasurably, square in the face and with refreshing clarity. It was relief. She patted her stomach.

As the rush departed, it left behind an acidic, burning backlash. Her place at the motel had reduced her to a mildly delusional version of herself, like a puppet prone to the whims of some hidden, deific puppeteer—and her master was clearly a sadist. Now, cut loose from the parasitic energy that had bound her there, the storm clouds cleared and she felt free—but also alone, left to ferment in the anger, sadness, and remorse that great storms always leave in their wake.

She wobbled unsteadily between affirmation and disgust:

I fucked up.

What else could I have done?

You did what you had to do.

She chugged half a liter of water, briny as it slipped down her throat.

What the hell was that thing?

I need to tell someone.

I can't.

Tears streamed down her face. She swabbed them away—her hands trembling, her upper lip quivering. She drifted clumsily off the road, clunking onto the shoulder of the freeway, grating against a row of rumble strips. Bolted back to her senses, she swerved to avoid smashing into the guardrail. Her rear bumper dipped out, scraping against the asphalt, and the car grated to a halt at the side of the road.

She rubbed her belly and shifted the car into park, lifting her foot up off the brake. She took a few deep breaths and regained her composure, eyeing her surroundings.

Not ten feet away was a parking lot, which dissolved a few meters out into sandy beach and, farther out, segued into a violent outthrust of pier. She perceived all this with wonder, and her gaze was especially drawn—as if by magnets—toward the colossal mass of the ferris wheel lurching above. It cast a wide shadow across the stanchions holding up the pier, as though reminding everyone of its authority in that realm.

The child inside of her flapped about. Living, growing, it urged her on, and it seemed to shout at her—*Don't Stop*—with a great, wordless pressure that felt like a tension headache. It reminded her of when she'd visited New York with Peter. They'd crossed under the East River on the L train, and her ears had popped. It freaked her out, being under all that water, and she wondered just how they kept it from surging down into the tunnels, from flooding and drowning the people traveling beneath it.

She sighed at the thought of Peter, rubbing her temples and pinching the bridge of her sniffling nose, holding back another fiery fountain of tears.

Her moist eyes trailed the promenade and settled their gaze upon a congregation of police cars and ambulances she'd somehow overlooked. They were assembled at the obvious scene of a crime. Yellow tape girdled them into a spotlight at the tip of her scrutiny. The swarm of medics and burly flatfeet all encircled a pimply, visibly addled, teenage boy. As detectives harangued the youth, he nervously shifted his weight back and forth from foot to foot. Reporters were just arriving on the scene and anxious deputies exercised their authority against them, their hands lifting up in warning: *STAY BACK*. A dozen pens scratched against notepads, filling them with words, while the boy cried with hands pressing down on his shoulders.

Her blast against the curb drew their attention, and some of them were moving toward her, perhaps mistaking her for the boy's mother; others were turned around to gawk at her, doing their best to idle on their notepads and laptops, pretending they weren't spying, checking for some diversion, ready to seize the next big news opportunity. The heat of their eyes on her was like the unblinking stare of a panther—or at least as unsettling.

A premonitory feeling crept back into her, like a snug, enduring buzz; it shook through her bowels and seemed to speak from deep within her. It shouted up from the depths, rising through her intestines in a voice not unlike her own—yet not quite a voice, more like a feeling, the same as when your conscience tells you (wordlessly) all about how you should or shouldn't say how you feel—how you really, really feel. In words that weren't words (yet that were whispering, and nibbling), she thought she heard the self-same plea:

Don't Stop!

She repeated it to herself, "Don't stop…"

It was an affirmation, punctuated by a thought:

Get out of here and don't look back. Drive home. Drive straight for Arizona.

She pushed the key forward in the ignition, expecting it to stall, but the engine sputtered only briefly, coughed, and caught, roaring briskly to life.

The bluecoats, the medics, and the teenage boy—they all disregarded her and returned to their goings-on; reports to complete, paperwork to file.

She pulled out and drove on, resisting the urge to stare back over her shoulder as she went. The desperate landscape dissolved away, and she felt it receding, sinking into the horizon's edge to Rest In Peace, alongside Darrell and The Peach Pacific. Alongside her dead husband, too.

The drive was slow-going. Congestion gathered to a head more than half a mile before the highway's on-ramp. Minutes dragged as she plodded and stopped, creeping inches forward only to screech to another halt. She kept checking the speedometer to make sure she wasn't speeding, despite the sluggish pattern of traffic. Heat quickly filled the confines of the truck; she rolled the window down a sliver. A breeze shot through the crack, flicking her hair about, combatively. Finally, biting her lip as she pulled onto the I-10 Eastbound ramp, she entered the swarm of gridlocked cars.

She thought back to all the little nuances of their bickering over the past days, the talking at cross purposes, and strived to remember the last thing she'd said to him before he left, before he came back as that *thing*.

She remembered. It had been, *I've always been like that, since before we even met. I used to think you were the cure...*

The truck crawled to a stop in traffic. A young blonde with giant sunglasses stared at her from a lane over. She looked like a giant insect; her hair was coiffed into a halo billowing around her face in the blast of her A/C.

Meredith stared back for a moment and rolled up the window. She turned on the radio, closed her eyes, and tried to zone out. Droplets of sweat bobbed up on her skin.

Since Meredith couldn't remember what Peter had said in response to her confession, she focused on something else, drawing her energies toward what he had looked like walking out the door: his perfectly average, hairy belly pushing out against the waistband of his swim shorts; his eyebrows merging ever closer together with each passing year, like unkempt (yet charming) hedges; his broad shoulders, glittered with freckles.

He's gone, she reminded herself, and was overcome with fresh grief.

The car behind her honked. She looked up to see that the traffic ahead had cleared. The man riding her ass, who'd honked, lifted up his middle finger in a gesture she knew well enough; it was one she calmly returned. He blushed at her counterblow.

Just as Meredith started to coast along at a comfortable 40 miles per hour, a polished silver Cadillac—an older model, a Seville with windows that were darkly tinted and rolled up tight—merged onto the highway and bolted across two lanes of traffic, grating against the bumpers and sides of cars as its driver pushed his way through, to pull in behind her.

Even without seeing through the car's windshield, she knew who drove it (she had a fifty-fifty chance of guessing, at least—whether she said John, or she said George). She'd seen their car once before, but wrote its existence off as a byproduct of fever dream.

Her palms slicked over with sweat and her upper lip dripped with it. She turned in her seat to look for an exit or a free lane, only to find neither. The silvery sedan screeched closer, and she was walled in with only one direction open to her: forward, and even that wasn't looking good. Her speeding quickly closed the gap on a VW compact, its driver glaring back at her through his rearview mirror; he stuck his arm half-way out the window, waving it backward as if to say, *SHOO! STOP! I'VE GOT NOWHERE TO GO!*

Neither do I, she realized.

As the Cadillac neared a point of impact with the truck—seconds from collision with no openings on either side—a blink of light shot through the blackness of its windshield, like a reflective mineral bathed in light, a diamond refracting sunshine. It revealed a flash of the driver's sunglasses, and the harsh contours of his face, before the sun drifted behind a cloud and the nebulous bow of glass darkened once more.

It was *them.* It had to be. She'd never been more sure of anything.

It no longer mattered that traffic confined her; she had to find a way out, even if it meant slamming through a handful of cars in the process.

The right! Move right!

By some miracle, the farmost lane opened a bit when a convertible stalled—its owner cursing, smashing a closed fist against the steering wheel. It represented her only (scant) chance of escape, and she took it, sliding into and coasting through the lane. Eighty yards ahead—and closing fast—an old jalopy labored to keep pace with traffic, puckering while it spewed a dingy trail of exhaust fumes. It crept along, its cautious driver maintaining a distance of two or three car links between the front bumper of his clunker and the vehicle just ahead: a giant SUV.

Meredith estimated her risks. Getting the slowpoke out of the way would be easy enough—she could just push it off the highway if need be. It was the SUV she was worried about. Drive too fast toward it and she'd end up ramming into the gas-guzzler (or folded up beneath it); drive too slow and she'd be caught, forced to face whatever torture her trappers had in store for her (a nice lampshade made from her skin, or perhaps a set of cutlery carved from her bones).

She made her choice, foot flattening against the gas as she shot forward and clipped the rear of the compact ahead of her. It swerved and slid off to the highway's shoulder. Meredith straightened out and picked up speed—but so did John and George, a precipitous hairline closing between them. With a quarter mile left before an exit and her two nemeses following in tow, she lay on the horn, shifting to merge into the exit lane and sending cars pitching for safety. They crashed, honked, and cursed behind her—a cacophony of howling, all of them moaning, machine and human alike. Still, the Cadillac persisted and was upon her, its headlights smashing against the truck's rear gate, which ripped off its hinges and rolled out of sight under the wheels of the Seville. Another impact—*WHAM!*—and the hood of the sedan snapped free, shot back, and flew into the air. It struck the windshield a quick blow on its way, shattering the glass to bursts, sending filaments flying like fireworks and leaving the front of the Seville ripped open.

Now she could see. She could see that it was them.

There they were again—in the same cramped getup, with the same slicked hair—and this time glaringly real. They were real, they were killers, and they were tailing her.

In the passenger seat, John's hooked nose hovered above his open, howling mouth, its disfigurement rendered doubly appalling by his screams. He beat at the dashboard like a caffeinated toddler who wasn't getting his way, and leaned forward, pointing his sausage-thick index finger out toward Meredith. He hoisted up a gun.

Meanwhile, George was driving with all the composure of a seasoned fighter pilot, his greased hair unmoved by the smack of wind pummeling against it through the shattered glass, his thin lips straight and steady.

She flattened the gas pedal, yet the gap between them still shrank.

Too late to stop.

(DON'T STOP!)

As the exit lane split and veered away, her two chimeral foes approached the left side of the truck. John rolled down his window and hoisted up his little 9mm, aiming it out and toward his quarry, tracing the length of his arm.

She fought the urge to look over again, to see if he would shoot. As she slid onto the off-ramp, the space behind her was swallowed up by another car exiting— its driver completely oblivious to the danger they faced, blind to the two hulking suits in her pursuit. The Cadillac fought for a spot, any small opening to slip through before the last eighteenth of a mile rocketed by, along with their last opportunity to follow after her. Smiling, she watched them fly by with traffic, John's face a crumpled gaussian blur of anger fading out of sight.

Home free, she thought, and calmed herself, but a well of pain burgeoned through her shoulder. Her clavicle felt sticky and hot; she touched it and her hand came away painted red.

Shit.

John had shot her and she didn't even feel it, at least not right away. A cascade of gore streamed from the hole in her side, and a muzzy sort of nausea choked her breath. Colorless confusion filled her head. Vibration suffocated her hearing. She wiped at her eyes to keep them from stamping shut, ordering them to stay open, willing her body to postpone the pain, to overlook the shock that was creeping over her.

A flash, cast by dying orange daylight on metal, drew her gaze back to the road ahead; it was the beaming curves of a convertible. Its grandeur mesmerized her, drawing her into fantasy—*coasting along carefree streets with the wind in her hair and her beau by her side.*

Shrill steel grinding on blacktop roused her as she realized, too late, that she was driving too fast to control her path. Hand over hand, she struggled to keep tread with the curving surface of the road, her foot pumping the brake for friction, decelerating too slowly. Her hands raised up, abandoning the wheel, and the truck spun out.

Tires screeching, alloy shattering.

She blasted into the rear of the convertible, its back end dipping against the force of the blow and propelling its driver out of his seat, arms flailing as his car spun around and he soared through the front of it toward her. He hit the windshield of the truck rear-end first, and shattered it just as Meredith's head bounced against the steering wheel. The two autos fractured to pieces as they—and their vehicles—flipped over. Meredith's arms swept out in a hopeless gesture of self-defense, watching as the truck slid, bottom end up, toward the base of the off-ramp.

Even as shrapnel and bits of flying glass caught on her face—ripping back open the fresh wounds in her neck and chin and cheek—she cradled her abdomen, protecting her child.

The bulk of the stranger's unconscious frame, still caught in the windshield, cushioned her against a new spray of debris as the collapsed vehicles coasted to collide with another car, passing by at the wrong moment, its windows exploding outward and adding to the mix of deadly detritus blasting through the air. The windshield that held the man was shucked from its casing and bisected him: at one end, a head and torso, arms torn to pieces, flattened to mush dripping off bone; on the other side, a pair of legs cut away, free to smack her in the chest.

Meredith hung against her seatbelt in the steel ossuary of the truck's compartment, cinched up like an accordion, waiting in slow motion for it all to finally end. She craned her neck and pushed all of her weight down into the seat from which she hung—which meant the direction she actually pushed was *up*—to minimize the pressure against her belly; it helped to alleviate the rush of blood filling her concussed head. Her fingers felt blindly for the *click* of a buckle, caught, and she was dumped onto the roof of the cabin, disoriented and sore, breath ragged.

The sound of wheels on gravel. The squeal of brakes.

She could just make out the shape of the Cadillac Seville, a late '70s model, pulling up to the wreckage of the crash. Four high-gloss, well-polished black leather oxfords tapped their way toward her, each one attached to legs which were perfectly sheathed by the hemmed, too-tight legs of their pressed black pants.

Their voices only dripped onto her perception—barely there, dissolving into the colorless backdrop of the landscape, like ambient sounds on an elevator.

Pull her out came through as a snippet of lucid speech, in the unmistakably country dialect of the tall man, John.

A plump set of dark-skinned hands hauled her free of the destruction and dropped her, prostrate across their hood.

Sirens wailed, drawing near. John and George looked at each other, their faces stretched into nearly comic bogeymens' masks by the torpor drawing her into its spell of quiet, lonely calm, of gray indifference. They hooked their arms through hers, lifted her off the hood, and tossed her into the back seat.

"Call it in." It was John again. "Let's get her the fuck outta here. Little bitch." She felt the unmistakable smack of thick, warm spit hit her square in the face.

The world dimmed around her. In those evanescent moments, all she could think of was her child, of its safety. She'd slaughtered her husband and practically killed herself to boot, yet all she could think of was the baby inside of her. She focused her energy on that life within her and what she found there, remarkably, was the recurrence of the voice that had coaxed her through the chaos. It had helped her endure the torture of killing Peter—or whatever had inhabited him. And it tried to help her to escape from George and John, from whatever evil biddings they deigned to fulfill. But now, it spoke in a different voice—it was almost Peter's, and it was repeating his last words to her.

She repeated after the voice in her mind, mumbling aloud the words it spoke and committing them to her memory, for whatever it was worth.

"If you leave, don't go too far."

CHAPTER XII

Meredith opened her eyes to a sterile, whitewashed environment. A gown hung loosely from her body, gathering into unflattering pools against the ratty cot she lay upon. A needle protruded from her arm. Tubing sloped from it, rising up to meet the body of water it supplied to her veins, a clear liquid dripping from an IV bag. The curtain surrounding her, which hung from rusted rods attached to the ceiling, was printed with a repeated, smiling yellow face that reminded her of the food she and Peter had delivered to The Peach Pacific.

THANK YOU ENJOY.

The curtains were drawn snugly around her cot, blocking out the rest of the room in which she lay at rest. It might have been a tiny space or a looming, open bunker, but the panels of the dropped ceiling—cracked and stained above her—hinted more toward the former.

A tight pressure along her spine prevented her from lifting up her head.

Scuttles and creaks. The sound of a distant newscast. Coughing.

Her entire body pulsated with bruises. Every muscle and nerve lit with an undeniable command: *REST*. But she fought the urge to drift back into numb sleep—perhaps even coma—and patted her way along the side of her bed, searching blindly. Her hand settled on a two-inch block of plastic, inlaid with a small depressible circle. It was a call button.

Push! she commanded.

It took every ounce of her diminished strength to press down on the mechanism, but it finally gave under her meager force. There was no satisfying click.

It's over, she thought. *I'm safe.*

She anticipated the arrival of some attendant—a smiling nurse, an encouraging doctor, *anyone*. When no one arrived, a sense of abandonment overcame her and, by its urgency, also brought back a brusque connection between her mind and wounded body. She strained against her attenuated back to lift herself up and her muscles responded, propping her up on both elbows. She hiked all of her weight into her flattened palms, flexing her abdomen forward, and leaned down to massage her dormant legs. Turning her head from side to side, she tested the elasticity of the muscles bunched together at the pith of her neck. All in all, she was intact.

Yet something still didn't feel right. A part of her felt hollowed, as though her core had been drilled into with an ice cream scoop. The bend of her stomach was slack, hanging from her like an empty plastic bag, a drooping paunch.

Suddenly, two young women appeared behind the white shade surrounding the bed, their silhouettes traced there like shadow puppets acting out the drama of Meredith's life.

She tried to speak, to urge them closer, but the words came out jumbled, "I, wha' happ—wha' hap-hap-pen…"

"You were in an accident," one of the nurses said with a high squeak. She pulled back the curtain to reveal herself—a common enough girl, sandy haired and teetering on the brink of obesity. "You'll be fine. You just need to rest."

The nurse turned from Meredith and whispered something into her colleague's ear, stretching to do so because the second nurse was tall (and thin, with no breasts and a toothy-grinned face floating on her ostrich neck).

"What about—" Meredith's voice caught in her throat. "What about my baby?"

"You incurred severe trauma to the abdomen during the accident." It was the fat one again. She had an air of obligation, not of empathy. "Among other places. Miss, your peritoneum ruptured, and your uterus was badly damaged. We had to induce labor by Cesarean section. There was no other choice, ma'am."

The other nurse advanced to stand beside her cohort, looming there with a giant hypodermic in her hand, still grinning from ear-to-ear, teeth beaming in the harsh light of the fluorescent lamps dangling loosely overhead. Both of the nurses' faces had the apathetic look of women too accustomed to a life dealing with trauma; they had the conditioned, stoical mouths and hardened brows of tired undertakers.

The needle pricked Meredith's forearm and a rush of leaden numbness coasted for her brain, blurring both the nurses into billowing, amorphous wraiths. Their voices took on grim depth, and their faces melted to gummy blobs.

"This will help you rest," one of them said, though Meredith couldn't quite tell which.

She fought against the claws of the sedative and managed to mumble, "What...happened to..." She couldn't complete her question—the drug was too strong. Anyway, it would only have been a repetition of the first one—*What happened to my baby?*—and they hadn't been telling at that.

The quarters folded up neatly around her as she sidled into dreamless chemical sleep.

CHAPTER XIII

Meredith woke up shivering and wheezing, patting at her face to confirm that it was still correctly assembled.

A heart monitor on the metallic bedside table beeped out a breakneck tone. It was an imminent threat: her own fast-beating heart. It would summon help—help she didn't want—so she calmed her breathing, imagining soft cirrus clouds enveloping her, cuddly blankets of sky stuff. The beeping slowed down.

She surveyed the room with a clearer head than before, blinking to rid her eyes of gunk, struggling to orient herself in the space.

There was a television, turned off; its reflection was too far away for her to make out the image of her own ragged, skinny reflection. A table—pushed against the wall by the door—was set with an empty vase, a cheap, pastel blue plastic telephone, and an empty cafeteria tray. A bedpan leaned against the far wall; it was empty. The door was cracked open by a brown plastic doorstop, yet few sounds made it through the sliver of the frame and to Meredith's ears: a whisper of electricity; a smidgen of air passing through the crack like wind through branches. The room's solitary window was drawn shut, its curtains gathered to darken the room. Still, daylight—even if it was scarce—was a welcome sensation, a mellow tickling of her skin. There were no other cots around her. She was alone.

Leaning clumsily over the guardrails of the bed, Meredith readied herself to escape. In her mind, she could simply get up, dust herself off, and run from the place, but her legs didn't want to listen. The idea of movement was ridiculous to them and, as she struggled to pry herself off the cot, she almost spilled across the floor. She lay back down and let the dizzy spell pass.

The feeling of lightness she experienced through her limbs told her something: it told her she'd been resting for a while, and her bony wrists confirmed it.

How long? she wondered.

She managed to slide herself closer to the side of the bed, but her movement pulled against the apparatuses binding her—a series of tubes running between the side rails. The stand to which they ran flipped over and, with a crash, sent urine running across the floor. She traced two of the tubes back to their home in her abdomen and, agonizingly, ripped them both out; they sputtered red fluid in intermittent bursts. One line was still attached to her, taped against the inside of her thigh. It was an indwelling urinary catheter. The narrow tubing disappeared into the fold of her vagina; it recalled the form of the thing that had leapt out of Peter's bashed-in skull.

She wrenched the needle out from her bladder. It ruptured and discharged a commixture of urine and blood. She tore out the IV that had long settled into the crook of her inner elbow; the serrated tip trickled. Beneath her soggy dressing gown, her bare figure was wired up with other devices—ones she didn't know the names of—but she knew one of them had to connect to the heart monitor, which was still blaring, essentially shouting *JAIL-BREAK!* beside her.

Meredith stood and ripped them all away. The monitor flatlined.

She scuttled for the door while gripping her crotch, christening the floor with droplets of blood as she floundered for stable footing. She ducked for the table, aiming for the telephone. It felt artificial in her grip—smooth and light, like a hollowed movie prop—and it carried no dial tone. Slamming the receiver down and lifting it back up, she tried again for a tone. Nothing. Pointless.

She fell back into the chair set alongside the table and sat there, unmoving for some moments, laughing at her own slow progress.

The monitor continued its high-pitched one-note shrill, but no one came to her aid.

Mobile at last, she trudged to the room's closest reflective surface, the television, and screamed at what she saw: her jaundiced eyes had sunken in, swathed by deep lines and dark circles; her nose was a thin strip of cartilage, the narrow bridge protruding from deep within the emaciated canyons of her cheeks; the medial line between her nose and lip was scaly and had become more pronounced, like the shadow of a steep cliff, it loomed above her scaly mouth and looked more like the philtrum of an ape. Her once curvaceous figure had dissolved away, liquefied to flabby skin hanging over bones, with only vestigial impressions of her beauty left behind, like yardage of silk without a form to hold it aloft.

An urge overcame her—to shatter the TV screen, to take up a thick shard of its glass and strike herself across both wrists. It would all be over quick; she'd bleed out too fast for them to intervene (besides which, according to the monitor she'd been "dying" for minutes, yet still no one had rushed to her bedside).

But something kept her from acting on the enticing possibility of a quick, quiet exit. It was the matter of the child, a large and looming question mark. She remembered the nurse's words:

severe trauma to the abdomen.

peritoneum ruptured.

uterus damaged.

Though her physical state was in shambles, a bolt of acuity formed at the front of her mind. It was a brute psychic wavelength, an invisible line of connection to the child that, somewhere, had lived on. She knew it, she felt it.

labor by Cesarean.

The likelihood of a second trimester fetus surviving a birth so premature was nil-to-none. But still, the nurse had said nothing about it passing.

The baby represented a chance for Meredith to expunge the evil forces assailing her, which had threatened to destroy her life. *Everyone loves a child,* she told herself. Even the most sinister of bastards melted at the sound of a newborn cooing in their arms. It—he or she—might also be what kept her from a life spent wasting away in prison. And it was her child, not anyone else's; they couldn't keep her from it. Not John and not George; not any cops or lawyers, judges, nor jury, jails, or worse.

More importantly, the life she'd so strived to protect had been a key to her survival. Somehow, all along, it had ensured her (relative) safe-keeping, and forestalled her death. Perhaps its safety had also been the reason why that barbaric pair, the Tall and Short Men, had decided to bring her to the hospital. If they wanted Meredith dead—and if the life of her child hadn't mattered to them—they would have ended her back at the crash site. They had ample time then to stomp in her skull, or shoot her between the eyes, or slice her neck wide open. But they hadn't.

They'll be back for me, she realized.

Meredith recalled the voice that had encouraged her during her hotfoot dash from the motel, and while she'd blasted across the highway. It had followed her all the way 'til the end, and some part of it still lingered, pulsating mildly within her. Only a feeling of it remained, an invisible sensation which breathed through the center of her brain—there but intangible, inexplicable, like an amputee's throbbing phantom limb.

Meredith grew ever certain: her baby was living and safe. And it was still— perhaps unintentionally—bolstering her on. If it really was alive, it might be her only remaining defense, her only protection from the wrath of whatever company the suited men kept.

Beside her, the heart monitor continued its blaring flatline. The patter of footsteps approaching meant the slow help had finally arrived.

She fumbled with the device, struggling to reaffix the pad of the sensor to her chest, but to no avail.

The door burst fully open and two nurses rushed in—a man, his eyes bulging at the scene, and a young woman, who sighed at the mess. They lifted and moved her (legs kicking, screaming curses) back to the cot. The man stood on one side and the woman at the other, locking Meredith's wrists down to her sides with thick leather shackles. The woman turned away for a moment to prep a hypodermic, affixing it to an oceanful of some languidly sloshing, cloudy potion. The needle easily found its way into Meredith's vein. The hammer was driven downward, the contents of the syringe swimming into her. The hypo's connector was pale blue—a blue which was cerulean, like the sky clearing after a storm.

Resisting the brawny pull of sleep, Meredith whipped up against her fetters and shouted:

"Where's my baby?"

The female nurse looked up at her workmate with uneasy eyes.

Whirls of the soporific numbed Meredith's face. The exchange of her tongue against her palate slowed like a slug's slow-baking death in the sun, impeding her ability to speak. Her mouth felt filled with chalky plaster. Despite the aphasic effect of the drug, she *felt* with increasing clarity: every hair on her head, every puff of air shooting out of the nurses' labored mouths, like the violent draught of twin tornadoes. Whatever amplified the sensorial link between her surroundings and her perception dissolved as soon as the sedative melted fully with her viscera. Then, it scrambled her impressions of the space around her, the details softening into wooly shadows.

As the opiate invaded her ever nook, her pupils constricted under their advice. Her breath slowed and a warm rush of blood rose throughout her body, moving up toward her drowsy head. An itch hooked through her eyelids, urging them downward and closed.

But the voice that wasn't quite a voice leapt up again. It appealed for her faculties and whispered words of encouragement, barely discernible behind the glimmer and glam of the powerful drug.

...not disappear...

...must...

...to leave...

Feet shuffled. The nurses moved away from her, their voices dissected to intermittent, receding peeps.

...fight...

...calm...

There was a sound of rubber gloves, their pliant shape stretching out and snapping against skin.

...one chance...

...now...NOW!

A flutter of clarity engulfed her, a divine epiphany. The lights buzzed blindingly overhead, struck with magic like a match in the dark. Every particle of dirt gleamed up from its place on the floor. She felt the movement of blood through every capillary running beneath her skin. But still—despite the tenacity of her will and the aid of her invisible guardian—Meredith couldn't move; all of her limbs hung loosely at her sides.

The female nurse was still in the room. She picked up the phone and dialed a number (it baffled Meredith how she so easily managed to catch a tone). After a pause, the woman spoke:

"Yes, she's woken up." She bit her thumbs, peeking out the door and making a shooing gesture while she covered up the phone's receiver, pausing before she continued. "About ten minutes ago. No, she's fast asleep again. We took care of that." Another pause. "Okay, that'll work, but for how long? I suppose that'll be fine. She'll probably come to by then."

With her cognizance slipping, Meredith fought against the drug's strong current, commanding her senses to endure for just a while longer—like a castaway clinging to the buoyant wreckage of her demolished sailboat, even as sharks swarmed around her. She hoped for some revelation—that the now silent voice (whatever it had been) would suddenly leap forth, with renewed strength—a genie summoned to fight by her master's side.

"…the child."

Those two words, which the woman had spoken, beckoned Meredith back from the hopeless jumble in her mind; they tore her from the quicksand pull of the narcotic.

"Yes, she asked about the girl." A longish pause. "No, you heard correctly… I said, *the girl*." A long pause, the longest so far. The woman stomped one of her feet and huffed. "Well, that's something you'll have to take up with him. I don't care what you say, we *can't* keep her here, not for very much longer—" Frustration had crept into the woman's voice, but whoever was on the other end of the line did a swell job of wrangling her back in. "I understand that… I'm sorry. Yes, I know he has a lot of pull, even here, but someone's *bound* to start asking questions if she carries on like this, locked away and screaming behind closed doors." This time the pause was only brief, and the woman's chest barely had time to rise as she drew in an anxious breath. "No, I won't do that, I refuse. Yes, okay, fine. I'll stand guard over her room, at least until you make it. Yes, sir, I understand. We'll see you soon."

Meredith was anesthetized—doped beyond recognizing the sound of her own heartbeat, which had just become inflamed—and her grasp of the telephone conversation had been largely inconstant, but it sounded as though they'd been discussing the sex of the child. Of *her* child. Her baby girl.

She, Meredith thought.

The tickling numbness of the drug rose again, fierce as a deluge. She succumbed at last to its somniferous grasp and let herself be submerged by it, drifting toward its yawning void. Its embrace was a solace, a cure-all with downy plumage; it swaddled her, and carried her away to another dreamless sleep.

CHAPTER XIV

A pair of ominously frowning figures greeted Meredith as she awoke—on the sweat-slick cot, in the increasingly familiar confines of her private hospital room—in her *prison*. Her former attendants had gone and left behind a glowering couple of grease-haired thugs.

John and George, seeing she was awake, smiled. In the room's harsh light, Mr. All-Angles John looked even more like coarse-chipped stone, sculptural and menacing as a gargoyle. And George: well, up close he was a different sort of scary. She was almost tempted to laugh at how his height diminished, standing alongside John.

The door was closed. Leather shackles—straight from the basement of some looney bin—still bound her arms to her sides, against the cot.

George and John sat at the table by the door, staring back at her from across the room. John looked like a viper, retracted, ready to pounce. He stood up and walked confidently toward her, carrying a plain manila folder which was drawn shut by a circle of red thread.

"You're awake," he said, and shook the bonds that held her to the cot, checking their efficiency. His mouth formed a check mark.

At his approach, Meredith's heart rate skipped. She pulled against the straps binding her and screamed, "Get away from me! Take these off of me!"

"Don't struggle," George said, still seated by the door, tinkering with the telephone. "It'll do you no good."

"Fuck you both!" She spat at John, hoping to repay the favor he'd offered her in kind, but the globule of saliva that shot from her mouth missed its mark, falling short to splash against his shoe.

"That wasn't very nice," John said. He leaned down and wiped away the spit using his bare index finger (the toe cap squeaking out a deafening peal in the suddenly silent room). He straightened up and, with a shake of his wrist, the globule slapped back against the floor. A steely composure hung upon his face. "As George was saying, struggling will do you no good."

George's thuggish accent broke loose as he backed up big-man John: "Yeah, give it up!"

John craned his neck to regard his accomplice and said, sarcastically, "Thanks a bunch, Georgey." He adjusted his sunglasses down the bridge of his nose, revealing those impossibly red, bedeviled eyes of his for a moment before covering them up once more. Then he was grinning; it was a long, wide grimace and it conjured up fresh dread in Meredith. She could almost imagine his face as a wolf, whispering, *The Better to Eat You With, My Dear!*

George stood up and walked over to stand beside John. The top of his head barely surpassed the crest of his alpine buddy's chin. He said, "It'll do you no good because, by all accounts, you're completely, irrevocably insane."

"Yep," John added. "Add to that the undeniable fact that your caretakers aren't rightly sane themselves, helping us as they have, and what do you end up with? Just what we've said: an inescapable situation, ma'am. Irrevocable, as Georgey said." He smiled down at her, his teeth full-on glinting, loosely vampiric.

"What do you want from me?" Meredith pleaded. She realized she was completely in their domain—irrevocably, as the thin-lipped one had said, licking his lecherous lips. In spite of all her inward cautions, she began to cry. "What did you do to my baby?"

"Au contraire, little Mare," George said, nudging his partner in the ribs (though John didn't register any sense of the pun and was far less than impressed). "Seems like *you're* the one want's something from *us.*"

"I want my baby," Meredith cooed. "I'll do anything. Just give me back my girl."

The men jolted back at that, but quickly recovered. John nodded to George again, and he leaned in very close, his breath foul and burning in Meredith's nostrils. He said, "Yer gettin' ahead of yerself, sweetheart." He patted her on one shackled wrist. "Why not see what's in the envelope?"

The crinkled edges of the file folder were soft, the corners worn to blurs as fuzzy as cotton. It lay resting on the hollow of her emptied gut, where John had gently placed it. She reached out for it, forgetting she was bound, and immediately swelled with hatred for them both; it was just beyond her reach. They were teasing her—like two evil little boys poking a chained-up puppy with some sticks—and loving every minute of it.

John and George looked at each other, lips pursed, all but shaking in their skins to hold back the enjoyment they got from playing their little game. Finally, unable to contain themselves further, they burst into booming, idiotic laughter.

Meredith was now certain (even without the omnipresent aid of her missing guardian) that neither John nor George were lenient men. They were callous, hard-boiled weasels. They were the kind of men who saw their business through to the end—rain or snow, fire or brimstone—even if it meant murder. The bullet hole they'd set through her was proof enough of that.

John grabbed the chair by the door and scraped it across the room. He sat down beside Meredith and told her, "Let's clear the air."

She waited for him to explain, but he only stared.

"Okay," she said nervously. "What's in the envelope?"

"In time," George said. "Play your cards right and you'll leave here alive, wiser than you were before."

"Now, now," John said. "Let's not rush into anything, George. How do you want this to go, Meredith?"

She wasn't sure what he meant, but she answered as best as she could: "Easy. I want it to go easy. I'll do what you say."

That seemed to satisfy John; he grinned again, and patted her square on the chin. It hurt more than a bit when he touched her there (she wondered how it looked, and if there wouldn't be a permanent, horrible scar where the creature had ripped her open). The touch of his skin almost seared, and drew her gaze into those eyes of his, which glowed even behind the comfort of his aviators.

"How do I know you?" Meredith asked. "You seem so familiar, but I'm sure we've never met."

John's grin flattened out.

George took up smacking his lips again, with renewed vigor.

"You've never known us," John said, "and you never will. Only one man can."

George nodded, adding, "But it's only natural you'd feel that way. We've been tracking you a while. You might have seen us, even if you didn't *see* us. Know what I mean?"

"Tracking me?" she asked.

"Yes," they said in unison.

"Ever since you met," John added.

"Since I met whom?" She was growing anxious, and pushed away the sense of knowing which crept up between her breasts and cloyed moistly down her neck.

They both laughed.

"Think hard," George said. "I insist."

"Meredith," John said, "you must have known. At least a little. You must have felt it: that he was so very *special*, in every single way. Some deep part of you must have realized *who* he was—how great he really was—else you wouldn't have kept comin' back, over and over, like a pet with its tail tucked low between its legs." He traced the aspect of her thigh with a cold finger.

She pictured *him*: his tight skin and leprous, bony wrists; his giving, open mouth, so ready and anxious to please her; his broad, skinny shoulders, so unlike Peter's. She said his name:

"Luke."

"Is that what he called himself with you?" John asked. "He goes by many names. None of them are real."

She felt the blood drain from her face.

So many trysts in dirty motel rooms, never understanding why she kept returning, as though she'd been drawn by some enchantment, against her own will.

"To name a thing," George said, "gives away its power. *Him* included."

She whimpered, "Why me?"

"He has investments all over the western United States, and expanding every year." John tapped the envelope still resting on her stomach. "It's all in there. You were one of his most promising prospects. We only just found out the baby you carried—*his* child—was a *girl*." He said the last word with a twinge, as though it hurt coming out of his mouth.

"But, you'll be happy to know," George said, "that she surprised us." He retrieved the envelope, unraveling the string that bound it shut and lifting back the flap. "Which means you don't *have* to die."

"Under certain circumstances," John added.

She blinked back at them and repeated herself: "So what do you want?"

"You've got quite the one-track mind," John said. "As George mentioned, she surprised us—"

"What did you do to her?" Meredith slammed against her fetters.

"Nothing she won't recover from—hasn't recovered from already, truth be told." John grabbed the envelope from George and told him, "Not yet."

"What John's trying to say," George continued, "is that we gave her a little test. Normally, in cases like these, we'd just get rid of you both, count our losses, and move on. But *he* was insistent—honestly, I think he might even have been a bit distraught over losing you. So here we are—"

"Get to the point, Georgey," John interrupted.

"Yeah, so, we took a short blade and we cut her, real deep across her leg—"

Meredith screamed—a resonant, high-pitched roar, veins popping out against her neck.

John covered her mouth until she quietened, screaming "Shut the fuck up!"

His palm tasted curiously like rosemary and mint. Slowly, she calmed down, reminding herself of what George had said: *she surprised them.*

"Go on," John said. "Finish what you were saying, George."

"So we cut her, like I said, real deep across her leg. Turns out she's human all right, but with a little something extra, something special."

Meredith let out the breath she'd been holding, snot and sweat running across her chin as she asked, begging, "What happened?"

"She passed the goddamn test," John said. "With flying fuckin' colors."

She regarded them in turns: George was nodding amicably and John was shaking his head.

"What do you mean, she passed the test?" Meredith asked, her voice little more than a whisper.

"Well she didn't die, if that's what you're worried about." John turned to George and smacked him on the back. "Finish 'er off, Georgey."

"The little bitch smacked the knife away, and the blood that shoulda poured out—well, it just didn't. A few drops maybe, but then she healed right up, good as new, like nothing even happened. None worse for wear and all of that."

"Left a nice scar," John added, "but not much mess to clean up."

Meredith struggled to digest what they were saying.

"Just tell me what you want!" she screamed. "Please, just let me see her."

"There goes that one-track mind again," George said.

"Which is it," John chided, "*just* tell you what we want, or *just* let you see her?"

Another spasm of misery welled up within her; a hopelessness, an overwhelming lassitude. She screamed, "I don't know!"

"Fickle thing, you," John said. "Firstly, what we want's what he wants, and that's for us to know and you to maybe, someday far away, find out."

"You might take a guess," George added, "and probably wouldn't settle too far from the truth, neither."

"Are you some kind of cult?" Meredith asked.

To that they only laughed, and then sat blinking quietly, awaiting her next guess.

She refused to play their game.

Finally, George said, "We're much more than that."

"That's a dirty, dirty word," John said, and he spit upon the floor again.

"Why not just kill me?" Meredith asked.

"Well, if I had my way—" John started, but was interrupted by George.

"He has a strange affinity for you. You remind him of someone, a person he once cared greatly for. Besides that, you presented us with a unique opportunity. It's obvious you possess some unique—um, we'll call them *gifts*. We think the girl has something to do with it."

The girl, she reflected. *My girl. And his. The nameless one, whom I let defile me...*

"You've been at death's door," John said, scratching the rip in his palate (Meredith realized disfigurement was a trait they now shared in common). "You're in no state to be up and about. We almost gave up hope that you'd awaken. All the drugs they pumped into you will take a while to leave your body." He stood and snatched up Meredith's shackled left hand; with a key which he produced from his breast pocket, he unshackled the fetter that bound her. "Tell you what. You want to get out of here, right? And, as you say, you want to see your girl?"

"Yes," she whispered skeptically, cautiously.

"Good," John said. He'd clearly taken over as leader of the pair, and George idled himself with tidying up the room (cleaning up the two neat rings of spit, scrubbing the stains of Meredith's blood). John reached over her and unbuckled the other binding, the expanse of his giant palm covering her frail wrist with a giant's shadow. "The link you share with her will serve us in our purpose—"

"Which is what?" she interrupted.

"Patience." He masked his agitation well, putting on to placate her with a half-assed smile, while his real emotion shortly betrayed him in the slope of his brow; it gathered together in a tight knot, presenting a sharp contrast to the beaming white of his teeth. She pretended not to notice. "It's all written down in there," he said, and handed her the manila envelope.

With the pain of her pierced shoulder still throbbing (along with most of her body), she felt for the scab covering up the bullet wound. She stumbled around inside her head, searching for the voice—the force that had somehow balanced her out before—but it just wasn't there. Only the dull pain remained, steadily emanating from the hole in her shoulder, along with a fathomless feeling of despair, like being trapped on the top floor of a quickly crumbling high-rise.

John and George stared, waiting for her to make the next move in their portentous scheme.

"You chased me down," she said, struggling to remain calm, "*and* you fucking shot me! And now you want me to be *patient?*"

"Yeah," John said. "Sorry about that. We couldn't let you get away."

Meredith wondered how deep their chase had gone, and how far back. They said it themselves, *they'd been tracking her a while.*

"Were you back there, at the motel?" she asked.

"*Which* motel?" George said.

So many trysts, nights she couldn't much recall.

"Not those," she said, knowing full well what George had meant. She nearly vomited, recalling what she'd done on those nights. "The Peach Pacific. Did you kill a man there?"

"If you mean Peter, no." George took to brushing his lips with the sleeve of his jacket. They left streaks of white behind, a snail's trail of dead skin and mucous. "We did kill someone else staying there, though. He might have done something to your beloved."

"Actually," John said, "*she* killed Peter, if memory serves. Things always seem to have a way of working themselves out for the best." He glided his hands through his hard-parted hair; it bobbed like a buoy floating on the sea, gelled in place atop his long skull.

She wanted to scream but knew she shouldn't, so she bit her tongue 'til it bled. A savory taste filled her mouth, perhaps more pronounced because it had been so long since she'd eaten solid food, and the only other things she had tasted were John's palms and her own sweat and snot. She whispered, "I don't want to talk about Peter."

"Fair 'nuff," John said. "Rules are rules. We've got ours and you've got yours."

"So tell me your rules."

"It's all there." He tapped on the wearied yellow pouch still resting on her lap.

"I want to see her." Meredith swung a leg over the edge of the cot, but George caught her by the knee, twisting instinctually for something buried in the waistband at the back of his pants, eyeing John, waiting for some silent, brotherly signal.

"Now hold on, missy." He looked from George to her, and back again. "It's just not possible."

"Why not?" she asked. "I won't agree to anything until I see that she's okay."

"You drive a hard bargain." John's high cheekbones seemed to grow more defined, and the chiseled tip of his cleft chin filled with shadows when he dipped his head in thought. He turned to George. "Tell her."

"What?" George asked. "Tell her what?"

"Tell her about the girl," John said. "Describe her."

"Uh, okay, I'll try." George's cheeks flushed, even through his thick, dark skin. "She's just a tiny thing. Underweight. But her eyes are full of life, and watery like a sliced-open orange, bleeding with zing. Her fingers look kinda like hooks, the way they bend together, so pleadingly, open-palmed and reaching."

Meredith's eyes filled with tears.

"We'll take good care of her," John said. "Don't you worry. She's a very important little girl. No one will harm her."

She felt a flicker of the link they'd mentioned—a psychic flare up—but it soon ebbed, and left her feeling desperate. All she could think of was the way she'd slaughtered Peter, and of the creature that had been inside his head.

"What was that thing—back at the motel, the worm inside of his head? Inside of Peter."

"It *was* Peter," John said, "and the man we killed before him. Only different than them, too. A better version of them both."

"Better? He was insane! I don't understand."

"All right, Meredith." He nodded toward George, who dipped his chin and scraped the chair away, back beside the table at the door. "You've asked enough questions." He nodded toward the file again. "You're in the right to want to know. And we've told you as much as you *need* to know. Now, if you have any real hope of meeting your daughter, you'll do what we say." He forced the envelope into her hand and left it hanging loosely in her grip, its red closure dangling like a premonitory banner.

"Okay," she said, nodding her head and wondering immediately if this would be her greatest failure.

"Good," John said, and stood. "I'll leave you with the file. Read it and do what it says. If you do, we'll be seeing you soon, and you'll be meeting your little girl. George here'll fill in the blanks on some loose ends." He nodded to his partner.

George nodded back.

"Be in the car," John said, and decamped, leaving a gaping, titan-sized hole in his wake.

A bit of weight was stripped away, like a heavy layer of chain mail. Meredith felt she could breathe a little lighter.

"Okay," George said. "From now on, you won't attempt to interact with the girl in any way, except where sanctioned by our leader, whose title you'll soon learn. If you in any way attempt to communicate with her, outside of our conditions, both of you may be killed." He had effortlessly and wholly erased whatever slim notion of calm she might still have been capable of, wiping it clear from her forever more. He added, "It's all written there, as Johnny Boy said. Do you understand?"

The word *killed* still bounced around inside her head. Nevertheless, she nodded.

"You're her mother, and that'll never change, so we want you to be near her. But she can't know you're there, and she can't know you're her mother. Ever. That's the gist of it." He pointed to the folder. "Still, read it."

"Then I'll never be her mother."

"What?"

"You just said, *I'm her mother, and that'll never change*, but it already has. I'll never be her mother. Not in any normal sense."

George smiled at this, his pervy tongue working briefly across his lips, retracting so he could say, "Normal? What's that?" He patted her on the cheek— the one that would always bear a deep pink, nebulous scar. "I think you'll see that she's more than you could ever handle on your own, Meredith."

As George stood to leave, Meredith glanced around the room. Its commonplace dressings seemed so out of place compared to the otherworldly conversation she'd been having. Something inside of her, though not the voice, told her to consent (though, chiefly, she already had). Their conditions were as vague as her intuition was, but her husband was dead and she didn't feel much like running home to mommy.

And then there was her daughter to consider.

"You'll always have that psychic link," George said, winking. "You'll need to learn to block it out, for the safety of the girl. She's a part of something greater than you and I, but she can't know it until she's much older. It would ruin everything if she understood that, and it might destroy her."

"I'm still not sure I understand," Meredith said.

George pointed again, at the envelope she gripped in her hand, its flap hanging open, its contents ready to be unveiled. "Soon. Now behave yourself and do as the document says."

What other choice do I have? Meredith thought.

She reached into the envelope, pausing with her fingers wrapped around the dry, thin pages within (they felt like the crumbling hearts of giant maple leaves). She stopped to sum things up, to paint a picture of her life up until that moment, and to imagine what might await her on the far end of her path. Wherever it led, her daughter would be there. Even as a background character—as a bit player in the avowedly epic story of her little girl's life—it was Meredith's best and only option.

PART TWO: THE ALERION
SIXTEEN YEARS LATER

The Alerion is considered to be Lord of the Birds, but there is only one pair in the world. It's larger than an eagle, with razor-sharp wings, and its feathers are the color of fire. When the female is sixty years old, she lays two eggs, which take sixty days to hatch. When the young are born, the parents—accompanied by a retinue of other birds—fly to the sea, plunge in, and drown. The other birds return to the nest to care for the young Alerion until they are old enough to fly and may repeat the pattern again.

—Pierre de Beauvais

...it was clear to the more astute alchemists that the prima materia of the art was man himself.

—Carl Jung

CHAPTER XV

"Yes, that *really* is my name. O-r-s-o-n. Orson. Just like the famous novelist, really and truly."

"Who?"

"The famous nov—"

"Never mind, I understood you. I've never heard of him, though."

"Oh. Maybe *not* so famous, then. Except perhaps with a certain circle of geeks, nerdy kids. A few of his novels were adapted into crappy, big-budget Hollywood movies. His most well-known novel was called—"

"No matter! I likely won't know its name, so hush. Besides, we aren't here to talk literature, are we? It's enough that you stick out here like hay on fire—with your white hair and skin—without your bringing up all this other nonsense. Focus."

Orson listened in awe to the rhythmic pattern of the giant's speech. He was a hard-bodied Native American whose broad, sloped forehead and black, age-salted strands of thick, coarse hair (pulled back behind a paisley-printed headband and gathered up in the back, against the slope of his occipital ridge, into a tight braid which danced at every slight movement he made) did little to disrupt the world of stereotypes he fulfilled. There was even a phoenix—rising from the guts of orange-and-yellow flames—hovering over his square, sun-darkened face, etched into the wide-sloping fabric of his headband. Like a mythical figure, it guarded his skull. The ends of the bandana were tucked behind his big, flat ears. Ochre-tinted aviator sunglasses blocked his eyes against the dim dusk light trickling through the lodge. He scribbled at a form with a mechanical pencil, wedged between two of his coarse, cindery fingers.

"Yes, sir," Orson said. "I'll do my best to keep my literary tastes to myself." He squinted against the harsh sun, which was setting and sending its last, most fertile rays down to Earth before heading off to sleep. He hovered onto the tips of his toes to see behind the Big Man's glasses. What registered there was, well, *not much*. It was clear the Big Man didn't care who Orson was, where he'd come from, or where he was headed—unless any of those details stood out as pertaining to the welfare and/or potential (mis)representation of the people the man protected: his community.

The native man was himself a kind of guardian (akin to the phoenix he so proudly wore), standing right before the single most important threshold Orson had ever crossed in his academic life. That stern and sturdy man was the only thing standing between completing his thesis and calling it quits. Finding a new topic, giving up, or switching the focus of his dissertation were his only other options, and any of those would mean a whole lot more work, time, and energy wasted.

Cultural anthropology, Orson thought. *What was I thinking?*

"Good. Fine. Great. You're right, I don't care much about your literary tastes, Orson. But I do need to get a better grasp on your academic interest in our community. I need to understand your intentions, to fully gather why you've chosen to come here."

"No problem," Orson said. "Whatever you need to know. Just ask. I'm an *open book*. Eh? Get it?"

Orson winked, but the man failed to comprehend his joke—or at least didn't intend on responding to it.

"I'll just need to fill out this form," the warden said. "And ask you a few questions. Then we can be on our way. That okay with you?"

"Sure. Shoot. Open book, remember?"

Still no response, no glimmer of good humor.

All business, that one, Orson thought.

"You're here for a glimpse into our community, yeah?" the Big Man asked. His lips were thin as phyllo and dark as coffee. He spat a kind of casual dread which

Orson appreciated.

"Well, not exactly. I mean, yes, I *do* want to learn from and immerse myself within your community. Integrate, even, if that's at all possible—from a strictly observational standpoint, of course. I'm not going to harshly judge whatever I see, if that's what you're worried about." He realized he was rambling.

"Who said I was worried?" the warden asked.

If the Big Man was trying to make Orson nervous, he was doing a damned fine job of it. Orson's hands felt slick with perspiration, which was always a tell-tale sign of his delicate disposition. The slightest anxiety had always been more than enough to send him to a land of headaches and tooth-gritting, and this was bigger than any term paper or nasty text message he'd been strained by in his past—*this* was the biggest risk he'd ever taken.

"Uh, no one? No one said that." Orson nibbled nervously at his lip.

The Big Man continued to scribble silently across his form.

"You go to NYU, a famously liberal institution," the Big Man said. It was strange how quickly he could shift between the simple, carefully enunciated dialect of a Native Man (almost iambic in rhythm and meter) and the rhetoric of a seasoned intellectual, flat-toned and matter-of-fact.

"Sure, that's the general consensus—the outside perspective. But you'd be surprised, sir. My program is fair and non-biased. Actually, my focus has always been on casting a more *positive* light on the lesser-known sects of modern religion."

"Sure," the Big Man said ineffectually, placing the clipboard between his legs for a moment to tighten his headband. He sighed, shook his head, and scribbled some more notes. He added, "Except we don't subscribe to that—modern religion, nor any of its sects."

"Oh, sorry," Orson said, reconsidering his approach at softening up the giant. "Ever seen *The Exorcist*? Well, if I'd been hanging around with them—with Damien and Merrin, even Regan, for that matter—well, let's just say there would've been a lot less hostility in that little girl's bedroom. A lot less head turning, too."

Orson waited for laughter that never came. Not even a hint of a smile spread across the warden's face.

The Big Man peeked up from his onerous form for long enough to make another judgmental pass, eyes sweeping briefly over Orson. They were critical eyes;

they flicked up and down like rolling pools of black matter. Orson could tell that, even behind the sheen of his glossy sunglass lenses.

"You must be about five feet, ten inches tall," the Big Man muttered.

"Come *oooooon*," Orson whined. "I'm at least a *little* taller than that. I'm no giant, sir, but no one is when they're standing next to you."

The Big Man jerked his head up. "Five feet, eleven inches, then."

"Fine," Orson said. "But back to the real issue: so I came here on the principle of interest, not looking to spread religious intolerance. I have zero predisposition to your customs. Actually, I don't know much about them. Like, nothing, at all. I was tipped off by a colleague—another academic type, but he's real mysterious, see? So I'm kind of shooting in the dark here, if you know what I mean."

That was a lie. He'd heard stories. He knew enough.

Enough to fly across the country, to leave his already hectic, cluttered life in New York behind for even more stress, in the form of uncertainty and sand in his boots. Enough to warrant two connecting flights and another nine hours of driving a rental car that was on the verge of breaking down, its exhaust leaving a scattered trail of smoke in the wake of his doubtful, squinting path.

"Not really, no, I *don't* know what you mean," the Big Man replied, his tongue sticking out while he erased something from the form.

"Okay, then," Orson said. "No problem. What I mean is, can you tell me a bit about what to expect?"

"The word you used—religion—is still the closest word to describe the experience in your language."

"The *experience?*"

"Yes, the experience. You've come to us at a good time. We're set to conduct a very important ritual of ours, a kind of rite, tonight. You can observe, maybe even participate, if we make it there in time."

This was exactly the sort of break Orson needed—something to wow his peers and finally get him published. To think, a bona fide cult's secret ceremony. He tried to erase the budding excitement forming on his mouth, and to hide it from his tone.

He asked, "So what's the rite all about, sir?"

"English doesn't allow us to combine our words with our emotions, not truly.

Only our native tongue allows it to be said. Explaining it so you'll understand would require more words than I know in your language."

"Well, shucks, can you at least try?" Orson was getting to be more than a little annoyed. Even if the big guy had a job to do—to protect and serve his people, to filter out the crazies from the legitimate academics, to keep evil from their gates— he must also respect the fact that, as a visitor and a scholar, Orson should be treated with a certain level of respect. Of course, he wouldn't say any of this. Not when the man he stood to insult could easily break Orson's nose with a fraction of the strength he had in one of his titanic thumbs. Instead, Orson batted his eyelashes in what he hoped would produce a comical *Pwetty Pwease* effect.

The warden dropped his clipboard, set his pencil at rest atop it, and took off his sunglasses. A necklace made of leather and feathers hung around his neck, which he clipped his eyewear to. He regarded Orson heavily, silently, and with deep-set, squinting eyes, as if the endmost dying rays of sunlight—still slipping through the tilted blinds—were causing him an undue, deathly strain. A behemoth of a man, and yet the sunset rendered him risible at best—like a tiger prostrated and ready to pounce, who unexpectedly emits the squeak of a kitten.

"I'll try, but we should get going soon. Here's the deal: religion, as I already said, is the easiest word to use. Sure, it's reli*gious*, but it's also much, much more. If I included all the ceremony's deep-set meaning, its long history, its impact on and connection to our community's traditions, to our culture—if I included all of that in its description, we would actually come somewhere closer to self-realization than religion."

As Orson listened to the warden's monologue, he thought, *Big Guy's got more English words than I'd have guessed.*

"Self-realization, huh? I know a thing or two about that," Orson said. "But can't one be self-realized *through* religion?"

"Maybe. To us, the rite—and everything else we do here—is about getting attuned with what's *inside* the mind, moving past simply *understanding* what we see and coming to know *why it is* that we see what we see, and in the way we see it. For some of us, it's a time to go even deeper than that: downward, toward the spirit."

"Toward the spirit," Orson repeated. "You lost me a little, but now it really *does* sound like religion."

"Not so much toward the *individual* spirit, but toward a kind of group spirit."

"Like a collective unconscious? That's been written about before—and thoroughly, through all the common philosophical, spiritual, *and* religious texts. But you're saying you have evidence of this occurring—of it actually, observably happening?"

"Mhm." The Big Man softened his expression and even, for the first time, smiled, warm and friendly. He slapped Orson playfully across the shoulder.

"And I'll be able to observe that occurring in the midst of this *experience*? In the proceedings of this rite?"

"You'll more than observe it, Orson, if it's so willed. Your participation—if those overseeing the rite deem you worthy—would mean that you *influence* the experience, too."

"Oh, great. I can't wait." Orson really couldn't; he was ready to go, anxious to get out of the lodge and on the sand, gliding over it and riding a wave of impossible dreams. He was ready to participate in whatever otherworldly experience this man had (almost) promised.

"Our nature, *human* nature, is what you'll come to face out in that desert, boy, and you'll come to understand its connection to that *other* nature, too. The one outside of us and around us, but also within us, if we look far enough back to our roots, to our ancestors. We believe that if one looks deeply into oneself, what one sees there—if the seeker is true, and looks with hard intentions—well, it would blow your academic notion of religion out of the water."

That was a lot of Ones, Orson thought, again swallowing his sense of humor, just in case a poorly-timed laugh could mean he wouldn't be allowed to taste their fire water after all. A quote jumped to the tip of his tongue, but he wasn't so sure he should share it. He weighed his options, considering how this calm, purposeful giant might respond, and landed on *Why the hell not?*

"What you said reminds me of a quote by a pretty famous guy—even more famous than the author I mentioned earlier. He's widely appreciated for his contributions to philosophy. You might know him—Nietzsche." When the warden only stared, Orson continued, "He was German and he wrote a lot of things, but the quote I remembered goes something like, 'When you look into an abyss, the abyss also looks into you.' I think that comes pretty close, at least."

"A lazy synopsis at best," the Big Man said. "Of course I know Nietzsche."

Full of surprises, Orson thought.

"Well, sorry for all the questions, sir," he said. "I'll let you finish up that form. Let me know if I need to, um, fill anything out?"

The man nodded unceremoniously, picked the document back up, and replaced his glasses on the bridge of his nose. Clipboard in tow, he walked over toward an antique oakwood roll-top desk sitting in the corner of the lodge. An old, rusty bronze lamp sat atop it. The Big Man pulled down on its thin ball chain; its green, mosaic-glass shade cast the room in a macabre light, like an old Italian giallo film. All was diffused with a shocking glow.

The Big Man unlocked and rolled back the cover of the desk, rifled through a few drawers, and finally found what he was looking for. He handed Orson a bottle of water and a small bag, about the same size as the tip envelopes Orson used to inconspicuously undercut his flamboyant hairdresser Gilbert (pronounced *Jill-Bear*, of course) back in Soho. But this one was made of plastic instead of soft manila; and this one was filled with a dense white powder instead of a single, folded one-dollar bill.

"What's this?" Orson asked.

He lifted the substance up in the musty emerald light. The powder inside the envelope was thick and clumpy.

"Aspirin. Trust me, you'll need it in the morning."

"Why?" Orson asked.

"Imagine the worst hangover you've ever had." The Big Man expanded his palms, fingers stretched, like the force of a slow explosion. "And multiply its hellishness by a hundred."

Orson zoned him out—hangovers were no big deal anymore for him, he'd had plenty of those—and instead imagined himself lying naked in the desert, retching viscous bile over the edge of a giant chasm, accompanied by a pair of Komodo dragons. Scorpions were there, too, except they were the size of toddlers and they crawled across his bare, fuzzy ass cheeks like his flabby butt was just another no-name dune in their domain, complete with hair serving as native grass.

Get a grip, he thought.

"I think I can handle it. I've had my share of hangovers. So we'll be drinking?"

119

"You're some kind of big, tough man, huh?" The warden tapped his pencil point against the paper and rolled his square head around on top of his neck, letting out a crackle like spit on fire. "Don't look so scared. I'm just the ranger, Orson. If you're already having second thoughts, maybe you should heft your stick of cloth-wrapped sundries right back over your shoulder and head home for The Big Apple."

Orson did most definitely *not* want to trek all the way back across the country to New York, empty-handed, to become his class's biggest loser: the failure whose dreams of academic grandeur hadn't at all paid off. He could just about see himself hunched over, cradling his own frowning face between his stretched-open palms while the rest of his answerable, upstanding classmates received grants for research on some idyllic European Paradise Island.

Always the sore thumb of the lot, he thought. *Not this time.*

"I'm not scared," Orson said. "I'm ready to look deep into My Ownmost Self and all of that. I just, y'know, kind of wanted to know what to expect. Thanks for sharing what you can, sir. Now I'm just anxious and excited." He shook his head, bit his lip, and wondered if his sad excuse for a testimony had convinced the sharp, judicious warden. Somehow, Orson doubted it.

"Good," the Big Man replied, short and sweet.

While the ranger finished off a last stitch of scribbles at the bottom of his form, Orson uncapped the bottle of water he'd been given and took a swill. He wondered what was taking so long with the document; he was more ready now than ever to be out in the open-skied desert, breathing clean air and experiencing what all the hubbub was about.

Orson had been planning this trip for the majority of his graduate career, having slowly saved up enough money (dipping into his booze budget where necessary) to rent some film and audio equipment from a shady shop in Chinatown. Once he'd crossed his T's in paperwork and dotted his I's in insurance, Orson finally made for the deep desert. He was ready to sip the mojo, the ayahuasca, the whatever-it-was-called-for-them, and to be exposed to that which so few had been allowed to taste, to feel, to *experience*.

But that *goddamn* form.

It must be some kind of test, to see if he'd crack under the pressure, under the scrutiny of time and deafening quiet—with nothing but the sound of graphite sliding over paper and his own pulsating ticker, beating close within his chest (threatening to rip his shirt open and reveal his own lying scoundrel's innards).

The ranger looked him over again and said, "Since I can see you're in a hurry, and since I'm guessing your last name comes with a history neither of us has time to sit through tonight, I'll need your ID. I want to get it down pat, famous novelists notwithstanding, so we can get on with it."

Snide prick, Orson thought. *If you weren't so massive, I'd come back with something twice as insulting, thrice as sarcastic, and so far over your head that you'd think it was the moon in the sky.*

He dug out his old California driver's license, from long before the days of three-day, coffee-fueled research papers at the graduate library. He handed it over, but was careful to obscure the ID's outdated photo with the outer edge of his thumb. In the picture, Orson sported dyed, blue-black hair, a too-chiseled goatee (which he'd spent thirty minutes grooming per day), and a pair of thick-rimmed, black eyeglasses that only enhanced the aspect of his always-ogling big brown eyes, dark as the cups of java he drank.

The ranger stared at the ID for a long time before he started to write again.

"I know what you're thinking," Orson said, raising an eyebrow, stomaching a chuckle. "When you looked at my photo, you twitched a little. I know, I know. Pretty dumb, right? It was just a phase, though. The lip piercing and the striped mime's shirt. I was exploring new ways of expressing myself. I'm sure you understand."

"Not really, no. But we can go now, if you're ready."

The magic words, Orson thought.

The Big Man handed back his driver's license and, astonishingly, smiled down at him again. This time it was wider, revealing two strips of meaty brown gums, inlaid with two rows of square, opalescent, too-small teeth which were flecked with chalky patterns of tartar buildup.

"Thanks, sir," Orson said, and gulped, careful to bury any expression that might have indicated his repugnance toward the state of the warden's oral health.

"You're welcome." The ranger ripped the form straight across its perforation, separating the yellow copy from the rest of the stack, and handed it over to Orson.

He folded the original up into a tiny square and shoved it into his breast pocket. At the threshold, he picked a shotgun off the rack (Orson had foolishly thought it was decorative), and a tan Stetson hat. He tucked it onto his big blockhead, hefted the weapon up against his shoulder, and said, "You ready?"

"Whoa, whoa, whoa. No, I'm not *ready!*"

"Well why not? It's getting late, let's go."

"Um, a *shotgun?*"

"Yeah. A *shotgun.*" The warden shifted it to his other shoulder.

"As in, with bullets, that kill people?"

"Don't worry, I'm not going to kill anyone."

"What, animals instead?"

"Maybe. Who knows." He shifted the gun back to his other shoulder. "Do you have a choice? Want to go home?"

"No! Look chief, I'm just not sure how comfortable I am with the whole shotgun thing, okay?" Orson quickly realized he shouldn't have called the man *chief*, and bit his tongue. Embarrassed, he whispered, "Sorry."

"Don't worry about it. But, like I said, I'm not planning on shooting anyone. It's just in case."

"In case of *what?*"

"Banshees and goblins," the warden joked.

Orson lightened up a little. Now he was starting to see the warden for who he truly was—a big, hulking *softie* who put on a good show. He eased into the idea of the weapon; it was just meant to scare him into his place, to ensure that Orson wouldn't act out of line during their little show—their so-called *experience.*

"Y'all believe in ghosts, too?"

"You never know. It can't hurt to have her on hand." Without another word, the warden walked away from the conversation, split open the batwing doors which barely separated them from the cold outside, and disappeared into the desert.

The doors swung—violently at first—then slowly sank back into place, losing their momentum and settling against one another like quarreling lovers who were finally ready to admit their unremitting interdependence. They reminded him, too, of the old Spaghetti Westerns he'd watched years ago. He could still envision Franco Nero's steely-blue, narrowed eyes, and could hear him declaring:

You can clean up the mess, but don't touch my coffin!

Orson chuckled and followed the Big Man out into the emerging twilight, full of a ticklishly cool breath, glowing by the light of a winking moon, but he was stopped in his tracks by the Big Man's dusty, coarse-palmed hand against the front of his neck.

"One more thing, Orson. There's something I need to make clear: this is no hippie commune. Formalities and forms aside, I'm warning you—and not at all because I like you. You may be as open-minded as you say but, at rock bottom, you're still just another one of the kids who come up here a couple times a year with your research grants and your big ideas, thinking you'll prove a theory that doesn't need the waste of your words. Your description of what happens here doesn't matter, kid. Neither does your opinion. This isn't about words and theory. It's about a feeling, and the only reason we're letting you up here is in the hopes that—someday—someone like you might take away more than inspiration for his thesis. Maybe you'll actually be *changed* by this. Did you ever think of that?"

Orson's voice caught in his throat. He'd meant to say, *No*.

"Yeah," the warden said. "I'm not holding my breath, either."

Maybe not the hulking softie after all.

Orson wriggled against the pressure of the warden's grip, sweat dripping across his shoulders, dribbling down his back, and drenching the fabric encircling his armpits. Finally, the warden released him. It hadn't been a life-threatening hold, and barely left a mark, but its message was clear enough.

In the aftermath, rubbing his throat, Orson realized he was completely under the control of this lone ranger—the Big Man, the warden, the stereotype he'd been foolish enough to dismiss. Orson was in his domain—not the scorpions' domain, and not the Komodo dragons' either—playing under the warden's rules, shotgun and all.

"All right," the warden said disinterestedly, "let's go. It's a long walk from here."

"No car?" Orson asked, half-joking but half-hoping there was one, rubbing his neck again, lips quivering.

"No car."

Orson still pictured the faces of his sniggering, bumptious classmates, wondering if he should leave after all. And he couldn't shake the embarrassment he'd faced, being held up by the warden like that.

The moon hung long and low above them as they darted over the crests of dunes, skipping over snake holes en route for what Orson hoped would be an experience as titillating as the Big Man had promised.

They made their way deeper, into the engulfing blackness of the desert, the ranger mumbling indistinctly to himself in a singsongy pulse, using words Orson couldn't quite hear over the roar of the dry winds buffeting his eardrums, hardening his joints with their harsh chill. Their trek drew into an enduring blur of unabating, cruelly sloped drifts. They measured their slow progress by the point of the moon in the sky, though it wasn't moving much.

Orson's legs ached and his lips had long chapped over, but he pressed on, following closely in tow of the warden's winking shadow, mirroring the pathway the giant carved and rejoicing at the occasions when his leader's back provided him with a momentary shield against the wind, against the flecks of sand filling in the creases of his eyelids and the flaps of his ears.

Face my ownmost self, Orson thought. *Yeah, right. If we ever get out of this mess.*

The wind picked up, beating more violently against his naked cheeks, chaffing them into two rosy mounds as arid and swollen as the environs through which they traversed. This was the closest thing to a sandstorm he'd ever seen. The spineless extremities of those harsh currents whipped into Orson like a cat-o-nine-tails, cutting through his skin like butter. But just when he was ready to give up, to call it quits, to tell the warden to pick him up like a helpless infant and head back toward the banal, unremarkable world—just before saying, "Um, excuse me, but I think I made a mistake in coming here, might we please go back?"—the warden mumbled some words Orson finally *did* comprehend, and they were welcome words, soothing as watermelon juice is to a fiercely burning hangover.

The warden said, "We're almost there. It's just past the next crest. Look out for the shape of the monument."

"Okay," Orson said. He tried to check on the camera peeking oh-so-subtly from under the front flap of his backpack, to confirm that its little eye was still squinting imperceptibly from behind a carefully punched-in silver grommet—recording their every move—but the warden kept turning toward him, his big hands urging them forward.

Orson was *almost* certain he'd powered it up when he parked the beat-up rental. He could remember the feel of the little plastic ridges on the side of the power switch, the feeling of his thumb sliding against it as it made a soundless shift to the right, toward the position labeled ON.

But he wasn't sure—just *almost* certain.

Ahead of Orson, the warden was mumbling again.

The moment was close—*just around the corner*, he said, *so close at hand, one drift of sand away.*

At last, it rose over the next dune like a golem's stony hand—its fingers separated and protruding from the pebbly ground. The monument swelled before them; it was made up of giant and sturdy, forbidding pillars connected together by moss-covered cactus arms, like some deity's barren canopy. It was an outcropping that evoked all the wonder of Stonehenge, but with an unequivocally violent undertone, as though whoever or whatever created the structure had been born with a seething madness which was so visible, so palpable in the form of the stones.

"There it is," the Big Man said. "There's the monument."

"I see it," Orson said, but almost wished he hadn't.

CHAPTER XVI

Birch sat at his desk, made of iron and reclaimed wood, staring out the floor-to-ceiling windows of his fifteenth floor apartment, overlooking the San Francisco Bay. He gazed out at the Ferry Building, just two blocks away, and stilled his writer's hands, running his damp palms across the porous desk and listening for the 11 o'clock chimes.

It was an exemplarily cloudy Tuesday, with fog rolling torpidly between the Financial District's familiar skyline. He squinted to make out the distant figures of business men and women scrambling across the ground far below him, marching their way out of their offices headed for early lunches, cinched up to the napes of their necks with ties or tailored into snug-fitting pinstripe skirts. He laughed at the formality of their outfits and considered his own get-up, surveying his reflection in the pristine glare of the window: a ripped, navy U-neck t-shirt—oversized and desultory—hung from his lanky shoulders; his tried-and-true snug-fitting jeans (in a washed-out black that hadn't started out so faded) were cuffed to just above his skinny ankles; and his prototypical heather gray hoodie—which had seen better days—had drawstrings that were ragged as the scraps of a mountain lion's prey. But it didn't matter how slovenly Birch dressed, because Birch had never walked into an office building—and, if he could help it, he didn't ever plan to, either. It was the part of his life which he most cherished—getting to work in the privacy and comfort of his own home, at his own pace, keeping his own schedule. As his own boss, he seldom had to face the rigors of the rest of the Herd. Their 9 to 5. Their boxed To-Go lunches (ham sandwiches, lettuce wilted; lukewarm tomato bisque soup, probably poured straight into a plastic container from a red-and-white soup can).

As the clock tower finished its song, he picked up where he'd left off writing on his story—a memoir of sorts—which is to say that he resumed *wondering* what he should write, where he should waste his time. Work on the project had been stop-and-go for over a decade, and a half. He'd been through draft after draft, written and rewritten the goddamn thing, and it still wasn't to his liking; it wasn't groundbreaking enough. And it wasn't grounded by facts.

Birch already published the article, in one of its earliest forms—in a gritty punk 'zine called *West Coast Hoax*. The title he'd chosen for his entry, which back then had only been a measly five pages, was "Cutting Through the Shit: Taking Back the Truth." He thought it would be his first big break, but it (unsurprisingly) hadn't turned out to be the impetus toward success he'd hoped for. If anything, it had been a joke. A joke that never made it off the ground.

He reassured himself, writing his failure off to a false start:

Lots of famous letters, essays, and novels started out as shitty drafts, only to mature later— into works that gained proper recognition.

Back then, his article had been nothing more than an immature and unapproachable hodgepodge of conspiracy theories and logical fallacies. He'd been writing from a narrow perspective, based off of one hazy, semi-traumatic experience he had as a kid. His only piece of physical evidence was a fuzzy, shaky cell phone video. The rest was based on hearsay, and leads that never quite panned out. Often his investigative tips were delivered by guys with ridiculous names like Spike, or Pike, or Serge. Not that he could talk; with a name like Birch, he'd drawn more than a few easy laughs of his own.

Birch's less-than-common name wasn't the only thing atypical about him. For starters, he wasn't your regular FiDi tenant—not by any means. As a 30-year-old college dropout (it just hadn't been for him—all the structure, the regimented standards, the useless subjects he knew he'd never use again) who worked from home, he was viewed as a freak by his neighbors, and was often the subject of their whispered conversations through the hallways of their well-to-do high-rise. The other tenants viewed him as a wart on the otherwise pristine countenance of the

127

building, and as the bane of their socialites' reputations. Theirs was an address which was highly esteemed; they protected its namesake fervently, guarding the halls with hawks' eyes, scouting for any excuse to get Birch booted out on his ass. To them, he was just a sewer rat. An uneducated oddball.

And Birch had another strike against him. Although it was established that he worked from home, no one quite knew the details of his business. This, of course, led to everyone on his floor—and even the doorman downstairs—wondering persistently about what he did all day, locked up in his room, emerging only to answer the door for whatever delivery-man-of-the-day was there to drop off his rice and dumplings.

Birch knew they wondered—and that they gossiped—because he could hear them doing their wondering, their gossiping. Oftentimes, during the ever-awkward, hushed elevator rides, he'd catch a snippet of some less-than-favorable slur (*slob*), whispered between two ladies. Sometimes when he left the apartment for a jog, he'd come across some snub-nosed bitches pointing out his door as they passed it by—saying things like *fucking hippie* or *get a real job*, even though they had *no clue* what he did for a living, nor how much he made doing it. Mostly, he ignored their verbal jabs; he was used to it.

Besides which, he was doing all right for himself. The luxuries he so enjoyed were many, no thanks to his ever-enduring pet project—the time-sucker, the article. But it wasn't money that brought meaning to Birch's life. He wasn't the kind of guy to lavish and luxuriate, to show off with fancy cars and expensive booze. Nope, it was the bus and beer for him, forever. His only real indulgence was on unique books, first editions, out-of-prints, and odd pieces of furniture—like the writing desk he loved so much, emblazoned with a strange mark at its center: a kind of pentagram, decorated with symbols like little hieroglyphs that no one seemed able to decipher.

It wasn't his life's work—his writing—that had secured him the financial security with which he so dispassionately and privately lived. His *oeuvre* was just the background music to his working life and, though it was a symphony redolent with potential, it still hadn't come to fruition. So he had another job, to make money the way any college dropout miscreant does: in stocks.

Since the prime age of 14, Birch had been experimenting with computers.

Networking, coding, hacking—the gamut. His aunt once told him (always the voice of reason in her knee-high stockings and matronly dress, evoking a mid-century grandma in a nightgown), "Birch, you oughta turn that brainy hobby of yours into something more lucrative," but mispronouncing *lucrative*: *luke-ray-teave*. So he did, and it wasn't long before he mastered *l'art du commerce*. Since the evolution of trading had seen new conveniences in his early adult years, he was able to continually keep up with and master the latest technologies as soon as they emerged.

Be it on a shift at the stand, funneling candy for a bored tourist, or late at night, tucked under his aunt's hand-quilted blanket and tapping away at his cell phone, Birch filled his time with computers—video cameras, cell phone hacks, coding, a new buffering technology for the cell phone recording:

the recording he'd captured that summer, when the boardwalk had stood empty until a bleeding man crawled out of the ocean—

The clock tower tolled its mid-hour chant, signaling 11:30 and interrupting Birch's stroll down memory lane. He realized he hadn't written more than a couple of sentences all day—and they were a pair all right, lurching and illogical:

"All signs point to impending disorder, outright chaos—riots looting, water scarcity, government secession. The anarchic mess that awaits us, if we do not act now, would completely obliterate all residents of the Bay Area in less than two weeks' time."

He sighed and thought back to the event that had created his obsession; it had planted a seed in his mind which, festering there, had grown to reveal a strange, invisible, and riotous world of conspiracy. It was the world Birch lived in every day, and yet no one else seemed to see things quite the same way. The ever-elusive, obscure secrets he guarded—really, that he grasped for—always gleamed right at his periphery, just out of reach. One of his tip-offs would start to pan out and he'd be getting close to solid, concrete evidence (an eerily abandoned warehouse or a thinly guised alien landing strip on an old parking lot, buried in dead leaves and debris), but then he'd realize the "evidence" wouldn't stand up against common reasoning, the majority rationale, the media. When he tried to publish again, it would have to quiet all the major questions. He'd have to be ready to answer any objection raised against his claims. And it would have to be big—national, large-circulation, print, TV, radio.

But still, Birch could never quite connect the dots.

All trails lead to nowhere.

Except for the video.

The grainy, fuzzy cell phone video from sixteen years ago, taken when Birch had lived in a sleepy Southern California suburb with his old aunt Greta, and the only recourse young Birch had against the itch to smoke dope every day—to forget the lonesome, awkward teenage hell he lived in—had been reading, video games, and his part-time job as a cotton candy vendor at the piers.

He watched it a million times—that day, and almost every day since it happened—and it still made no sense. There was something more than surreal about the whole experience. There was something impossible about it: namely, everything. He only vaguely remembered being there, being present, standing and watching the whole thing as it happened, as though his cognizance had been severed from him for those few minutes, a blip in the timeline of his temporality carved away, an eraser dragged across his consciousness—across his memory. He'd stood by and watched like a soulless, mindless dolt—a numbskull—while the stranger was ripped apart and eaten alive by some violent alien *thing*. He'd watched a man die and didn't do a single thing to help him.

Guilt was one of the reasons he lied to the cops about what he saw, but a bigger part of the lie had stemmed from Birch's inborn inkling to uncover the *thing*'s true origin. He knew just by looking at it—and by its ravenous movement— that it wasn't some as of yet unclassified sea creature, one that had chosen to crawl up and out from the ocean's depths, that had coincidentally decided to make a lunch of the man on Birch's watch. It had to be much more than a leftover dinosaur. The thing was vicious. Small, but vicious. And sentient, intentional; it knew what it was doing when it went for the brain or the spine or whatever it had attacked, when it rendered the man unconscious—when it killed him. It ate through flesh like a red-hot laser. It opened the man up and made his insides its home, as effortlessly as a snail slides into a vacant shell, except the man's body had *not* been vacant when the creature decided to invade and make it its own.

To Birch, re-watching the video he'd captured of the incident was the first step in investigating the creature's roots and discovering the cause of its attack.

Watching the recording had also been an escape from the otherwise droll aspects of his humdrum, teenage life. It was something truly exciting (though morbid), and it had happened to him. He felt as though he'd been right at the center of it all for a reason, as if he'd been drawn toward his ultimate calling, as if he'd been chosen to witness that man's death. If Birch believed in predestination (which he didn't), he would have called that day—and all the long days since, of research, of false starts—his fate. But Birch wasn't like that. Sure, he'd been at the right place, at the right time, but to believe in the idea of *fate* meant believing in God, and Birch couldn't force himself to recognize—or even to speculate—on that front. There was no God in a world that could make a thing like that, nor one that exists in a universe that could take his mom away from him. Instead, Birch believed in conscious human choice. That meant he made the *willful* decision to lie to the cops—and to take it further, to research the creature on his own.

So he searched and traded, searched and traded, stumbling ever forward, hopefully—no, willfully—awaiting the day when he could prove he wasn't crazy, that he'd really seen the thing, and that it might be the end of them all, just as his gut had always told him. Sometimes he got caught up, thinking things like, *If only I'd known back then what I know now*—thinking he'd wasted sixteen years of his life, aching to solve the mystery of the monster he'd caught on film, when he wasn't even sure about calling it that: a monster. That was a bold word. Maybe it was something else—a random aberration; an evolutionary mishap; an optical illusion, or a hallucination caused by the boredom with which he'd lived his entire life. So many days, weeks, months, and years of aching, always ready for a new revelation that never fucking came, and yet he was just as eager, as anxious, to unravel the secrets of the *thing* he'd caught on film.

Birch hovered over a folder on his notebook's desktop; it was illusively named *Tom's Wedding* (he didn't even know a Tom). He single-clicked on and off the folder, selecting and deselecting the archive, shading and un-shading the folder's cunning caption as he gnawed at his bottom lip. He thought about how much time he'd spent poring over the thing, analyzing each and every still-frame snapshot for missing clues. He couldn't be exactly sure how long he'd spent—since he hadn't kept a log—but, by estimation, it very likely exceeded a quarter of his waking life.

Oh well, he thought. *One millionth time's the charm.*

It was a giant file, and his laptop lagged while opening it. He'd flattened and sharpened and blurred the thing beyond recognition of its earliest form, and still, all he could make out were the blurry, painful movements of the dying man. A sharp convulsion here, an agonizing jolt there, and then it was all over, just as before. Fade to black.

He squinted, adjusting the blinds to dim out the sunlight finally breaking through the fog. The screen adapted to its new ambience, brightening up a bit.

The stranger's screams were what had first drawn Birch's attention from his stand, before he even saw the man. And then he emerged, crawling along the shoreline, waterlogged and frantic. Sixteen years ago a man—whose name it seemed Birch may never come to know—struggled against the current, slowly lurched up the shore, tumbled over the boardwalk, and crawled toward him, fingers lifting up, twitching with entreaty.

"Help me, please," he'd begged.

The sound was gritty, even after submitting the file to the best audiophiles in the industry—across the country, around the world. The damn thing had been processed and reprocessed more times than he could count, but only behind a guise of fiction. Everyone involved on the project, except for himself (and except for his own aunt, who'd so predictably told him to call the cops, and that had been the end of her involvement) assumed it to be some cheaply constructed horror film. They were only sent the raw audio to work with, isolated from the video component; or, conversely, they were only given the video—what Birch told them was low-budget science fiction *crap* to edit.

Perhaps, he thought, *if they'd known the magnitude of the real subject matter they were dealing with, they'd have given it an extra level of care, extra attention to detail.*

They might have told Birch something more. Still, full disclosure was too risky.

Outside, the herd of professionals were trundling back to work, jogging for their offices. It was a familiar signal: the end of the early lunch crowd and what would soon become the real lunch hour, noon. Mid-day. Five hours of writing and a sidebar—a refresher with *the tape*—yet, as usual, Birch hadn't accomplished *anything* on the project.

The dying man on his screen was still screaming, his face a blur of movement and thrashing pain, while the worm-like thing gnawed its way through him. If Birch didn't know what he was looking at (if he hadn't seen it all first hand), the subtle tunnel popping up across the surface of the stranger's skin might not stand out in the footage. Like the gentle caress of a feather, its presence only hinted at the agony the man endured. Until the thing finally reached his head; then the man's suffering became more than apparent. His eyes rolled up into his skull, showing only slivers of white like shattered, slimy cue balls. He convulsed against the ground with enough force to splinter the wood panels beneath him. Little shards of oak sprayed up around him like a throttled jar of toothpicks, sprinkling across the sand.

As the man's seizures abated, Birch had begun to cry.

He remembered feeling helpless, not knowing what to do, and—once it was all over, when the stranger grew still—Birch also felt guilt. He filmed the whole thing, stood by and watched. He knew he'd be implicated in the crime, perhaps even tried with murder, unless he relinquished the evidence and told the authorities what he'd seen. Yet he wouldn't. Even in his murky state of mind, as cloudy and scared as he'd been, Birch was (and always would be) driven by his interests in the unknown. He was driven enough by these interests to hide his phone and lie to the cops.

The gravity of the situation—its real, mortal implications—had been affirmed by the fast approach of police sirens (though he didn't know who'd called them, and it certainly hadn't been him). When they searched him, they found no traces of evidence. He'd been sure to tuck the little device away at his kiosk, sandwiched between the blue raspberry and green watermelon jars of flossine.

Raspberry watermelon, he'd thought distractedly, all he could do to keep cool. *I should try that out.*

Their questions had been imprecise at best.

Was anyone else here with you?

Did you see anyone leaving the area before or while this was happening?

Did you know the victim in any way?

And perhaps most importantly, What happened to the body?

No, no, no. It had all been *No!* from Birch (and "I don't know," on the last count), and they'd been more than convinced, patting him lightly on the shoulder, whispering to one another that he'd entered a mild state of shock. They were further assured of Birch's innocence by his mild speech impediment, which—little did they know—was completely unrelated to his observance of the "crime."

As soon as they let him be, which hadn't taken long, Birch devised his own line of questions, a series of internal wonderings that burned at him deeply, intensely enough to warrant the sixteen years of research he'd invested. They were questions he *had* to answer, and ones that required diligence, scouring the deep-dark nooks of the internet for likeminded cronies (most of them cranks, junkies, clinically insane).

And so it was that he'd started on his journey. He'd been searching ever since, and re-watching the same old, fuzzy video. Officially, now, for the one-million-and-second time.

He closed out the clip and sighed, tying his overgrown hair into a little samurai knot at the top of his skull, like a prince's undersized crown. He hid the bun under the hood of his sweatshirt and stood up to stretch, bending down at the waist; he locked his knees and tickled the floor with his wide open palms. It felt good to lengthen his spine after so many hours of inactivity. With all the time he put into the project, sessile and hunched, Birch required some extra reaching and pulling to care for his irregular back.

He'd been born with a hunch; granted, he was no Quasimodo, but it was there if you looked hard enough, from the right angle. Because it was slight, and because he wore such shabby clothing, it created an aura of aloof disregard more than one of lumbering disfigurement. Unless you knew Birch well, you wouldn't know how much it bothered him, how hard he tried to hide it—as if he wasn't shy enough.

Part of the reason Birch always kept to himself was what had happened, witnessing that man's death. It was a grave responsibility and a burden, so he locked himself away in his room, scouring the web for photos of monsters matching the description of his subject, but none of them were right. They were too large, too small, too simian, too reptilian, or too downright *fake*-looking to match the profile of the beast he was after. Besides a few quirky films he found clips of—where gelatinous space creatures snatched up the bodies of their human hosts by the dozens, transforming them into catatonic, wide-eyed replicas of their former selves—nothing came remotely close to the thing.

Aunt Greta would sometimes knock gingerly at his door, peeking her pointy little face through the crack of its frame. She'd say, "Birch, why don't you come for a walk with me, down the pier?" He'd say no and she'd ask him *Why*, never seeming to grasp that he had more than his fair share and fill of the boardwalk on his four hour shifts.

Sometimes she'd make him his favorite meal (spaghetti and meatballs, but with soy protein balls instead, because she was vegan—a philosophy about which she was almost as adamant as her religious views) to try and lure him out from his dungeon, away from the speculative fiction he'd be reading. On those rare occasions when her strategy *did* work, she'd give him just enough time to settle fully into his meal, to really get a mouthful of mock meat going between his chompers, before she laid into him with her line of gentle reproaches—questions shaped like needles, statements sharp as rapiers pricking at his patience, but only enough to draw up some anger.

Why do you read that fluff?

You know that's rotting your brain?

Why not read the Bible instead?

I ran into my friend Becky at the grocery store and, well, she's been bringing her grandson to this thing called a "youth group"—have you heard of it?

Birch, why aren't you out playing football like other boys your age?

Did you know girls aren't really into all that space technology stuff?

You know, you'll never get a girlfriend if you sit inside reading all day.

But Birch knew Greta's intentions were pure, and never reproached her for her concern. Hell, looking back now, he realized he may really *have* been a bit too absorbed in the alien theory bit. Now that he was older and wiser, he'd outgrown the phase and moved onto other possibilities. Cults. Psychic manipulation. Brainwashing.

As soon as Birch turned 18, he decided to try out college at a small, private liberal arts school a few hours north of Los Angeles, smack dab in the middle of the Central Valley, near Fresno. He'd already coasted through high school's pedestrian course load, earning mostly A's and was rewarded with a free ride at the university. His excitement waned and, in the end, he fell flat on his face, earning all F's and losing all of his grants. But that was okay, because it just *wasn't for him*. Rules. Regulations. He *was* a rebel, after all; at least, he liked to think so.

When he turned 21, he made it the rest of the way up the PCH toward San Francisco, and had since lived a mostly happy life, earning his more-than-stable income, sailing comfortably along through his 20's, and entering his dreaded early-30's with less fanfare than the average California boy. He felt that (pardoning himself the usage of another cliché) age was *nothin' but a number*, and he lived his life accordingly. Whereas most men even moderately concerned with signs of aging, in either Los Angeles or San Francisco, would already be starting their first (or sometimes tenth) batch of *botulinum toxin* injections, Birch would rather save his expendable cash, storing it away for the rainy (apocalyptic) days he imagined weren't far ahead.

The bleep of an e-mail—nothing but junk—brought Birch out of recollection and reminded him that he needed to close down his article and get to work—his real work. He already lost two hours in reminiscence, with no hope of progress on his weary disquisition, so he needed to work extra hard to make up some slack. Fresh cup of coffee in tow, he readied himself for the daily grind.

Like some dreaded chore, committed by obligation, earning his living by trading was something he had to commit himself to daily and by force, calendar reminders and timers included. Otherwise, he'd carry on researching outer space conspiracies and de facto zombie possessions well into the night.

As he reopened the blinds, the clock tower began its 12 o'clock toll, but the close of its iconic ditty—the "Westminster Chimes"—was interrupted by a blaring siren, and the carefully articulated recording of a man's voice.

"THIS IS A TEST.

"THIS IS A TEST OF THE OUTDOOR WARNING SYSTEM.

"THIS IS ONLY A TEST."

It drowned out the first eight tolls of the hour.

The message blared down the Embarcadero, sending out-of-towners into a quick panic (as it always did), their fears subsiding only once they'd frozen in place for long enough to grasp the meaning of the words buried in the static of the deafening sound (and long enough to piss off some locals, ready for their hard-earned lunch breaks, shouting "Move outta the way!"). The last four chimes reappeared just as the man's pre-recorded voice vanished back to the shallow, digital grave from which it had crept. It would hibernate there for another week before it repeated the cycle all over again, and again and again and again.

The end of the Tuesday Test signaled the last minute start of Birch's self-scheduled trading. He sat down to *really* work, but found himself still wondering about the morning's failed attempt at writing. Although he still hadn't deciphered the hidden meaning of the video—and even though none of it was any closer to coming into a clearly focused picture—he was more certain than ever: his threadbare premonitions would soon come true.

One day, he thought, *that won't be a test message. Unless I do something about it.*

Birch had always felt certain that the man's death wasn't a one-off fluke. He felt this even more strongly as of late. There were little peeks at the less-than-pleasant future he foretold, trickling through the grid work of the media. Two weeks earlier, a crazy man was seen running naked through the Powell St. BART station. He stabbed two strangers in the neck before he slashed his own throat. A month earlier, over 1,000 dead fish were seen floating on the surface of the waters around Pier 1, stinking up the area and driving out the tourists. But the news and radio stations all came up with some half-assed explanations for what they called *minor disturbances*.

There was a bigger picture, a hidden message, and it was Birch's job to figure it out. After all, there hadn't been any news flashes way back then either. The man's death had been brushed under the rug. No one had ever made a fuss about it.

Like a hidden picture game, where the shape of the image is clouded by a massive crowd of clutter, by thousands of other meaningless bits of data floating around the canvas, Birch knew he was growing close—just a worm's length away from sorting it all out, bringing the answer out of the shadows and into the unobstructed light of his sixteen year sight line.

He closed out of his gain-loss calculator and opened up the video again, then dragged the file of his unwieldy opus back to the icon of his word processor. It bobbed in place on the computer's dock for a full ten seconds before the program spit all two-hundred unfocused pages back across the screen.

Trading can wait, he thought. *Duty calls.*

Birch decided to watch the damn thing for the one-million-and-third time, just in case he'd missed something. He took a full hour, clicking through each frame, analyzing every split second of the three minute recording.

The man washes ashore; seen it all before.

The man writhes in pain; isn't that a shame.

The man slips away, limp as sand that day.

He laughed, in spite of himself. It wasn't that he found the contents of the clip to be humorous, but he'd seen the footage so many times that most of the shock had been taken away. He still respected the stranger, even if the dead man had sucked away any chance Birch might otherwise have had at a normal romantic—or social—life. And he wasn't afraid of death.

He'd read enough books, seen enough of the gut-wrenching, sometimes purely evil underbelly of the internet that raised him to know what death looked like; he realized that (most of the time) it wasn't altogether *that bad* to die. In some ways, dying was just as important as living. It was a final stamp, a real and tangible *end* to all the hard work and shit-kicking ingrained in life. Yeah, he was *okay* with dying; not so much ready for it as he was resigned to it, shooting irretrievably off toward it. *Come what may*, and all that. Just as long as he didn't die at the hands (or mouths) of one of those *creatures*—right at the moment of understanding their history— Birch figured he'd be fine with drowning, starving, or being burned alive.

Bring it on, he thought, *but make it surprising.*

"Earth to Birch," he told himself.

He refocused his energies on assessing the last few seconds of the footage, not really expecting to find anything earth-shattering hidden there, but always at least hoping for something new—something he hadn't seen before, even if it was just an inconsequential detail. He wished to see a crab which he'd never noticed, crawling across the bottom of the screen, or a rebel seagull diving into the ocean, splashing back out holding a pair of flopping fish in its long-billed mouth.

Hope notwithstanding, he got nothing. The same dreary sky presented itself on his screen. The same plodding static, which no one could remove, darted intermittently across the screen, sometimes blocking the edges of the frame. Another glance at the same tall weeds swaying gently, their calm lilt juxtaposed against the harsh tremors of the man dying on the boardwalk, center frame. Same old, same old.

Birch was ready to close up shop, to sleep away the remnants of the afternoon, to wake up at 5 or 6 o'clock, and to shoot for his regularly-scheduled evening run along the bay.

But then, something *did* catch his eye. Just out of view, peeking out from between the shaggy mane of wild marram grass flanking the wooden planks of the on-off ramp, something appeared—visible for just a moment before it vanished from sight. It wasn't the cute crab he'd halfheartedly wished for, but its ill-defined shape might as well have made it some other odd crustacean. Perhaps it was *another* freakish creature.

Birch back-tracked by fractions of a second to find the clearest moment, grasping for a flash of certainty where he knew there wouldn't be one. The file was decrepit, moldering; he was probably just overreacting. Still, he took several screenshots of the video and dragged them over to his image editing software. He sharpened them all and messed with the levels, struggling to drown out the static, to bring the shape of the thing into better focus—to reveal some discernible feature: an ear, a claw, a beak, a nose.

What was clear was this: it was animate, some living thing after all. He knew this to be true because it had moved, though cautiously and only subtly. It was here in one frame, there in another—movement. He also saw, thanks to his quick tinkering, that it had two eyes—big, bulging black eyes, like a doe. But the smears of movement, caused back then by his own unsteady hand, made it nearly impossible to tell much more than that. Despite his best guesses (a condor or vulture awaiting the spoon-fed meal of the man's corpse; an owl, awakened from its slumber, curious about what the heck was happening; an escaped bear, or one who'd wandered undetected from its habitat for a season of rest at the beach), Birch had no clue what it was. It could have been anything.

He thought he'd try one last ditch effort, even though the greater part of his common sense told him it would be a complete waste of time (and of money, too). Birch logged into his e-mail to find the man who'd been most competent in his attempt to overhaul the video. His name was Crispin and he wore a toupee and he did not take *anything* but wire transfer for his fees.

Birch wrote:

Hey Crisp,

Any chance you can clean these up for me? I tried my best, but I'm no whiz. There's something in the background, buried in those weeds, and I'd like to know what it is.

Think you can help?

Name your price—I can go as high as $75/image if they come back clear.
Let me know!
- Birch

He attached the four clearest snapshots to the body of the message before he clicked on **SEND**. He was sure Crispin would shoot something back that was at least a marginal improvement over the original. Crisp was brilliant and fast, but also expensive, charging double what he should have for a half hour's work. Birch had since wised up, and he always named his price ahead of time. In this case, a whopping three hundred bucks if the images came back. It wouldn't break the bank, but it was a pretty penny for four measly photos. The only reason Birch was willing to go so high was to drive up the sense of urgency—Crispin would know this one was important when he saw that price—and because this *could* be the biggest lead of Birch's whole investigation.

Or it could just be a fluke, he told himself. *A bit of dirt stuck to the lens.*

Even if it wasn't some other monster—even if it turned out to be a goddamn common turtle—at least it was *something*. Something new, something exciting. If it turned out to be more than drifting sand, that would mean *something* else had watched the man die, too. At least he wouldn't be completely alone in his burden. Somewhere out there, if the thing hiding in the grass was still alive, there might be some animal who shared in his duty.

A bird to share my albatross.

He laughed at himself again, but his enjoyment was hindered by a thunderclap, which heralded a fast-approaching storm. Clouds ballooned threateningly across the sky, foaming over the bay like God's ready-to-rupture vesicle.

So much for that run.

Before he could come up with a backup plan for the evening, his inbox flashed the warmly welcome indication of incoming mail. It was Crispin. No surprise there; the bastard really was fast.

Birch,
Easy peasy, lemon squeezy!
Check out the attached images. I think you'll be more than pleased, but see for yourself. I

can definitely make out what they are now. Sunglasses!

Looks like someone was peeking in on your humble little low-budget pic. Paparazzo, maybe?

Let me know if you need anything else.

Wire me the money ASAP. You know what to do.

Technically Yours,

- Crispin

Sunglasses. He was right. They definitely *were*, without question, sunglasses.

Crispin managed to bring the shape of two aviator lenses into clear focus, like a pair of coals glowing in the weeds. Behind those plastic-or-glass orbs, Birch could even make out the contour of two conclusively human eyes, set under bushy black brows and bent into an oddly familiar scowl.

Each of the four photos confirmed it: Birch had not been alone on that day, sixteen years ago. Some*one*—not some*thing*—had seen the whole thing happen, had witnessed the man die. A Peeping Tom, who'd neither intervened nor raised a hand. Just as Birch had sat by, so had the stranger—seemingly unconcerned, creeping in the shadows.

Three hundred dollars well spent, Birch thought.

He closed his laptop and sat, overpowered with wonder, while the sound of thunder grew louder and nearer outside. Birch was unmoved by the clamor, enrapt as he was with the limitless pit of questions that opened in the center of his mind.

He realized with certainty that he *had* to find the man behind those sunglasses.

Somehow, Birch had to find him and learn why he'd kept silent all those years.

Perhaps they would be colleagues, searching together for the answers to Birch's burning questions.

Or they might be adversaries.

Outside, the clouds swelled into ominous gray masses, heavy with dread. Like colossal steel dish sponges hovering in the air, they threatened to crush whoever walked—ill-fatedly—beneath them. They were waiting for just the right moment to loose their heavy tears, when the wonder of their innate power would find the most befitting head to strike.

That was too bad for Birch. He really needed his run.

CHAPTER XVII

The ocean floor was littered with the debris of a costive, wasting world: a thousand straws jutting up from the sand like morose plastic trees; dull plastic bags caught against vibrant coral, flailing dreary flags on living neon pole masts; hundreds of thousands of plastic soda pop caps, sugary shrapnel dotting every sandy surface like an army of inebriates' inert eyes staring up at Jezebel; millions and millions of cigarettes, slow-oozing their resinous black tar trails, floating in a foul egress across the sea's stage, burning along a course of Marlboro menthol malignancy toward her, toward the spot where she dangled from the mast of a sunken ship, its crumbling deck slowly eroded through the centuries, its sail mast cracked and bent over like a wooden wishbone, the longer "winning" end threatening to separate completely from the ship at any moment—to drift away with the wizened whales and ornery octopi living down there—scooping up scallops and schlock in its long-shredded sails along the way. She surveyed these surroundings with a calm, collected outlook, as a pacific spectator.

Despite her cool disposition, Jezebel found that she couldn't move. Something deep within her kept her body from responding to the synapses her mind sent. The signals said, *MOVE*, yet only her eyes responded, darting left and right, searching her surroundings for help. Whether some autonomous self-defense mechanism or a foreign presence—an intruder—had caused her reflexive mesmerism, she did not know. The latter theory, for however idiotic or inelegant its possibility might have seemed to someone other than herself (someone not as inclined to believe in the extraordinary as she), stood out as the more probable cause of her stupor. Stranger things had happened.

To Jezebel, this was just the sort of thing she'd grown used to: another trip through the fluky landscape of her imagination, plodding across faraway landscapes without weaponry, left to fend for herself, unarmed and naked, strapped for weaponry in her fight against some new (and undoubtedly ferocious) beast. It was a fine example of how fucked up the challenges could be, and arguably as annoying as the time she'd been set in an immense cornfield and tied to a barrel, a tornado zipping toward her—but back then, she'd at least had her legs to rely on.

A sensation like boiling, a bubbling in her brains which she'd lately grown accustomed to, told her the solution to her predicament was right at the tip of her tongue, dangling in plain sight. It was a kind of prescience that guided her, a little tingle of knowing—there, yet not there, lost in the folds between memory and cognition. Just like the small, old scar she had at the top of her left thigh: she couldn't deprogram it from her embodiment—its form was forever visible, in plain sight, and yet the story of its making still eluded her.

She wandered through the vast encyclopedia of her head for some advice on what to do, smashing open doors along the hallways in her mind—little tunnels of knowledge she'd created for herself, alcoves of information she'd stockpiled like a harbinger of doom collects his cans of tomato soup. All the knowledge she'd absorbed through hours of tireless research was hers to use at will; and yet, not a single shred of it was of any use to her down at the bottom of the sea. Poseidon had died a long time ago, and so had good ol' Cthulhu. Frankly, she was on her own. Despairingly, hopelessly alone, a prisoner in her own body, staring out through the windows of her eyes.

Her limbs were loose, floppy as cooked spaghetti dangling against the sides of her body. She hung like a mermaid from the pointed bow of the ancient shipwreck, carved into its prow, a sentient yet silent figurehead trapped to wonder impossibly at the resolution of her dilemma. She thought back to stories she'd read of Haitian zombies, people poisoned and rendered paralyzed, their pulse slowed to an undetectable rate so they could be buried alive and dredged up again later, to do the biddings of their master.

Not far away, a crab jumped down from the ship's deck toward her, the masthead. It crawled onto her right arm and painfully dragged its knobby pincers into her skin the way a dog kicks up dirt after it defecates. It shredded open her forearm and burrowed its fine-tapered appendages deep within her flesh. The pain lit a fuse inside her head, with all the warmth of direct summer sun against skin—a throbbing thread of awareness, swelling up from the depths of her nervous system, tickling the muscles of her forearm with pins and needles. Suddenly, she felt a renewed connection to her limb—a burning pit in the hole the crab had crafted. She lifted up her arm. It was only for a moment, but the slight movement was abrupt enough to dislodge the crab from its fresh, warm home in her skin. It wobbled away, disgruntled, and disappeared into a crack in the fetid, festering wood, slipping back into the bowels of the ghost ship.

In the wake of the crustacean's brutal greeting, Jezebel leaked an abundant stream of inky blood, dark copper flipping through the water, dense as her own brooding spirit. The blood flowed freely from the soft nook of her inner arm, swirling away from her in dramatic floating arcs, traveling away to finally merge with the cigarette current, drifting into the throng to live alongside the deep sea folk and swim with the debris dumped down by man. Her blood became one with a giant accretion of life and death: a nearby floating trail of living and inanimate shapes composed of flesh and bone, of plastic and metal. It was a fully-functional, giant traveling death machine; it was a two-for-the-price-of-one attraction: a graveyard-slash-amusement park ride; it was a hulking trash mass that lured you in with its size and strangeness—lured you in 'til you became stuck in the muck of it and couldn't break free.

But not her—she wouldn't fall for that. She wouldn't wonder at the magnitude of that floating, funereal trash mound. She possessed enough common sense to know where that trail led: it was nowhere good, not by anyone's definition of the word. The mass of dead and dying matter drifted away from her before she realized it was gone.

That's not the challenge, then.

Perhaps it had just been some overflow, a leak in her imagination, a representation of her tendency to dramatize what she'd been reading about lately—about the state of the outside world, how it had been slowly devolving into a polluted, festering mess since well before her birth, and how it wasn't getting better any time soon.

The world was headed straight to hell, some articles said.

That's why we're here, she remembered. Someone had told her that before, but not in a dream, nor a challenge. They'd confessed, in a not-unkind tone, that her *purpose* was to purge this world of all its villainous, murderous, damned tenants— the ones causing continents of floating trash like the one she'd just seen; the ones waging baseless wars over gasoline. Those ones. All of them.

It was her purpose to *purify*, they'd said, which was a heavy encumbrance for one teenage girl. Nonetheless, she held her composure and bit her tongue, obeyed their commands and did as she was told (*what other choice did she have?*). She studied hard, and she always finished these things, the challenges. Always. Perhaps as much a result of her psychological makeup as by her birthright, Jezebel always wanted to win, and did.

So this one should be no problem.

The wad of trash had drifted by without incident, so that was neither here nor there. Her blood had vanished forever into the swarm of dross and nature as though it had never been a part of her to begin with. Its absconding was apropos— her spilt blood was still living, if only temporarily so, and yet useless to her because it no longer served her any purpose. The bloodletting was a perfectly symbolic commingling of the two disparate facets that had comprised that growing, ovoid mass; and it was a perfect parallel to her predicament: she was fully cognizant, present and aware, yet she was useless, trapped, immobilized.

She felt drained, but it wasn't from loss of blood; the fresh aperture of the wound she'd received from the cruel crab shrank up tight, all of its own accord. It must have been a pre-programmed favor, an advantage built into the challenge, which said she wasn't meant to die *that way* today.

So the crab wasn't the culprit either.

A last puff of watered-down blood escaped from the crook of her arm, shooting out from the yonic slit before it fully closed, mimicking a vulgar abstract painting: a pair of lips exhaling, ejecting a cloud of ochre smoke, then vanishing altogether behind a veil of fumes.

Vacant and receptive, Jezebel felt as if the whole episode with the barnacled bottom feeder had robbed her of some small, invisible—yet essential—vitality.

Perhaps it *was* the missing component, the bit that would have helped her to quickly solve the challenge, so she could get the hell off the slab of tainted timber from which she still hung. That damn crab had stolen her enjoyment of the challenge, of her journey to the depths of the sea; more than that, it had also tipped her off. Even though its actions now seemed cursory, its presence had told her there was something more dwelling down there than met the eye, something she couldn't quite put her (paralyzed) finger on, like listening to static and hearing a blip of some faraway signal—knowing it's out there without fully grasping its message.

She surveyed her surroundings again, searching this time both for savage sea life (a mutant shark who might eat her, or a frenzied patch of seaweed that might rip her apart) and for any hidden clues. Clusters of words formed like dots in her vision; she repeated them to herself, hoping the buzzwords would dislodge a bit of significance from the annals of her mind:

shipwreck.

immobile.

seabed.

Jezebel suddenly became very conscious of the fact that she'd been able to breathe for the last half hour, while submerged. Under normal circumstances, this wouldn't have been alarming (she'd already swum through rivers of molten lava, flown across the sky, and jumped along eighty-story skylines), but this latest miracle held a special significance; it rubbed her in all the wrong ways.

The fact that she was in the ocean felt crucial.

She had a vague notion that she'd been there before. Like déjà vu, particulars of the environment jumped out at her in moments of vibrant, fleeting clarity.

A trail of waste, cigarettes and trash.

Bits of shattered glass, sprayed around her in vaguely familiar patterns.

Far away, in the wake of the trash mound's trail, a plethora of dead fish, turned belly-up and rising. Hundreds of them, bobbing upside-down as they rode an invisible current toward the ocean's interface with the air above. A devastating contagion must have circulated amongst them, seeped into the tide—perhaps a byproduct of the floating island of waste.

No, that didn't feel right. This was something more *intentional*, more *immediate*. There were all the token signals of a challenge, little shavings of her fears and memories, but there were also elements at play that were unlike anything she'd seen before.

It felt like she was watching her own fears play out through someone else's eyes.

Rather than waste more time guessing, Jezebel decided to try for a change—to address and find a remedy for her immobility. As a major part of what barred her from effectively exploring her options, she knew that fixing that and getting moving was her first step toward beating the challenge. If she could just get her feet wiggling and climb down from the mast of the slow-rotting wreck, she'd stand a far greater chance of success.

Using her most basic instruction, one of the first disciplines she'd been taught—what they called the Singular Method—she focused only on herself. Turning inward, she blocked out all the other distractions of the underwater world: the leviathan sea snails crawling by, like giant cinnamon swirls, disappeared; a school of nurse sharks swimming by vanished at her inward instructions. All the crazy sights, the subdued sounds of the ocean, melted into a perfect quiet, a soothing shade of gray behind her eyelids, and finally into a harmonious mantra echoing at the pit her head.

That is infinite, and this is infinite.
The infinite proceeds from the infinite.
Taking the infinitude of the infinite,
It remains as the infinite alone.

The saying came as a scrap of knowledge hefted off a shelf in her mind, straight from the hallway marked "H," under the special topic of "Hindu Mantras." It was not a topic of her regular studies; it was not in the materials they chose for her.

The Overseer would not be pleased with Jezebel for mixing Hinduism with their own special breed of theology. He'd probably have labeled the mantra "Nothing More Than a Silly Poem." In Jezebel's mind, it was fine to mix the Singular Method, or any concept from their long list of rituals, with the practices of other religions, philosophies, cosmogonies. Whatever instilled the inspiration—and provided the desired effect—was well worth the focus and effort.

As she opened her eyes, the seabed shook around her. Her teeth chattered in her skull. A shoal of ancient squids shivered past, shattering the scant rays of sunlight that had made it so far down. The ground trembled as though it might crack to loose a sleeping titan. The crests of sand holding up the ship took on more finite, concrete shapes as, without warning, the sea evaporated, creating a dense, all-encompassing cloud of steamy hot mist. In moments, even that disappeared, leaving thousands of sea creatures gasping for breath—dying—and loosening the shipwreck's grip on the ocean floor. It toppled over, carrying Jezebel with it, cemented to its prow; she squeezed her eyes shut just before smashing against *terra firma*. Strangely, the impact was like slamming into a cloud: it did her no harm. The ground succumbed nicely to the shape of her, cocooning her in a foam of dry earth and grit. It swallowed her, prying her off the prow of the ship, drawing her downward. The sand was scalding, dry and fiery, as though it had been baking in full sun for hours, not moments.

With an effort, Jezebel used her only mobile arm to drag herself against the pull of the earth, prying herself back upon the prow. In the distance, Jezebel noticed a dip in the sand.

There, the dunes shrank and flattened into what looked like a bulls-eye. Her eyes were drawn to that spot. At its center stood a structure, but it was too far away to make out the intention of its design.

She fell from the prow again—this time landing, thankfully and safely, on a patch of land that was a bit less eager to eat her—and rolled toward a sprout of jagged rocks in the distance. Lying in the shade they afforded, she listened to the rows of lifeforms scattered around her in sad little clusters, most of them dying of suffocation.

At her foot, a pair of eels puffed at the poisonous air, their cheeks distending in painful gasps. One of the eels ensconced her foot. Its unhinged jaw seemed to mimic an infant gasping for its mother's teat. It sought comfort, nourishment, support; it clung to life, writhed for it, but failed. It died attached to her. She kicked it off her foot.

Intuitively, Jezebel picked the dead thing up, regarding its admirable girth; it filled her palm nicely. The animal looked like a worm—like an oversized, slime-green worm, but with a mouth and eyes. Eyes that somehow still held a trickle of life, a stubborn gesture of imprecation burning out of them, boring into her. She dropped the eel and, staring down at her empty left palm, realized the importance of her gesture.

She crawled onto her knees, rising to stand, and exclaimed, "I can move!"

She shook off the question of *How* and tried for a strong footing, first quivering on knees like jelly, then teetering like a child's spinning toy until she pushed herself up.

"What next?" she said, to no one in particular.

A school of sharks—lumbering house-sized beasts—struggled to breathe nearby, cursing the transformation Jezebel had somehow caused to their environment, tails thrashing. She walked toward them and, placing her palm against one of the beast's fins, felt the potent sinew lurking there. He looked like a creature ripped straight from a horror film, with rows and rows of glinting razors lining his screaming maw. His thrashing made it hard for her to maintain a sturdy grip on his fin.

She walked away from the rude fish, headed for the down-sloped dune and the structure she noticed before. Behind her, the ship moaned out an angry, rotten fart. Thanks to the sharp light of the sun, which had slammed abruptly against the seabed, the wreck was dissolving, crumbling to bits. Jezebel reflected cursorily on the well-being of the crab that had clawed at her, but she kept on her course, entranced by the newest mystery in a growing lineup of them.

As she closed the distance, the sand beneath her dissipated and was replaced by a clean-poured shelf of concrete lined with perfectly spaced rows of white paint, which all pointed toward an oddly fluorescent building. Up close, Jezebel still couldn't tell what it was. It was a multi-storied, U-shaped structure, a building with an attached glass-enclosed room at its center. Looking at it made her palms grow slick with sweat.

There were other strange objects there, too, like auguries dropped onto the scene, glowing with subtle meaning.

A rose-red truck, beat up and parked in between two of those white-painted lines. It was the only vehicle on the square-paved lot.

She knew what this was called: a parking lot.

Her heart rate rose.

Rows of palm trees—she'd read about them, but never actually seen one—

shot up into the sky, impossibly tall, apocalyptically so.

Her eyelids twitched. More than ever, she was certain of the irregularity of the challenge. This was more than the usual *face your fears* formula which they subjected her to once or twice a month. This was a new kind of torture: they were having her face the uncertainty of the real world, giving her exposure to some of its most frivolous details. These were not the things she feared, and they weren't the objects of her everyday concern. Their glaring presence was pointed.

The building, with its nauseating, salmon-pink paint job, somehow conjured up stories of ruins from a long-dead age, of ancient civilizations. Maybe it was because of the fact that the windows were crusted over with dirt and sand, or the way the corners of the building had been blasted into curves. The whole structure looked and felt abandoned, drowned in dread. Its peachy color was simultaneously sad and jarring, both repellent and captivating. She didn't want to look toward the place, but an impulse compelled her to. A searing hook gnawed at her heart. The walls of the place hummed with the lingering scent of infirmity. Something bad happened there, and the force of that incident still beat off the dead truck parked outside, and hummed off the stuccoed walls like ghosts, whispering to Jezebel.

These weren't details she could create. Someone had programmed this place for her—had crafted her very own ugly Atlantis.

Behind her, a small creature knocked over a pile of rocks and disappeared beneath the truck in a sideways scramble.

It was the crab.

It trailed her, the creepy little bastard. It crawled back out and surveyed her, stretching upward on its legs, genuflecting in place.

She glanced around, waiting for the Overseer to jump out and scream, "Joke's on you!" but he didn't. *So no joke, then.*

The crab's beady eyes squinted up at her, its mouth puckered in a long question of, *Wellllllllll?* as its claws snapped out a staccato rhythm, raised into the air. It continued lifting and lowering its body in place, humping away at nothing.

Jezebel took a couple of steps toward the depraved decapod and sat down on her heels. She stuck one tentative finger out toward it, cautiously—the memory of the damned thing's barrage against her forearm still fresh in her mind. It punched her finger away with the blunt end of its right claw (which looked swollen compared to the left one). It raised and waved its arms in a critical gesture before it scurried off between her legs, scuttling up the side of the peach building and disappearing down one of its dark hallways, leaving Jezebel behind in the dust.

"Wait!" she screamed, running after it.

She ran for the second floor, skipping the stairs two at a time, arriving just in time to see a glimpse of her bipolar friend's flat crimson body as it rounded the corner of the hallway ahead and stopped outside a closed door marked—just like her chamber at the compound—in silver, serifed numbers.

The room was number 210.

210. 210. 210. No matter how many times she ran the three digits through her head, Jezebel couldn't distinguish if, when, or where she'd heard them before, much less what they meant. Still, with each recitation, her throat felt tighter, her joints more clenched.

A puzzle inside a puzzle inside a goddamn labyrinth.

The challenges weren't normally like that; normally they were easy. The Overseer chose a topic—something simple, like climbing a mountain or swimming across a lake. The participant would be read the prompt as they dozed off into rattled sleep. The challenger's mind was typically loaded with enough anxiety, enough happenstance, to do the rest of the work—the rest of the so-called challenging—on its own. The safe mountain became a deadly active volcano; the lake became infested with ferocious piranha. It was the participant, or challenger, who did himself in.

In rare instances, when the challenger's particular neuroses didn't quite line up with the Overseer's overall vision for the challenge—or when things weren't getting to be quite scary enough, quite quickly enough—whoever was assigned to observe the challenger's activity (they called them *monitors*) would feed some fresh stimuli to the challenger with simple mermerism, whispering a few dark words into their ears.

Jezebel wasn't one hundred percent on the particulars of how that bit worked, nor did she know if they had ever employed this tactic with her. Usually, she coasted right into a lull state, ready to tackle any obstacle. Whatever words they might be whispering, back in the real world, were totally lost on her.

This challenge—the building, the crab—all of it was unquestionably more lurid than anything Jezebel had experienced before. It was loaded with numbers and symbols and plain objects—simple, everyday things like *trucks*—things people at the compound didn't much care about, things they didn't have everyday exposure to, especially not Jezebel.

If anyone was projecting this set of curiosities *into* her challenge, they were undeniably stronger than Jezebel. Maybe even stronger than the Overseer himself.

The crab pushed against the door to Room 210, straining with every fibre of his being until the frame peeled back into a sliver of black. He vanished into the dark, leaving Jezebel outside, wondering whether or not to follow. Her instincts told her not to enter, but something clawed at her spine with the urgency of a soaring nuclear missile and whispered,

go.

She held back a shiver, a feeling of imminent doom, as she stuck the tip of her bare foot over the threshold. Nothing happened. No one bit off her little toe; no one grabbed her ankle and dragged her in against her will. Retrieving her foot back out of the darkness, Jezebel pressed into the door with the weight of her shoulder and slinked her neck around, peering inside for a peek.

The crab was there, clawing its way up the side of the bed, which was huge—at least three times wider than her cot at the compound. When the crab reached its destination, dead-center atop the mattress, it jumped up and down in place, tearing holes into the faded duvet cover with each impact of its sharp little legs.

Anxious to be rid of the nausea swelling up from her stomach, Jezebel slinked into the room and approached the bedside. Instead of abating, the sense that she'd soon upchuck grew stronger once she entered the quarters.

Her eyes adapted slowly to the blackness inside. She waited patiently for them to acclimate and spun around for a better look:

The walls were the same effervescent orange as the building's exterior. Cheap prints of generic coastlines and still-life photos of glossy fake-fruit baskets hung crookedly on the walls.

The bedclothes: peach.

The shower curtain: peach.

The foot-flattened, still-damp floor mat around the molded, nauseatingly sulfurous toilet: peach.

The window treatments, surprisingly, were purple.

It was all so cartoonish, so otherworldly, that it couldn't possibly be real. And yet there were small details that bespoke the truth, that wholeheartedly screamed this was *real*: the memory of cigarette smoke embedded in the ashen, musty walls; a single sandal upturned against the carpet, sulking in the corner of the room, its foam sole and plastic thong coated in brown dust; a little sketchbook, left open to a page with a dachshund puppy scribbled in black ink, its eyes wide-set and drooping with sadness. That last detail in particular sent her reeling; she couldn't stop staring at the little character, scrawled so many aeons ago.

It had to be real. This had to exist somewhere, or some when. It was an actual place—if not physically so, then at least in someone's mind space, as the memory of a distant moment. And with that realization, Jezebel finally came to understand that, despite her earlier doubts, this was very likely a situation where someone had entered her mind, had influenced her experience of the challenge, and was barring her escape.

The room felt hot and dry, filled with a screen of sharp dust that stuck against her sweaty skin. Jezebel missed the cool dampness of the ocean and wished it would come crashing back down.

The crab caught her attention, waving its claws all about.

"What?" she asked it, and covered up her mouth. She glanced around the room, checking its corners for onlookers. Heaven forbid she talk to a crab in a peach-painted motel at the bottom of the dried-up ocean. "What is it?"

He responded with a lonely clicking sound.

"Are you trying to tell me something, crab?"

She crept closer to sit beside her sadistic little friend. He jumped up at her, a flying disc of red, spines of his legs ready to slice her again, but she crawled back in time to avoid his charge.

"Don't go clawing me, you little bastard!"

He looked up at her with the saddest eyes in the world, brimming with impossible tears. His whole body shivered. Before her very eyes, his hardened carapace melted into a heart.

"You've got to be kidding me."

Jezebel crouched down low, ready to console the capricious creature, even willing to put her inner elbow back on the line, if it meant she could get him to share whatever secrets he held.

Shit, she thought. *Now I'm anthropomorphizing a crab. Get it together, Jezebel. Crabs don't talk, and they don't keep secrets.*

As if to contradict her, and to prove his vast intellect, the crab jumped up for her lowered face, barely missing the tip of her nose. He scuttled under the bed.

"That's it! You're going down, you prickly little prick—" She stopped herself, realizing she needed to find him fast, before he crept back out of 210's front door for the open-aired Atlantis outside.

She slammed the door shut to prevent his escape and lowered herself onto all fours, tilting her head sideways, peering beneath the bed frame. The puce-red brute was there all right, lying in wait, pounced low to the ground on all six of his legs, kicking back against the ground and shredding the carpet into bits of fluff which seemed to float in place, like impossibly sedate dandelion puffs.

Just when she thought he'd charge, her hand rising to protect her face, he didn't. Instead, he ran around in circles beneath the bed, and pointed with his big right claw at a spot on the floor.

"What? You make no sense, crab. Hell, you shouldn't even exist. I've never seen a crab, not even in a photograph. In fact, who knows if that's what you are. Somehow I'm guessing that's what you are…"

He shrugged, tilting himself up on one set of his legs before recommencing his frenzied race in place, coiling round and round, clicking his claws overhead in a trio of even-timed claps.

Click-Click-Click.

He ran around once more, and stopped at the same spot, just outside the little ring he'd created. This time, when he emitted the quavering beat, the sounds came farther apart.

Click. Click. Click.

"I'm not crawling under there with you, crab. Whatever it is you have to say, you'll have to bring it out here in the open."

She sat on her feet and crossed her arms, waiting for the stubborn imp to join her. Instead, he only continued on his repetitive course beneath the mattress, running an endless cyclical marathon punctuated with alternating sets of clicks—

fast, then slow.

Sprint, *click.click.click.* Sprint, *click-click-click.*

Irritated, Jezebel sat up and slouched against the bed, resigning herself to what was beginning to look like a lifetime of quiet suffering, with only a deranged crab for company.

"C'mon. Get out of there and tell me what you know."

Sprint, *click.* Sprint, *click.*

"Okay, fine. Don't come out. See if I care." She cracked her neck, twiddled her thumbs. "I'll just be waiting over here, in case you change your mind. Come see me when you're ready to fess up. I already know there's someone else down here. There's someone else inside my head, and not just my monitor. So whenever you're ready, come help me understand what the hell's going on."

Sprint, *click.* Sprint, *click.*

Jezebel's blood boiled. If the crab didn't get out from under the bed—and soon—she was liable to pluck him out herself, and to rip each of his ugly limbs right off his body.

"Last chance, crab. I'm warning you."

Although she'd never had a mother of her own, Jezebel thought for sure that her threat would lure him out. It should have worked because—in the films they let her watch—the *mom* characters usually gave a similar "final warning," and it always did the trick. In the novels they let her read, the *mother* always counted backward from ten and the kid would—inevitably, begrudgingly—come crawling out from underneath the kitchen sink, ready to apologize for whatever misdeed he or she had committed.

But a crab was not a kid, not any more than Jezebel was a mom, so he stayed put instead, circling and clicking, circling and clicking.

Jezebel stood up, dusting her knees off, scraping away the film of dirt which had formed across her palms, and peered beneath the bed. Dipped low to the ground, she scooped her forearms under the bed frame as, with a single driving force, she upturned the bed, sending its whole hulking mass flying to the far side of the room where it slammed against the wall and dislodged a painting. Now that the bed was gone, the crab abandoned its repetitive relay and jumped to rest at her side.

She looked down at it, just as it looked up at her. Its eyes bulged with urgency, drooping from their stalks as its colossal claw pointed back toward the spot of its erstwhile show. There—centered in the violent ring of shredded carpet the crab had created—was the word *TUCSON* written in what looked like blood. Somewhere at the back of Jezebel's mind, recognition tickled her as she read out that name, but it was not the same sort of recognition as she had when seeing the truck, nor the building. The vestige of memory those things had scrubbed was faint. This was a brighter burn, a clearer hunch.

It was a word she'd *definitely* seen before, and she knew exactly where: on a map of the United States. That was the country she lived in, and where the compound was. On her map—which hung prominently and proudly on her cell wall—there were lots of tiny words and different colored shapes. She'd learned (way back when she was just a kid, maybe seven years old) that those shapes and colors designated things called *states*. States were run—just like the United States—by a community of rule-makers. However, their power to influence was levied on a much smaller scale. Each state's rule-makers dictated what people who lived in their state could and could not do, but the government of the country had final say over any rule the state created—at least, that's how she understood it. Someone (Jezebel wasn't sure who) at some point (and she didn't know when) had given each of these colored shapes, called states, a name. There was Florida, way down in the southeast corner; that one looked like a boy's privates. Then there was New York, which was said to house one of the world's most bustling cities. Strangely enough, that huge city shared the name of its governing state—it was also called New York. There were lots more of them, too. But at the compound, none of the states mattered more than the one in which they resided. It was named *Arizona*. She probably shouldn't have known this, but a few years earlier Jezebel overheard snippets of the Overseer's conversations with some of his attendants—something about recruiting in Phoenix—and she'd put two and two together to figure out which state they were in.

And so she'd studied up on the great state of Arizona. Its nickname was The Grand Canyon state, named so for the canyons that were there. Canyons were basically a kind of giant crevice in the earth. Some of Arizona's stretched on for miles and miles. The *grandest* of them was called The Grand Canyon, and it stretched across some 270-plus miles of Arizona land, and counting (she also learned about what caused these rifts in the earth, things called tectonic plates, which were always creeping together, or apart, inch-by-inch, moving the giant land masses that comprised the inhabitable parts of the planet). Arizona's flag looked like a glowing orange star floating in a deep-blue ocean. On the map, the state was approximately located in the southwestern region of the United States. The record high temperature in summer occurred eight years ago and was 125 degrees Fahrenheit (a western unit for measuring the weather); it occurred on a Wednesday in late July. Of course, there might have been a more recent edition of her beloved Encyclopedia, which contained a higher, record-breaking temperature.

She'd learned a whole bunch more about Arizona, too—the topography, the state bird, the lakes, the rivers, the (mostly deserted) highways. She even knew about the deeply spiritual indigenous communities that lingered in the drylands, buried deep in the canyons; she liked to envision them smoking long pipes, their hair (coarse as a horse's mane) braided into long ropes. And she knew Tucson was a city, located in the south of Arizona, seemingly far from the plateau of dried-up trees by which the compound sat, hidden from passersby.

Based on all that she learned, Jezebel had guessed at their position on the map: roughly the northwestern corner of Arizona. Aside from the great distance separating them from Tucson, Jezebel knew relatively little about the place. There'd been no reason to take especial care in learning about it.

But now the name *Tucson* had been delivered to her—or she'd been brought to it, by her crabby pal—not so much served on a platter as splashed on a swatch of ratty fabric and ensconced by the crazy path of that conniving, violent trickster. She crouched to pat the still-damp word, feeling the indentation in the ground; she lifted up her fingers, soiled, and smeared the fluid between thumb and forefinger. It smelled oreish, metallic, like blood should smell, but it was thicker than the kind she'd experienced before (her own, but nothing serious—from scraping her knee or pricking her finger). She traced the shape of the loop the crab had crafted, mirroring the path he'd carved with his knifish legs, feeling her way through the moat he'd drawn.

"What does this mean, crab?"

Of course, he only stared dumbly back at her, lifting himself onto his side once more, in an expression that seemed to say,

157

You got me. Just doin' my job.

"Is there something else? Something I'm not seeing? I must be missing something—*oh*, what is it?"

The crab made his little clicking sound again and leapt into the air, landing in a split on the base of his knobby thorax with his legs splayed out beneath him and spinning like a hockey puck. If he'd been capable, Jezebel guessed he'd have also drawn those arms of his up inside of himself, like a turtle hiding from danger. The decapod couldn't do this, so he chose to freeze instead, playing dead against the carpet.

"Really now? Well then, tell whoever sent you this: go screw yourself. And he can screw you, too, for all I care. I'm not playing into this. It makes no sense and I won't have anything more to do with it." It felt good to use those curses; she rarely had occasion for it.

Jezebel hooked her arms above her still-developing breasts (she was a late bloomer), using them as shelves upon which to rest her frustrated limbs. She refused to make eye contact with the crab and used the strength of her calves to lift herself back up, off the ground, and moved for the door.

"If this is some morbid game of the Overseer's, I'm going to be pissed." She said this more for her own benefit than the crab's. Besides which, she said it to abate the growing fear that this was *not* a game at all, at least not in the usual sense of the challenges.

There was no longer a question: this was something more than that—more than a challenge. She got the sense also that whoever was there with her, feeding her those strange riddles, didn't mean to trick her. They would—very likely—rather spell it out for her, to tell her exactly whatever message they were trying to convey, without having to use all the cryptic clues—but that would be difficult. It was hard enough to influence someone in a challenge to see something they wouldn't otherwise fear, that they wouldn't otherwise imagine as a possibility for disaster or death. To directly engage in conversation, to speak clearly and without the guise of the challenge (without the odd creatures, the natural disasters)—well, that would mean a few things.

It would mean that the person invading the challenge was putting himself at risk; it would mean that he'd exposed himself. There would no longer be doubt as to whether this was an unlicensed incursion, which would mean the intruder would be exposed to the full wrath of the Overseer, and to that of all his pitiful bootlickers.

It would also mean they could damage her—that whoever was there, peeping into the playground of her head, could hurt Jezebel—even if unintentionally. If she hadn't adjusted as slowly to the concept of a foreign entity, occupying the same mind-space as her, she might have gone into shock, or been prematurely ejected from the challenge by the sudden, jarring influence of the intruder. She might even have accidentally trapped the other person's mind within hers; they might have been stuck to live as a prisoner to her percipience.

So the intruder might be friendly—probably was—and *Tucson* was their message.

"What's Tucson got to do with anything, crab? Did something bad happen there—at this place in Tucson, inside of this strange building?"

Unsurprisingly, the crab didn't have much to say on the topic. By way of a response, he raised his dominant claw to what could be called, in human terms, his forehead. He scratched himself there, adding a single click as punctuation.

"You know about as much as me, then. Completely useless."

He snapped his claws together and uttered a long series of clicks which seemed to say, *Watch it!*

"Sorry, crab. *You're* not useless. You did good bringing me here. It's just that I've about had it with this fever dream. I want to go back home, back to the compound." Mumbling to herself, she added, "Never thought I'd say that…" Tears welled at the corners of her eyes, even as she remembered what the Overseer had always told her about her emotions: *Never let them get the best of you, Jezebel. Remember your duty and your birthright. Be strong,* along with some other claptrap. Even though she had a habit of letting what the Overseer said pass through one ear and out the other, she realized he'd been through a lot in life and, oftentimes, knew just what he was talking about. So she channeled the great man himself, pushing back the sharp saline sting and swallowing a lump in her throat.

Across the room from her, a mirror lay at rest, leaning against the wall. Its surface was streaked with a menacing swatch of copper jelly. She stared into it for a long time, struggling to grasp the source of the congealed fluid, before realizing what else felt askew about what she saw: her reflection didn't show there, and it wasn't because of the goop.

She waved her hands in front of the mirror. Nothing. No matter how hard she tried to will herself into the image it cast of the space labeled 210, she wouldn't materialize. All the peachiness was fully represented there, bouncing against her vision in the tall pane of glass, and so was the crab, but Jezebel was not. Her tears metamorphosed into tooth-gritting, knee-clenching focus. Whenever she was irritated, she found it difficult to implement the Singular Method. She clenched her eyelids more tightly. Rather than a calm shade of gray, all she could see was that word: *Tucson*.

She opened up her eyes. Still no Jezebel there.

What the hell does that mean?

"Hey crab, any idea on this one?"

Of course, the crab was oblivious to the meaning of this latest anomaly, though he did decide to take up residence on her thigh, tucking his legs beneath him as if ready for a nap. His stemmed eyes bent back to look up into her face.

"I see we're getting cozy now. Good friends, huh?"

His eyes bowed low, then raised back up: *Uh-huh*.

She wrapped her hand around him, gripping him like a brick, fingers sliding down between each of his legs. In a fit of vein-popping rage, she threw him against the mirror.

"If you can't answer any of my questions, go the hell away!"

He squeaked as he arced through the air, never breaking eye contact with Jezebel. His legs hit first, shattering the glass to bits. Fragments showered the room, dousing her bare legs with flickering pellets that nicked into her skin. A Pollock painting revealed itself in the flesh of her torso via budding blood, and this time there didn't seem to be any self-healing power at play.

Dizzily, Jezebel rose to her knees, wobbling for support against the upturned bed frame, but the mattress slipped and so did she, sliding to the ground, bashing her forehead against the edge of the bed. Her perception of the room grew bleary, but she made it to the room's entryway and out—down the stairway, past the beat-up pickup truck.

She collapsed against the sand, a stone's throw from the concrete lot. As her consciousness faded, replaced by a gray beyond her control, Jezebel found herself wondering again about the crab; she found herself feeling guilty for throwing him. She couldn't help also feeling that this was her due punishment, and that whoever had created this strange world for her would soon put her to death.

The sand tasted gritty, warm and mealy against her lolling tongue, pungent as fresh-ground pepper. Its flavor and coarseness were all too real.

That word repeated again in her mind, over and over:

Tucson. Tucson. Tucson.

But another word rose and replaced it, in a voice than wasn't her own.

It was calling out her name, and the voice was the Overseer's:

Jezebel. Jezebel. Jezebel.

The world around her melted into a gaussian blur, the ornery octopi and wizened whales bleeding into disorienting streaks, swirling together in a kaleidoscope of grays and blues. The Overseer repeated his call, beckoning her out of the deep well of her mind:

Jezebel. Jezebel. Jezebel.

She landed back in her physical body, where it had all started—where it always started, every challenge—reminding herself that everything was a-okay again, squeezing a bunch of her bouncing crimson curls with a two-fisted grip; pinching her shoulders, bony but broad and purposeful, graceful; even patting her pert little breasts, which were free of lacerations.

"Jezebel! Jezebel! You're back." It wasn't the Overseer after all. It was her monitor, Hopper, screaming in her ear. "Tell me you're back!"

"I'm fine. Gimme a minute." Huffing and puffing, she flattened her cream-colored attendant's robe against her sweat-damp flesh, then rose to smooth her wild mane, regarding herself in the narrow, ovular mirror mounted over her desk. Thankfully, this one *did* show her reflection: her blessed, fair-faced complexion, beaming from the simple cut of frameless glass; thick eyebrows, subtly arched, gifting her with an always impassive, androgynous expression; heterochromic eyes—one clear blue and the other a bubbling gray; button-nose, speckled with brown dots like the finest sprinkling of cinnamon over white bread, even though she was rarely exposed to the sun; and plump, rosy lips—her most revered asset, her most feminine attribute.

A static buzz erupted from the wall, from an intercom set just beside the door to Jezebel's cell. Hopper rose to see who called, though they both knew who it would be.

"Hello?" Hopper said, in his always cordial voice, hand half-raised to his mouth.

"It's me—" The Overseer. "Is she back?"

"Yes, sir."

"Good."

With an abrupt cackle of static, the intercom cut back out.

"What did you tell him?" Jezebel asked.

Hopper paused. "Jezebel, you know I had to."

"What did you say?"

"That you were in deep, that you weren't responding to my signals. He'll be by to check on you—"

"That's not necessary, Hopper. I'm fine—"

"All the same, you know he won't take no for an answer."

Jezebel cringed. She hated being near him—near the Overseer.

"Jezebel," Hopper said. "Are you going to tidy up? It's a rare treat to be paid a one-on-one visit, you know."

"Yes, I know." She brushed her palms over her desk, her bookcase, the little window—its sill and the iron bars which filled it, barred it. "Better?"

Now it was Hopper's turn to sigh. He said, "I suppose…"

Jezebel stuck out her tongue, more playfully than with any real menace, but Hopper raised his hand to smack her anyway—a punishment which was customary at the compound, when a young girl stepped so far out of line.

But Hopper wasn't like the rest. He stilled his shaking palm and lowered it slowly, just as the Overseer knocked on her door.

Though their leader entered calmly, a shift in his gait betrayed his concern.

"Jezebel," the Overseer said, matter-of-factly, with that suave accent of his. She wasn't worldly enough to place it, but it was nothing like the other people who lived at the compound—and they'd come from all over the world. No, his was extra special, left over from another time. "You're back to us."

"Sorry, sir," Jezebel said. "Really, though, I'm fine."

"I couldn't bring her out," Hopper said, "no matter what I did. I tried everything—"

"What happened?" the Overseer asked.

Jezebel didn't need more than her right hand to count the number of times she'd seen him up close, face-to-face, and without all the others around. He was usually much higher, towering above them, standing far off at his lectern on the stage, a safe distance from his followers. She now saw that his eyes (which she'd previously mistaken to be a common brown) were a rare tan, like wet sand—almost gray—and held a searing quality of madness; she found it difficult to look directly into them. He was uncommonly tall, with clavicles that poked up behind his robes; they made him look skeletal.

"Jezebel! I asked you a question?"

"What?"

"Yes, exactly that—*what*? What happened?"

She *did* want to tell him, to let him know what happened, to explain how awry the challenge had gone. If only she opened her mouth, just a sliver, the words would come tumbling out. But something else, another part of her, kept her from telling the truth, though she wasn't one to lie in the first place and—when she did—she wasn't very good at it. An inkling of foreboding crept into her, and her head tingled with something less intense than headache, but more staggering.

Still, he was their Overseer, and she was his One—the one to purify, the one to purge. She opened her mouth to speak—

WAIT. PLEASE, DON'T.

It was a clearly articulated, feminine voice inside her head—at once soft and hard, full of intensity yet placating. Somehow its command outweighed her obligations to the Order, to the compound, and to the Overseer himself.

"Nothing happened," she lied, picking at her brow. "I failed, that's all."

"Jezebel, if something—" Hopper started, but the Overseer cut him off.

"If something *unusual* happened during the challenge, you should tell me. You *need* to tell me."

"Nothing unusual happened, sir. Except that I failed." She bowed her head low.

The Overseer seemed to consider her announcement, calculating his response with unpleasant silence.

"You're lying," he said. "But it's okay. Sometimes we need to lie, don't we? For the greater good—"

"I'm not lying, sir."

"Do *NOT* interrupt me, Jezebel." His nostrils flared, growing impossibly wide beneath his file-thin nose. He surveyed her with eyes that felt wet and dense—like the quicksand that had nearly suffocated her during the challenge. They sucked at her soul. "I know what it is to be an outsider, how lonely it can feel. But you're the chosen one, Jezebel. Even though we've not yet fully drawn you into the workings of the Order—and even though you may not yet be aware of how truly important you are—I trust that you'll believe me when I say this: I understand what you feel. Surely you can recognize the truth in these old man's words." His lipless mouth showed a hint of gratitude, only one corner slightly raised.

"Okay," she said, not quite sure what she should say. "So you know what it feels like to be an outsider? Good for you, but that's not the way I feel."

Another long silence. The Overseer leaned low to pick up the book she'd been reading lately: *Twenty Thousand Leagues Under the Sea*. He smiled as he flicked through the novel and read a passage aloud:

"The sea is everything. It covers seven tenths of the terrestrial globe. Its breath is pure and healthy. It is an immense desert, where man is never lonely, for he feels life stirring on all sides. The sea is only the embodiment of a supernatural and wonderful existence. It is nothing but love and emotion; it is the Living Infinite."

He closed the book with a flick of his wrist and set it gingerly back where he'd found it, at the foot of her bed.

She still didn't know what to say, but she felt pretty strongly that she'd had enough of the sea, and of the Infinite, for one lifetime.

"Very well, then. So you've failed the challenge. *How* did you fail it?"

"Funny enough, it was an underwater challenge." She turned to Hopper for proof and he nodded. "I drowned. I've never been swimming, so I didn't know what to do. I blacked out and I drowned. I have no idea why Hop—sorry, Hopper—couldn't bring me out."

"Anything else?" the Overseer asked.

"That's it."

"What did it feel like to drown?"

"What did it feel like?" *Morbid fucker.* "Why?"

"Just. Answer. The question."

"Well, it wasn't at all like Jules Verne says in there. I mean, I definitely felt the hugeness of the sea, but it was a lot more than lonely. It was cold and stark—there were other creatures, but they were all vicious, conniving."

"That's not what I asked you." The Overseer waved Hopper away with one gray hand, covered in rings.

Hopper slipped out without a peep, more than likely glad to be free from the tense mood of the room.

"Drowning," Jezebel said. "It felt like being born. Suffocating darkness first, and then just brightness, all around. It felt like being cozy and fine with the way things are, and then getting shoved out of comfort and left to fend for yourself."

"Interesting." He turned to leave, without a word.

"It didn't hurt!" she called out, unclear why she'd felt the need to add that last detail.

He turned and looked at her with concern, sadness. Those lurid, crazy eyes of his might even have been a little bit scared.

"You've never failed a challenge before," he reminded her.

"I know. I'm sorry, sir."

"It's okay." Something kept him from turning to leave again. He said, "Jezebel, I know I've not been very present in your life, perhaps not as present as I should have been. I want to make sure you know how important you are to me."

"I know, I know. I'm *destined* to change the world."

"You seem dissatisfied with this." The hood he always wore fast around his head shook a little, and almost fell back. He straightened it peevishly.

"What if I don't want to be part of this? What if there's still some hope for the world out there? What if there's someone else who's *destined* to do the opposite, to save humanity from the brink of destruction?"

"It's not just that, my dear." He touched her shoulder. His fingers were icy and wet. A quiver pierced through her heart. "You're more than just your fate. I understand your compulsions toward these, uh, nihilists of yours—" He nodded toward her bookshelf. "And even your need to seriously consider their retrograde philosophies. You feel as though you've been dealt an unfair hand, that you didn't have a choice in the matter, because you were born to this world—a world of confinement and boredom. Is that it?"

That about sums it up, she thought, and nodded.

"You feel conditioned to it," he carried on. "Bullied into it—a prisoner to our whims, yeah?" He opened his mouth to say something else, but stopped himself. The look on his face was worse than the feel of his cold hands; it was an expression of feeling. Specifically, it was a mien of sadness, something she hadn't thought him capable of. "One day, what I hope you'll realize is this: your ideals *are* mirrored in ours. Your vision is ours, too. We are very much, as the saying goes, cut from the same cloth, Jezebel. We want the very same things."

"You don't know what I want."

CAREFUL. That voice again, repeating the same word. *CAREFUL.*

"You might not have noticed," the Overseer said, "but I've been watching you—" Oh, she had noticed, all right. At his lectures, he always seemed to be staring straight at her, boring his fire-filled words through her. "Since before you could even speak, I saw greatness in you, Jezebel. I certainly know what you want. Freedom. And you want to know where you came from, how you came to be with us. You want fulfillment, and history, and lineage. You especially want to feel *normal*, as if that was what mattered most. Sex, family, love. Those are mortal diversions; they're beneath you."

"You're wrong. You don't know me at all. Those aren't the things I want." She was lying; he had read her perfectly. Still, it was beginning to feel nice defying him, and now that she had the invisible voice, it was easier, too.

"What *do* you want, then? What is it that you crave above all else? Tell me, and I'll give it to you, and more."

DON'T SAY. DON'T SAY.

"Nothing," she said.

"There was once a great king," the Overseer said, turning his back to her, pausing at the door. "A prophet named Solomon. I'm sure you've already heard of him; you're an apt pupil. Something you might *not* know is this: his rule was only made possible by the intervention of certain spectacular forces. Some believe he possessed a ring, and in the ring lived a jinn, sometimes called a genie. Solomon used the jinn to assist his armies in battle. You are that jinn, Jezebel—you're our jinn, our enchanted jewel, our great key."

EVIL. EVIL. LIES. LIES.

Reflexively, she repeated the words of the voice, shouting them:

"EVIL! EVIL! LIES! LIES!"

He was facing her again—though she hadn't seen him move—and slapped her firm across the cheek. She flew across her small chamber, landing sprawled across her cot, in the shadows at the corner of the room.

"Evil is human will," he said. "Neither gods nor demons have an ethical value; toward humans, they're ambivalent." He seemed to float—*POOF*—soaring over her bed, fast as a gazelle, his face looming threateningly above her. "I don't know what you're hiding from me, but I'll have it out of you, even if I have to rip it from your skull. There's no way you failed. You're Jezebel."

With that, he absconded, leaving her alone to paw at the throbbing ache in her cheek.

STAND, the voice said, and she did, forgetting the pain.

She hated him, absolutely and irrevocably. Before, she'd only hated her circumstances—and sometimes the way he looked at her—but now it was full-blown, boiling loathing. He was a monster and, even without knowing how or why they were planning to do what they were planning to do, she was done with it. She wouldn't participate further.

Something—not quite the voice—beckoned her toward her desk. She sat down and stared at the map of the United States hanging crinkled on the wall above her. He'd been right about her: she wanted freedom. Perhaps that place, the one from her challenge (which had felt more like a dream—like someone else's dream) would give her the answers she yearned for.

Tucson, the crab had written.

TUCSON, the voice said.

"Tucson," Jezebel said, jabbing her finger at the little black dot beside it on the map.

Her door opened a crack. That shouldn't happen; doors were kept locked there, especially hers. She moved toward it, peeking out through the fracture, scared to walk through it.

"Hello," she whispered. "Hello?"

No one responded.

That great longing returned, stronger than it had ever been. She slipped through the door, barely making out the scrap of an acolyte's garb, the hem of their robe fluttering as they fled round the corner and out of sight.

TUCSON.

Jezebel fled, running as fast as her legs could carry her, down the hall where the acolyte had disappeared, across the grounds with her hood pulled low across her face, hoping no one would see her and repeating the word in her head—*Tucson, Tucson, Tucson.* Then she was out, through the front archways and past the dead husks of trees which surrounded their camp—their fortress, and what had been her home.

She remembered the Jules Verne quote the Overseer had read:

It is an immense desert, where man is never lonely, for he feels life stirring on all sides.

Perhaps what they said about the desert of the sea did not apply also to the deep desert proper. All she saw around her were endless slopes, barren dunes, infertile hillocks that writhed and morphed with the changing winds.

She said it again, "Tucson," and listened for the voice.

It wasn't there. It seemed to have left her, so she wandered forward, on her own.

CHAPTER XVIII

Orson's lips were dry, so he sipped some more water. They were making the last stretch toward the monument, and the wind settled into an eerie calm.

"Easy on the H$_2$O," the warden said. "What's in there'll be the last of it for you 'til tomorrow."

"S'okay, I have more in my pack." Orson patted the rucksack slung loosely across his back.

The ranger stopped in his tracks and sprung toward Orson.

"Boy!" he shouted, nearly butting heads with Orson. "Don't expect this to be a walk in the park. You won't be sitting around a campfire singing Kumbaya, getting off on some new kick. This is serious, real shit."

Serious. Real. Shit. Finally, some words I can relate to. Orson chuckled inwardly, but was also genuinely (and increasingly) freaked out by the bipolar shifts in the Big Man's attitude.

"Sorry," Orson said. "Let's just hurry and get down there."

He kept slipping in the loose-packed sand. It swallowed him up to his ankles, his sneakers filled with bits of it, weighing him down. He felt as though he'd never get a good grip, but knew he shouldn't complain with the warden heading up the front—with ears like a hawk. Suddenly, an idea occurred to him. A realization, really. Namely, that Orson didn't even know his name. *Humanize the brute,* he thought.

"Do you have a name, sir?"

"Yes," the warden said, without turning, without telling.

Orson ventured a guess, laughing to himself.

Little Big Guy.

Star Wanderer.

Wind Numbfuck River.

After a while, the Big Man finally *did* speak.

"Askuwheteau. He Who Keeps Watch. But that's all you'll get from me, white-hair. I won't be sharing my family's history with you."

Orson touched himself on the top of his head, double-checking that his blond hair hadn't turned white, since He Who Keeps Watch kept calling him that.

"*Ask-You-We-Toe,*" Orson repeated, sounding it out.

"Close enough."

They moved briskly, the ranger—Askuwheteau—still leading the way, closing in on the massive structure, which glowed orange from afar. Smoke rose from its center, through the night sky, casting up a watercolor aura of purple and gray. As they drew nearer, Orson could see between the cracks in the formation. There within, smolder and fumes emerged from a fire lit at its epicenter. Up close, it loomed above them like a giant boulder-capped castle, blocking out the stars in the sky.

Centered between ten monolithic stone pillars, a flame-pit blazed, spewing forth its hellish spits, which shifted the shadows of the twelve acolytes gathered in a circle across the space. Each of them were seated, their feet scrunched beneath them, their knees pointing straight ahead. Side by side, thigh-against-thigh, they lay in wait, ascetic disciples resting with palms supine against the hallowed ground. The hulking stones ensconcing them seemed to move, too, with every flickering dance of the flames.

Each attendant wore his own unique robe—one with a snake stitched across its front, its rattler poised and dancing in the lambent flames; one with an otter, its small but vicious mouth opened to reveal its glinting white teeth; one with a deer, its long horns bowed elegantly before it; one with a bear, its small, methodical arms holding up a fish; one with a raven, its black wings spread in flight; one with an owl, its eyes stitched in gold thread, glowing in the firelight; one with a goose, its neck curlicued about itself in a gesture of protection; one with a crocodile, big and wizened, lurching and looming; one with a turtle, the tip of its nose beaked, sharp as a knife; one with a dolphin, gentle but fast, ready to jump right off the fabric; one with a frog, its legs impossibly long; and one with a shark, its fin struck with a fresh, giant gash, as though it had just been injured by a hunter's flying harpoon.

A withered woman stood poised above them, on top of a boulder, her braid lowered close to the tip of the flames. She held a twisted sandalwood staff and was meditating; her eyes were closed, locked in concentration, and her body did not move. Her robe was built of the same cloth, a durable, coarse burlap, but hers was *not* emblazoned with an animal. Instead, hers housed an image of the sun, its shape perfectly clear, round and bright yellow. Swirling lines of orange and red emanated in every which direction, representing its powerful, life-giving rays.

Askuwheteau grabbed Orson by the shoulder and whispered in his ear, "They've already begun. I'll stand guard over the ceremony from here. There's room for you, across from the shaman. Go there now. Kneel down before her."

"And then what do I do?" he asked.

"Just follow her instructions." Askuwheteau pushed Orson forward.

Tripping over the shoulders of a disciple—the Turtle—Orson apologized with an uncertain smile and a quiet wave. He regained his composure, setting one foot forward, and immediately felt himself pulled into the ring, as if by some irresistible charm, a magnetism. He was on the ground before he had a chance to check the status of his hidden camera. Since he knew his visit would end abruptly, if they were alerted to the device, he'd just have to hope he remembered to turn it on earlier in the car, before he entered the lodge and met Askuwheteau.

The *shaman*, as Askuwheteau had called her, rose from her place of reflection and kneeled beside Orson. She swept his bag off his back and—while keeping her stony gaze locked on his—she tossed it outside the circle, back to the warden, who picked it up and nodded back at them.

Her eyes were cloudy with glaucomatous veins, and punctuated with silvery cataracts whose edges seemed to quaver cooly, like two ice cubes melting their way into the hot, sweating skin of Orson's face, calming his concern. They searched him, read him to his core, memorizing every faintly twitching muscle and swooping mound of flesh on his face, every line from cheek to chin. Down, across the long sweep of his crane's neck, and over the length of his narrow chest. She seemed to appraise him favorably there, despite his lanky build, a gummy smile tugging at the corners of her lipless mouth.

Her grin distracted Orson from the spell of her eyes, but it also aged her. He'd initially guessed that she was somewhere around sixty (in the warm cast of the blaze, she'd looked smooth and angelic), but now that she revealed her leathery, toothless gums, she looked more like eighty (and more like a witch than an angel).

Regardless of her age, she still managed to move lithely, as though time had neither withered her muscles nor stiffened her joints. Her arms painted the air with the movement of her liturgy; like two spectral birds in soundless flight, each wrist rotated around an axis that was impossibly broad—as though her hands and arms were boneless, elastic. Her movement picked up speed as she clipped around the bonfire, spinning away from Orson in quick circles, twirling around and around the blaze, her coarse-braided hair bouncing against the back of her robe. She jumped up and up, her feet raised impossibly high into the air, above all of their heads, and she licked at the flames with the tips of her spritely finger tips, like a pianist massaging her instrument's beloved keys, pounding out a loving, racing tempo.

Each of the members of the circle took up the beat of her step-and-jump, patting against the length of his own stretched thighs—creating a rhythm that reminded Orson of the subway performers he'd grown used to seeing (even bored of) back in New York. But here, their thrumming pattern entranced him, its cadence gaining momentum and speed as the old woman—the shaman, their chieftain—dissolved in a blur of quickening steps and leaps, around and even across the sharp tip of the flames. She leapt again and again, back and forth, until—abruptly and simultaneously—all of their movement stopped. The skidding break of the shaman's heels against the sand kicked a flurry through the air. Slowly, she settled back against her boulder in a seated position, humming surreptitiously to herself.

Orson's heart beat frantically against the inside of his shirt. Although he was exhilarated—and could feel every rushing drop of his own hot blood coursing through his veins—he was still no closer to understanding the meaning of life, or whatever the warden had promised. Not even a glimmer of epiphany poked through the buzz of his adrenaline. Surely this wasn't the *experience* Askuwheteau had promised.

As the flitting ring of elation drained from Orson's head, he felt the impulse for more thrills, like the evanescent hit of a cocaine bump leaves the addict craving more. In answer to that longing, a new—and even stranger—stimulus entered upon the scene.

A man was dragged almost imperceptibly out from a fold of black, from between a pair of the tall stone columns at the perimeter of the monument. A trio of escorts followed in tow and one of them, the centermost, shoved him from behind, sending the man flapping toward the ground. He buckled into a heap of grime a foot from the edge of the circle. He was bound by a tight-fitting choker, fashioned in metal. He looked like a medieval torture victim, his bruised body tossed to the masses. Stumbling back to his feet, he briefly scanned their company, eyes flashing like a wild animal, his wounded mouth diminishing to a pathetic little O. Silently, he stood there, like a pet who's been punished before and knows full well the chastisement that awaits him.

No one moved; no one spoke. Everyone sat, mostly ignoring the dazed, confused, bare-chested man whose unwashed body seeped with fluids radiating the scent of offal.

"He's hurt!" Orson screamed, scanning the group for some indication that this might be a joke, or a test to see if he was worthy to receive their beloved *experience*; but no one flinched. "Someone has to do something. Someone help him—"

At the sound of Orson's voice, the newcomer lunged toward him, the links of the chain that bound the man clicking together in a quick race across the ground until the tether could extend no farther—stretched taut from his keepers' hands to the shackle around the man's neck. The man fell backward to the ground.

Orson screamed, his chest feeling like it might explode, his head pounding with panic. He scanned the edge of the ring for Askuwheteau and found him standing, shotgun lifted peaceably against his shoulder, hands folded together. Their eyes met; Askuwheteau nodded, and unwrapped his hands to lift up one finger in a commanding gesture: *Back toward the ring.*

Orson was on his own.

The men ministering to the prisoner were costumed like the rest of the group, their robes embellished respectively with a falcon, a wolf, and a scorpion—all animals of distinguishable power, renowned and feared for one reason or another.

It took all three of them to restrain their victim, to subdue his sudden outbursts. Any time they came near the edge of the circle, the shaman shrieked horribly, raising her hands to the heavens above.

The Scorpion—gripping the chain with leather-gloved hands, his feet grating into the sand beneath him with the pressure of the man's convulsions—shouted something in another language. It sounded like *Heck-Hey-Hermes*.

The Falcon and the Wolf followed the Scorpion's lead, repeating it after him. Orson caught a bit more of it this time:

"*Heck-Hey-Vermees, Heck-Hey-Vermees, Heck-Hey-Vermees.*"

It still made no sense to Orson, but judging by the circle's response, it was their call to arms. They repeated the phrase, shouting it in unison with their fists raised high above their heads. The chant grew clearer, louder:

"*Heck-Hey-Vermis, Heck-Hey-Vermis, Heck-Hey-Vermis.*"

The Scorpion drew in a span of the chain separating him from his victim and, gripping the vise that surrounded the prisoner's neck, twisted a sort of key which protruded almost imperceptibly from the side of the shackle. Slowly, like torture, the fetter's clasp grew ever-tighter against the distended skin of the wild stranger's throat. Each minute rotation meant the metal gripping him grew closer to choking him out.

"They're hurting him!" Orson screamed again. "Stop it, you sick bastards!"

The shaman, the chieftain—whatever she was—pressed her hand against Orson's mouth, stamping out his cries. Her palm felt papery and dry, and she chanted more of her mumbled words.

Tranquility overcame Orson, smoother and stronger than a shot of skag; he lulled.

She removed her hand and nodded toward the Falcon, the Wolf, and the Scorpion. They resumed the chant:

"*Eck-Hey-Vermis, Eck-Hey-Vermis, Eck-Hey-Vermis.*"

The gravelly shrine filled with a clamor as all of their company howled it out, their voices echoing around the circle in a chain reaction, reverberating through the pit of Orson's skull—louder than heavy metal and more ghoulish, too. The Scorpion, the Wolf, and the Falcon beat their fists against their chests, screaming along with the crowd.

All of a sudden, the real words of their mantra opened up to Orson, like the answer to a riddle whose solution had been haunting him for hours, yet was right in front of him all along. They were chanting:

"ECCE VERMIS, ECCE VERMIS, ECCE VERMIS."

It wasn't their native tongue at all. It was Latin, and Orson knew this because of the very man he'd mentioned earlier, in his conversation with Askuwheteau at the lodge. Friedrich Nietzsche's last book had been named *Ecce Homo*, meaning "Behold the man," and was a reference to Pontius Pilate's fateful words as he offered up the scourged Christ for crucifixion.

But *Vermis?* Orson scoured every recess of his mind for some literary reference—combing the annals of his years-worth of studying for philosophy tests. Nothing in his background told him the word's meaning, but it was definitely Latin—he was sure of that much.

Vermis. Vermis. Vermis, he thought, repeating it to himself, over and over, rolling it over the inside of his mouth like fine wine across the tongue, feeling it for flavor or a jolt of memory. And then he remembered. *Vermis* was the name of the lobe bisecting the cerebellum, right at the forefront of the brain.

Jesus, he thought. *They're either going to crucify him, or lobotomize him.*

Their shouting faded to a whisper and finally into silence, leaving only the sound of the gagging man, gasping for breath, to echo endlessly around them.

He—the man, their oblation—regarded all of them, his bulging eyes flicking round the circle from face to face; he whimpered and sniveled, snot hanging from his nose, until his stare settled on the shaman, whereupon he gurgled—a waterfall of spit splashing to the ground—and passed out.

The Wolf stepped forward and produced a glass canister, a Florentine flask. In his other hand, he hoisted up a metal grille: a grate whose metallic latticework looked home-spun, loose, like he'd warmed the material and constructed it himself. It was lifted up by a set of foot-long legs. He entered the circle—heads ducking, shoulders parting to let him pass—and threw the grate over the flames, which licked their way eagerly through and around its interlacing strips of wirework. Then the Wolf set the flask on top the grill.

Inside the glass was a dark fluid, which began to bubble as the heat rose. The flask fogged; it sent up a bilious miasma of green, vegetative rot, with a cloying smell of mold.

The Falcon stepped forward and entered the circle. He approached the fire and held out his hand, lowering it unwaveringly toward the lip of the glass container while, with his other hand, he withdrew a hooked dagger from the belt of rope running across his waist. Light glinted off the weapon's sharp edge.

Orson blocked his eyes against the glare and missed the blade's impact.

Blood oozed evenly from the Falcon's palm, into the stinking admixture, tinting it a ruddy ochre.

A stretch of silence passed, during which all eyes were locked on the slow-trickling flow of lifeblood filling up the glass. Then the shaman spoke—this time in English.

"Stanch the blood flow," she said. Lifting her own hand palm-upward to demonstrate, she pantomimed his recourse, draping a bandana over her "injured" hand and pressing it firmly down. She passed him the bandana and he followed suit, trading the blood-smeared tool for the dressing.

She wiggled up and off her boulder, creeping toward the flame, where she followed suit: slicing open her palm, watching her fluids drip into the brimming vessel. After she bandaged her hand with another swatch of fabric, the knife found its way into Orson's hand. Swinging him up by his armpits, she cast him toward the flames and the libation they were drafting.

He was dazed, but sure the shaman would accept nothing but compliance. She expected Orson to follow their lead, drugged as he was by her strange spell. They wanted him to cut open his own flesh, to let the grit of him slip away, into their esoteric brew.

The blade's wooden grip was already moist with so many bodily fluids—his sweat, their blood, and dribbling spit which fell from his own pathetic, puckered mouth.

"You must do it!" she screamed. "If you can't, you'll leave us, now." She pointed to the warden, who stood closer to the edge of the circle than before, his feet spaced farther apart, knees slightly bent, with one hand lifted to the butt of his shotgun.

Even though part of Orson thought they might kill him as soon as he left the circle—or worse, they might turn him into their next victim—he still wanted to leave. But he pictured the face of his roommate Brian, and all of his academic peers, smiling smugly as Orson arrived empty-handed, defeated, beat-up. They'd laugh at his failure, though they expected it all along. If he could just get through it, follow their orders, and walk away smiling in the morning, he might be able to use the evidence of his recording against them and come out the victor. It would mean national attention, and he'd be the last one laughing.

He approached the edge of the fire pit and tipped his head over it, peering down through the top of the flask, through its wide-brimmed aperture and into the concoction. It frothed, its head of foam iridescent with the look of grease, bubbles squelching up with fat and gristle. Reluctantly, he pressed the edge of the dagger against his opened palm, but flinched at the pain; only a drop was released, and altogether missed the decanter. He gazed around pleadingly from his place at the center of the circle, but saw only a dozen stoic faces, eyes lilted hazily closed like a battalion of somnambulants awaiting their master's order.

"Do it!" the shaman screamed, both arms lifted, hanging skin flapping. She looked like the Wicked Witch, her leathery skin stretched into a tight, inhuman grimace.

Her scream made Orson flinch, and before he had the chance to willfully *do it*, he'd already—unfeelingly—done it. The keen blade bit numbly into the meat of his hand. It was a deep cut. A river of red welled up, brimming over the arch of his palm, falling from each fingertip in rapid driblets, and swirling down in their biotic concoction, which was boiling ever faster, ready to spill up over the rim. He watched his contribution streak its way across the surface of the mix for a moment, red stripes of blood across oleaginous bubbles, the constituents coalescing to become something whole: an evil, breathing goop which spumed and coughed in Orson's face.

Nausea overcame him. He was falling to the ground, the world spinning.

The shaman approached and retrieved the knife from him. She offered Orson his own square of fabric, with which to slow the blood flow. The corners of her full, brown mouth slanted downward.

"I'm woozy," Orson said. Indeed, his muscles felt slack, muddy, melting off the bone and dissolving into the sand.

"You'll be fine," the shaman said, patting him on the shoulder. She hooked an arm round his neck, ushering him back to his spot on the ground below her, beneath the boulder. There, she spread her arms out widely—and looked like an eagle at full wingspan. She shouted, *"ECCE VERMIS!* Now we begin." She lowered her arms slowly, still holding the knife in one hand and her sandalwood staff in the other—a knotted stick, a wizard's scepter, she pointed it down toward the fire and the object of their undertaking. "Are you prepared to share in the joys of our ceremony? To taste the wonders of the bitten man, the *tatane*, and to join us in celebration?"

All fifteen of them—the Snake, the Otter, the Deer, the Bear, the Raven, the Owl, the Goose, the Crocodile, the Turtle, the Dolphin, the Frog, the Shark, the Scorpion, the Falcon, the Wolf, the warden, and the shaman—let loose a trickle of guffaws, a horde of wild animals greeting one another with malefic cackles and squawks.

The sound of it made Orson cringe. He covered up his ears but, even through the flesh and bone of his hands, the pitch of their laughter grew into a roar. It took on a hymnal quality—an animalic song of birds cawing, wolves howling, snakes rattling, geese honking, frogs ribbiting. They smiled broadly at him, like the pack of wild beasts that they were.

Something was happening. It felt as though something was changing within him, as though his very chemical makeup was being altered. He felt himself joining them in laughter, yet he didn't recognize the sound of his own voice. It was a stranger's hysterics—a gluttonous, blood-thirsty fit.

Through the flames of the fire, Orson could just make out their victim, growing frenzied, snapping at the air, his jaws clacking together with the sound of a steel baseball bat hitting a home run. His three jailers dragged him closer, to the center of the circle and up to the edge of the fire. The wild man still pulled helplessly against his chains, hard enough to draw blood, which hissed on the flames, and he emitted a grating, drawn out clicking sound like the call of an insect army. His cheeks puffed out with each incomprehensible, inhuman clack, the veins on his forehead protruding against the surface of his sallow skin. His neck was a strenuous, bloated mess of tension, bulging against its cuff covering like love handles over a too-tight belt.

As whatever trick they had executed over Orson bored its way deeper into him—the stars glimmering overhead with ever-brighter brilliancy—all of the strangers' expressions stretched into one ghostly, transparent gauze, bearing only a dim impression of their once-human features. What remained instead—in the shapes of their meshed-together heads—took on a gray cast, like a mound of corpses at a burial site. They blended into a hulking, donut-shaped blob of amorphous, writhing meat, cackling and spitting.

Something was *definitely* happening. He'd ingested enough psychotropics in his personal and academic life to know that his vision had fully melted into the unreliably bleary aberration of a drug haze, a hallucination—yet he hadn't taken anything. He couldn't feel his heart, but he knew it must be beating rapidly because his hands were shaking, and his teeth were chattering, and his eyes were crossing. It wasn't from blood loss—in fact, the opening across his palm had already scabbed over like yesterday's stigmata, old news. This was something fresher, and unfamiliar. This was something preternatural. It was the start of the *experience* Askuwheteau had promised.

The shaman approached their prey and tossed down her sandalwood staff. She lifted the knife against his throat, rotating the tiny, lethal tine of its tip into the fraught muscles of his neck. A thin line of blood crept over his Adam's apple and pooled in the lake of his pronounced, bony clavicles, but the man appeared unfazed. He stared deeply into the shaman's eyes, with all the forbearing of an invalid—one who can no longer feel the impulse of pain. She moved the weapon upward, sliding its blade over the curve of his cheeks, the bridge of his nose, and pausing at the center of his forehead—its tip only a half inch from the surface of his skin. She drew in a deep breath and held it, tightening her grip on the handle of the blade. Hefting it high in the air, she drove it straight into his head.

When the knife made impact with his skull, it disappeared effortlessly into him, up to the hilt, with a sound like a watermelon smashing against concrete. Twisting it into him, she drilled him open, bone crushing—spraying into the air, coating her hair with gray, fibrous tissue, hanging in clumps from her braid.

Impossibly, the man was still alive. He flailed his arms and legs against the six strong grips which the Scorpion, the Wolf, and the Falcon held him in. His eyes rotated within their sockets, flashing white-black-white-black, rolling like eggs boiling in a giant pot. As his seizures grew more rapid, they gained momentum too, and the three restraining him had to lift him up in the air, cushioning him between their bodies to prevent his escape.

The circle resumed their frantic shouting:

"*ECCE VERMIS. ECCE VERMIS. ECCE VERMIS.*"

Orson loosed the sparse contents of his stomach across the sand, a splash of water and some gas station pastries, watching in horror as the little old woman hacked away at the man's skull—and he, still wide awake while she burrowed casually into him like a jackhammer into a sidewalk. Her skinny, sagging arms flapped back and forth as she lifted, drove, lifted, and drove her fist—and the blade—in and out of him.

In and out. In and out. Mashing and pulping and blending his scalp and his hair and his skull and his brain into one chunky, gruesome maceration—a gooping amalgamation of all the bits of a person no one's ever supposed to see.

Finally, once she managed to create a hole which could accommodate her entire fist, she stopped. She dropped the knife and fell quickly to her knees, peering into him like a girl who's lost her most prized piece of jewelry, a microscopic but invaluable diamond. Using her fingers, she swiped across the fresh aperture of the gaping wound, pulling out bits of his skull and tossing them carelessly over her shoulder until she found what she was searching for—what she'd beaten him wide open for, for all of them.

She pulled it out of him. She pulled out the *Vermis.*

Orson remembered; it didn't just mean a part of the human brain. It was so named for the creature it resembled: a worm.

The thing didn't come out easily from where it lay, not without a fight. She had to tug and pull, as did the men holding onto the (finally) slackened body of their victim. It was as though the creature had suction-cupped itself to the inside of his head, holding on for dear life. When the shaman, her skin slick with sweat, finally separated the worm from its host, she hoisted it up proudly, its fat-ringed form wriggling in her grip, and she shouted it again, "*ECCE VERMIS!*"

All the attendants mirrored the mantra in a final, booming hoorah:

"*ECCE VERMIS, ECCE VERMIS, ECCE VERMIS!*"

Behold the Worm.

The Scorpion handed the knife back to the shaman—now encrusted with sand—and she hefted it up with the worm. She hardened her grip on both objects, careful to hold the odd being as far away from her body as possible, careful to avoid a stray nip from one of its pulsating, tooth-ringed mouths.

Mouths, Orson thought, reeling. *It has two mouths.*

When she drove the blade into the worm, it let out a squealing click, not dissimilar to the insectile noises its host had formerly made, but this one was more pronounced—the shrill whine of a tea kettle over too much heat, ready to explode. Both of its circles of teeth spasmed in the sphincters of its twin mouths.

Orson teetered, right at the border between waking and dreaming. He regarded his own throbbing, injured palm, and caressed it gently with the fingers of his other hand. Since the emergence of the creature—from the sanguine gap in the stranger's head—Orson's wound seemed to pulsate with life, and the modicum of hallucinatory images increased. He was ready for it—to slip into the comfort of unconsciousness, to melt into mindlessness, a soft and downy cloud—but when the thing's viscous innards began to drip down into the bubbling vat, his head quietened, as though in a drunkard's fleeting calm. Just as its brackish fluids drained from its body, to commingle with their own at the bottom of the glass, the anxious sensation of needles, which had pricked at Orson's every nerve, was replaced by a sense of effortless repose, as though he could feel the very deep fibers of every living entity on the scene; as though he'd somehow gained an omniscient perspective, one far-removed from the gritty goings-on—where he could see every tick and movement of the shaman, squeezing the last drops of the worm's insides out, draining it into the mix; where he could see every undiluted hair-splitting contortion of the Scorpion's facial muscles as he readied himself for whatever terror came next; and where, in an instant, he could count all the prickly hairs on the warden's head. Orson was high—impossibly, effusively, floatingly high.

The shaman approached the piping hot decanter and, using her bare hands, lifted it up from the flames. She transferred its contents into a calabash gourd whose snarled waistline was tied with a thin blue ribbon, and she shook it about, swirling the liquid across the inner walls of its new home, cooling it off before she did what Orson knew she was going to do.

The shaman drank deeply, her lips pressed firmly against the rim of the timeworn receptacle, her head lifted back and her chin stretched upward, diminishing the severity of her elderly, slackened jawline. Both her hands embraced the hardened gourd, with all the tenderness of a mother holding her newborn child, as she voraciously gulped down its contents. With each slurp of the viscous ink she drank, the shaman seemed to brighten a bit, lighting up like a firefly. She glowed with the golden, preeminent aura of a seraphim.

It was passed around the circle. They drank eagerly, their necks glugging with the force of their deep drafts. It came to Orson last.

The neck of the gourd felt elastic, giving to his touch, drooping as though made of soft plastic. He gripped its base with one hand as he lifted up its mouth, pausing before the first drop of the stuff hit his tongue, because all those around him had changed: their plodding black eyes without irises swelling to the size of melons, swallowing the rest of their faces; their hair lighting up in flames, dissolving to ash, and their skulls sprouting long, curving, knobby horns whose points stretched endlessly up toward the sky.

It tasted like shit and blood, and its texture was at once coarse and chewy, greasy with clumps of fat. It burned down his throat and hit his stomach like lava on water, with a hiss. The sensation of knowing which he'd already endured grew stronger. He could count the stars overhead; he could hear in every direction for miles—every lizard scratching itself, every snake slithering out of its skin, every coyote panting as it ripped apart its prey. The darkness of night overhead was replaced with glowing, an impossible brightness that was alive, vibrating through his skull and shaking all his bones.

He saw some wondrous things, and many that were horrendous:

A pillar made of human skulls, rising toward the sky, parting the clouds.

A man with the head of a goat, baying loudly as it stampeded toward the edge of a cliff and fell down to its death.

The circle rising, disrobing, and masturbating—some taking turns on the shaman, who moaned like a heifer in heat—beating at one another's crotches 'til they were bruised and bleeding. The circle eating their victim, tearing his limbs apart, gnashing at his flesh with their serrated, grisly teeth.

It was a long night, filled with the barbarous dreams of the drug, blurring the lines between what was truly happening on that hidden slope, between the tall stones, and what was just a figment of Orson's metamorphosing mind.

The blood of the worm was the key, and he'd been left its most pungent, swirling tannins, at the bottom of the gourd. He felt it take hold, wrenching up every buried secret, every deep and dark desire. It spoke to him, in a voice that felt like smoke blowing pleasurably over his skin.

Rest, it said. *Be at peace.*

So Orson did. He closed his eyes, and he drifted away, unguarded, trusting his fate to the hands of his captors. Trusting the word of the voice.

CHAPTER XIX

The rain fell, dampening Birch to the core. His hair—tied up in a customary knot atop his head—was suction-cupped to his scalp with wetness. The sweats he'd slid into were hanging from him, slopping comedically, making him look like a saggy-skinned sumo wrestler, the fabric swinging around his body with every racing stride. Birch wondered shortly if he'd have been better off staying at home, but when his run called—when it beckoned him to its calming, dreamy lull of speed, of racing heart, of sweat and grinding frenzy that drowned all else out—he could do nothing to avoid it; he had to run.

Down the Embarcadero he rushed, calves burning with the urgency of his pace, mind abuzz with possibilities. Crispin had truly hit a home run. All those years of wondering, of exploration, of false starts, of money down the drain—all that time, and the biggest clue of all had been sitting right before him. He felt like the world's biggest oaf and, now that he was drenched to his pits and to his crotch, he probably looked like it, too.

He slowed down to wring out his sleeves and considered taking his shirt off, to feel the refreshing bite of raindrops on his chest, but he was too ashamed of his lanky figure and slanted back to actually follow through. Instead, he hiked up the arms of his sweatshirt and stretched the elastic apertures of his sweatpant's legs, pulling them up above the outward curve of his knees. Now he thought he looked even sillier, dorky as a zit-faced kid at the Renaissance Fair wearing harlequin pants, but at least he could feel the joy of the wind cutting against his uncovered limbs.

He regained his pace and jolted past the giant, iconic bow and arrow sculpture at Rincon Park on his left. The tip of the bolt was forever buried below the ground, its aspect left up to one's imagination. Only the red-feathered fletchings and chipped silver shaft were exposed, locked in place by the careless golden slope of the bow, and by the bondage of the bowstring. Every time Birch ran past the 60-foot fiberglass sculpture, which was meant to evoke the aspect of cupid's bow, he was reminded of the clear absence of love in his own life. He'd dedicated so much of his time—and of himself—to solving the lifelong mystery of the creature that he'd entered his 30's without the everyman's customary patch of year-long relationships etched into his belt. For a fellow as good-looking as he was (and not in the conventional biceps-and-abs kind of way, more like an odd, modelish handsome), it was more than a little bizarre that he hadn't attracted a mate, let alone a handful of lovers. But sex was something altogether foreign to Birch—and unwanted, unnecessary, like drinking or drugs; in Birch's opinion, they all sucked dry your vital bits.

He flew by his favorite drunken hobo, whose long, curved toenails were looking yellower than ever, hanging over the edge of his sandals.

The man shouted at Birch as he passed by, "Mistah, gummie uh sangwich terday?"

Birch ignored him, picking up speed and feeling a little guilty for not responding—it had been over a week since he'd brought the guy a scrap—but telling himself the man didn't remember him anyway.

Birch strode past a group of teenagers, geared up in Giants attire from head to toe. They were running late for the game, keeping pace with Birch for a few blocks south toward the stadium before he finally accelerated past them. He was glad to break away; not only could Birch not care less about sports, but Giants fans were also the *worst*: notoriously loud and proud. The group of kids had been a particularly annoying reminder of the often inelegant nature of sports fans. They'd mocked him, whispering to one another and calling him *scrawny fag, scrawny fag,* over and over.

Their insults didn't hurt Birch, but they did bring him momentarily back to when he'd been a shy, introverted kid—as opposed to the shy, introverted adult he'd grown into. The teens reminded him of the time in his life when he'd been more concerned with learning about the universe than about going to the gym, when he would rather read comics than watch action films—and of the time in his life when he'd seen the worm, the thing, and when he'd seen the man. They reminded him of when he'd watched a stranger die, when someone—some hulk of a stranger wearing sunglasses, even though it hadn't been too sunny that day—had spied on him from the cover of the brush, hidden alongside the boardwalk.

Why didn't he help?

Why didn't he scream?

Why didn't I see him?

These questions looped through Birch's mind on repeat, gnawing at him like Aunt Greta's incessant interrogations at the dinner table.

He passed under the Bay Bridge and by a smattering of tourist traps: cafés and dive bars he'd never visit—real rat traps, with foreign drunkards gagging on rotten-smelling oysters, feeling special because they were eating on the water, and at a place that somehow (despite its sour-smelling urinals and over-salted food) made them feel more *fancy*, more *local*.

How could you not have seen?

He cursed himself again for overlooking such a glaring, obvious detail, fantasizing about a Birch who *had* seen the man, and who had saved himself more than a decade of mindless, desperate searching. But that wasn't Birch—not the real one, running like a mad man through the rain, stamping his frustration out across the Embarcadero.

At a crack in the path, he twisted his ankle and almost veered off the sidewalk into oncoming traffic. He slowed down a moment to clear his head, hunched over with his hands on his knees. He lifted up his sweatshirt, fanning it open to let in the breeze, lifting his open-mouthed face to taste the clouds' jetsam. His heart was pounding.

It was tempting to call it quits, to head back home and go to sleep—to forget about the frustration of all those wasted years—but he reminded himself of how much *possibility* the detail Crispin uncovered would finally open up, and he redoubled his efforts, running ever-faster, closing his approach on South Beach Park. The modern structure of the yacht club lurched into view, a mass of glass and wood; it contrasted against the classic design of the baseball stadium glowering behind it—that brick and steel coliseum gazing out toward the bay, greeting foreign aircraft, welcoming alien visitors. It said, *Please, come. Stay a while.*

Birch swung below Pier 40, close to the water, so he could get a good look at the boats anchored to the wharfs, slowing his pace to appreciate the way the schooners dipped in the bucking waves, like elegant fowl floating along the dock, undisturbed by the petulant thrashing of the current. Overhead, the storm clouds bloated and spilled their excreta down on the heads of the fans packed into the stadium. Their far-off cheers liquified under a bellow of crashing thunder. Birch stopped running altogether to wait for a flash of light across the sky—doubled over again to catch his breath—but no lightning cracked the somber gray firmament above him. The sound of the thunder fizzled out and, in its wake, the fanfare of the game rose again to take its place.

Birch sat down to rest at a bench facing the water and closed his eyes, picturing the blurry yet undeniable shape of those glasses—watching him, watching the dying man. Years and years now separated them whereas, back then, it had only been a span of several feet. The bridge of the man's nose was just visible between those two aviator lenses. Birch could picture it with his eyes closed; it was that distinct. It sloped outward from the brow ridge at an almost horizontal pace and hooked abruptly downward, like a narrow cliff that dropped off toward his lips far below, invisible behind the cover of the tall weeds among which he crouched. The man's nostrils looked distended—huge, as if he had been scared.

Birch felt certain he'd seen a nose like it before, but he couldn't quite place where.

One of the benefits of introversion and an adolescence devoid of drugs and sex—devoid of distractions—was a crystal-clear memory. Birch could recall about every event of his youth with sparkling clarity, right down to all of his ugly haircuts ($9.99 at the mall, once at the hands of a gentle giant—a transvestite named Betty whom Birch actually rather liked, despite her bad breath; and she'd done a fine job on his hair) and back-to-school shopping trips (at the thrift store, with Aunt Greta insisting he try *everything* on). He was still able to remember snippets of conversations with his sixth-grade teacher (Mrs. Thompson—*the P was silent*—who'd required them to plant time capsules under their middle school's bleachers; he buried a Hanson CD, his school photo, and a pack of sour candy in his; later, when they dug them up, Birch's capsule had been overgrown with mold and he'd cried), and recalled the exact shape formed by a cluster of zits on the forehead of his favorite fast food cashier (after school, he'd detour on his walk home from the bus stop to order a medium french fry and small lemon soda with his allowance— every day, without fail), and the way Greta's mouth sloped, brows drawn together, veins popping out of her neck (so predictably, like clockwork) whenever he came home late, grease and salt on his fingers, reeking of fast food (*you've spoiled your dinner*, she'd say). So it should have been easy for him to recall where he'd seen that nose before. Yet he couldn't.

It's not just the nose, he thought. *It's also the glasses.*

An unequivocal combination: the classic aviator shape of his shades perched against that narrow, hooked nose. It was an image that bothered him. Another growl of thunder rumbled overhead, like an old car's engine; the sound of it dislodged a hidden memory, a gem. It unlocked the memory of the man.

He knew exactly where and when he'd seen the brute before. Crossing the street, on his way home from school. Crossing the intersection of Madrid Avenue and Segovia Street. He'd seen the man there, a countless number of times, idled in his long, silver car, sitting there waiting for the light to change and wearing his aviators on the edge of his hooked nose.

After the incident, for the few years of high school Birch still had left, he'd walked home from school. Rather than take the bus and suffer the unending punishment of his peers—punching his arms and calling him names—he'd resolved to walk the full five miles between his school and Greta's house, their home, every day. Rain or shine, he walked, and though it didn't show in his slim physique, he carried on in the tradition of his fries, too.

The trip was always a quiet one, but sometimes there was a single moment of dread, at the end of that stretch of mental repose: when he reached the intersection of Madrid and Segovia, Birch had always been struck by the odd coincidence of the same ugly nose peeking out from between the same pair of aviator sunglasses. The man had a horrible face. Even though Birch had never seen it up close, he could still recall feeling that there was something mangled about it.

Back then, Birch had assumed the man was headed home from work, or that he must have lived nearby; he figured it was just a fluke.

The man stared at him. With intention, with intensity. And he hadn't been alone.

On most days, there had been someone else with him, sitting beside the giant who drove the car. The other man's nose was less pronounced but, still, his features made him equally memorable: a rather squat figure, and he wore his hair slicked back. It reminded Birch of the sort of films Aunt Greta loved so much. Gangster pics: De Niro and Pesci in *GoodFellas*, Brando and Pacino in *The Godfather*. For a woman as modest as she was, her taste in movies was strangely brutal. If *she* had seen those guys—the two men in their shining sedan, buttoned up in all-black suits—Aunt Greta would likely have told Birch to run. They looked just like the actors in all those films, full of rage and style.

Now Birch wondered if the two of them hadn't *both* been there, on that day at the beach, spying on him through the brush. Perhaps the little one had been leaning up close behind the giant, whispering to his crony (just as the dying man drew his last breath), *What's he doing now, boss?*

Fucking bastards, Birch thought. *They should have helped.*

Another crash of well-timed thunder brought him once more out of reverie. A woman passed by, pretty in a two-kids-in-two-years kind of way, lugging an armful of groceries toward her boat docked at the piers. She was decked out in red pumps and a form-fitting burgundy skirt made of tweed, pilling at the hemline. Up top was a frilly-collared white blouse that was just a bit too tight, showing off flashes of her modest paunch. It was strangely formal attire for a trip to the grocers, though this wasn't the first time Birch had seen a woman dressed to the nines for such a prosaic task.

Beloved Greta—bless her heart and rest her soul—had also treated trips to the supermarket as though they were fashion shows, except dear Auntie's sense of fashion was about as *couture* as a 60-year-old from Mayberry. She channeled Aunt Bee, down to the pearls, pillbox hats, and tops that looked like doilies. In the absence of a nice purse (she was too frugal to buy more than a simple satchel), she had always dragged Birch along as her *most* prized gem. Although they didn't have a yacht, their Cadillac Calais was about as sturdy—and about as weathered, as stalwart, as Greta was herself.

More thunder sounded overhead. It agitated Birch's fugue trance, like a thin sieve shaking the rubble apart from the diamonds of memory in his mind, and it reminded him of one such trip to the market. They'd been driving in stormy weather, and Birch had been struck by the familiarity of the lumbering argent vehicle that was trailing behind them. The roads were otherwise clear of traffic on that rainy afternoon, so it seemed odd to Birch that a driver would risk collision by tailgating in blustery weather—especially when he could glide around them easily enough. He turned to look through the car's rear window and immediately recognized the giant and his small-fry sidekick, polished as usual in their tailored suits, their slicked hair glistening, even in the overcast light. For a moment, Birch had considered telling his aunt about the men, about the intersection of Madrid and Segovia, but he quickly realized how preposterous his allegations would sound— *they're stalking me; they follow me; they're everywhere I go.*

As if they'd sensed his thoughts, the car turned down a side street and disappeared.

It now seemed obvious to Birch: they'd both been there, on the day his life had changed, and had been following him ever since. With all the clarity of the thunder crying overheard, and all the crispness of the icy rain biting his skin, Birch knew that the two men had been with him for ages, as persistent, hidden shadows in his life.

Birch snapped away from the twister of his memories, ripped from reflection by a change in his surroundings. The rain stopped abruptly, but the clouds still swirled overhead, gathering into a hefty ball, which hung low over the stadium and throbbed gently. The subtle, swirling motion hypnotized Birch, drawing him toward the arena.

The cars driving by on the Embarcadero sounded impossibly far away, the sound of their engines engulfed by a faint buzzing that screeched and slowly built up to a full-blown scream. It was like a thousand nails on a thousand chalkboards, like a train grinding along its tracks with sparks flying off the brakes. Even with his ears plugged, the painful boom of the mechanical wail bounced inside Birch's head.

From where he stood, he was at the perfect angle to see the stadium's Jumbotron. But instead of slow-mo replays, instead of sing-a-long words lighting up the lyrics to classic stadium anthems, Birch saw the horrified expressions forming on thousands of orange-and-black-clad fans, their lips rolled up to their gums, their tongues absconding for the calm black of the backs of their throats, their eyelids folded into rolls of pain as they squinted, hands raised to their ears, nails digging into their skulls, ripping their hair out in clumps. The closer he got, the louder the sound grew, and the more he could relate to the pain those people felt. The frequency of the racket had him crouching on the floor. There was little he could do to escape it. Crawling, he was drawn toward the arena—with a feeling like someone was repeatedly stabbing his inner ears with shards of glass, or scrambling his brains with a power-drill. Birch pushed his hands flat against his ears, smoothing them against the sides of his head with all the strength he could muster, quivering through to the tips of his fingers.

Overhead, the ring of lights illuminating the stands exploded in a shower of sparks and glass, raining down across the stadium and maiming its occupants. The Jumbotron, still intact, flashed a few images—of men with their eyes hanging out of their sockets, bleeding and oozing into their wives' laps, children hunched immobile in their chairs with chunks of glass lodged in their skullcaps—but then it burst, too, with streams of plastic melting into fiery tentacles, connecting the display to the grass below, lighting the field in flames. The handful of players still on the green lay prostrated, helplessly engulfed by the blaze, their bodies lighting up in pillars and then wrinkling, flesh caving in and leaving nothing behind, like scraps of paper dissolving in a wildfire.

The clouds tumbled agitatedly overhead, like a living cake batter of metallic gray, sparking occasionally, gloaming with what looked like sun sparks, little flares of immaculate light.

All at once, the buzzing subsided. Birch could hear the cars again, driving by as though nothing out of the ordinary had just occurred—*just another day of screaming rainclouds.*

Then, instead of the otherworldly, grating screech, Birch picked up another sound: the deathly moans of the masses, lifting up their pained cries from inside the stadium, enhanced by the building's shape, rising into an abominable mixture of dying screams and vicious, gut-churning roars—of thousands sobbing in unison. And another noise drew closer. It was a vibration of deep bass, like a giant subwoofer shaking the ground, loosening Birch's footing.

No, it was less of a sound and more of a feeling, a sensation of floating on choppy water. Like the few minor earthquakes Birch had endured, it created a sense of nausea, of disorientation. He fell to the grass again and placed his head between his knees, breathing purposefully and deeply, in and out, willing away the rumbling, but its intensity only grew, kicking his guts around inside of him 'til he couldn't help but puke.

The first of the survivors shoved their way through the turnstiles of the stadium exit, skipping at a modest clip, warbling on injured but able legs, darting past Birch without so much as a passing glance. A few of them carried children, either in their blood-soaked arms or heaved across their backs. One couple had almost passed him by, almost freed themselves from the growing throng, but the young woman—who was late in pregnancy—fell to the ground. Lifting herself up on one elbow, she vomited neon strings of bile. Her partner tried to lift her up, but she only pushed him away, swatting at his ankles with one hand, dragging her nails into her own cheeks to help her endure the pain. All the while, she continued to spout a fountain of stinking fluid.

The trickle of people turned to a stream, and then to a rushing flood as the intensity of the crowd swelled. All around Birch, they surged, swarming the promenade and rushing the streets. A group of teenagers—uninjured, though deeply affected, screaming and crying—bolted up Second Street, with the clear goal of getting away, as fast as possible. They were hit by a light rail, the train screeching to a halt and spraying their limbs across the intersection.

More and more people rushed by—a flood of bleeding men, women, and children, a mob of vomiting, sweating, crying, stampeding victims seeking the cool solace of the outer world, away from the hell they'd just endured.

Birch realized he'd soon be trampled, yet he couldn't move to avoid it. For the first time in his life, he experienced the true meaning of a "deer in headlights," and in the time it took him to fully process the impending crisis of the addled, injured, and dying crowd that was fast-approaching his spot (overwhelming his options for escape), he'd managed little to prepare for the inevitable injury they'd inflict.

When they fully engulfed him in the swarm, it felt like the air was being sucked from the Earth, that the temperature was rising by a degree per passing second, and that the atmosphere was growing dense, balmy, wet, and salty. Their bodies were drowning him, suffocating him, pinning him claustrophobically to the spot. No matter how he nudged, elbowed, or bumped, Birch was stuck at the center of their growing mob. It was a slow death by drowning, without water. His muscles ached under the pressure they were dealt, to resist being caught up in and pulled away by the current of the crowd. He stretched for escape. His hair was ripped out in handfuls; his sweatpants and shirt hung in tatters from his body.

Just when Birch lost all hope (when he'd felt enough closed fists and elbows bruising his ribs, bashing his jaw)—just when he knew it was the end, and that he'd soon die under the blow of a thousand dirty sneakers, stamping out his life, fracturing his skull, with the smell of human stink and fear rising in his nose—the horde waned, thinning out to small clusters of limping civilians. Twenty or thirty, scattered here and there; a circle of five, a line holding hands. In small numbers, they were more able (and generous enough) to avoid a path straight for Birch, though still none of them offered to help.

Surveying the aftermath of the evacuation, Birch saw how many lay dead alongside him, or dying. They were a pathetic array of moribund sufferers, the left behind. A young man beside him wailed inarticulately, his right leg flattened below the knee into a mass of white and cruddy flesh where there had once been a lithe, responsive limb. Farther away, a little girl with pigtails, wearing a blue-and-white gingham dress drenched in her own red, screamed for her mother—each syllable punctuated with a hiccup, "Mom-ma! Mom-ma!"

Cops and firemen finally arrived, more than a little late, and lifted the injured onto gurneys, doing their best to calm those who were still on the edge of shock.

Birch lurched toward the little girl, scooping her up in his arms, and quickly weighed his options. He knew from his experience at the beach—sixteen years ago—that cops didn't do well with things of this nature: things that fell outside the bounds of everyday disaster.

He made it to the girl and blanketed her with his arms.

"We'll find your mom," he whispered. "Don't worry, we'll find her, I promise."

"Mom-ma!" she cried again, ignoring Birch, swatting away his conciliatory grip, wriggling to break free.

"Calm down," he assured her, patting her on the back. "It's going to be okay."

She melted in his arms a little, calming when she heard his honest tone. She assessed his bony shoulders, running her hands over them as the left corner of her mouth lifted up into a curve which said, *He's okay. Couldn't hurt a fly.*

The girl had scraped her knees pretty badly—and worse, when he set her down, she fell flat on her palms, wailing in agony as she abraded her hands.

He picked her back up and patted her uncertainly on the top of her head.

"Where does it hurt?" he asked.

"Ankle," she said, calling it *anne-cuh* and pointing down to her feet, snot dripping over her mouth.

"I can carry you, 'til we find her." *If we find her,* he thought.

He lifted her up, holding her as best as he could—more like a newborn than a toddler, though she didn't seem to mind any form of support.

"Where do you live?" he asked.

She gave no indication that she heard Birch, and only carried on sucking up snot at the back of her throat.

His apartment wasn't far; they could go there. It was doable, although the mass of the crowd had also seemed to move in that direction. They'd just have to hope most of the pandemonium had already slipped away.

A hand settled on Birch's shoulder, with nails that felt like pointed talons. He turned around, thinking it would be a cop or—even better—the little girl's mom, come to take her away. Instead, an old woman stared at him with her mouth opened, and her eyes full of tears. Her shirt had been ripped open to expose her bare and flaccid breasts. The left one was hanging by a thread, just a flap of loose skin dangling from her torso. A mass of spongy, moving grub worked their way through the flesh there, tightening around the fatty tissue of her loosened bust and squeezing it into a tight, purple ball. A few of the creatures abandoned the cradle of her bosom and slithered their way up toward her neck, the flesh along their trail bubbling up into red tunnels of distended skin. She managed to get out the word *Help* before the things had cinched themselves around her throat, but the word *me* was crushed before she could say it, by their hold across her trachea.

Birch swatted her hand off his shoulder, tightening his grip on the little girl, and watched in horror—covering the child's eyes—as the woman fell to her knees, gripping her throat with both hands and, with such strength as to rip herself open, exposed the delicate web of muscle and tendon in her neck. Her eyes rolled into the back of her head as, with all too much familiarity, the *things* took full hold of her.

Birch backed away, a stab of dread tightening in his chest, staggering his breath.

Before he had a chance to connect the dots, to wonder how the things had invaded his life yet again—had killed another stranger right before his eyes—some of the injured, who'd regained enough of their composure to make a break for it, sprinted by him and knocked him onto his back.

Everywhere, the guttural croaks of others choking filled the air; they clicked with their chins upraised, batting at passersby and loved ones alike, ripping each other apart in the midst of their death throes. At least thirty were so afflicted, fading around him. Some even lunged at the cops, at the paramedics, not as much with malice as with unsullied impulse, reaching for any hope of survival.

Birch didn't wait to see what would happen next. He scooped the girl up (she tucked her face against his chest, her plump little arms wrapped around his neck) and bolted north toward his apartment, following the crowd. He was glad for the feel of the wind again, for the return of the trickling droplets of rain splashing against his face. He was glad to be running with his eyes closed and leading with his breath.

An explosion erupted, back where they'd come from, somewhere near the wharfs. The cops had drawn their guns. Another boom. One of the civilians flew back against a tree, painting its trunk red as he slid lifelessly toward the ground.

As they approached the Ferry Building, their progress slowed and then halted altogether. Ahead of them, the mass of people were looking for shelter. They'd stopped directly beneath the Bay Bridge, its shade barring the dribble of the clouds overhead. Everywhere, people were bleeding, cupping their limbs with their shirts to stanch the blood flow; they were crying, rubbing each other's backs in filial support; they were coughing, hacking up chunks of lung and throat.

Another rumble lifted up—this one more tenebrous than the two before it. It was unlike anything Birch had heard before, a mixture between the sound of an imploding skyscraper and a crackling, dial-up modem, full of static. It came from the stadium, where the mass of gloom suspended in the sky had melted into the shape of a perfect circle, with a hole cut from its center like the eye of a hurricane.

But the clouds weren't moving: they just sat there, perfectly still, awaiting some command.

The sound, though; it hadn't come from the clouds. It had come from the screen, the Jumbotron. A fissure split down the middle of the screen, sparking, shooting out fireworks. Gouts and gobs of the worm-things slithered all around it, crawling and dragging their way across the structure, covering it with their wriggling, spongiform masses. Somehow, amazingly, the screen still managed to display some images—flashes of horror showing momentarily through the shapes of the creatures covering them up. It showed the people left behind, who were retching, their eyes rolled back, convulsing; they were attacking one another, ripping out clumps of one another's hair. And, occasionally, it showed images of nothing: vacant seats where the crowd had already fled.

Birch gripped the little girl closer, pushing her face against his chest.

He thought back to that morning, when he'd told himself that something big was coming.

Someday soon, he had thought.

Overhead, the outdoor warning system crackled on.

It screamed, "THIS IS NOT A TEST!"

Yeah, Birch thought, *no shit*.

CHAPTER XX

Desert. Endless desert.

Jezebel had read about them in her studies, about how spending too much time in any of them (Arizona's included) could make you feel like you'd gone crazy—or worse, could kill you. She'd heard of mirages, of seeing things and hearing things once the heat finally started to get to you, but she thought herself immune to those effects. The great, powerful, (pre)destined savior of the world, of mankind: Jezebel. Surely *she* couldn't fall victim to the slow pain of dehydration, nor succumb to the deep anguish of sunburn so severe it melted skin off of flesh.

She thought wrong. Her fair skin had already turned pink—within the first half hour—and now she was doing all she could to keep cool—spitting on her palms, rubbing them across her face. A part of her said that was dumb, that she should save all her spit.

Since she didn't need a heat stroke to see and hear things (that pretty well came with the territory of growing up at the compound, under the guidance of people who could make it rain, or make it storm, or any number of other unholy things), she'd always felt pretty certain that she could handle any challenge. If Jezebel could take on a tornado and swim through lava (even if in her dreams), she could take on a plain old desert. But now that she was out there, with sweat covering every square inch of her being—dripping down her butt cheeks, sliding off her neck, pooling in the cavity of her milky-white collar bones—she found it more difficult than she'd expected. And she found a new appreciation for a term she'd never understood: "hotter than hell."

She'd learned her fair share of idioms, of little catechisms; pop-culture references, acronyms, emoticons, memes. Her knowledge of the world outside extended beyond what she garnered from the Overseer's academia, beyond the esoterica her mentors shoved down her throat. More than book smart, Jezebel also liked to think of herself as *street smart*, learned of the world's trends, of its fads—at least, as much as someone in her situation could be. She did her best to get her hands on magazines, popular novels, and compact discs. They were her *bad* education, so to speak, and the schooling that gave her the most pleasure, that made her feel just a bit normal, that let her escape from the path she was so "destined" for—a path she hadn't chosen, that she'd been forced, begrudgingly, toward. Her trinkets were treasures: jelly bracelets crammed under her pillow case, pop songs and chewing gum. They let her see the world with different eyes, or at least let her pretend to do so, if only for a while. She could imagine she was someone else, a different Jezebel, one that went to the mall and kissed boys and loved to eat out at Italian restaurants with her best girlfriends.

So he had been right; that *was* what she wanted.

Freedom. A family. Friends. A boyfriend.

Although her protectors did their best to guard her from gaining access to the little leaks she sneaked, the vestiges of the outer world, they came—like water slipping invisibly through cracks in the compound's brick facade. She had her ways.

The Overseer wouldn't have liked it, not one bit. He'd have bashed the jewel case of her favorite Alanis Morissette CD. He'd have set her magazines on fire with a single snap of his bony fingers. Yet somehow she got away with it. She knew he had to know, that he must object to her spending so much time with such useless artifacts—*wasting time*, he'd have called it. Yet he never addressed it with her directly.

Jezebel gushed at the possibility of the world that existed outside the compound's walls, where women wore makeup and their primary concerns were which new cell phone to buy and finding a new hairdresser. She knew those girls' concerns were trivial, especially compared to her own, and that they'd do better occupying their time with some more meaningful cause, but it gave her comfort to know that somehow—some way, some day—she might enjoy those freedoms, too.

Now was her chance. Thanks to the nameless hero who'd set her free, she could take on an alias, explore the world, and find a *new* calling. She could paint her nails, talk on the phone, swim in a pool.

Except she was lost, with dreadful heat and endless stretches of sand standing in her way. She was adrift in a new kind of sea, a real desert, and she struggled to understand how Jules Verne could call the ocean *loving*. There was nothing in the desert—no shade, no comfort, just endless slopes of yellow, and the occasional dried-up husk of what had once been a living plant. Not even a snake came to greet her. She'd take a serpent for a friend over this new solitude—or, better yet, her crab.

At least the isolation of her quarters held some hidden treasures—her little bounty of knickknacks—and the assurance of water, a meal, a bed. In the desert, there was nothing and no one to occupy her time.

Earlier, when Jezebel had first stepped outside the gates and felt the real, prolonged contact of sun on her skin, she'd run as fast as her legs could carry her—in a random southeasterly direction, past the copse of rattled, dead trees surrounding the compound. She just wanted to get away—as far from the Overseer, and as far from the compound as she could get before anyone noticed she was gone. Now that she was a safe distance away, she was beginning to regret the impulsiveness of her actions.

Badlands rose and fell in the distance, casting their crescendo of bright clay and dark coal, striating the hills around her. The bit of color they lent to the landscape was welcome. No trace of wind, dead still and silent. But far off in the distance, a sign of hope: the appearance of branches rising over a dune.

She ran toward them, making out the appearance of some sparse-leaved torchwoods. As she grew closer, she realized there was only one, a solitary tree. It wasn't much. Still, perhaps it could lend her a scrap of shade, to keep her milky skin from burning any worse. Breathlessly, she closed the distance, limping slowly toward it.

Under its sparse shadows, Jezebel realized she was alone. For the first time in her life, she was completely free, without the charge of another. Even when she'd been in isolation, on those long stretches of introspection they so often prescribed to her, there had always been an occasional sound outside her door, a blip of conversation, or some other distant signal of human life—the far-off laughter of a group of guards on break; the sound of her meal being shoved through the grates, plastic clanging against metal; an indrawn breath and a raspy yelp as some new trainee took their first fist to the gut.

Jezebel did her best to venture inward, to search through the endless channels of knowledge she'd drawn in her mind, tripping down her invisible halls of information for some bit that would help her survive this.

A compass, she thought.

She knew that she was, roughly, in the northwestern part of Arizona. And she knew that word, the word which had been burnt behind her eyes, dripping wet like its image carved into the carpet of that strange, dark room—Room 210. The word *Tucson*, a city somewhere south and east. She needed to get there, to head for Tucson. A compass would help.

She pictured a page from her encyclopedia, from the volume marked *C*.

Compass:

A navigational instrument displaying directions relative to the surface of Earth. A stationary frame of reference helps its user determine the four cardinal directions in relation to his or her place on the Earth, and relative to the direction he or she is facing. Some compasses utilize angle markings—

The rest was superfluous. She skipped ahead, to the bit she really needed.

There are two kinds of easy-to-make magnetic compasses: dry and liquid. Both require a needle—

She closed the book in her mind, gazing around for something to use as her needle. A dried-up cactus protruded from the sand, standing off in the distance by itself, leaning over slightly like a lone ranger with a backache. She walked toward it and pricked off one of its spines, spinning it between her fingers.

Rub the point of your needle along the south pole of your magnet and the eye of the needle along the north pole of your magnet. If you don't happen to have a magnet on hand, you can also use a bit of silk or wool from your clothing to magnetize the needle. Massage the full length of your needle about one hundred times to fully magnetize the needle.

Things just weren't working out for her. Not only was her needle *not* made of metal, but she was also pretty sure that her attendant's robe was made of cotton.

Still, the inward voice of her memory drifted on:

Pierce the needle through a cork or a leaf—anything that floats in water will do. Lastly, float your compass in a still body of water. The tip of your needle will spin to face north—

"Shut up!" she shouted. The voice subsided. She let out a sigh and rolled out from under the torchwood, ready to wander again. The sun had begun a sharp descent toward sunset, which meant it was heading westward, which meant she was walking east. She adjusted her position to ensure that she was walking equal parts south and east, and carried on.

A few minutes later, a pair of half-baked desert hackberry trees appeared in the distance. It was odd for them to grow so far out, and in the open, barren drylands. She approached them cautiously and checked their lowest hanging branches for bright orange fruit, but found none. A handful of immature green berries fell to the sand, tempting Jezebel with their plumpness—*That'll do just fine*, she thought.

She battened down under the stretching shade of sunset, waiting for the temperature to drop. When it did, she wiped the sweat off her brow and struggled to build her first fire with the skinny twigs of the adolescent hackberries, blowing on and spinning the wood, but it didn't want to catch. Remembering she was Touched—and knowing that brought certain gifts—she abandoned her struggle and stared at the pile of wood, with intensity, until it lit up with a spark.

Overhead, a lone bird squawked. She shot it down with a thought, and skinned it with a rock.

She stared down at her bloodied hands, imagining what it would feel like to receive a manicure, chewing on cotton candy gum. But the word burnt its way back up behind her eyelids, and the voice was back to whisper:

GO TO TUCSON. GO.

CHAPTER XXI

Orson awoke upon a wafer-thin cot, set atop a flat stretch of wooden pylons, with a blanket wrapped tightly around him and a bucket at his feet. He sat up and rubbed his temples to clear away the haze, clenching his eyes to bring them back to life, gripping his knotted stomach too, to keep down a churning vitriol, resisting the temptation to reach for the container and loose the contents of his gurgling guts.

His head was full of the tight, throbbing pain of a balls-shattering hangover—as Askuwheteau had promised, the worst of his life. But his mind was also tinged with something else, something new, something Orson had never felt before. It was a sensation like floating, an out-of-body feeling similar to what he'd experienced at the ceremony, though not as pronounced as before. Just a hint of that preternatural buzz remained, not the overwhelming flood of omniscient awareness he'd felt when they all drank from the gourd. When they—

When they fucking killed him.

That feeling of awakening burned, but burned faintly, like pins and needles trickling through his limbs—little ricochets of energy bounding along his nerves with minute electric shocks. It felt as though the connections between his mind and body had been tweaked, renewed, adjusted and made adroit—the kind of change he imagined people returning from New Age retreats must sometimes experience: a heightened awareness, an elevated conduit between all the senses. He flexed his arms, examining them for change, half-expecting to see a brand-new pair of bulging biceps. Sadly disappointed, Orson saw that he was just as scraggly as before.

The tips of his fingers tickled, like someone was tugging against the end of each digit, as though they were bound by strings, like a marionette's wood-carved hands. Forming a fist, then releasing it, shaking them on their wrists and tickling a piano through the air, Orson fought to rid his body of the nauseating feeling of lightness permeating through it.

The fluttery feeling was most pronounced in the ends of his thumbs and index fingers. He touched them together, forming a pair of A-OK signs with his hands, and lifted them up to his eyes, peering through them. He surveyed the room.

Back at the lodge. It looked like someone had ransacked the place, and gotten into a bloody scuffle. The ornate desk in the corner of the room was smashed to bits and the glass lamp was crushed, too. Green glass was scattered across the floor. The warden was nowhere to be seen.

Orson gathered his balled up shirt and pants from where they lay underneath the cot. He was naked—or mostly so, save for his worn-out, sweat-stained underpants. The mystery of why and how he'd been stripped bare, exposed without his knowledge of the act, seemed less important than getting out of there—and fast.

Lifting his jeans up over his thighs, Orson noticed that his legs were bruised all over, and lacerated; his knees, too, looked as though they'd been dragged over jagged rocks. He followed the perpendicular scabs, running in lines across his hips, up to his torso where someone had really gone to town on him:

Smack dab in the middle of his chest was a giant symbol, carved right into his flesh—probably using the same blade with which they'd sliced open their palms, and the stranger's head. Orson had been mutilated into a living canvas, branded with the strange shapes of their ritual.

A narrow, scabby rhombus—its acute angles pointing up toward his sternal notch and down to his naval, respectively—was set above a bloody isosceles triangle. The former shape, almost a diamond, was bisected by a straight, horizontal line running through its center and piercing through both of its obtuse angles, reaching outward for his nipples on either side. The rhombus was connected by its bottommost point to the vertex angle of the triangle below it. Both ends of the simple line had little embellishments: dashes adorned both ends, hanging like tails from it. The same was true of the triangle's base—the long end of the isosceles, running perpendicular to his happy trail, had the same tattooed tails hanging from it.

It wasn't until he found the door to the bathroom and looked into the medicine cabinet mirror (daubed with an ominous, chestnut-colored film) that he could stand back and, regarding his own reflection ruefully, see what the pictogram meant to convey: it was a crude drawing of a bird, its body formed by the rhombus, its tail formed by the triangle, its plumage fashioned by those little hanging lines.

So they'd carved him up like a holiday ham—bedazzled him with a scar that was sure to draw attention at the beach—and then dragged him back there, to where it all began. At some point, he must have fought back, thrashed about, wreaked some due havoc. At least they hadn't defiled him without a fight.

He touched his face in the mirror. Something about his physiognomy was different; his long neck looked longer, his bird chest wider, and his head of light hair overgrown. That tingle rose up again, starting under his nails—it felt like digging the tip of a pen into the soft pink tissue hiding under there—and flailed through his every vein, climbing up to his brain. The room spun.

He settled against the turquoise-tiled ground, leaning with his back against the toilet, seated in what children sometimes called—bunglingly enough, given the circumstances—"Indian style." Orson gripped both of his knees and waited for the flood of nausea to pass. He forced himself to stand back up, pulled his plain white t-shirt over his head and across his chest, dragging chunks of scab off the hardened wounds there. Minute droplets of blood crept through the shirt in slow motion, staining it from within.

In the dim light of the bathroom, he looked like an offbeat superhero—the hum of the long fluorescent bulbs over the mirror crackling, morphing his narrow face into a surreal parody of himself, distorted with vengefulness (*eyelids twitching, hands shaking*), yet awash with all the burning strength of a champion.

A creaking sound came from somewhere outside, someone parting the batwing doors, shuffling as quietly as they could. Orson listened for the sound of the doors swinging back into place, grazing against one another and tugging against their hinges with each recurrent arc. He peeked out from his hiding spot.

The unmistakable form of the giant warden, Askuwheteau, was there and fast-approaching him. The titanic man's face fluttered with annoyance as his eyes locked with Orson's.

"I see you're awake," Askuwheteau said, noncommittally. He made no move to pry open the bathroom door.

"Yeah, I am…" Orson's eyes flicked over the warden's protuberant shoulders, scanning for an escape route. There were two windows in the lodge, but they were far away, in the kitchen of the studio-style living space, on the opposite side of the property. Both were drawn open, sputtering with tufts of sandy breeze, and they were blocked off from the outside by thick metal bars.

"Good," Askuwheteau said. "We weren't sure you'd make it. Now, why don't you come out here so we can talk about all of this." It wasn't a question; it was a demand. Still, his tone wasn't quite threatening—but neither was it soothing. He sounded like a cop talking a jumper down from his suicidal ledge.

Orson had to obey. He was fatigued and confused, lost in the cage of his slowly metamorphosing mind. Besides which, even if he tried to run, the man could easily squash him.

"Okay, I'm coming out," Orson said. He emerged, head hanging low against the tip of his dripping shirt.

"Sit down." A huge finger pointed across the packed room, back toward the cot.

Orson moved silently toward the bed—which was still damp with his sweat and stinking to high hell—but he didn't sit down. He hovered by it expectantly, his head exploding with questions. "Tell me why—"

"Why what?" the warden interrupted.

"Why'd you kill that man? And why the hell did you shank me?" He pointed down to his weeping upper chest.

"*I* didn't slaughter that imp. You saw it for yourself: I was only there as a protector of the rite, to prevent any accidents. With my shotgun." Askuwheteau winked. "Besides, he was already dead. A husk of a person, a man trapped in the prison of his soulless body, locked there by the evil forces you saw at work. They were tearing him apart."

Orson recalled the way the man had thrashed about, like a feral animal, and the guttural, croaking click he'd released before his death—almost the same sound the creature had produced once they pulled it from his skull.

The warden approached the bedside, taking his time, unnerving Orson more with each of his pronouncements—so perfectly, cooly, and unemotionally articulated. He rested a coarse, opened palm against the surface of Orson's bleeding chest and said, "We did him a favor, really."

Askuwheteau's hand might as well have been a barrelful of salt, thrown upon Orson's freshly bloodied wound. He slapped away the warden and screamed: "Don't touch me! You're fucking crazy—all of you!"

"It wasn't a choice we made alone. He came to us for help. We offered a solution, which you saw. We freed him of his burden. It was unavoidable. Together, and according to the agreement he made with the shaman, we freed him. It's what he wanted. Such are the ways of our people." Askuwheteau's tone lifted up to something just below a shout when he said, "And you've played your part, too."

"What'll you do with me?" Orson asked. *Murder me. Torture me and eat me.* "Did you put one of those things in my head?"

Askuwheteau's stolid expression snapped—his brown gums and tiny teeth revealed in a minatory scream as he reached out to pacify Orson with a punch. But he missed.

Orson spun away with a store of energy he didn't know he had; he backed himself against the far wall of the lodge, by the fireplace. His hand settled against the grip of a rusted steel poker lying by the hearth. He picked it up and lifted it high, with all the wild frenzy of Perseus fighting the Kraken. Swinging the metal rod like a baseball bat, he shouted, "Don't you fucking touch me!"

"Calm down, Orson." Askuwheteau was treading carefully, tiptoeing closer. "You're lucky, really. Few are allowed to see as much as you saw that night, much less participate as you have. We don't want to hurt you. You're one of us now. You've been forever changed."

Forever changed. That tingle in his palm, and the feeling of knowing he'd experienced.

"I'll never be like you!" Orson shouted, but his imprecation slouched with uncertainty at its end. There had been a glimmer of something askew, buried in the warden's statement. He replayed it through his still-leering brain, fast as a bullet train busting through the end of a mountain tunnel, careening toward the daylight.

Few are allowed to see as much as you saw that night—

as much as you saw that night—

you saw that night—

that night—

"That night?" Orson asked. "You mean *last* night?"

"No. The ceremony was more than a week ago. You've been sleeping here ever since. Well, mostly sleeping—there were a few times you woke up and stirred quite a—"

"Wait," Orson interrupted. "A week? You've gotta be shitting me."

"No, I'm not *shitting you*." The warden sighed. He was only a few feet away now, with his giant's hands lifted up into a *We Come In Peace* gesture that didn't convince Orson.

"That's impossible!"

"Is it? Truth is verily unknowable, and logic here with it."

"I don't know what you're talking about." For a moment, Orson tried to dismiss the warden's claim—surely he couldn't have lain on that cot, unconscious for a week—but the little details he'd forced himself to overlook, which he'd uncaringly brushed aside in the immediacy of danger, now began to stack up in his mind like so many incriminating clues.

His face was coated with a generous swathe of hair—longer than a single night's growth of stubble. It felt dirty, coated in sweat and grime. Then there were the scabs. Even though he'd only barely managed to drag them open while putting on his clothes, they were further along than they should have been, too close to healed. Though they were still tender and bruised, those cuts had already puffed up around the edges, a surefire sign of the presence of his white blood cells, gathered there to clean and heal the injury. The edges of the scabs were lifted up and flaking off in places, having largely completed their function at the spots where the blade hadn't sunk too deep.

"Why did you do this to me? And I don't understand what you mean—he was *already dead?*"

"The mark on your body—" the warden paused, struggling for words. "You might call it a rite of passage. A symbol, linked to your re-birth. You've been given a very precious gift, Orson, and the image on your chest is evidence of the pathways you'll carve as you work to reach your full potential. It will always be a reminder of what you've endured, that you might cherish the experience. I was wrong about you before; the shaman saw that right away. I apologize for having doubted you."

"So let me get this straight—" Orson's grip on the poker tightened, the odd tingle returning to his fingertips and surging through his bunched-up fists. "You cut me open because I'm the lucky recipient of some gift. This precious present of yours—does it come with a contract? 'Cause I'm not so sure I want anything to do with you people anymore—"

"You don't have a choice!" The warden lifted up his fists, squinting shut his eyes.

For a moment, the poker shifted in Orson's grip, wiggling only slightly.

Askuwheteau reopened his eyes and said, "You're already very strong. Even in your senseless state, you were resistant to our ways. Near comatose, yet still you fought against us. In time, I hope you'll come to understand—perhaps even cherish—the hardships you've faced, the necessity of our ways. We need someone like you." The warden's eyes floated between Orson's face and hands, watching to see if he really had the gall to strike out with the poker. "I see not much has changed. Not yet. Only give us some time and I promise, you'll come to appreciate what we do. No further harm will come to you. The rest will only be good."

"The rest? What, I make some verbal agreement with you—just like the last guy? So I can become your next victim? What are you thinking, man? You're going down for this. You're going to die slowly in a prison somewhere, and then you'll burn in hell."

Just as he cursed them, Orson realized the futility of what he said. He could claim retribution with all his might, screaming their travesties from a mountaintop, but he knew it would never happen. Who would believe a washed-up ex-junkie whose circuitous tale included a trippy ritualistic murder? And at the hands of these private, peaceable people? They were locked away from the vulgarities and violence of modern man, and by choice; they were supposed to be connected to nature, suffused with love. No one would believe him. No one would believe that, instead of a dovish clan, he'd found a dark coven of murderers buried between the dunes.

Anger welled up through Orson's throat, choking his breath, tinting the room a blooming shade of pink. The warden backed away, both hands raised in entreaty, with his gummy, small-toothed mouth open in an expression of ill-fated shock.

The blunt end of the poker flew high above Orson's head, its pointed end directed straight down at Askuwheteau.

"Wait—" the warden said, covering up his face, knowing full what might come next. "You can't control it. You'll hurt yourself and me, unduly."

control it.

can't control it.

The warden was right: Orson couldn't. His rage grew into a buzzing bulls-eye, like the perfectly aimed scope of a sniper's rifle, with his redress directed straight at Askuwheteau. A smell of burning filled the room. Orson's hands charred, alight with the sweltering heat of the poker melding to his skin—melted alloy, cauterized flesh. The choleric force burgeoning its way through his body carried the same blistery heat as the rod, now gleaming an impossibly bright, solar flare orange, dripping its liquified substance onto the floor and tearing craters through the floor boards.

Askuwheteau shifted from the mollifying tone he'd feigned to one of a fire fighter dashing with exigency—stamping shut his mouth, grinding his knuckles together as he cried, *"STOP NOW, OR I'LL STOP YOU MYSELF!"* He dug his heels into the floor, pawing like a bull prepping to strike.

Orson's will to destroy the warden—to protect himself, to forestall his own death, to escape—drew together, into a picture of the giant man's agonized death. Nerves sparked, electrons firing, jolting down his spine, brooding at the pits of his shoulders, bubbling across his scapulae, and launching down the length of his outstretched arms. Sizzling spider legs of blinding light flew through his fingertips, shooting through the poker and balling together at its tip, forming a florid, energetic orb. The pale-burning fireball flew across the room, ripping straight through the pit of the warden's chest and shooting out the other side with a spray of gore.

Faster than a blink, Askuwheteau fell against the bed. The sheets smoked beneath him, charred by the blast and the warden's flaming chest. He was ripped clean through from sternum to spine, chest to back; he was cleaved open to show the bubbling, dripping tips of each of his dissevered ribs.

Orson dropped the rod—now a twisted, bending mess. As the violent energy within him abated, he approached the bedside and knelt down, watching the warden's breath expire, his thin dark lips locked forever in an ugly gesture of pain. Orson gazed into Askuwheteau's cracked-open, dripping torso; it gaped back like the jaws of a hungry dragon.

If you stare into the abyss, Orson remembered, but left the rest out.

Impulse and reflex kicked into gear. He grabbed his rucksack from where it hung on the coatrack by the door. The camera had been found, plucked from the subtle grommet he'd punched into the flap of the bag—

Fuck it, he thought. He held the proof. He was the proof.

But maybe he had it all wrong. The warden had tried to assure him that the man they cut open was *already dead*, implying that he'd been taken over in some way. Askuwheteau also suggested that an evil spirit had invaded the man's flesh and locked the helpless fellow in a prison of insentience, like the old wives' tales of men buried alive—their breath and heart rate slowed to measures unrecognizable by science—and later dug up, made to do the biddings of some evil magician. But this was no myth; this was reality, and he'd seen the way the stranger behaved, kicking all about, screaming like a rabid dog threatening to break free from his leash.

There would be naysayers. The world wasn't ready for the otherworldly truth of what he'd found, out there in the desert. Even if he did complete his thesis, he'd be treading on dangerous waters if he published. All he had to rely on as his evidence was his (drug-addled) memory of the scene.

Perhaps a new focus *was* in order. Perhaps he was ready to move on from the part of his life that was so accustomed to darkness, madness, folklore, and magic. Now that he'd seen it, and been changed by it, he wasn't sure it had been worth the enterprise.

Orson took in his surroundings once more—a giant dead man, and a bed burnt to crisps—and tapped himself down to check for injury. The carving on his chest still tingled with inflammation. His eyes were puffy, like they were pumped full of air, about to burst. The lightness in his head had transformed to a more complex sensation, of simultaneous pleasure and pain, as though he'd at once been gratified and harmed by the surge of energy that had rushed through his body. His hands were badly burnt—the skin peeling back to reveal the raw pink flesh underneath—and the meat around his nails was melted away. Some of his fingernails had fallen off or were sticking out at jagged angles, in places they weren't supposed to be.

He moved to the window and saw—to his surprise and delight—the beat-up rental, a sand-crusted blue Pinto. Its tires were half-buried in the sand and there were piles of desert burying the windshield wipers, but its presence was an unexpected blessing, and his only chance of escape. The driver side door opened easily enough, save for the grit of sand loosened by its being freed after such a long stretch of quiet. Orson settled into the chair, admiring the peace and quiet of the car's interior, sitting silently, gripping the armrest with his eyes closed, picturing what his life might be like now that he'd been changed.

Sighing, he dug into the bottom of his pack for the keys, but they were nowhere to be found. They were probably at the bottom of some pit now, resting alongside his camera and a pile of corpses, the victims of their rite.

He was no better off than when he lay helplessly back in the lodge, whimpering and wondering alongside the stiffening corpse of the warden. He might as well wait for them to come for him. He envisioned it—the shaman skipping around the room as though floating on air, whispering arcane words before she cracked open Orson's skull, digging around to find it—

The worm.

Orson wondered again if there wasn't some slithery creature pitted at the center of his skull, its toothed mouths interlocked, its body looped around his temporal lobe, or perhaps glutting on his pineal gland, feeding off the invisible energy it was supposed to produce. He wondered if he would succumb slowly to its will, or if it would be quick.

But no, that didn't feel right.

He was very much—despite the multiple injuries—attuned, aware, and connected. He felt turned on, lit up; he was more Orson than he'd ever been, and it felt good—as good as was possible, given the circumstances. Massaging the center of his forehead, as if feeling there for foreign inhabitants, Orson focused on how the hell he'd get out of his mess, stickier and trickier than anything he'd ever been mixed up with. Worse than the illness he'd faced, worse than the drugs he'd taken, worse than the debt he'd accrued—worse than any of it.

I'm fucked, he thought. *Unless...*

He rubbed his fingers together again, letting the light fill him—the essence of the world distilled into his senses. Like with the first sip of the drug they had drafted, he could instantly count every grain of sand gathered across the dash. Every inflection of shadow was suddenly consequential. Every skittering lizard's path was purposeful.

Then, a flicker of blue-white light. Orson opened his eyes and raised his quopping fingers. Slowly, each digit began to glow as if lit from within. He could almost see through the flesh, to the bone, as each finger was transformed into a roiling electric stick. He tossed the sputtering embers of light back and forth, between each palm, like Thor's own voltaic yo-yo.

This'll do, he thought. *This'll do just fine.*

He folded all but one of his beaming fingers away, into the safety of his palms, and shoved the remaining one straight in the ignition. It molded to the form of the metal inlet, flesh bending as malleably as clay, as though the bones and meat of his finger had flown away, swapped for this celestial juice. A grinding sound filled the air, and the car lurched against the sparks surging through it. Rotating his hand clockwise against the ignition, he brought the engine to life. The car grumbled as it awakened, yawning against the great nap it had endured and scattering sand off its hood.

Orson extracted his finger and slowed his breathing, watching as the soft bits came back in a wash, a slow gradient of flesh rising outward from palm to fingertips. The buzzing white light succumbed to the normalcy of his own human hand, creeping out of his body as quickly as it had come. Finally, the energy fizzled out in wisps of smoke which scattered through the air.

He remembered Nietzsche again, for the fourth time since arriving in that arenaceous hell.

Overman, he thought, and almost felt guilty for his gift, and for not letting the warden explain himself. Perhaps Askuwheteau had meant what he said, that no harm would come to him. Still, he wanted nothing to do with these people. And no, he decided it *wasn't* guilt that had emerged. It was something else altogether: it was deepest shame, the kind of humiliation that keeps a man up at night.

As he shifted into drive and pulled away—shoulders hunched, eyes flicking left-to-right-to-left, searching for any of them who might jump out toward him from behind the cover of a sand dune, bashing his windshield, smashing in his skull—he wondered how long it would be before they came for him. The shaman, the Snake, the Otter, the Deer, the Bear, the Raven, the Owl, the Goose, the Crocodile, the Turtle, the Dolphin, the Frog, the Shark, the Scorpion, the Falcon, the Wolf—and whoever else among them he hadn't been privileged enough to meet. He wondered how long it would be before they, or the police, came around asking questions, beating down his door.

But no one barred his escape. He pulled casually, if not a bit cautiously, out from the parking lot and drove onto the freeway.

"Time to get the hell outta Dodge," he told himself, chuckling but eyeing the rearview mirror skeptically, still half expecting the shaman to leap into view, flying on the back of a magic carpet.

Where the hell are you crazies hiding? he wondered.

Perhaps they were all hibernating, suffused as they likely were with one another's blood, full and flush with the fresh sustenance of their kill. Orson pushed concern for the future momentarily aside—buried back with the shaman and her abettors, covered in the sand—and he drove, switching the radio on to a classics station which played his favorite song (*Ch-ch-changes*).

He used to really zone to that one, blunt in one hand, beer in the other.

Changes were right. Those days had come abruptly to a close when, after a trip to the doctor for a routine physical, his life had been altered.

Cancer, they told him. Esophageal. A tumor had metastasized its way across his entire throat, lymph nodes, and sinuses. It was a hulking chunk of a thing and was—as a result of its immensity—largely inoperable. After more than two years of radio- and chemotherapy, of going it alone (none of the "friends" he'd made in his wayward days seemed to care much for the sober, sicker version of Orson, and he hadn't talked to his family in years), the growth had abated. They treated him with surgery, and another slew of palliative and preventative treatments. He stuck it out, stayed strong, got clean. It was a long and hard struggle, and it toughened him against the dependence he'd developed to the skag.

Skirting with death had helped him change his ways for the better. But even as he closed out a less-than-joyful chapter of his life, optimistically, he still felt lonely;

he was more alone than ever before.

So Orson drowned himself in study, gaining fulfillment through the rigors of a rarefied subject that most scholars had long abandoned. Researching those lesser-known fields gave him a feeling less of joy than of exceptionalism. He didn't feel the need to fit anyone else's mold, nor to be financially "successful." Instead, he found metaphysical fortunes, solace, and a new sense of fellowship in the niche community of like minds who still found allure in the esoterica of bygone ages. And when his peers weren't dependable, he always fell back on the texts, on his research, and on the experience he gained in the field, working with communities to understand their belief systems, their ways of life, their ancient traditions and sometimes odd customs.

There were hippies still out there, wearing tie-dye and lost in a world that had left Flower Power behind in favor of social networking; there were polygamist communes living down isolated backwoods roads, filled with men and women (but mostly women) who'd managed to trick themselves into believing the world wouldn't care about them, just so long as they left it alone; there was even the occasional suicide cult, filled with conspiracy theorists who thought the government was poisoning the water, or that a passing comet could be their personal stagecoach to heaven. Those were the people who most fascinated him.

And then there was this—the real deal. A giant, a shaman, a bloody rite.

Orson had come face-to-face with an otherworldly, ethereal force—one that was swiftly panning out to be a game-changer, and not just for him, but for the whole world. He wasn't sure whether he should move into the woods to live a life of isolation, or if he should find a way to share his gift with the rest of humankind. The latter sounded great, in concept. If only there wasn't the niggling detail of the warden, whom he'd so thoughtlessly killed (it had been surprisingly easy to do, almost instinctive—a thought, an impulse).

Just as Askuwheteau said, he needed to learn to better control it, regardless of whether he kept it to himself. And he'd need a game plan, in advance, before his anger ever caught up with him as badly as it had at the lodge.

Bunnies, he thought. *Think of thousands of adorable bunnies.*

Something flicked by, a momentary flutter at Orson's periphery, like a spirit glimmering at the far corner of an ill-lit room—some premonitory vision. He shook his head, dismissing it to illusion, a mirage, or perhaps his wracked nerves. He tuned back into the radio, which was still playing the Bowie tune. All those memories, and time had barely skipped a beat.

"*it seems the taste was not so sweet*

"*so I turned myself to face me*

"*but I've never caught a glimpse of*

"*how the others must see the faker*

"*I'm much too fast to take that test*"

As he eased into the jam, forcing concern out of his mind and zoning, Orson envisioned his loose escape plan: get out of that wicked wasteland, back to the airport, and back to New York.

And then what? he thought. There was no easy answer.

The Pinto gained speed, traveling fast along the sandy stretch of empty desert road, the quiet highway—vastly empty and humblingly hushed.

He cranked it up to catch the bridge of the song:

"*strange fascination, fascinatin'*

"*ah, changes are takin'*

"*the pace I'm goin' through—*"

The song cut out with a blast of static, replaced by a thrice repeated blaring beep. Then, a message came on:

"Civil authorities in San Francisco have reported that a natural phenomenon has killed or injured several thousand citizens in or around the city's downtown and financial districts. It is reported that the symptoms of those affected include seizure and extreme violence. Do not approach or attempt to apprehend anyone you may know who exhibits these symptoms. If you do observe this behavior in citizens of your area, or begin to experience the symptoms yourself, it has been advised that you immediately dial 911."

"What the fuck?" Orson whispered, and turned up the volume to listen to the message again.

It repeated:

"Civil authorities in San Francisco have reported that a natural phenomenon has killed or injured—"

THUD! Something slammed against the front bumper—loudly enough to

215

overwhelm the blaring Emergency Broadcast Signal—and shook the car. It flew into the air, limbs flailing, and crashed against the windshield, shattering it to bits. Orson skittered across both narrow lanes of the freeway, nearly driving off the road.

A tall, fair-skinned girl was half-lodged in his windshield. Remarkably, she writhed, still conscious, and gripped his shoulders with her blood-soaked hands, tugging and tugging 'til she fell through the glass and into the car's cabin, her long hair pitching about and obscuring her face. She tumbled into his already tender chest, pinning his arms and legs against the driver's seat, mashing his foot flat against the gas.

Orson looked down and saw through a fold in her wild hair: her eyelids were twitching, flitting faster than a hummingbird's wings, and it sounded like she was whispering something but—with the uproar of their careening across the road—it was impossible to make out.

They swerved on- and off-road. Like a rookie stunt driver, he struggled to maintain control, to keep his grip on the steering wheel with her heavy, flaccid weight cramming against him.

In a final outrageous, howling skid, the Pinto spun out and rolled onto its side, grinding against the time- and tire-worn asphalt, spitting fountains of sparking metal as it spiraled off the pavement and plunged headfirst into a drift of sand.

CHAPTER XXII

Birch stretched his back as best he could, massaging out a gnawing cramp while holding in his lap the little girl, whose name he still didn't know. He pet her head, wondering if she'd ever give up crying. Not that he could blame her; it wasn't every day a child saw hundreds of injured people running en masse, their limbs stamped off, their eyes bleeding, or worse.

The Ferry Building was crammed with people sobbing, shouting for their spouses, their brothers and sisters—*David! Heather! Mom! Dad!*—a blur of names, titles, relationships, all coalescing into one hapless scream. Finding the girl's mom there was starting to seem hopeless. If anything, it was the worst possible scenario: they were corralled into a huge public building with nothing but strangers, awaiting news from the outside. They were sitting ducks, a bulls-eye for whoever (or whatever) had caused the pandemonium.

The so-called "disaster relief" crew had shown up abruptly, wearing stark, shiny hazmat suits. Wrapped in those plasticine yellow cocoons, completely encasing their bodies, they looked a bit like aliens themselves. Understandably, the girl was terrified by them, and latched against Birch's torso with all the frenzy of a wet cat, digging her claws into the soft flesh of his sides, only letting go once they'd made it safely inside. The only trace of humanity which leaked out of those men was the clear plastic sliver cut out of their masks, which showed off their eyes. Most of them looked about as frightened as the civilians were, but they did their job all the same, herding the lot of them down the Embarcadero, hobos included, shoving them in droves through the doors of the Ferry Building. The outdoor public warning system still blared ominously overhead, a five- or six-minute drone of sirens followed by the same repeated recording:

"REMAIN CALM.

"THIS IS NOT A TEST.

"FOLLOW THE ORDERS OF THE POLICE AND SAFETY OFFICIALS AROUND YOU.

"REMAIN CALM.

"THIS IS NOT A TEST."

Shut up and sit down, basically.

But they couldn't sit; they had to stand because the hallways were packed to brimming with people, many still injured and bleeding. Birch wondered if their fluids carried whatever disease or parasite had caused this; whether any of them had those worms crawling through them, hiding in the pit of their soft bellies and waiting to break free, to wreak havoc. In the cramped space, it would be nearly impossible to tell who was and wasn't affected.

But Birch had an advantage over the rest of them: he knew more about the symptoms, how the things moved, and the way they ravaged the body of their host. Even if his last encounter had been sixteen years ago, the impression which those moments had cast over him had been severe enough to affect him for the rest of his life. He would never forget it. Still, he was cautious, and his attentions were drawn equally between care for the girl and scrutiny against the strangers who hemmed them in.

"You okay?" he asked her. She finally started to calm down, her cries dissolving into little hiccups and only an occasionally raspy breath.

She didn't respond.

"Listen," Birch said. "I know you miss your mom, but we're going to find her. There are lots of people in here, so it might take a little while. Is that okay?" Still no response. Birch added, "Eventually, everyone's going to find their mom or their dad, their brothers and their sisters, and we'll all get to go home. Do you have a brother or sister?"

She pressed her pathetic, tear-swollen eyes down against his neck. The few bits of moisture still falling from them tingled against his hot skin, trailing over his distended veins—so full of fast-beating blood—and cooling him off, stilling his temper a fraction. In a way, it was good that they'd been brought together—that Birch had been audacious enough to scoop her up, to rescue her. The girl was an elixir for his anxiety.

Birch had always been notoriously jittery, awkward and uncomfortable around others. His disinterest in girls and penchant for all things nerdy had guaranteed him an adolescence full of hectoring from his peers. If he didn't have a book to read on the bus, he would grit his teeth and clench-unclench-clench-unclench his fists forever, sweating buckets even if no one was pestering him. He believed he was naturally predisposed to the ill will of others.

Since he was just a wee thing, every interaction Birch had with kids his age had created an idea that most people—if not all of them—were nothing but hungry, self-serving wolves. Except for Aunt Greta, who was always kind to him (if not a bit bothersome in her approach at parenting), and who didn't mind constantly reminding Birch of the fact that she'd saved him from a life of endless suffering.

The details were fuzzy, but from what he surmised—and had been told by Aunt Greta—his mother had been a drug addict and a harlot. She slept her way around town and was eventually disowned by her family. After working her way through most of the men in the neighborhood (married men not to be excluded; Greta even recounted one or two incidents of pissed off wives coming 'round with shovels, bashing in the front windows and such), his mother had left their home town in the southwest of Utah. The last his aunt had heard from her, she was somewhere in Arizona, and she'd finally met a man who was "taking good care of her," whatever that meant.

Some time passed, the family mostly forgetting their black sheep had ever existed. And then Birch had shown up, dropped on Greta's front door without warning when he was only a couple years old.

Birch had few memories of his time before Greta, and they were all hazy.

He remembered living surrounded by sand, and surrounded by men. He didn't remember any of them hurting his mom—at least not in the ways Greta had hinted at—but there were too many of them to keep track of who was who, or to discern their relationships to his mother.

Her name had been Susan—though he wasn't sure how he knew this; it might have just been his aunt who'd mentioned that. The details he could recall of her appearance were in accordance with the impression Greta cast over the years (inimical accounts of her gaunt face and sleepless eye sockets, always covered in bruises). But there was some beauty buried there, too: Birch could recall her thick hair, which was long and wavy—the kind of hair a kid could sink his whole fist in, all the way up to his wrists, and tug on without hurting his mom too terribly; the kind a kid could use as a pillow when she holds him (though that didn't happen enough, not nearly often enough). Milky-skinned, short and thin, his mom had given him his complexion and—according to Greta, as this last detail escaped him—the color of his eyes, full of gray austerity, yet bouncing with light, big orbs which "sucked you right in," said Greta.

There were only a couple memories of specific events. Even though he'd only been one or two—about half as old as a child *should* be before he starts to experience moments that really stick—they were there. Like cruel scars, he could still recall the look of his mother's face—beaten, sobbing, throwing things across a cold, dark room made of cheerless gray cinderblocks. The ferocity of those images would sometimes creep back to him, unexpectedly, uninvited. And they would always render him somber, no matter where he was or what he was doing.

How he made it all the way to California, and into Greta's stern but loving arms, remained a mystery. Birch had no recollection of that long journey, nor of being left on Greta's charmingly garish front porch—full of knick-knacks: little hand-painted gnomes and plastic flamingos, ceramic stepping-stones leading to a flower bed of wilted, dying sunflowers in much need of care. There was no clear moment of abandonment, no sad *adieu*, full of tears. Maybe it was better that way— that he didn't have the additional grief of remembering the expression on his mom's face before she deserted him forever. But the absence of that memory didn't make it any less painful to deal with growing up without her—sure, he could have had it worse; he always heard horror stories about abusive foster homes and homeless kids whoring themselves out in bus stop bathrooms to get by. He was thankful for the hospitality and safety Greta created in their home, but it was no substitute for her—for a *real* mother.

Birch knew how the little girl felt. He knew how her heart must ache, how it felt to be ripped from her kin so abruptly and left in the arms of a stranger.

Beholden to protect the child, Birch was determined to keep her from a parentless fate—one which would be even worse than his had been. He would do whatever it took to prevent either of them from being attacked by one of those things.

Her wet eyes were finally starting to close up, the stream of water formerly bursting from them now calmed to just a trickle. Her sniveling abated, too; what had been deep, heaving sobs turned into a sniffle here and there, punctuated still by her adorable hiccups.

"What's your name?" she asked. Her voice was surprisingly adult, sensible and composed, especially for a girl who'd been crying her head off only moments earlier. She brushed off her dress, stood up tall, and spoke with a clear, evenly articulated timbre, shocking Birch with her maturity.

"I'm Birch." He stuck out his hand, which she reluctantly took. "Funny name, right?"

"Kinda weird, yeah." She wriggled free from his grip and stood on her own, arms crossed, wiping snot from her upper lip. All three-and-a-half feet of her glowed with innocence.

"What's your name?" Birch asked.

"Isabella."

"That's a very pretty name." Despite the fact that Birch had little experience with children (and by choice; he usually detested them), he somehow felt an intuitive bond with the girl.

"Thanks. It's Italian." *Eat-al-yen.*

"How old are you, Isabella?"

"Four'n a half."

So young, he thought. He wasn't sure how to respond.

"Wow," he started, scratching his head. "I'd have guessed five, at least. You're very smart for your age, and tall."

Isabella ignored the compliments, her focus drawn away by fresh sounds of disorder: someone at the far end of the hallway had broken into a cheese and meat shop. People were rushing the gate, looting the store for its savory snacks.

A few hours, Birch thought. *A few hours, and they're already rioting.*

A squat man with a giant boil on the tip of his nose reemerged from the shop first, crawling under its half-raised gate with a tube of salami clamped tightly in his jaws. Before he could take his first bite, a group of teenage boys appeared, kicked him in the sides, and were prying it away. One of them lodged his boot in the crook of the fat man's undulating back while another, using his bare hands, wrenched open the man's mouth.

"What're they doing?" Isabella asked.

Birch picked her back up and pushed his way through the crowd, backing as far away from the commotion as he could.

Let them have their fight, he thought.

The teenagers bragged about their haul, slapping one another on the back while the fat man covered up his bleeding mouth, cradling his broken jaw, rocking back and forth as runnels of blood leaked out between his fingers. He moved his hand away and—to the audible, gasping horror of those standing around, not helping—revealed the damage the boys had done. They had reduced his mouth to a meaty, shredded orifice—exposed nerves protruding from the jagged ridges of his broken and missing teeth.

Crawling across the floor, pulling himself away, the man pleaded muddily for help, "Please…help me." He coughed, showering the floor with his blood. "Please, someone." But no one moved to help. Instead, the horde split, their multitude dispersing like oil in vinegar, repelled by the poor man's grotesque display of frailty, or perhaps afraid of facing a similar wrath at the hands of the rampaging boys.

Birch covered up the little girl's face, scooping her into his arms and pulling her in toward his body, cooing into her ear, "*Shhhh*, don't look." He managed to shove his way through the host of civilians blocking the hall that led toward the northern exit, and peeked past the bright yellow shoulders of the hazmat suits guarding the doorway.

Outside, towering above the office buildings, he could just make out the tippy top of his high-rise apartment building—so close, yet so far away. If only they could break free, make a dash for it. But there was no way past the guards. Cops, military, government—whatever they were and whoever they worked for was unclear, but what *was* clear was the fact that they were everywhere outside, corralling passersby together like lost sheep, pushing them through the western doors of the Ferry Building in droves, packing them in.

The sky overhead looked no less forbidding than before, striped with billowing silver clouds that sparked with occasional yellow brilliance, the same way the massive, swirling cumulonimbus had flashed over the stadium.

"Anyone else want to cause a problem?" one of the kids shouted, hoisting his meat tube in the air like a darkly comic sword.

Birch realized something: whoever said there was "safety in numbers" must have suffered through a natural disaster themselves—or a war zone, or two—because Birch knew their odds of being singled out were less severe amidst the crowd, especially as long as there were assholes like those kids strutting about, causing a scene.

"Why didn't you help the man?" Isabella asked.

Birch hadn't anticipated the girl's broaching the subject of the attack, nor did he even expect her to understand what had occurred. She was proving herself to be full of surprises.

"It's hard to explain," he said, sighing heavily. If only little girls could see the world for all its shades of gray, she might understand how difficult it would have been to step up in the situation, to put *both* of their asses on the line. "Let's talk about something else. Can you tell me about your mom and dad?"

"Mommy's a teacher. She works hard and has to do other stuff on the weekend to support us both."

"What about your daddy, Isabella?"

Isabella looked away, rubbing her button nose with the back of her hand and then tugging on the ends of her pigtails as if she hadn't heard him at all.

Dad's gone, he thought, and he asked her, "What grade does your mom teach?"

"Middle school. She teaches about books, teaches English." *In-grish.*

"That explains why you're such a smart little girl."

Isabella smiled at that. Clearly, she didn't mind the compliments he'd been laying on so thick. He wondered what her mom was like: someone smart, but modest. She probably could have been a lot more in life, except for the little girl she'd had so young, unplanned, unexpected. Even though her daughter meant the world to her—gave her life some real meaning—Birch could picture Isabella's mother crying in bed at night, alone, wondering if this was really the best that life had to offer her.

A woman's scream reverberated across the high ceiling.

Somewhere far away, at the other end of the main hallway, Birch imagined another vendor was being looted. This time—perhaps due in part to Isabella's pure-hearted reproach—he felt compelled to act, if not at least to investigate.

He pulled Isabella along by her soft, miniature hand, moving toward a coffee shop at the first intersection in the hallway south of where they stood. The scream continued, just outside the restrooms, which were sealed off by officials.

The plastic-coated men stationed there wore suits of the same fit and construction as their yellow brethren, except theirs were an aquatic green instead. A few of them hoisted up a bone-thin, writhing woman and dumped her onto a narrow stretcher. The woman screamed; it was the same throaty wail they'd heard before, but up close it was much louder, full of torment, and somehow animalistic, like the whinny of a corralled stallion.

It took three of the men to move her from the hallway toward the entrance of the women's restroom. A green-suited man stood at each end of the gurney and one hovered alongside her, reaching over her, pinning her upper body down to the stretcher. Just as they made it to the entrance of the toilets, a man broke free of his friends' clutches and leapt toward them, screaming.

"Let her go!" he wailed, face purple with anger, veins popping out on his forehead.

Without hesitation, a guard moved from his spot by the men's bathroom and bashed the butt of a rifle against the man's forehead. For as much hysteria as the man had possessed—legitimate concern for his loved one's safety—he put up little fight, dropping like a fly at the first blow.

Isabella was crying again.

Birch set her down and, addressing her face-to-face, pleaded, "Calm down. Calm down, Isabella."

"Where'd they take the lady? Why'd they take her away?"

"I don't know! I don't know!"

"Help her, Birch—" *Boych*, and the first time she'd said his name. "Help her, please."

Some of the what looked like the woman's friends stepped forward, incensed but afraid to face a fate similar to the man's, should they speak up. They formed a little ring around the guard who'd bashed their friend's forehead, shouting threats at the guard and spitting on him.

A man with a purple mohawk stepped up—a kid, really, who couldn't have been more than twenty-one—and slapped the guard across the side of his plastic-covered head. Using one knuckle-tattooed hand, he pinned the guard up against the wall—feet kicking below him—and, much to the guard's horror, tore away the mask. The hazmat crewman, crying like a baby, dropped his rifle and puffed out his cheeks, holding his breath like a child prepping for a cannonball into a pool. Before long, his face had turned the color of beet juice, yet the group of civilians could do little to get him to speak. No matter how they pried at his mouth, pleading for answers (*"What'll they do with her?"* and *"Is she going to be okay?"*), they produced no result. The guard would only re-clamp his mouth shut with a snap. They punched him in the gut, but still he drew no breath.

They thinks it's airborne, Birch realized, but doubted it himself. He'd seen the creatures before; he'd been right at the wellspring of their madness all those years ago, and neither brush with death—with those miry, nasty things—had resulted in his becoming infected. If it was an airborne contagion, Birch would have been among the first victims.

Isabella was still screaming in his ear—and stomping her feet, pushing into Birch's sides—screaming, "Help her, Birch. Please!"

"Okay, okay. Stay right here. Don't move." He gave her a final soothing pat across her shoulders.

Seizing the opportunity which the woman's friends had created, Birch neared the restrooms. Since their colleague had lost hold of his headgear, the two green-suited men guarding the entryway had largely abandoned their stations. They still hovered near the restrooms, but they no longer blocked the passageway outright. Circling past, Birch peeked into the bathroom.

The floors were covered in tarpaulin; the walls were sheathed in hazy plastic sheeting.

A crew of the green- and yellow-suited men surrounded the woman. All of them had steel cylinders strapped to their backs, and the hoses which linked to those canisters were what they utilized to wash her down. Their system was largely inchoate—one of them squeezing a handle to loose a high pressure gout from the nozzle of his device, squirting her in the face with a frothy brown substance, before

225

the next one blasted it away with what must have just been water. None of them seemed to know whether they'd achieved the desired effect—they kept glancing back and forth at one another, shrugging and shaking their heads—and the woman carried on screaming throughout the proceedings while sheets of her skin sizzled, washing away with each corrosive blow of the chemical bath they gave her. Through it all, she spit the same guttural croaking sound, alternating it with an insectile, throaty clicking that sent chills of remembrance down Birch's spine.

Part of him wanted to bust through and grab her, to throw her across his back and run from that place like an indestructible superman, but he knew he wouldn't make it far and—besides which—he had a little girl to look out for. Further, he knew the woman was too far gone. Soon, she'd be just like the man on the boardwalk.

A similar roar—but much closer—erupted through the hall and knocked any hope of saving the woman clear from Birch's mind. Whoever had been afflicted next wasn't far away. People were screaming, pushing and punching, falling down, getting trampled worse than they had been at the stadium. In the crammed confines of the Ferry Building, avoiding the path of a scattering crowd became much more difficult.

Ironically, there was so much space overhead. The Ferry Building had tall, gaping, modern ceilings made of glass and metal, and yet there was no space left to move at ground level.

Overhead, Birch thought. *That's it!* He grabbed Isabella by the wrist and, with as much serenity as he could fake, skipped casually around clusters of civilians, moving as quickly as possible away from the rising commotion, without creating a scene.

Peering over the tops of civilians' heads as they moved, Birch observed some of the hazmat crew leaving their posts to investigate the noise. They carved a circle out of the crowd and were trying to heft up one of the teenagers who'd stolen the fat man's salami. More than the kid's knuckles were now bloody, and it didn't look like the fat man's blood; streams of it passed over his lips, squirting up from his throat in bilious, chunky spatters, splashing against the clear screens covering up the faces of the crewmen. The boy convulsed against the hard concrete floor, flattening out the back of his skull by his paroxysms yet somehow still alive, his eyes rolling around inside their sockets like loose marbles.

"Where we going?" Isabella asked, tugging back against Birch's grip. Clearly, she'd had enough of running.

"Just a little farther. I promise we'll rest soon."

"I don't want to run." She broke free and leaned against a vacant stretch of wall, right between a closed-down ceramics shop and a safe-and-sound grow-your-own-mushrooms kiosk (apparently neither had been appealing enough to loot).

"Come on, we're almost there. I want to make sure you're safe, until we get you back to your mom."

Isabella wouldn't budge, and she slid down the wall to rest on the floor, wrapping her legs together and crossing her arms. Soundlessly, she looked up at him with full, wet eyes that seethed with real annoyance.

"Isabella," Birch said. "You have to stand up. Trust me."

As much as he wanted to grab her by both arms and toss her over his shoulder, he also knew it would likely draw unwanted attention. He was very clearly unrelated to Isabella. Whereas she had thick, curly hair (especially for someone so young), and was undeniably Italian—with passionate brown eyes and warm, tanned skin—Birch was pasty, white, and as far from Mediterranean as they came.

"I'm not gonna see her again, am I?" Isabella asked. "Is she dead, Birch?"

The pair of questions bit at him hard. Just as he was growing accustomed to her childlike mood, she demonstrated how eerily mature—how logically competent—she was for a girl under five years old.

"I think you'll see her again, if we can just find a way out of here. It's not safe anymore. Will you leave with me, Isabella? I'll do all I can to keep you safe."

She weighed her options heavily before squeaking, "Yes."

"All right then, let's go."

Hefting herself up with little of his help, Isabella brushed off and stretched her legs, rising onto the tips of her toes before she said, "Okay, I'm ready now."

Tough little girl, he thought.

Hands clenched tightly together, the two of them progressed toward the southernmost wing of the building, passing by groups of people who so far appeared uninjured. To the best of Birch's passing estimation, no one was smashed against the floor, foaming at the mouth, getting ripped apart, nor being sprayed in the face with volatile solvents; not at that wing of the building. The guards, too, were less on edge, chatting comfortably with one another. None of the green-suited men were down there; it was all yellow suits.

Birch surveyed the second-floor hall above them. He'd been to the Ferry Building often enough to have already noticed its top story, but most passersby paid no heed to anything but the overpriced restaurants, the novelties and knick-knacks, the world-famous slow-drip coffee, and the ferries. But hidden above them—yet in plain sight—were other tenants, set far enough back from the railings to suggest some meaningless architectural detail. The wash of gray which suffused the modern style of the building helped erase the offices' presence from view, too.

There had to be a way up there. An elevator, a stairway. Something.

One of the yellow suits noticed them and, approaching with his right palm raised, ordered Birch to stop. He'd come too close to the exit, apparently, and hadn't noticed how much he stood out, separated from the civilians as he was, looking like a fish out of water while the rest of them were packed like sardines behind steel-slatted barricades.

The yellow suit eased Isabella and Birch back toward the crowd, back into the throng from whence they'd snuck, but in his doing so, the guard also revealed a small detail—though one substantial enough to give Birch the exact location of their route.

Once the yellow suit corralled them back behind the partition, he moved to resume his station by the exit; but instead of outright blocking the outlet, he looked up and toward his right, toward a set of hidden doors, painted to match the walls of the hall. Even the lever-handled doorknob blended in, its metal grip painted to match the grayish-tawny brick archways separating each vendor down the length of the halls. When the guard settled fully into his post, massaging the back of his neck through the thick plastic of his suit, he angled his body to perfectly block both sets of doors: those that opened to the outside world, and those that would undoubtedly lead them up, to the second floor.

Think, Birch, he told himself. *There's got to be a way past him.*

Another gutted wail echoed through the hall. The three men guarding the exit from the inside—more were outside, their backs turned to them, facing whatever terrors still lurked and loped down the Embarcadero—looked at one another soundlessly. Apparently they had no means of communicating, other than with vague head nods, pointing, and urgent hand gestures, because the one who'd so graciously swept them back into the crowd was shaking his neighbor's shoulder and stabbing at the air in the direction of the screams.

The sound grew louder and, as it did, the yellow men itched in their pants, nervously shaking their heads, stomping in place, lifting their guns up out of their belts with expressions that proved they didn't have the balls to shoot another living being, especially not a human, even if the man or woman stampeding toward them *did* have some alien creature slithering around his spine.

Birch bent to whisper into Isabella's ear, moving a soft ringlet out of the way and cupping his palm to say, "Get ready, we're going to run over there." He lifted his chin an imperceptible fraction of an inch and, locking his eyes with hers, traced a line toward the set of doors in the far corner. Blood boiling in his face, he scooped Isabella into both of his arms, lifting her up (her legs dangling in front of him) and out of the path of two men—

One of them—the fat man from the sausage tussle, who'd most definitely been beaten to unconsciousness and who shouldn't, by any means, be walking around, much less running and screaming—charged like a cripple with ropes tied to his wrists and ankles, as though some god, reclined across the roof of the building, was carrying him along on his savage path. The man's disinterested face was slack and sliced from the bludgeoning he'd received, yet his mouth slavered actively, foaming, clicking open and shut as he neared the guards.

The other man had clearly been sprayed by whatever corrosive substance the green-suited men had strapped across their backs. His face was half-melted, the flesh charred into dripping, fatty mounds. Bones poked visibly through the ravages of what had once been his cheeks, and his lips were split open to show his bloodied gums and chipped teeth, cracked and splintered from the awful, violent stamping motion he made with his mouth—

CLAMP. CLAMP. CLAMP.

The afflicted men took down a guard each, tackling them to the ground, leaving just one yellow man to fend for himself. But the last man chose a coward's route, banging on the door for the officers outside, begging to be set loose.

One of the men outside unlocked the door and slid it back a sliver to let his colleague through, but the latter slammed his full weight against the door, sending it flying wide open.

The rest happened in a blur. The mob of civilians saw an opportunity to flee and took it, forming a charging spearhead, cinching together at the aperture of the door, forcing it further loose and ballooning outside, into an explosion of overwrought, insensate citizens, too great in number for the yellow men there to subdue.

"This is our chance!" Birch shouted above the din. He set Isabella down and pointed toward the door, tugging her by the elbow.

She stood rooted to the spot, her jaw hanging loose with shock at what she witnessed: the two pinned guards were being torn apart. One of the unwell men—the melted-face man—extracted an exceptionally fat creature, one of the worms, from the back of his own throat. It squelched its way up his esophagus and past his wide-parted, sliced-open lips, plopping wetly against the plastic guard of the yellow man's mask like the semi-solid turd of a cow. The thing struggled to bore its rows and rows of jagged teeth through the guard's mask before it finally found an easier route inside, through the seam where the suit's mask and body met, at the back of the guard's neck.

"Don't watch!" Birch screamed, forcing Isabella to turn away from the violent scene.

He dragged Isabella to the camouflaged doors and, struggling to maintain a grip on her with his sweat-slick hands, plowed against the threshold with a solid kick. It didn't even rattle in its sturdy frame.

"Try the handle!" she shouted.

Birch gripped the doorknob, pausing for a moment with his eyes clamped shut—hoping, praying, perhaps unrealistically—before he pressed down on the lever. It didn't move a millimeter.

Fuck, he thought, and told her the obvious, "It's locked."

The other guard—whose head was being beaten against the floor by the fat man—had a glint of keys attached by an o-ring to his belt but, even *with* luck, Birch couldn't make it past the first of them, the agile, melted one—

Except, now that he'd given the guard a taste of his worm, the melted man was wilting. It was as though he'd spent all of his reserves to expel the creature; the man lay still, prostrate on his back but still blinking, still *somewhat* alive.

"Stay here," Birch said. "I'll be right back."

"No!" Isabella gripped Birch's wrist with all the strength of an Olympian. "Don't go."

"I have to. I'll be right back. I promise."

Birch knew—just as he decided on what to do—that she would be unlikely to trust him again. Not fully, not ever. Still, he'd promised to do his best, to get them out of the mess they were in, and if she wouldn't come around later—if they even lived that long—well, he'd deal with the repercussions then.

He shoved Isabella to the ground. She skittered to a halt against the locked doors. The look on her face, which he barely had time to absorb as he turned to run for the keys, was one he wouldn't soon forget. It was the singular look of the orphan: of the betrayed, the child whose guardian leaves her for selfish gain. Except, Birch's act wasn't selfish at all. Isabella might not have known it, but this was their only hope.

He hopped over the first yellow man (whose limbs twitched as the creature made its final cinch around his brain) and the charred man, and broke through the panicking clusters of people (some of them only making it a few feet past the entrance, shot down by the guards outside or sprayed with their noxious spumes).

Birch came upon the fat man—who was still lifting and flattening the guard's head against the ground—and kneed him in his side, sending him flying across the hall, tripping civilians.

Instead of rising and turning to charge Birch, the fat man seized the opportunity of fresh and easy prey, sinking his rotten face into the necks of passersby, ripping open their throats to plant new *things* in them, to spread its wormish offspring.

Birch lifted the keys off the guard's belt loop, and his eyes were dragged down to meet the guard's fast-flickering lids. For the second time in his life, Birch watched a man die, practically in his arms, and did nothing to help him live.

"Hurry!" Isabella screamed from across the hall.

With the small metal question mark of the keys in his hands, Birch loped back to the corner, the door, and the girl. He left his apology for later and wrested her up, onto her feet.

He tried one, two, three keys—but none of them fit.

With only one left to go, the danger rose: the fat man stood up again, fully recuperated, recharged and ready for action, with hell in his eyes as he warbled toward them.

As the distance between them lessened, Isabella shouted, "He's coming! He's coming!"

The last key slid into the lock and, no matter how Birch wrestled with it, the door still wouldn't budge.

Shit, he thought. *Shit shit shit.*

They were out of options, with the afflicted fast approaching.

Crouching beside Isabella, Birch squeezed her tight by both of her trembling shoulders.

"What do we do, Birch?" she asked, shaking from head to toe in his hands, like a barren, wind-rattled twig—pathetic, so easily broken.

"Hold on," he said, rubbing her arms to soothe her. "Trust me."

The fat man lumbered toward them, less than three feet away—his gut bouncing heinously with each craggy stride.

Birch lunged out of his path of destruction, falling onto his back, pinning Isabella to his chest as they skidded across the floor and to safety. He bobbed his neck, peeking back toward the spot of their leadoff, where the fat man lay face-down across the smashed-open doorway: his dead weight had done it, had knocked the double doors free of their casing.

Nervously, Birch and Isabella moved back toward his body, which lay still atop the felled set of doors. They tiptoed over him. Birch pushed him back into the hall and did his best to lift the doors back into their frame. They wobbled, then settled. It would have to do, and they'd have to hope the man remained unconscious or that, if he did reawaken, he'd lack the faculty of memory to know where to follow.

Birch held the doors in place for a while, just to be safe, to ensure that no one came after them. The chill sensation between his hand and the door was a welcome feeling, an equitable, simple grounding—like splashing into a still, cool lake or drinking lemon iced tea. No one rapped at nor pushed upon the door, so he let his grip fade. Again, it stayed mostly in place, only teetering for a second before it grew still.

Isabella sat waiting behind him, on the first step of a cold, ill-lit stairwell.

"Isabella, I'm sorry. I didn't meant to leave you back there, I—"

"It's okay, Birch," she interrupted.

Rubbing her own knees, the remarkably composed little girl (a far cry from the sobbing, wailing pre-schooler Birch had met, not long ago) waltzed toward Birch and embraced him in a hug. It felt warm. That combination—cold, metal door and soft, warm skin—was a nice juxtaposition; it easily erased much of the anxiety of their quick brush with death. Whatever bond had already begun to form between them was solidified in that quiet moment of forgiveness.

"Let's go," Birch said.

"Okay."

Without a question about *where* or another cry for her mother, Isabella followed Birch up the dark stairwell. Though neither of them felt certain where it led, nor knew who might be awaiting them up top, they were comfortable and unafraid, protected by one another's companionship and the assurance of their mutual safekeeping. It was reciprocative; she'd proven herself capable, and he trusted her fully. If it came down to it, Isabella would protect him, without a doubt.

Up and up they went, without pause, equally calmed and encouraged by the enduring silence around them. The stairwell seemed never-ending, a perpetual loop of the same pattern: ten narrow stone steps leading up to a rectangular slab of concrete ten feet wide, connected to another set of ten narrow stone steps leading up and in the opposite direction, which connected to another rectangular slab of concrete—and so on, and so on. They must have climbed for five whole minutes, though the fresh quiet of their environment might also have enhanced the feeling of wandering, of timelessness.

Finally, they came upon a new set of sterile, steel doors. The landing before it was illumined by the only window they'd crossed in their whole passage. It was behind them, set high along the wall, nearly touching the ceiling.

Outside, the sky swirled with the same charcoal-tinged foam as before. Birch could just make out the tallest tips of the faraway Bay Bridge. Only the points of each of its towers, and the uppermost reaches of its suspenders, were within view.

We're definitely not on the second floor, he thought.

Isabella tugged at his elbow and said, "Are we almost there?"

"Yeah," he said, but he really couldn't tell. He lied, "It's just a little farther."

"You keep saying that." She tugged at her socks, pulling them half-way up her calves. "But I don't think you really *know* where we're going."

Birch hid whatever shock he felt at her continued and uncanny insights; he only tapped her on the top of her head, a gesture he remembered hating when he was a kid, and one he immediately regretted subjecting her to.

"Sorry, I know that was probably annoying—" They exchanged a smile. "I'm *pretty sure* we're near the top of the building, near the clock tower. I just didn't know we could go this high…"

Isabella's smirk stretched into an unchecked, beaming smile, its authenticity reinforced by a sudden indrawn breath, an expectant one. She pried excitedly at the handle before them. The door gave easily to her push, and she dove through it into darkness.

Birch, chasing after her, crossed into a narrow, dim hall that smelled like rosemary and sage, but tinged with a meaty undertone, like an Italian deli. The walls were made up of wire-mesh and metal rods. Through the thousands of manifold apertures the mesh created, Birch could just make out the shapes of boxes, of cartons stacked high toward the domed ceiling overhead.

Afraid of losing pace with Isabella, he quickened his stride to catch up with her, but his toe met with a chip in the floor, at just the right angle to trip him. Scraping against the coarse-graded concrete, he managed to avert severe injury but, in doing so, took a nice chunk out of both his kneecaps, leaving a smear of blood along his bounding path.

"Isabella, wait!"

Ahead, the rows and rows of industrial storage drowned the minute figure of Isabella. Her silhouette paused, at the edge of vanishing in the darkness, before her restless voice echoed through the hall as she said, "Come on! I see another door up there."

"Wait, I fell! Come back here, I—" he started, lifting himself up onto his elbows, legs still dripping generously, but she was gone, out of sight.

Dammit, you stupid girl, Birch thought, but immediately felt sorry. She was anything but dumb. Since they met, this was the first time she'd been so immature, so selfish, and Birch knew he shouldn't reproach her for a little bit of enthusiasm, a flash of excitement. It was only natural for a kid to act that way, perhaps especially so, in light of the travesties she'd been faced with.

A whimper drew his ear off to the right; it came from behind one of the many mesh enclosures. It was followed by a sound like water flowing—*water*, he thought, something neither of them had consumed for hours, something they'd need to find if they expected to survive. Tracing the trickling tone to a doorway set into one of the storage spaces, Birch saw what he'd thought had been water. It was something else entirely—something liquid, but not of the same thirst-quenching quality as good old H_2O.

It was a stream of urine, which crept toward Birch from under the rail of the wire mesh wall. Behind the web of metal, as though locked in a zoo, a little girl—perhaps only one or two years older than Isabella—sat on the lap of a dark, muscular man. Their skin tone mostly hid them from sight, but the thing that hadn't been water was what helped Birch discern them from the gloom. The trail of piss led straight toward them, to where the girl sat; she'd peed in her pants. Her face was wrought with fear—though, mostly, it was in her eyes: they welled up, bulging from their sockets like two moist, shelled hard-boiled eggs. Those blinders of hers burned through the darkness of the space and screamed with petition against the man's hands, which were clamped tightly against her mouth.

Birch said, "What's going on in there? Everything okay?"

"You jus' keep on walkin' on your way," the man said, with the wiry inflection of a geriatric. "You don't pay her no mind. Keep on your way now, y'hear me?"

The girl whimpered again, and beat both of her opened inner palms against the surface of her captor's thighs.

"I don't think she can breathe," Birch said. "Let her go."

"Back away from where you stand, and then I may, mistuh." He was southern, for sure. A good ol' boy.

"I'll leave you alone, I promise. There's nothing you can give me, there's nothing I want from you." He paused, awaiting a response. Only silence from the man. Birch pleaded, "I'm with a little girl, too. Did you see her run by here, just a minute ago?"

Still no response, just the same whimpering, pleading cries, barely making it past the hard mask of the old man's calloused palms.

It was unclear how the two of them had gotten in there, but they'd made out quite nicely with supplies—stacks and stacks of produce (bartlett pears, pink lady apples, fresh Hawaiian pineapples), bags of jerky, and cases of what Birch craved most: water. Clean, pure water. An upturned bottle by their feet dripped slowly against the floor, absorbing into the porous concrete, wasted. Next to it, a worn Holy Bible sat closed but ready, its creased black cover lovingly marred with the folds of frequent usage.

"I ain't seen no little girls 'round here, 'cept mine. Besides which, if we did, we ain't dumb enough to stick our necks out at 'er. Could be one of them demons. You seen her?" He looked down at the girl in his lap who—still struggling to breathe against her captor's firm grip—did her best to shake her head no, tears streaming down her cheeks. "Nope, neither of us've seen 'er. All clear here. Mosey on…" The old man's eyes pulsated with urgency, pointing toward a stack of boxes off to his right. His gaze settled on a .22 Magnum revolver, the glory of its stainless steel draped in shadow yet still pulsating with dangerous possibilities. The old man nodded his head in its direction and smiled out at Birch. "Go on," he chirped. "Leave us in peace."

Birch took a step back, his hands raised up, and said, "All right, listen. I understand what you're doing. We need to protect ourselves, and look out for the ones we love. I'll keep walking."

He moved to walk away, but the old man stopped him:

"S'right, mistuh. You go on after that girl of yers, and I'll keep after mine."

Birch backed off, headed in the direction of Isabella, toward the far end of the hall. As he limped away from the storeroom, the girl drew in a sharp breath, finally free of the old man's grip. Wheezing and sniffling, she said, "Grampa, that hurt!"

Grampa hushed her with an urgent, *Shhhhh!*

Demons, Birch thought. A new concept—one he hadn't considered more than in passing. But the flinty old fellow believed it, with all his heart. He believed it with enough certainty to find his way up here, to lock himself up with his grandbaby and feign hazard against her; to pray over them with his Bible, to pretend he'd kill her if he had to, even though he likely loved her more than anything else in the world.

Maybe the old man was right. Maybe they were demons, come to purge the Earth of its mortals and their sins. To reap. Birch chuckled, bent over to massage his shins and check that his knees had finally scabbed over.

Demons, my ass, he thought. Somehow aliens still seemed more plausible to Birch.

He reached the door Isabella had run to; it was sliced open a thread, and a weak but promising halo of light filtered through. It opened with ease and led to yet another flight of stairs. This one was substantially narrower, winding its way steeply upwards. Traversing it reminded Birch of when he first moved to San Francisco and he'd done all the touristy stuff in a day. He took his first ascent up the high stairwell to reach the Coit tower back then, marching endlessly up to reach its observation platform and the panoramic skyline it offered. He'd absorbed the skyline with such wonder. Back then, the day had been bright and warm, and the sky had been clear. He'd thought this was the best place in the world. The City by the Bay, full of promise and beauty.

Overcrowded, swarming with hobos and drug addicts and whores. And now, monsters.

With each laborious step, Birch ascended higher, wondering how Isabella and he made it so far without passing any security—*luck!*—and without any of the *whatever-they-were* getting in their way. Things were going too easy, too smoothly; he half-expected a yellow-suited man to jump out at him.

He struggled to maintain a steady pace, his bruised knees throbbing, his throat dry and raspy, burning as he screamed, "Isabella!" The word echoed through the cylindrical walls of the structure he ascended. Overhead, only a few stories of stairwell remained, crowned by a smattering of bilious, moving shadows.

At the top—finally, collapsing—Birch sat down next to Isabella, resting his hand on her shoulder, feeling its aspect for comfort, for the assurance of her safety.

She pushed his hand off her shoulder. Her face looked deflated, as though the youth had been sucked out of it, leaving behind a colorless, dry husk—skeletal, reticent. Little of her exuberance remained.

"What's wrong?" Birch asked hoarsely, still catching his breath.

Isabella only hooked her thumb over her shoulder, pointing through a narrow opening in the wall, toward a space Birch hadn't examined yet.

He labored to stand, studying their new setting.

The room was square. Each of its walls contained three tall, rectangular notches, thin cut-outs which opened onto a view of the city below—a view perhaps as wondrous as Coit's had once been, but in a grim, orderless sense of the word. Leaning out through one of the windows, Birch saw how things had changed outside since their anarchic arrival at the Ferry Building.

Emptied of life, the streets stood cluttered by abandoned cars, their doors hanging open, left behind in the sudden chaos triggered back at the stadium. A few green-suited men stood in a ring alongside the amorphous shape of the Vaillancourt Fountain, hefting their deadly squirt guns up before them, looking like child soldiers playing a post-apocalyptic dress up game, ready to coat any passersby with their volatile goop. Off to the south, a plume of smoke drifted from the center of the arena, coating the sky gray, floating to coalesce with the clouds overhead. The Jumbotron in the distance writhed visibly with life, still coated by the worms; sparks still shot from the great schism through the center of the screen.

From the east-facing wall of the tower, Birch could see the Bay Bridge, jutting across the inlet to stab through the center of Yerba Buena Island. More cars were stalled along the bridge, lying still as corpses, crushed in accidents or hanging off the edge of the bridge by a single tire, scrunched into accordions. Leaning out, with his body hanging over the edge of the tower—hoping none of the plastic-coated men on the ground below would notice him—Birch could just make out one of the four enormous clock dials of the tower ticking below him. Its diameter was more than twice his own height. Its hands' minute shifts were visible from so close, and their movement emphasized the elevation of their vantage point.

He gripped Isabella's hand and reassured her, "It's going to be okay. I don't know how, but I'll figure a way out of this."

She looked up at him, her big eyes like black holes—full of nothing, full of everything—drowning him in innocence, foreboding. The feel of her uncalloused skin in his hand reminded him how delicate she was—how vulnerable, benevolent and trusting.

Forcing a smile, she settled her head into his lap and said, "Okay, Birch. I trust you."

He knew that she did; wholly, like a child of his own, despite how he'd shoved her before. She would follow him wherever he went, and would do just as he said.

"Don't run away like that again," he told her. "Okay?"

"I won't."

"You promise?"

She lifted her head up and nodded before returning it to the nest of warmth in his lap and wrapping her arms around his waist. They settled in for some rest, Birch's mind swarming with questions, with loads of conjecture but no immediate answer to the predicament they faced. Before the hopelessness of their post had time to settle into any real insight, a wail sounded, close at hand.

The siren of the warning system was loud enough to explode their eardrums. Isabella sat up, pressing her palms deep into the sides of her skull, wincing in pain. Birch followed suit, but paid attention to the message as it played, hoping for an update:

"REMAIN CALM.

"THIS IS NOT A TEST.

"FOLLOW THE ORDERS OF THE POLICE AND SAFETY OFFICIALS AROUND YOU.

"REMAIN CALM.

"THIS IS NOT A—"

The message cut out, skittering into static which was no less discomforting than the sound of the siren. It lingered, grating through the air until the speakers blew out, exploding just below their wing of the tower like fireworks, shooting outward in all directions around them, and attracting the unwanted attention of the "safety officials" on the ground below. But their focus was quickly diverted by a fresh terror, a howl that was at once lupine and aeriform, as though a pterodactyl had somehow made its way through a portal to their time.

Far in the distance—off toward the south, above the stadium—a new beast emerged. Through the wriggling mass of worms still coating the Jumbotron, a pair of jaundice-yellow hands protruded, anthropomorphic fists cusped by long, pointed fingers—not quite talons, they were jagged, but composed of the same coarse-skinned flesh as the rest of its fists. There were no claws, no fingernails, just skin over muscle over bone. Its wrists emerged next from the sparking crack, pushing through the fatty mass of the worms, two impossibly thin *carpi* with skin that segued into brownish-blue by gradient. The forearms came next, stringy, sinewy limbs (which were a deeper, bubbling oxford blue); they bent down across the screen, latching onto the miry slab to pull out the rest of its atrocious body. Its head emerged, a grimy and slimy night-black raven's head the size of a panther, with two grapefruit-sized, gaping eyes, encased with the fluids of its otherworldly birth, its transference to the place called Earth. It had a sharp-curved oreish beak whose tip glinted with violence.

With a single powerful leap, it launched itself out the rest of the way—a hulking, naked freak with the ripped physique of a bodybuilder. Its human-like torso and legs were the same deep Monastral blue as its upper arms, and its crotch was complete with purplish male genitalia, swaying grotesquely, distended between its burly thighs. Its feet had the same freakish points as its hands, like ten little knives crowning each digit. Perhaps most frightening of all was its back, a tightly wound mass of tendon and flexed muscle, furnished with tall, feathered wings as long as its body and dripping with putrescent, brown muck. It stretched them majestically, up and out around it, flicking off the coating of spectral ectoplasm, and crawled up to perch atop the screen.

More of them cinched their way out of the portal—which had been turned, by their constant clawing through it, from a thin crack into a gaping, swirling hole of gleaming light, of cindery ash and incomprehensible sputters. In total, twelve emerged from the gateway above the stadium, and they were stationed in a menacing row across the length of the Jumbotron, flicking their massive bird-heads to and fro, crouched down on their hands and knees and screaming their call to arms, as if bedamning this strange world, as if awaiting their unseen master's orders.

Birch clutched Isabella close to him, squinting to make out the indistinct shapes of the winged things lifting off their perch, swooping down low to pluck off the heads of the plastic-coated men as easily as snapping a twig off a low-hanging branch, circling the tips of skyscrapers for prey. One crashed its way into a window on the tenth floor of Birch's apartment building, spraying glass like confetti through the air and re-emerging, seconds later, with a woman in each arm; it plucked at them, alternating between blonde and brunette, transforming their faces into bloody pulp before dropping them to the ground far below—satiated, done.

A few green-suited men succeeded at their task, fearlessly confronting the beasts, spraying their feathered faces and leathery skin with their volatile back-strapped brew. But the beasts who were sprayed surmounted the caustic sprayers, shaking off the sizzling stuff and wailing their assailants away, as though they were only flimsy paper dolls.

Isabella crawled over Birch to peek at the chaos outside, but he clamped her around the waist and told her not to look. She, of course, fearlessly assured him she could handle it, and that she just wanted to see what was happening. Eventually he gave up, knowing the girl had grown up more in the past eight hours than she would for years to come, but also aware that the sight of the flying horrors could be the last strand of straw to break her bulldogged back.

"What are they?" she asked, eyes wide with wonder, though with little fear.

"I don't know, but they're dangerous. We need to lay low and wait it out."

"Wait it out?"

"Yeah. Someone will come to help us eventually. The government, the military. They have to." He looked at Isabella, whose knees began to shake, her fearless countenance once more cracked. She seemed more afraid of the idea of the government coming to their aid than she did of the winged creatures outside.

A silence passed between them, punctuated repeatedly by the winged things' tenebrous shrieks. Birch knew what she was thinking. Even if she didn't yet have a grasp on uncouth cusses, her furrowed brows and her hands, raking through her scalp, said it well enough:

Bullshit. No one's coming to help.

From the shadows of garages and from the coffins of cars, the creatures who had once been human began to emerge—the ones Birch called *afflicted*—with their slackened jaws and wandering eyes, clicking and stomping mindlessly, looking for new flesh upon which to spew their vile offspring, searching for new minds in which to propagate.

Birch couldn't help feeling that they were truly and completely fucked. He wondered about the old man and little girl, somewhere down below them, locked away in their cage—free of concern for the outside world—with their generous month's worth of rations.

Where'll they shit? he wondered. *How long will they last?*

The husks of men and women marched down Main Street, congregating where they once took coffee breaks; where they ate their boxed lunches, called their mistresses, texted their spouses. Sadly, there would be no recognition of those so-familiar surroundings, no tick of memory at the pit of their skulls, no recollection of the many occasions upon which they frequented the bagel shop, the park bench, the bar for just one drink.

Above them, the flying things soared up and down, plucking off more of the last vagrant heroes' heads, green- and yellow-clad men whose masks were torn off with a single strike, leaving only the stalks of their necks exposed, squirting like geysers.

He hid Isabella's head against his chest as a trio of the bird-men flew higher, closing the safe space separating them, approaching their vantage point with their sharp hands outstretched—reaching for their secret place, where the two of them were tucked away. One of the things perched high on the edge of the clock tower, clinging to the building's facade—within arm's reach, its wings flapping in support of its treacherous spot, filling their cramped citadel with the stinking wind of its fetid, excited excretions. Its skin smelled like fresh-tanned leather, its hanging privates like soured milk. So near at hand, its rebellious yell was a fatidic reminder of their helplessness, a hellbound screech that erased any still-lingering hope of rescue. Its brethren drew near, too; all twelve of them surrounded Birch and Isabella, filling in the various interstices cut from the walls of the tower. They blotted out the murky light of the storm-clouded sky.

Isabella quivered in his arms, sobbing and limp, fully abandoned to dismay and fast approaching shock. Birch ensconced her more tightly, sliding to the center of the room and moaning loudly to drown out the ever-increasing pitch of the creatures' screeching. He dove for the stairwell leading down—for the safe quiet back below, the cage-lined hall of the storerooms—but the door was locked from within. They were stuck.

The creatures' fearsome beaks cracked open, crying out for blood, revealing black tongues, spotty gums, and their open-throated, pulsating tracheas, lined with scraps of green and yellow plastic. Their sharp-pointed, wand-like fingers lashed through the air, swiping out with as much ferocity as a many-pointed guillotine or a flesh-bound cat-o-nine-tails, but their behemoth girth kept them from fitting easily through the slivers of the glassless windows encircling the tower—perhaps the only blessing Birch and Isabella were afforded, and the only thing that kept them from being ripped apart. Primordial anger, raw and unbridled, overcame the creatures;

they slapped and snipped at one another like untrained beasts fighting over scraps.

Thinking quickly, and using the creatures' careless quarrels to their advantage, Birch set Isabella down and whispered in her, "They'll break through soon. We have to fight back. Try to find something we can use as a weapon."

Isabella's shoulders tightened close against her frame and her hands fell limp to the ground. Her eyes rolled into the back of her head. Birch shook her, trying to coax her back into awareness of their surroundings, but her flushed skin and rapid heartbeat meant she'd slipped away, into mental shock.

"A weapon!" he shouted to himself, but there was nothing useful around: an old dish rag, tossed into a corner; a short plastic step-stool; a chrome fountain pen, its shiny surface long-dulled and scratched.

Their tufted wings whipped through the air, still filling the cramped space with noise like a hedge trimmer. Dark feathers, mottled with brown grime and flecks of blood, swirled past Birch's face; they were longer than his forearm and floated through the air at a crawl.

The smallest of their company—its eyes almond-shaped, almost human, and impossibly green, like glinting emeralds—snuck past its quarreling brethren and, drawing its wings in close against its body, managed to fit half way in before the others realized it had almost passed them by, through the slender cutouts which barred their entrance.

Enraged by the small one's near success, and filled with jealousy, they reached out and dug their fine-edged beaks and pointy-fingered hands into its left calf. A tug-of-war ensued, where the monstrosity fought against the grip of its kin, screeching at them in a whole new octave, its beak stretched to capacity—as though its skull might crack in two, should its mandibles part any farther.

Birch rolled to the right edge of the room, pushing himself as far from the bird-man as he could, dragging Isabella behind him by both of her ankles. She hit her head several times on the way across the space, leaving a sparse trail of her bloodied hair behind her. He folded her arms and limbs inward, manipulating her into a fetal shape, and shielded her with his body. If the things wanted her for their snack, they would have to go through him.

The small one's head was turning back and forth with rapidity, assessing how to most easily break from its kin. Hovering in mid-air, ferociously beating its wings (its testicles flapping about between its muscular thighs like two fleshy, purple boulders), the beast managed to finally break free, but the impetus of its resistance—against the others' clutches—caused it to fly sharply upward. It smashed against the ceiling, loosening bits of cement overhead. It shook its head to reorient itself and, with eyes full of delight, set a course for Birch before it dove, quick as a lightning bolt—soundlessly, with its feathered wings folded up and its round face pointed downward, beak aimed straight for the neck, swooping backward, pulling up at the last moment, landing on its feet, crouched low over the prostrated Birch.

As its hungry little tongue clicked across the coarse inside of its rhinotheca, its upper beak, Birch pushed out in defense. Clasping the rusty old fountain pen, unsheathing it hopefully, he stabbed down toward the creature's discomfiting gaze. The pen tore through its glaucous cornea, shredding open its eye.

The beast fell back, covering its injured eyeball with both hands, hovering in place with the aid of its slow-pulsing pinions. It lashed at the air, disoriented and unsure where to aim.

Birch stood up, filled with a buzz of adrenaline. He dove for the beast; he stabbed it again, embedding the rusted point of his stylographic saber in the pit of its neck, right where the frill of its collar began to merge with the rough-textured, bluish skin of its body.

It reached out to swat Birch away, falling backward in pain, and withdrew the pen, tossing it out the window behind it.

Birch flew across the room under the impact of its fist, crashing back into Isabella.

She opened her eyes again, just in time to see their greatest portent yet: the other beasts, incensed by their brother's pained cries, ripping open the space between two of the slender portholes that dotted the walls, creating an entrance wide enough that any of them might finally fit through.

They piled in, spilling onto the wounded one, burying it with their weight, in a pile of gradient flesh and feathers, ripping it apart. They gorged themselves on their spoiled kin, somehow oblivious to the fresh, living meat which still quivered off in the corner.

Birch and Isabella sat there, limbs intertwined, holding hands, waiting to see what would happen.

Satiated, the creatures turned to face them with fire in their eyes, and made for their fresh prey.

Birch rose to protect Isabella, shielding his face against the blow of the foremost beast, which sank its claws into Birch's shoulders and, lifting him off the ground, sliced into his cheek, cutting all the way through in one swipe, cracking a few of his teeth and nicking his tongue. Another one of the beasts, eager to taste a kill, tackled the first one, which loosened its grip on Birch. Wriggling free, Birch ducked and swaddled back toward Isabella, who was curled up, shivering in the corner, a blur of a girl in the shadows. They'd spared her so far, but one of them—perhaps noticing Birch's course toward her, hopped over Birch and plucked her away, jumping out of the wide hole they'd ripped in the side of the building. Its escape, however, was barred by the entrance of two more creatures.

Nearly an inversion of the winged things, the two who entered were vastly closer to human than their predecessors. They both had human heads, which were set atop black-feathered bodies; their wings were bony and leathery, pock-marked with pustules and veins; and they both wore glasses—dark-lensed aviators. They barged through the raucous ranks of the other bird-men, snatching Isabella from her captor, and headed straight for Birch.

One of them was taller than the other, with reddish eyes that burned through the lenses of his glasses and a distorted face—a ragged, deformed mouth with a cleft that exposed his jagged, hungry teeth. The shorter one followed in tow, slapping Isabella 'til she finally fainted, all the while licking his lips with a slender, forked tongue.

The tall one hoisted up Isabella and threw her out, over the crumbling wall of the tower, down to the ground far below. But she didn't make it far: the winged things, which Birch was now more than comfortable calling *demons*, tore her apart long before she knew where she was headed.

"Remember us?" the tall one asked.

Birch did, though he could scarcely believe what he saw—nor confirm it with a response, as shocked as he was. These were the men from before: from the tall weeds by the beach; from the intersection of Madrid Avenue and Segovia Street. The men who'd followed him, all those years, but who'd never attempted to make their presence known.

They beat Birch mercilessly, until he was barely alive, floating in the dream of an ocean of the wriggling things, the fatty wormlike beasts who bored into his flesh. He dipped in and out of consciousness, sometimes aware of the feeling of movement, of brisk wind against his face and the unpleasant feeling of knives digging into his chest, and sometimes seeing the face of his mother, bruised and beaten; or Greta, scooping faux-meatballs onto his plate; or Isabella, whom he'd so badly failed.

—

He came to, chained at the feet of what he first mistook for a skeleton. It was a man—a rail-thin man who almost disappeared, turning and pacing as he was, robed in sable, face obscured by the shadows of his hood. The two men—who'd beaten him, who'd killed Isabella, who'd followed him for sixteen years—stood in the background, looking mostly normal. Their feathers were gone, and their arms were crossed.

"What—" Birch's voice caught in his throat and transformed into a cough. The air was dry, like a tomb sealed off for many decades, with the dust of bones tumbling through the air after so many moons of solitude. He managed to get it all out: "What do you want from me?"

"You're going to help me find a girl." It was the skeleton speaking. His voice was icy, and it lifted every hair on Birch's neck. "And in return, I'm going to help you."

I don't need your help. Birch thought it, but didn't manage to speak the words before his mouth was stamped shut.

The stranger shoved a wet rag deep into his mouth; it coated Birch's tongue with a zesty flavor, like peppers and lemons. The skeleton man bowed low and backed away, receding into the shadows of the chamber's far wall.

The other two men, his stalkers, stepped forward. Waltzing in opposite directions, they poured out the contents of the red velvet bags they both held, spilling a circle around Birch, until he was girdled by a ring of what looked like lard—thick, chunky, and rancid with the smell of grease.

"Yer lucky," the tall one said. Up close, Birch could hear a yokel accent come through, and could see that his narrow-set, inbred eyes meant he was terribly, hopelessly dumb, a fact which he strived (in vain) to make up for with his brawny physique.

"He's right, you know," the short one said. "Say a prayer, you scrawny thing. Pray that you can take it, pray that you're Touched, and not Taken."

"What are you idiots rambling on about?" It was the stranger again—the skeleton—returned with his hood pushed back to reveal a thinning head of wispy gray hair.

They shouted in unison, "Nothing!"

The stranger moved close, ushering back his underlings. His breath smelled of onion and rot.

"An ancient tome," he said, "tells us of the End Times, brought unto Earth not by the evil of Satan, but by the evil of man. No, it's not the book you're thinking of. This is something else—something altogether baleful." A tight, thin grin spun across the man's face. "It's our belief that every one of us carries a seed of good *and* of evil; they are complementary. You have a germ of both, Birch, but weigh more heavily on the side of evil. Today you'll be Touched, given gifts that will show off your true potential. You'll use these gifts to bring me a girl."

"Why?" Birch managed.

"Why? Because she's the key, of course."

"The key to what?"

"To our whole endeavor."

His cronies cackled maniacally behind him.

The stranger's eyes were an odd gray, tan as sand. Birch felt hot when he stared into them for long, yet he couldn't look away.

"Just relax," the stranger said, lifting his hood back over his head. "I'm putting you under. You'll soon feel heavy, weighed with exhaustion. Don't fight it. Give in to the pull of the drug swimming through you. When you wake up, everything will have changed."

Birch faded, lulled by the soporific they'd stuffed in his mouth, and dreamed only of Isabella. Sweet, innocent Isabella, who died because of him.

CHAPTER XXIII

Jezebel stretched open her punch-drunk eyes and, beckoning her limbs to follow suit, ushered her body back to life, craning her neck and swooshing her hair out of her face to make out the figure of the man whose arms encased her. She disentangled herself from his lap and lifted herself up, still befuddled, over the driver side chair, and plopped into the rear of the car's cabin—*A car! A real car!*—bashing her shoulder against the left passenger side window below her. It had shattered during the car's grating passage across the pavement, and sand now flitted through the cramped space, settling in mounds against the worn gray upholstery of the vehicle. Peering over the archway of space between the two front seats, she wondered about the man's safety. He was breathing, but shallowly, and a generous trail of blood poured from an injury in his chest, spurting out from around the edges of a palm-sized shard of glass, deeply lodged there.

She was compelled to help him, but was equally dumbfounded by her predicament, and confounded by him. He wore a white t-shirt, though that was quickly being dyed garnet by his wound—red spreading like food colorant in water, or like a puff of smoke diffusing through the air, soundlessly, creepingly. The garment's simple construction barely covered up his arms, its sleeves ending in form-fitting loops across the middle of his biceps. Its collar was a no-frills, boring shape, a utilitarian neckline against which his unconscious chin lulled. Altogether, the effect his countenance produced was underwhelming—thin fractures for lips, pasty skin (though this, perhaps, was enhanced by the severity of his blood loss), and common sandy hair, disheveled and unmaintained. A far cry from the attire Jezebel had grown so accustomed to—long hoods and wide sleeves, well-brushed hair, skin aglow, swathed in the ceremonial oils of olive, patchouli, frankincense, vetiver.

Jezebel decided she'd at least tend his wounds before she went on her way. She slipped her robe up over her head and wrapped the fabric firmly, in a white-knuckled grip, around the icicle of glass protruding from the man's sternum. She tugged until—with a sound like a free weight plopping into wet sand—the fragment came flying out. Before the opening in his frame could bud further, she pressed the rough-hewn cloth of her robe against the injury to slow the blood flow. In doing so, she took a moment to close her eyes; she savored the fresh feel of warm sand against her uncovered skin. The only bit of cloth separating her from nudity was the scant undergarment of her slip, which she was required to wear under her robe at all times. In lieu of traditional lingerie, it was modest but efficacious in providing support and contour to her developing curves. Sexuality was not something the Overseer shunned—in fact, he encouraged it—but it was meant to be handled with class. The sheer fabric hung to her bosom by its spindly shoulder straps; its length was modest, capping her legs at mid-thigh.

As the blood congealed to form the beginnings of a scab, the man roused. He looked up at Jezebel with bulging eyes full of fear, as though what he saw in her face was inhuman, an abstruse apparition.

"Who—who the hell are you?" His eyes trailed across her shoulders and locked onto the budding mounds of her breasts, whereupon he settled into a fit of coughs.

"My name's Jezebel. You hit me with your...car." She crossed her arms, jolted by the unexpected energy which emanated from him. It was unlike anything she'd felt at the compound before—it oozed from the pit of his mind and it budded from the mound of his groin.

"Impossible." The man gripped her robe to his chest and craned his head around, rotating it on his stiff neck, recovering from his throaty convulsion. His gaze flitted from the fractured windshield to the passenger side door above them. "We crashed, but you're not injured. I remember—you crashed through the windshield." He pointed toward the cracked glass, at the wide hole Jezebel had

249

created, through which she'd careened to land against his lap, and he rested his gaze on the blanket of sand coating the dashboard. "We're sideways," he said, stating the rather obvious fact as he grew accustomed to his topsy-turvy surroundings.

Lifting her hair away from her brow, she showed him the lingering impact of her blow against the glass. It was a thin line of scuffs, a bit of chaffing and a trail of scabs dancing across the edge of her hairline. Largely, though, she'd already healed—one of the blessings of being Touched, at least for her.

"I'm fine," she said. "But you're not."

He lifted back the robe; his fingers settled against the center of his chest, and he tickled the still-malleable mound of the blood clot forming there.

"Fuck!" he screamed, pounding a closed fist against the ground below him— which was actually the driver side door—and re-covering the wound with her robe.

Jezebel jumped, startled not only by the suddenness of his exultation, but by an upswell of that energy she'd sensed. It surged, as though his fist had been charged with electricity, and for a moment he'd transferred that power through the metal skeleton of the vehicle encasing them. The violence of the outburst swatted her, like an open-palmed slap across her face, and in the wake of its force she felt rejuvenated, as though he'd somehow charged her, too.

He's Touched, she realized.

"We need to get out of here," the man said.

"Okay." She pointed toward the right side of the car, which was facing skyward. It was their best route, considering the front of the car was still embedded in the face of a sand drift, and the driver side was squashed against the ground.

"How the hell—" Squeezing himself up onto his knees, he reached up for the handle of the door above him, shouting through gritted teeth, "It's stuck."

He drew in an angry, rattled breath. Jezebel sensed the energy swelling through his limbs again, gathering into his clamped fists.

"Let me try." Standing, she pressed against the right rear door above her using both of her palms. Straining for a better grip, she stood on the edge of the driver's seat and lifted with all her might, jaws clamped and eyes squeezed shut, stretching through her heels, pushing all the way up through her spine until, with an invisible vibration—the marginal space between her fingertips and the door tingling with energy—the door flew up and off its hinges. It soared through the sky in a tall arc and crashed against the two-lane road, twenty feet away.

Squinting against the vibrancy of the freshly exposed sun—it was the hour before sunset, when the Earth's star seemed to emanate most violently—Jezebel pulled herself up and out of the car. She stuck one of her thin arms back in to offer the man some assistance and noticed the question mark in his eyes. He was shocked, but not that shocked—as though he'd seen this sort of thing before, but he hadn't expected to see it from her.

"How did you—" he started, but cut himself short, opting instead to accept her support and to seek the immediate comfort of escape from their sand-bound tomb. "Never mind."

She hefted him up alongside her.

They surveyed the damage: the front of the overturned car was buried in sand up to the base of the windshield, its hood completely embedded. One of the rear tires had flown off the car and lay atop the crest of the hill, as though it were the crown of their haphazard achievement. The door which Jezebel launched from the car was bent into the shape of a U, and it teetered back and forth in the wind like a miniature see-saw.

"But really, how did you do that?" he asked again, scratching his head. "Who are you?"

Knowing that he knew—at least partially—how she *"did that,"* Jezebel let his questions linger in the air, partly because she wasn't sure how to answer either of them and partly because she wanted to savor the moment. The latter question was one she hadn't really thought about, and the situation demonstrated the possibilities of her response. She was a work-in-progress, standing at the threshold of the rest of her life. If only the man hadn't hit her.

"Like I said, I'm Jezebel." She stuck her hand out, in the way she thought was right. When their hands touched, her spine tingled. "I'll explain later—it looks like we have company."

The color drained from his face as he let go of her hand and spun around, searching for their visitors. When he finally saw them, pulling up in a rusted blue Camaro, his eyes burst into shallow pools of dread. As the car wound its way closer, the threat it offered beat more palpably through its front windshield, where an old woman sat, leaning forward across the dash. Their tires kicked up dust as they pulled up alongside the wreck and parked.

No one moved. All the passengers in the Camaro sat in silence. The old woman, with tanned skin full of creases and eyes full of fire, bowed her head. Her escort, a young man with coral-striped cheeks, placed one palm against her shoulder and followed suit while the three headbanded, ferociously built men who were lined up along the backseat alternately flexed their arms, pushed against the pilled fabric hanging from the roof of the vehicle, and cracked their necks.

Jezebel waited to see if her new friend would make the first move, but the man only stood there stiffly, like someone who's just broken an oath, who's stared into Medusa's eyes and was stone-bound—or spellbound, she couldn't tell which. His chest had already completely healed, which was a good sign that he *could* be as strong as she was—eventually. For the moment, though, she knew she'd have to take matters into her own hands.

She crept back toward the man's overturned car and slipped her arm through the top of the cracked windshield, careful to maneuver through the small space left between sand and glass, straining to close a fist around the robe he had left behind. Withdrawing it, she slipped covertly back to stand alongside the man, and waited to see what would happen next, preparing herself for an attack she hoped wouldn't be necessary.

It was the shaman who emerged first—a deceptively fragile croon who walked with a slump and a sandalwood staff. She was the kind of woman who thought it better to act on instinct; to kill now and ask questions later, with whom Jezebel knew to tread lightly.

"Boy. Orson," the woman said, her throat crackling with age and resentment. "You killed our Askuwheteau."

The man—Orson—replied soundlessly, with a slight unhinging of his jaws. His tongue lolled dumbly across his lower lip, as though he'd just been reminded of something he'd been trying desperately to forget. Perhaps the gravity of his alleged murder had yet to sink in. Jezebel was uncertain about trusting him, especially now that she knew he'd killed a man, but her options were limited and the sense she got from the old woman was worse than the one she got from him.

"What do you want with him?" Jezebel cried out, as the others emerged from the Camaro. The driver, she saw, was uncommonly tall standing beside the squat old woman, whose curved back lessened her height to that of a pubescent girl. The other three were of average-to-short height, but each one had a fine-tuned physique, sculpted to the state of Apollonian perfection. The contours of their muscles were even more pronounced in the amber light of dusk.

Orson gulped audibly, staring back and forth between his predators and Jezebel, his new friend, who was the only thing keeping those lunatics from grabbing and dragging him back to whatever hell he'd escaped from.

Turning toward Jezebel, their leader addressed her: "That's no concern of yours," but, as their eyes locked, the woman's composure cracked. Perhaps sensing—through an unconscious exchange—a bit of the great power Jezebel possessed, the woman abdicated her right to an easy retrieval. She showed a weakness, which Jezebel would shortly exploit. The shaman continued, "He took something dear to us and, for that, he should receive his due recourse. Send him over to us, girl."

There was something familiar about the group. Jezebel could feel the same aberrant energy pulsing off of them as she did from Orson, yet their power was somehow more fiendish, less pure; it was the same feeling she'd get back at the compound from groups of the High Order, when those most prestigious of acolytes would enter or pass her room to deliver her tray of cold lunch, or to communicate the terms of a challenge—and she *especially* felt it when the Overseer was near. There would always be a pulse of energy, of adrenaline, which lasted as long as they were in close proximity; but it would fade as quickly as it had come, as soon as they left. She always got a buzz from those interactions, a little leeching of their powers.

But here was a band of the Touched who very clearly lived outside the walls—and the conventions—of the compound. Nowhere were the customary cream-colored robes; instead, they each wore an almost affable rendition of a textbook native outfit: braided hair, leather boots, beaded tunics. They masqueraded behind stereotypes.

Reminded by their farce of her own near-nakedness, Jezebel slipped her own robe back on. Something about the familiarity of its coarse-wound fabric pressing against her skin, even bloodied as it was, gave her a boost of stamina, a readiness, a jubilance, and produced a potent, opposite effect on the group who challenged them: their stern faces cracked into worried ones; the shaman peered back at her cohorts, nervously leaning against the tall one for support; they whispered quietly to one another.

"You won't be taking him," Jezebel said. It was clear now: they were more than a little astonished by her presence with the man, with Orson. They were afraid—but it was unclear whether it was because of her blood-stained robe or because of the affiliations her outfit prescribed.

They know something about it, she thought. *About the compound, the Order.*

The tall one stepped forward, his hands interlocked and lifted against his chest as he pleaded, "We don't wish to disgrace your Order, nor to sully our relationship with it. If we'd known of your relationship with this one—" He pointed at Orson. "—we would certainly not have involved him in our customs."

Their tone had moved from savage to helpless, at a clip. Something wasn't right.

"Whatever he did," Jezebel said, "is none of our concern." The natives all stared at the Rorschach blot on her clotted, bloody robe. Aiming to weigh the extent of their servility to the Order, Jezebel added, "And if you leave now, I won't need to bring the Overseer in on this."

The five of them gasped and—again leaning close together—conferred at a whisper.

Orson slanted over to Jezebel and muttered, "What's going on? Do you know what you're doing?"

"Yeah," she assured him. "I think so. We'll get out of this one easy, I'm sure...Pretty sure."

He sighed and backed up, leaning against his overturned car, caressing the top of its fractured, sand-embedded hood like a dead pet.

You can handle this, Jezebel convinced herself, cracking her knuckles.

"Go back now, and I won't tell the Overseer what you've done."

At the second mention of his title, the lot of them shivered and, clearly inspired by her threat, even bowed. The shaman herself—who Jezebel knew, from first glance, was not the sort of woman to beg—shimmied closer, on her knees. Tears welled at the corners of her eyes. She bent to lay her face against the sand. When she sat back up, Jezebel had to curb a bout of laughter at what she saw: the old woman's face looked like a crackled, crumbling mummy, encased with granules of grit. She grabbed at the hem of Jezebel's robe and stared up at her.

"I beseech you. I'm no supplicant, but please, don't say a word of this to *him*. I promise we'll never, ever bring common folk into our ring again. As Baal is my witness, we'll keep to ourselves, to the caves and sandy interstices we've carved into the dunes. I pray, let us be."

Baal. Jezebel weighed his name in her mind. He was a Taker—one Jezebel knew quite well. They'd invoked him before, a long time ago—before her time— but found his prowess unmatched to the gifts of the others they'd since discovered—the older ones, whom their patronage supported, whom they exalted. So they'd abandoned Baal like wilted lettuce; they threw him to the curb.

They're defectors, she realized. *Rebels.*

They were a sect who'd deviated from the will of the compound, a group who'd survived the first schism, from the original teachings of the first Overseer. They lived in fear and they lived in cover, hiding from the will of the one from whom Jezebel fled. But they wouldn't get very far under Baal's old, ratty banner. She was happy to send them on their way, to let them continue on their endless quest for power in Baal. If it meant she could still escape, Jezebel would turn a blind eye. She pried the old woman's hands from the hem of her robe and lifted her up by her elbows. Jezebel stared into the shaman's beady, glaucomic eyes, and saw that the woman was priggish; the bitch prided herself on the domain she held over others and lauded the gifts Baal bestowed upon them, like a happy dictator. The woman's down-sloped mouth and lifted brows betrayed the abasement she so desperately aimed to convey with her couched, sobbing words; her half-assed body language gave her up, exposed her as a fraud. The woman feared the Overseer from whom she hid—but in the end, she wasn't so very unlike him.

"Leave now, deserters," Jezebel commanded, not realizing the double-entendre of her mandate.

The old woman patted her eyes, drying whatever sham tears hadn't yet been absorbed by the sand which coated her face, and she ambled back toward their old blue Camaro. She opened the passenger side door and glared over it, staring across the arch of its topmost surface, snarling and knowing how little she could do— nothing against the will of the great, powerful Overseer. Her abettors followed suit, packing back into the car.

As they drove away, Jezebel was left with a lingering feeling of terrible wonder, at the power of the man she'd escaped from. He could command legions, even from afar, even out of sight. The mention of his name was enough to send wizened old shamans into shivers.

Jezebel was frightened by his preeminence, by his potential wrath against her. Should he decide to pursue her, to reel her back into his dastardly clutches, there would be little hope of escape left for her. Yet she was also encouraged; if she'd already made it so far without anyone coming for her, she would at least remain optimistic. Perhaps they'd already dismissed her case as hopeless, and found a new prophetic lamb to torture—to beat into submission, to fulfill their awful plans. Maybe, after all that she'd endured, they would let her be free.

Maybe, but probably not.

"—ou okay? Hello! Jezebel, was it?" Orson waved his hands in front of her face, bringing her back into the immediacy of their predicament—lost in the heart of a desert.

"Yes, that's me. What did you say?"

"I said, are you okay? That was pretty intense, what you did there."

"Yeah." She sucked in a deep gulp of air, holding onto its vital, alimental stuff until she had to let it out. "I'm fine. We should get moving. Sorry to've been so informally introduced. Our handshake got cut a little short..." Jezebel stuck her hand out again, this time anticipating the jolt of his energy, but it was no longer there. In the absence of stress or threat, Orson seemed to be handling his powers well enough, even masking them.

He sized her up and stared at his crusted blood, which had soaked in and hardened at the center of her robe.

"Thanks for your help," he said. "I don't even know what's happening anymore." He bit his lip and appeared genuinely freaked out. For a moment, his energy pulsed again, alighting at the tips of his fingers.

"You know," she said, staring at his hands. "I think I can help you with that, Orson."

"Help me...with what?"

She pointed at his hands, which he lifted toward his face. The last pulse of electric light was fading down from each finger, absorbed to the pit of his palms.

"This…" He choked up a bit, his cheeks burning red, wetness budding across his lower lashes. "It's funny, I've dedicated my life to this. Trying to understand how people can believe in the extraordinary. I never thought I'd actually find out there was something bigger out there—something that so far exceeds our understanding of the way things tick." His head hung low against his chest, and he seemed to finally understand the preternatural wonder of his mostly-healed chest, picking there at the scarred tissue, peeling away the last traces of scab which barely clung there.

"It's hard to believe, but it's real."

He drew in a heavy breath, but expelled it fast, as though it pained him to *need* to breathe. Like a patient at hospital whose condition is terminal, he seemed to have given up.

"What's wrong?" she asked.

"I didn't ask for this."

She touched his shoulder, but he swatted her away.

"It's because of what you did—isn't it?" Jezebel asked. "The old woman mentioned a guy with a crazy name—not that we should talk." She chuckled, hoping he'd enjoy the joke, but he didn't respond to it at all.

Orson walked abruptly away, scuffling down the highway in an easterly direction.

The sun and moon lay at opposite ends of the horizon; the two of them—the satellite and the star—equidistant in the sky, like estranged lovers lamenting their separate woes from far, far away. Jezebel ran to catch up to him.

"We don't have to talk about it, if you don't want to," she said, skipping to keep step with his long strides. A silence hung between them before she added, "I've never had to do that before. To kill someone…"

He stopped walking and turned to face her. "It's not just that. It's the whole thing. I can't shake the feeling that it wasn't even real—like the whole situation was just a crazy dream. What they did was fucked up, and it changed me. I don't want to understand it and I don't want to discuss it."

"Okay," she said, walking in front of Orson to face him. "But it won't just go away. You're Touched now, and you can't ignore it."

"Touched?" His face crinkled into discomfiture. "I drank this awful brew of theirs. It had their blood in it, and mine. I thought it was a poison, and I just—I just woke up, like this."

"What else happened?" Jezebel gripped him by the front of his shoulders, staring at him with intention, encouraging him to say more, to discover how they'd affected Orson's change, how they'd summoned Baal.

"There was a man. They dragged him out and cracked his head open. Inside of his brains, there was this worm, this thing. The shaman went crazy, like a wild animal. She moved so quickly. It was impossible that she could move that way. It was awful." He sobbed, covering his mouth with his palms, mumbling through them, "They killed him."

Jezebel let his shoulders go, uncertain how to handle the situation. Here was a man who could very likely help her, and whom she could help, too, but he was unstable—like a newborn separated from its mother, left to crawl on its own. They would be stronger together than apart, even if he wasn't very firmly anchored, nor acclimatized to his special gifts; he would still be an asset. Besides which, there was that certain level of what she wouldn't call fate—but rather, synchronicity—involved.

Orson said he hadn't chosen his path for himself—at least, he hadn't chosen the outcome of it—just as she hadn't chosen her lot in life. They could work together to utilize their separate gifts to greater effect, and toward a cause that was worthwhile. That, at least, was willful.

There was something cataclysmic, something dire, about her desire to nurture him, to coach and develop him, to bring him into the know—but she ignored that tickle of foreboding, focusing instead on the positive sense she had, that their meeting felt rightly aligned. Like the sun and the moon play their part in the balance of the world—with the cycles of day and night, the rise and the fall of the tide—Jezebel felt the same pull and push from him, simultaneous, contemporaneous, organic, budding. Together, they could affect balance; they could help and heal one another.

She touched his face and, surprisingly, he didn't flinch. For a gesture so tender, coming from someone he didn't really know, Orson melted readily into her soothing hands.

"He was already dead," she said, searching his overwhelmed expression for understanding. Since Jezebel could remember, living at the compound had always meant she was the one learning—constantly growing, never teaching—and so she never had to explain it before; she never had to describe what it meant to be Touched, or to be Taken. She thought hard, back to when she'd first learned about their special gifts. She told Orson, "He was Taken."

"Now you sound as crazy as them." He gripped his hips and gritted his teeth at her. "Taken? By their Baal?"

She craned her head to the top of her neck. "What do you know about that?"

"I studied this stuff, you know. It's kind of my…specialty. Divination, conjuration. Crowley to de Plancey. But I never thought any of it was *real*…"

"Makes sense how you ended up with that crowd, then."

"That's right. I was tipped off to come here by a friend of mine. He said they'd be able to show me something *out of this world*. I thought maybe I'd get high off some ayahuasca and then head home with some new insights on the *'Power of Belief'*…" He was talking more to himself than to Jezebel.

"So you've heard of Baal?"

"Roughly. That name could mean anything, though." His gaze drew inward and off to the left, to nowhere in particular, as he searched his memory for traces of Baal. "Its Hebrew meaning is *master* or *owner*. It's a name that can be used to describe anything from deities to a boss, like the head of a family. But based on where you're headed with this, I'm guessing the object of their worship is the imagined prince of Hell, whose name comes from the same Hebrew Ba'al—but this one's said to be a many-faced liar with three heads: of a crowned prince, a toad, and a cat. And he has the legs of a spider. I played a video game with him in it once." Orson chuckled at this admission, but Jezebel had only heard of video games—and, at the time, hadn't much understood why anyone would waste their time on one.

"You don't seem to believe a word you're saying," Jezebel said. "Yet you saw evidence of Baal's existence with your own eyes."

Orson stared upward for a long moment before he turned back to Jezebel and shook his head.

"Why not?" she asked.

"The thing is, I can't force myself to believe in some omniscient, bearded powerhouse living high up in the sky. I've been through enough to know that there's no one looking out for me. I know that, for sure. Especially now."

"But you've dedicated your life and studies to researching the topic—"

"Indirectly. What fascinates me is *belief*, and its power; how it can completely consume someone, to the point that they might act in ways they wouldn't normally act. It's like self-induced hypnotism, or group psychosis. Cults, pataphysics, the preternatural—it's always allured me because of the fanfare surrounding it. But, what I've mostly learned is this: anything with so much smoke and mirrors usually ends up a bust—just like the Wizard of Oz."

She didn't know the reference. Oz must be somewhere outside the country, or else she'd have heard of this wizard.

"Orson, you don't have to *believe* in the existence of an otherworldly power in order to *know* it's out there, hiding in the little shadowed pockets of our world. Just look at your hands."

His fingertips pulsated at her reminder, buzzing briefly with white light. Turning to hide them from her, he knotted his fists together and, pushing them between his thighs, rubbed out their innate glow, stifling the powers which he still didn't understand.

Jezebel drew closer and touched his shoulder. Her hand rested there peacefully; she felt an anger building up, brimming there against the edge of his will.

"You know what I think?" He turned and gripped her arm, but not in a gesture of kindness. Instead, his grip was filled with resentment, misdirected at the single person who could protect him, who wouldn't manipulate him, nor lock him up. "In order to believe in the existence of a demon like Baal, you have to first believe in God. And I don't believe in God."

His blasphemous words didn't stir her. Not long ago, Jezebel had gone through her own religious crises. The Overseer hadn't been particularly fond of her taking to the tenets of philosophy to feed her quest for meaning in life, especially when she chose thinkers who tended to look less-than-favorably upon religion of any sort. Although her quandary had come at a much younger age than Orson's— no thanks in part to the fact that her whole existence was immersed in the continual questioning of faith, spirituality, good, and evil—it was still no less painful than his. At the end of her inward conferences, she'd decided that belief was less important than openness, and that her will to do good for herself and to others usurped the negative influence her companions pushed onto her. She needed only to bide her time, which she did, and wait for the right moment to escape. And that had brought her there, to where she stood, standing alongside a man almost twice her age who was on the verge of tears—who was hating himself and begrudging the world for the cards it had dealt him.

She could protect him—from being locked up, or from falling into the wrong crowd. If only he'd let her, she could keep him away from the ones who'd use him as a pawn in their heinous plots. They wouldn't hesitate to scrape him dry of his vitals, 'til all that remained was a husk of the man who'd once been called Orson.

"That doesn't matter right now," she said. "I know exactly how you feel, Orson, but you have to stop hating whoever's wronged you in the past. Those people back there won't be bothering you again. So please, for your own good, forget about them. At least for now. Trust me, there are others who would do you greater harm than they would."

He avoided her gaze.

She continued:

"You weren't drawn to this dark world by coincidence. You chose to pursue this road, and it led you here, for better or worse. Deal with that for now, and ask yourself those other questions later, once we're somewhere safe. Maybe I'll even give you my insight, if you care to have it. I've had lots of experience handling these things."

He smiled a little, like a kid who realizes he might not be in *too* much trouble after all.

"You're right. I'll calm down." His clawed grip on her forearm loosened into one less savage, more appreciative.

As he let her go, his fingers caressed her wrists and sent a shiver through her spine. A charge of light shot through him and into her, from hand to elbow to shoulder, like a rocket of bliss aimed straight for her brain.

"What do we do now?" he asked.

"We should get moving," she said, wondering how to explain her predicament, should he ask where she was headed. "That car's not going anywhere. We'll have to walk."

"Wait, wait," he said. "Where will we go? We can't just walk out here—I did that for hours with their warden, and almost died. Besides, how do I know I can trust you?"

Just be honest, she thought. And somewhere, at a deeper level, a reassurance came that wasn't her own.

"Calm down, please," she said. "I'll explain more once we gain our bearings. Do you know where Tucson is?"

"Roughly. I mean, I've never been there, but I could pick it out on a map."

"And do you know where we are, right now?"

"Again, roughly. I know, based on the way the sun's setting, that we're facing eastward, and that I was driving in that direction, too, before you ran out in front of my—"

EAST.

Somehow, she knew that would take them where they needed to go. Whether it was that familiar, distant voice commanding her—perhaps her little friend, the crab, guiding her along—or someone new, another invisible supporter, was hard to tell. But she'd take its word, since she'd already made it so far on presentiment alone.

"Eastward," she cut him off. "Yeah, that feels right."

"Okay, so we'll head east. I was going to the airport before, but I'm not in a rush to get back to New York; to face the wrath of the rental agency and the police, not to mention my classmates' simpering faces when they find out how badly I've fucked up."

Somehow I doubt you'll be seeing them anytime soon, she thought, and asked him, "You've got a lot of angst, you know that?"

"So I've been told."

"Want to talk about it?"

"Not particularly."

"Somehow I'm not surprised." Jezebel patted him on the shoulder. "We should get moving anyway."

The sun had fully set, drowning their world of dull sand dunes in a blanket of cool, in a breath of calm. As the temperature dropped, Jezebel realized how greatly she'd under-appreciated the warmth of the outdoors, of the desert sun, and wished her attire had included something with a bit more cushion from the bite of the night breeze.

"Jezebel?" Orson was struggling to keep pace with her, skipping along in short bursts and then falling far behind.

"Yeah."

"I have about a million questions for you, and I'm largely trying to keep them to myself for now, but you have to understand—this whole mindlessly-wandering-through-the-desert thing is fairly new to me. Don't get me wrong, I'm already starting to get used to it, but I can't help wondering if you even know what the hell you're doing."

She kept walking, leading him on like her own abiding pet, pleased with the servility she'd so quickly affected in him, but not maliciously so.

"Not really," she admitted. "You're right." She listened for the voice in her head again, but nothing was there, just an inkling of self-doubt tempered by the excitement of what was to come, of what might be waiting for them in Tucson, Arizona. "Just trust me for now, okay?"

A long silence.

"I guess I don't have a choice," he said. After another pause, he asked her, "Am I Taken, too? By Baal?"

"No, you're what we call Touched—at least, I think so." She held in a spit of laughter that was about ready to emerge, and challenged his earlier doubts: "But I thought you don't *believe?*"

"I'm a little shellshocked, so I'm not really sure." He pursed his lips and squinted one eye at her in a playful grimace. "Let's put it on the shelf, okay? So, for now I'll agree that I've been Touched by the demon named Baal. Sounds pretty crazy, and not dissimilar from the name of this religious television show from a few decades ago, except instead of demons it was angels—" He stopped abruptly in his path, as if inwardly shocked, or suddenly stricken with the gravity of his conundrum. "Wait, don't tell me there's angels in the world, too?"

"Not that I know of, no." She'd heard talk of them before, but had never seen one herself. With all the fire and brimstone the Overseer kept at, it wasn't very shocking that talk of them was sparse. They were the antithesis of their pursuits—and reputedly lazy, notoriously officious.

"Okay. So, one step at a time. I'm Touched. Tell me what that means, exactly."

"Well, it's always different, depending on who you are and *how* you've been Touched. But think of it this way: the man you saw—who wasn't quite himself, who was Taken—he'd been completely overcome, whereas you only ingested a bit of the Taker, assimilated with its recesses, absorbed some of its power. You're still able to function, independent of the Taker's will, but with a bit of his extraordinary, *um*, talents."

Orson kept walking, but was visibly shaken by the understanding that was budding across his consciousness. Like a man who's received unexpected news at an STD clinic, his face took on a pallor of dread.

"Will I always be like this?" he asked.

"Yes, mostly, but it's not so bad. It might seem terrible right now, but that's just because you killed a man and wrecked a car. There are ways to get past all that, though. And I'll help you. I'll help you learn to control it."

They were just passing a sign, dry and dusty, coated in heaps of grime and speckled with the bullet holes of bored passersby, rednecks practicing their shot. The mile marker informed them that they would hit Flagstaff in a week's worth of walking, at their current pace. Although Jezebel didn't know exactly where Flagstaff was in relation to Tucson, she could vaguely remember it on her map: it was much farther north than they needed to be.

They needed an alternate route, an accelerated path.

"Looks like we're nowhere near where we need to be, huh?" Orson asked.

"I was just thinking the same thing. It's okay, though. I have an idea."

The sun had fully set, and the night was full of stars that were brighter than she'd ever seen. Even when she strained to peek out of the slatted bars of her window coverings at the compound, the bits of light she could pick up paled by comparison. Without the pollution of other lights, the patterns they painted across the black canvas of night looked like fat raindrops speckled over glass.

"Good," Orson said. "I'm getting pretty hungry, are you?"

"Yes, of course I am." In fact, her stomach had been growling for the last half hour.

Her idea would be an easy one to execute, given the right conditions. All but one puzzle piece was missing. She'd prepared herself over the last mile's stretch for what it would entail, imagining how she would utilize her training—and her own set of "special gifts"—to manipulate their trek across the dry state into a more rapid one, a less time-consuming one.

And then it happened. A semi's giant headlights budded into view, like two far-off prehistoric fireflies, growing ever-closer as it sped across the highway toward them. That word she hated so much kept popping back into her mind: *fate*, but she scratched it out and counted their blessings instead—one.

"What I wouldn't give for a giant bowl of peanut butter cereal," Orson said.

"Gross! Is that what you guys eat out here?"

Orson had zoned out, his eyes turned upward, completely absorbed in his daydream of food.

"Wait, *out here*?" he asked, shaken from his fantasy. "What do you mean, *out here*?"

The truck screeched up alongside them, brakes grating. A thin, long-necked man, with a pair of bulging yellow eyes protruding from the deep wells of his raccoonish eye sockets, leaned out toward them. Orson staggered backward, shocked by the sudden appearance of the truck and the interruption of his hungry daydream.

"Questions later. Our chariot awaits," Jezebel said, flourishing dramatically toward the opened passenger side door the driver had flung outward.

"Are you sure about this?" Orson asked.

"All a part of the plan," she reassured him.

The truck driver grinned oafishly down at them with his gummy, toothless smile. It reminded Jezebel of one of the older acolytes at the compound, Robert, who'd always creeped her out, the way he would linger in the shadows at the corners of the halls, grinning at her with salacious ill-will. His was a more primal urge than the Overseer's was toward her. She didn't need to read minds to know what Robert imagined doing with her; even if she'd never done it before, she'd read enough about it to know what he wanted. So she'd envision it in horrific detail, the way he'd enter her—his flabby legs shaking with each thrust. Not the best image to have before being ushered off to sleep. Sometimes she'd even dream of Robert, imagining that he'd broken into her room and was rubbing against her in her sleep, molesting her, but she could never wake up.

"Y'all gettin' in or what?" the driver asked.

"Ladies first," Orson said.

"Quite the gentlemen, aren't you?"

"Self-taught, too."

The two men exchanged a knowing wink, its meaning completely lost to Jezebel. There must be some unspoken, psychic language between the male gender, one that kept outsiders like Jezebel from knowing what they did—a secret code, a subtle movement of the eyebrows.

She climbed in after Orson, struggling to reach the high step-up to enter the cabin of the gargantuan truck. The side of it said:

STOCKYARD SHIPPING

FURNITURE, IMPORTS, & TREASURES

The truck's rims, over two feet in diameter themselves, were painted black and covered up the innards of its 40-inch, soot-covered tires, creating an ambiguous effect of movement, as though the trailer being hauled was suspended by some supernatural means, floating like a giant metal coffin behind the blaring headlights of the tractor conveying it forth, across the midnight roads.

The front of the articulated lorry had enough space for the three of them, but it was cramped nonetheless. Orson was squashed between them, his shoulders drawn upward and inward, close to his body like a scared turtle. He leaned over to Jezebel and whispered something into her ear, but she couldn't hear him over the din of the trucker's blaring radio.

She learned forward, peering across Orson's lap, and said, "Do you mind turning it down?"

"Whassat?" the driver asked.

"I SAID, DO YOU MIND TURNING THE MUSIC DOWN?"

It was a blue-grassy tune, all twang and yodel, harmonica and accordion. The driver seemed to really enjoy it; he bopped his giant, loose-skinned head atop his skinny neck like the bobble head of Betty Boop glued to his dash. Nevertheless, per Jezebel's request, he reached forward and dimmed the music.

"Better?" he asked.

"Yes, thank you," she said, and whispering to Orson: "Now, what did you say?"

Orson leaned close and cupped his hand around her ear, his eyes flicking backward to see if the trucker was listening. "I said, now what?"

She pushed him away, angry at his impatience and embarrassed by his very obvious display of scheming.

"Sir," she said. The trucker turned to face her, his mouth lolled open with his tongue sliding back and forth across his shiny gums, like a slug in a wet jar. "Sir, we're headed for Tucson. Do you think you can take us there?"

"Well, hell." The man chuckled, drawing his elbows up parallel to his hands, at two 'n' ten. "Tha's quite a request, quite a ways outta my way, ma'am. I can take you as far as Phoenix on I-17, but you'll want to swing a ride down highway 10 from there."

Jezebel and Orson stared at one another—he with a look that screamed of thanks and diffidence, she with one of plotting.

"That'll have to do," she said. "Thanks very much."

"Don't even mention it, little lady."

Orson leaned up close to her again, the tip of his nose pressing against her temple as he murmured, "That's good, right? Part of the plan?"

Again, she nodded and shoved him away, but this time more gently. She mouthed the words *Stop It* and turned to stare out her window, drawing up her energies, closing her eyes in focus, readying herself to try it out on a real human for the first time. Jezebel tried not to panic, promising herself it would be fine, that all would work out and end well.

A focal point formed at the pit of her brow, in alignment with the frontal lobe and the pineal gland not far behind it. Both parts of her mind pulsated with choice and consequence, and with the marginal association between this world and theirs: the Takers, the demons—who, unbeknownst to most, lived scattered round the world, invisibly. They were there, waiting, and she looked to them, beseeching their power, to carry it through and to bend the rules of time—just a bit, for only a while.

"I'm Tom," the trucker offered, but his voice was faint, like shouting through water, diffused by the time it reached Jezebel's ears.

She lifted a finger to her lips, blocking out the distraction of his words—and of the sound the sixteen tires sent up while they ground along the road, kicking up pebbles beneath them; and of Orson's touch against her thigh, his nails digging into the skin to snap her out of it.

And then it worked. Like crashing through the frozen surface of a winter lake, the atmosphere of the truck swerved toward nameless territory. There was a pause between the thought of her intention and her willing it to occur. In that frozen place, she felt every tiny hair across her cheeks sizzle and all the subcutaneous nerves across her eyelids, pulsating with feeling.

The driver's mouth was frozen in place, halfway to completing the word *names* in the question, "What's yer names?"

Orson sat beside her, oblivious to the temporal shift that occurred. He waved his hands in front of the driver's face, but the man didn't blink; his lips remained puckered over the sound of the *a* in *names*. Outside, the rest of the world flew by as though nothing at all had changed inside the truck's cabin. Oblivious to its driver's sudden calm, the truck carried on at a normal rate, heading toward Phoenix; and, if Jezebel had done it right, Tom would drive even farther than that, carrying them down to I-10 and then southeast and round to Tucson, where fortunes untold might await them.

"What the—holy shit! What did you do, Jezebel?" Orson was standing up, his butt squished into her face as he tried to pry the driver's hands off the wheel, to shove him over and take control of the gas. "We'll crash!"

Jezebel watched him struggle in vain for a moment and then calmed him with a pat on the top of the skull. "We won't crash," she said. "It's fine. He knows the way to Tucson and he's taking us there. When we get there, he'll drop us off and he'll drive all the way back to Phoenix before he even realizes where he's been. He won't remember us much, if at all—like the vague memory of a bad dream. He'll think he only imagined us."

Orson looked a bit like the old man himself, the way his lips hung agape, his tongue lolling out. Except the expression on Orson's face was less buffoonish and more bewildered.

"Who the hell are you?" he asked.

"I'm Jezebel. You already know that."

"And you're Touched, too? How did you do that?"

"I'm not sure, exactly." She struggled for words to explain it. "It's one of the methods we're taught, but I've already forgotten its name. Anyway, they're mostly all the same. It's sort of like willing something so strongly that it comes to be—it becomes real, it happens."

"Sounds too easy to be true. Do you think I could do that, too?"

"Maybe. It's different for everyone. The Overseer left Baal behind a long time ago, in favor of new Takers."

Orson scratched his head, turning to get a closer look at their frozen, mute concierge, Tom the trucker. He held his ear up close to Tom's mouth, listening for breath, and must have found it. Falling back into Jezebel, Orson screamed, "He's still breathing."

"Well, yeah. You'd prefer that he was dead? We wouldn't get very far like that, would we?" She chuckled inwardly.

"I guess not. So, these other Takers you mentioned are the ones who helped you to do this?"

"In a way. It's hard to explain."

Jezebel idled to a place of meditation, careful to feel out the energy still pulsating (weakly) from Tom, to check that his trance didn't run too deep. When they veered up onto an overpass, or merged lanes, Tom's eyes would unfreeze while he checked his blind spot; they'd move, and then he'd revert back to his mummified state. Like an automaton fulfilling its most basic inbuilt impulses— programmed with only basic motor skills—he maneuvered without emotion.

"Who's the Overseer?" Orson asked. "You seem to respect him a lot. Except, it seems that you've run away from him. Why would you run away from a man you admire?"

She scrunched her eyes closed, wondering how she could possibly explain the Overseer when she didn't even understand him herself. All those years under his supervision, yet she never fully knew him—not in the way a clergyman knows his pastor. But Orson was right, she did respect him. And feared him, a lot.

Orson took to waving his hands again, but this time in front of *her* face.

"What did he do to you, Jezebel?"

"Nothing," she said, her eyes fluttering back open, back to life. "He didn't do a thing. I just couldn't stand it there anymore."

"Where?"

"The compound. All cold stone and gray, fire and brimstone, the end of the world. Blah."

Orson laughed and said, "You're going to have to give me a little more than that if I'm supposed to follow along, blindly."

"Remember the group who changed you?"

"Of course." Orson scrunched his eyebrows together. "They didn't seem to care much for the mention of his name—*er*, his title."

"That's because he's a real bastard. My guess would be the old woman, the shaman—she was a dissenter. She wanted some of that power for herself, and she left, or was banished. Either way, the Overseer doesn't take kindly to those who disagree with him. Hence, I'm seated alongside you."

"Did he do something similar to you? With a—one of those *things*, the worms? To make you Touched?"

"No." Jezebel gnawed at her lip and thought, *Odd that it looked like a worm...*

"Well, how did it happen then, for you?"

"I don't remember. I was sort of born into this."

"What do you mean?"

"I don't remember anything from before the compound. Someone left me there—or brought me there, I don't really know."

Orson's lips parted, and his chest heaved with heavy realization. "So then, this is your first time outside, isn't it?" His pupils were pools of feeling; they opened toward her.

"That's right."

"Well, I'd say you're handling it pretty well."

Jezebel appreciated his empathy, but felt stifled by the sense of caring he exuded. She wasn't used to so much care—undiluted, without ulterior motives— and it riled her a bit, like a dog who's been abused is often skeptical toward new owners.

"Thanks," she said. "I probably have as many questions as you do, but on some pretty dull topics. Like nail polish, movie theaters, sex."

Orson blushed a little. "I'm an open book..." He paused. "Wait—how old are you, anyway?"

"Somewhere around sixteen, I guess."

"You guess?" He laughed. "What are you, like a Jehovah's Witness or something? No birthday celebrations at the compound?"

"None," she murmured. Her heart burned a little, with equal parts embarrassment and resentment toward the man who'd kept her from experiencing so much. "I know my age based on certain rituals, which are only prescribed once a member of our Order has grown past adolescence."

Doing his best to hide a grin from her, Orson covered his mouth and bit his tongue.

Still, she saw it.

"What?" she asked. "Did I say something funny?"

"Oh, nothing. It's just the driver over here. He farted, and it smells pretty bad."

No one at the compound would talk like that. They were neither repulsed nor amused by a bodily function as base as that, yet—judging by Orson's childish giggles—she understood it must be a subject of certain taboo for people outside the compound's walls.

"I'm surprised it worked so well," she said, changing the subject. "I've never done it before, not in real life."

A stern glare from Orson, his head twisting toward her faster than a wind-up spinner, his eyes narrowed into slivers like almonds.

"What the—? You've never—" He stopped himself, turning to focus instead on prying Tom the trucker's solid grip from the wheel.

"Stop it, Orson!"

Prying his fingers off of Tom's, Jezebel did her best to reassure Orson of the efficacy of her work, demonstrating the depth of his trance—and the efficiency of his unconscious maneuvers across the highway—by covering up the trucker's eyes. Tom lifted up a hand, turning the wheel as they veered over a curve in the highway, his eyes not leaving their place of purposeful direction, gazing forward with the stoic depth of a martyr. Jezebel finally removed her hands. With his gaze freed and her palms removed from its pathway, the trucker continued wordlessly along on his silent, mesmeric journey toward Tucson.

"See? It's fine," she said. "Calm down."

"What do you expect me to do when you say you've *never done this?*" Orson huffed, his bottom lip protruding. He crossed his arms together. "Is this how you people work, with trial and error? Experimentation? Not while I'm around, okay? Stick to the shit you know."

Jezebel wondered if she should tell him, and decided transparency with her new friend was the best policy. He'd done nothing that should worry her, and his tender rapport was enough to calm any concerns she had of being found out in his company. They were safe together.

"At the compound," she said, "we're not allowed to practice on other living beings. Not until you've passed a long series of challenges."

"Challenges," Orson repeated the word, sucking in his bottom lip and unfolding his arms. "Challenges. I'm listening."

"They sort of *prep* you for the real thing."

"How?"

"It's difficult to explain—"

"Big surprise there," he interrupted her.

"But I'll try." She smoothed the front of her robe, picking at the blood clot on its center, scratching away little red flakes of Orson. "I don't know exactly how it works, but we have these codes. Certain specific words—"

"Like a spell?"

"Will you let me finish?"

"Sorry…" He pouted facetiously.

She continued:

"We don't call them that, but I guess they're similar, yes. Every challenger is assigned a monitor, who whispers a series of words in your ear, just as you're drifting away. We take a soporific—that's like a sleep-inducing drug—so it doesn't take very long to fall asleep. Then, sometimes in English, sometimes in Latin, sometimes in tongues whose names I don't even know, we're read the words that send us away. To the challenge."

She looked across the space of the cabin to check on Tom again. His unblinking gaze confirmed that they were still on track.

"Then what happens?" Orson asked.

"It's different every time. Sometimes you're flying, fighting winged demons, or other horrific things that aren't even real—figments of the mind. Other times there aren't any beasts, and you're just made to overcome extreme odds. Natural disasters. Pain and dismemberment. Paralysis. Things like that."

"What were some of yours?"

"Most recently—just before I escaped—I was underwater. There was a crab, which might seem trivial to you, but it was somewhat important to me. This crab was so realistic, even though I've never seen one before in my life, and that's sort of key to why I was so bothered by its presence in the challenge. Usually, you wouldn't see something you couldn't otherwise imagine, on your own. Anyway, the crab leads me along—after I've drained the ocean of water at an impulse, mind you—and we come to this strange, deserted building with stairs wrapped around its outer walls. It was painted an awful coral color, and there were so many rooms. Each of them were numbered, and the metal plates that signified the room numbers were reminiscent of the cells in which we lived at the compound." She looked toward Orson, to check that he was still following along.

"I have questions already," he said, his nostrils flaring. "But go on…"

"It was there that the word Tucson was shown to me—sort of."

"Is that it?"

Jezebel ran the top of her tongue across the outer surface of her incisors. They felt gritty, like fuzzy blankets encasing her teeth.

"Yes," she said, "mostly," and thought, *Better not to mention the voice, for now. One step at a time.*

She could hear it again—the voice. Feel it, really, like a lead ball at the back of her skull, heavy and bulky with implication.

"So we're heading to Tucson," Orson said. "On a hunch."

"More or less, yes."

Orson shook his head before the corners of his mouth turned up in what looked like the forced smile of a yearbook photo.

"Well," he said. "For better or worse, we'll go there. I don't know why I trust you, other than because you're maybe the only one who understands what's happening to me. We'll see what we find there." He patted Tom the trucker on the top of his trucker head, saluting the dead air. "To Tucson!"

"Thanks, Orson. I know it sounds crazy, but there's definitely *something* waiting for me there."

She imagined a big-bosomed, apron-wearing mother would be there, sliding open a white picket fence, welcoming Jezebel into her warm arms. Those were the makings of fantasy, and—despite all of Jezebel's best cautions—they occupied the fancy of her lonesome mind.

"Will you know it when you see it?" Orson asked. "What we're meant to find?"

"I think so." She weighed his question heavily and wasn't certain she was telling the truth when she said, "Yes, I'm pretty sure I will."

"That's good."

Things grew quiet for a stretch of some forty-odd miles, until the trucker stirred, as though the enchantment she effected was beginning to wear off—a trickle of movement in his upper lip, his index finger rising a quarter of an inch, resting in place for some few moments, floating for three or four seconds before it fell back to its place against the steering wheel.

Orson looked at her knowingly, with concern that showed through the three parallel lines across his forehead.

"We're almost there," she said. "Don't worry. Why don't you close your eyes for a while? Take a rest."

"Okay. One more question, though—"

Jezebel prepared herself for what it might be—more about the Overseer or more about her abandonment. She wasn't exactly glowing with excitement for either topic. She said, "Shoot."

"Who named you Jezebel? If you just, sort of, grew up in the company of the people at your compound, who decided on a name like that?"

"I'm not sure. Y'know, in her time Jezebel was associated less with whores and harlots than she's come to be nowadays. Even I know what a name like mine means to someone who's unschooled in our ways."

Orson scratched his nose, squinting uncomfortably.

"I don't know," she continued. "It could have been anyone. Could have been the Overseer himself, but I'm really not sure. A long time ago—before I was around—the Order invested a great deal of time in praise of the Taker Baal, which is how your friends back there must have grown acquainted with him, too.

"The queen Jezebel encouraged worship of the deity Baal, as I'm sure you know. Her name even meant, 'Where is the prince?' Even though it's not precisely the same entity as the prince of Hell, to whose cause we once worked, there could be some connection buried there."

Orson's face told her he wasn't quite satisfied, and he rubbed his thighs through the worn, stained covering of his jeans, emitting a loose-lipped trill. But he didn't pry.

"Actually," Jezebel said, "I have a question for *you*." She hesitated. "If it's okay."

"Sure." He smiled. "Shoot."

"Actually, it's one I already hinted at. What's sex like?"

The rush of blood that immediately swelled to Orson's cheeks meant she should be embarrassed talking about it—but she'd been raised in company who never showed signs of modesty, by people who placed personal fulfillment and betterment over the comfort of others.

"Do you really want me to answer that?" Orson leaned back, deep into his seat. Drowned in the shadow of the ill-lit truck, he looked more like a specter than human, as though he could disintegrate at any moment—so great was the extent of his humiliation.

"If you can," she said.

"Oh, I can." Orson licked his lips. "I've had plenty of experience, but I've never tried to describe it. As you said of the ones who are Touched, it's always different. You get a different feeling from everyone you're with, and of course it depends on the *kind* of sex you're having..." For a moment, his embarrassment dissolved, replaced by unrestrained delight at the recollection of so many pleasant encounters. His eyelids swelled and the tint of his complexion took on an even, rosy glow.

Jezebel felt a twinge, a dull throbbing, at the base of her belly and the sudden urge to clamp his mouth shut. She said, "We don't have to talk about it anymore—not if you don't want to."

It was as close to a feeling of chagrin as she'd ever experienced.

"Yeah," Orson said. "Maybe not for a while. I think I'll take your advice and catch some shut-eye."

She was careful to take note of the idioms Orson used, to acclimate herself to the new language of the outside world. *Shut-eye*, she thought, tittering inwardly at the saying. She found it cute.

"No problem," Jezebel said. "I'll wake you when we get there—when we make it to Tucson."

"Thanks."

Although his eyes were closed, she could still feel his wakefulness, like a restless insomniac grinding his teeth, eyes flitting wildly about beneath their lids. She wanted to reach out to him, to ask what was on his mind, but she reminded herself of all that he'd been through, and respected his privacy instead, idling herself by picking at her nails, imagining which shade of pink she'd paint them first—bubblegum, cherry blossom, rose cupcake, or the soft and fleshy pink of a kitten's wet rhinarium.

"Jezebel," Orson moaned, with his eyes still closed.

"Yeah? I'm here." She almost grabbed his hand; wanted to squeeze him tight, to juice all the kindliness right out of him, to delight in its warm, fuzzy, comforting glow.

"I don't feel guilty. About killing the warden." He opened his eyes a sliver, and the vacant gaze he projected toward her was enough to suck all the gumdrop-and-lollipop sweetness she'd been feeling right back out. It was the look of an unfeeling reprobate, brows drawn into a harsh-slanted V. "Shouldn't I feel bad?"

Jezebel felt a tightening along her abdomen, a looming wariness across her spine. She said, "I guess that's relative, Orson. They did some pretty awful things to you. I think guilt is personal, and intuitive."

His eyes slid shut again, and he curled his neck upward to reveal the slope of his scraggly chin.

"Is this normal?" he asked. "Being so cold? Does it come with the territory of being Touched?"

She weighed his question with as much care as a baker does his proportions, careful not to disrupt or destroy the balance of the mix. In the same way, she knew how delicate Orson's equanimity was, and factored that into her response.

"Maybe," she said. "Why don't you just rest?"

"Okay." It came out as a breathy whisper.

Strained and exhausted, Orson passed into sleep and—left alone to wonder about the heartless statement he'd just made—Jezebel decided then that she would distance herself from him, at least for a while. She would treat him with respect, and help him to hone and control his gifts, but would also not hesitate to sever all ties, if it suddenly became necessary to do so. Without a moment's hesitation, she knew she could send him off, knock him out, carve out a chunk of time in which she might escape, unbeknownst to him. As tempting as it was to let go and connect, to bond over their shared questions—to be in the company of someone from outside the compound, to open herself up to him—she would remember to always treat their relationship with a speculative mind, and to look out for signs of declining mental health or instability in him, little red flags like the one he'd just raised.

He sounds like the Overseer, she realized. *Guiltless.*

While Orson slept soundlessly beside her, Jezebel drifted into her own moony, waking state of distress. Addled by the questions he'd raised—about her upbringing and lineage, about the Overseer and his dreadful prowess—and stirred by the promise of things yet to come, of sex and manicures and peanut butter cereal, she struggled to find a spot of inward comfort. Just as Orson struggled to get a firm grasp on his new place in the strange world of the Touched and Taken, she had a hard time finding any stable footing upon which to stand. Out in the real world, there were miles of distractions, and she'd only gotten a taste of them so far.

The car crash, the shaman, the truck and its driver. And, of course, Orson. As far as Knights-In-Shining-Armor went, he'd failed to stack up. If this was what the rest of the people outside were like, she'd have a hard time finding solace in their company. Orson was reckless, self-absorbed, and damaged. Though she didn't know what ate at him, she could feel the pain of prior hurts, and knew that inner pollution would get in the way of fully realizing his potential.

Drawing her faculties inward once more, she nestled herself in a cocoon of peace, of quiet and solitude, drowning out the growl of the semi's trek across the midnight highway. There, in the perfect pit of blackness at the center of her mind, she drew a picture of what she wanted:

A quiet life, a home, a family.

Half-way there, she thought. Freed from the cave of her dwellings at the compound, and from the paralyzing grip of the Overseer, yet she still felt she had a million miles to run before she realized her dreams.

All there was to go on was Tucson—dry, dusty Tucson, a place she'd never even dreamt of, 'til the ornery crab had carved its name into the imaginary carpet of her mind. In a way, she felt she was still floating along, coasting through another challenge, haplessly and without concern for what might occur if she failed in her waking endeavor. It didn't quite feel real, not yet. The gravity of her situation had not quite sunk in, and she consoled herself against the most dire of her cares by ignoring the threats slowly rising alongside her—Orson's recklessness, rebellious as a teenager in his new shoes, and the threadbare glimmer of power she struggled to project. It all felt different—more difficult—in reality. It was altogether burdensome to cast her mental prowess across the wide, open world, like a fisherman's net cast over a miles-long school of fish—whether he succeeds in dragging back his catch or losing it against the forceful pull of the fish, his ambitions remain unmatched by his profits.

Although the voice guiding her hadn't spoken in a while, she felt its calming reemergence in the form of a soft caress, as though a pair of fine-fingered, slender hands coaxed her out of her cocoon of indrawn ignorance and back into the real, cramped seat of the truck. They were uncalloused, clear, painterly hands. They told her to get a grip, to stay alert, and to realize the miracle of those unforeseen proceedings.

Wide awake and ready for whatever came next, she checked on Orson, whose upper lip quavered in his sleep like the tremor of a slight earthquake, infinitesimal enough as to go unnoticed by those used to such things. The driver, Tom, carried on, astute as ever, driving without thought or care across the night.

Just as the sun peeked over the horizon, a mile marker declared:

TUCSON—34 MILES

As they drew near The Old Pueblo—Tucson, Arizona—enchantment and speculation suffused their way through Jezebel. As though those invisible hands had gotten their hold upon great chunks of her hair and were pulling her closer, dragging her by the crown of her head, beckoning her near.

CHAPTER XXIV

Birch dangled by a thread, between consciousness and dream. All the sulfurous explosions and maniacal shouts, which the stranger effected in his invocations, were drowned out by the drug Birch had been given. But the pain—oh, the pain still endured, biting through the veil of the sedative and sticking into him like barbed wires, dragging at his skin.

Too, there was the voice, telling him:

REST.

BE AT PEACE.

LET ME IN.

So he did, and felt with great accuracy the rending of his back, the tearing open and reconfiguration of his skeletal system to make way for an evolution, for the emergence of a chthonic addendum to his deepest being—a scrambling of his heredity, a deprogramming of his DNA. The pain was unbearable. He collapsed into boundless dark.

When he awakened, after an unknowable stretch of time, it was to bright, welcome warmth: filling his vision and tingling across his skin. Shouting, too, helped part the curtains of his slumber—the shouting of a massive crowd, screaming:

"BRING HIM OUT!"

"SHOW HIM TO US!"

He was raised on display, at center stage in the middle of a sandy courtyard, surrounded by a mass of people robed in a fashion similar to the stranger—the skeleton. There were some among them who exhibited gross aberrations from normal human physiognomy—a flattened nose, without any nostrils; a gargantuan man whose thin limbs contrasted against the huge trunk of his body—though mostly they all looked normal, their hungry heads hovering at the borders of their hoods.

The exception was the row of thrashing, blood-soaked men who were chained-up naked along one of the courtyard's enclosing walls, tied to metal stakes which shot up from the sand. They had lost all trace of normalcy, of courtesy and decorum; they were just like the man on the beach, and all the others Birch had seen dying on the bay.

"Behold—" It was the voice of the stranger, somewhere behind him, but Birch couldn't turn his head to look; he was bound up tightly with rope. "Behold, the Touch of Andras!" The stranger approached with a leather scabbard lifted high above him.

The crowd shouted again, their fists raised high:

"PRAISE THE OVERSEER! PRAISE ANDRAS!"

Only one of them was unaffected. A woman, her hood dropped back to reveal her long, curly hair—brown with jarring streaks of gray—and the aspect of her face: a full mouth, even for her age, and a graceful, soft skin marred by pink scars running all around her cheek and neck. Her left eat was malformed, the lobe sheared off.

The stranger—the Overseer, it seemed—spoke again, this time addressing Birch:

"You have been Touched, a blessing few are lucky enough to receive, especially one as unlearned to our ways as you. What have you to say of your gifts?"

Birch strained to clear his throat, spitting a gob of chunky green mucous far off the stage, into the sand before the attendants. He whispered, still choking against the cord cutting into his throat, "Fu—*fuck you*…"

The crowd gasped, shouting at their arbiter, "KILL HIM!" and "SLICE HIM OPEN!"

The Overseer shooed the crowd, his hands lifted up where Birch could make out every purple liver spot and yellow, pointed nail. His left hand still gripped the black sheath, whose throat and chape were embellished with ornate silver, swirling with the letters of a foreign tongue.

"Quiet, friends. His body is still seething with mortal poison, but he'll soon come to his senses." The Overseer looked down at Birch and unsheathed the blade, its honed edge glinting with sun and suffering. "Isn't that right?"

When the Overseer held the tip of the blade tight against Birch's throat, the woman—whose disaffection had already been so apparent—raised a delicate hand to her mouth and almost dashed forward, but she caught herself in a grip around her stomach and, hunched over, held her tongue.

"The boy will bring us back the girl!" the Overseer shouted. He slid the blade under the tight-cinched ropes that bound Birch.

With an audible snap, Birch was freed. He flexed his arms and back, surveyed his body for missing pieces and found none. Instead, he found a couple of *extra* bits: a pair of pinions, feathered and all, which he scarcely needed to think about before they took up a pulse behind him, fiercely beating out the cadence of his rage. His back felt stronger—less hunched than before—but so did the rest of him; he was imbued with a frenetic strength, amped up and irked.

The Overseer smiled, watching as his creation juggled with its newfound potential.

Birch made to fly, to flee from the courtyard, but the Overseer gripped his wrist. The feel of that cold, dry skin melted all of his will to take flight, crushed all his strength.

"If you want to go on living, you'll bring us back the girl."

"What girl?" Birch asked.

"Jezebel." He said it with a hiss on the *z*, his festering tongue hanging off the tip of his top incisors for far too long as he drew out the sound of her name. Though he'd barely whispered it, the buzz of the crowd died down, and those standing near to the wavy-haired woman backed away, leaving her on display, fully exposed.

Birch turned to face her; so did the Overseer.

"Go," the Overseer said. "Fly to her, and use this bitch as your guide. I'm certain she'll bring you to Jezebel. She and the girl have a *special* kind of bond." He pushed Birch off the stage.

The woman moved toward Birch, her gentle hands helping to lift him back up to his feet. She directed him through the crowd, robes parting to make way—mouths gaping with execration, tongues lolling at the edge of curses, though no one touched them nor shouted their anathemas.

"Can you try to fly?" the woman whispered into his ear.

Birch's wings tingled with the suggestion of flight, recommencing their repeating pattern 'til his feet raised off the ground. Gripping the scarred, gentle woman in his arms, they lifted off and arced over the high walls and battlements of the enclosure, over a smattering of dried-up trees surrounding the compound and then into the drylands, the endless rippling sea of sand.

It was impossible to hear the woman over the roar of the wind, but she pointed out directions as best she could, nodding her head and aiming imploringly this way, then in that, then over again and back. They seemed to wander for hours, yet Birch's body never grew weak—nor did his latest apparatuses, appendages, or whatever he should call them: his wings. Ceaselessly, they beat, carrying him and the woman over wave after wave, dune after endless dune of the granular ridges below them.

At last, she pointed with greater urgency, toward a distant outcropping of rock which rose sharply before them. Like the head of a titan, it advanced: a lone and lofty stone bluff, whose sharp ascent afforded a welcome curtain of shadow as they flew beneath it. They alighted at the mouth of a cave, carved almost invisibly into the side of the cliff, and both immediately lay down to rest—to revel in the luxury of freedom, of the cool shadows blanketing them, and in the quiet of the desolate landscape.

There, at the lip of the entrance to the cavern, Birch closed his eyes and swooned, exhausted, drifting off to sleep—dreamless, deep, and much needed sleep.

The smell of meat roused him. The woman was cooking something, the twinkle of her humble fire exaggerating the aspect of the cave in which they sat, lighting up its hollow interior with frantic shadows. It was a bird she was roasting, defeathered and decapitated, its slight body skewered through with a stick. The aroma made Birch's mouth water.

"You're awake," she said.

Birch moved close to the fire and sat alongside the woman, on the uncomfortably bumpy surface of a rock she must have dragged there.

"Yes," he said, his eyes straining, adjusting in the dim light. It was settling into dusk outside, and bringing along a chill wind which yelled through the mouth of the cave.

"I'm Meredith," she said. They shook hands. "You must have a million questions."

"I'm Birch—"

"I know who you are." With one wandering finger, she unconsciously traced the shape of the scars running along her neck, chin, and cheek.

"How?"

"I make it my business to know everything *he* knows, or as much as I possibly can."

"You're against him." Birch's statement was basic, almost childlike, perhaps because he was still rousing from his rest.

"Yes," she said, lifting the bird off the fire and sliding it off the stick with a single tug. She brushed off a nearby, flattened stone and set it down to cool. "He took something from me. Something very important to me."

Birch wondered momentarily if this wasn't just the latest circle of his life in hell—some fresh torture for him to endure, another game to make him slowly go insane. Still, he was curious what she meant and asked her: "What did he take?"

"My daughter. The *girl* he's hectored you into bringing back. Jezebel."

"I don't understand any of this." Birch lifted up a bothered hand; his head was still reeling with the changes he'd so recently undergone.

Meredith tore off both the bird's wings—a gesture which made Birch cringe, his pinions fluttering with dismay—and dug her fingers into the breast of the animal, tearing away the skin to expose its teeny chest muscles. She delicately pulled off the flesh, and lifted up a chunk in offering: "Want some?"

Despite his inward disgust at the savagery she displayed, Birch couldn't say no to her present, and sucked down the meat in a flash.

"He took something from me, too," Birch said, between bites. "At least, I think he did. Things are just beginning to make sense—things I've always wanted to know about—but now I'm not so sure I want the answers."

"What do you mean?" She cast the remnants of their meal into the fire.

"My mother abandoned me when I was young. I barely remember her at all, except that I know we lived somewhere surrounded by sand, and with a man who abused her."

"I knew it," Meredith said, at once thrilled by her foresight and disheartened—half-smiling, yet the corners of her eyes cast down with sadness.

"Knew what?"

"You're his son. The Overseer's."

"No way. There's no way that's my father." Still, the odds were growing in favor of Meredith's declaration. Revulsion coursed through Birch; he was on the verge of puking. "Okay, maybe. You said you knew, but how?"

"Don't worry, you must have gotten the looks of your mother. It's the eyes, though—you have those piercing, hollow gray eyes, though yours have a bit more feeling."

"It's funny," Birch said. "My aunt used to always say I had my mother's eyes. Do you think she's still there?"

"Who? Your mother?" Meredith grew quiet, considering her response carefully before she continued, "I don't know. It's possible, but I doubt it. Women enter and leave his life with the seasons—I should know."

"You were with him, too?"

"Yes." She lowered her face, ashamed.

"Then that means—"

"Yes, Jezebel's his daughter." Her shame transformed to urgency, her eyes lighting up. "But she doesn't know. She can't know."

"I understand." Birch's mouth was a straight line. He felt as though he might implode. "Wait, then that means—"

"Yes, you're related; you and Jezebel are half-siblings." She smiled for a moment, but the hint of satisfaction quickly dissolved and was replaced again with dread.

"Wow…" For his entire life, he'd never known his family—besides Greta—and now, in the span of an hour, he'd discovered that his father was a plodding doomsdayer and his sister was a fugitive of their Order. Still, for as desperate as he felt at those revelations, he could also see that Meredith was going through it. Her mouth was quivering, on the verge of outburst. He asked, "Is there something else?"

"No." Her chest rose and fell sharply with her breath. "No, it's just—I've lived the majority of my life with lies."

"It's never too late to change." Birch remembered Isabella, and wondered if what he said wasn't completely wrong. Sometimes, it was too late—irrevocably so. "At least she had *you* all this time. Jezebel doesn't need to know who her father is, especially not if he'd cause her harm. Maybe there's something we can do to settle this, so that you and your daughter don't have to live in fear—"

"No!" she interrupted. "That's not possible..."

"Why not?"

Meredith didn't respond, yet Birch felt he knew the answer to her question anyway. The Overseer would never allow it.

Neither of them said anything for a while. Meredith rose and drifted away, following the light of the moon outside and settling into a crouched position—gazing at the stars, her legs dangling over the bluff below her.

Birch approached, folding his wings up behind him, drawing them as near to his body as he could. In this way, they were barely there.

"You can tell me whatever you want," he said, placing his hand gently upon her back. "I know we only just met, but I can already tell you're not like them. Unless you're a world-class liar—" He realized what he said was wrong, and immediately stamped his mouth shut. "I'm sorry..."

"It's okay." She rotated to face him. "I'm tired of lying. Maybe it's time I finally told someone the truth."

"Might as well be me," he offered, smiling. "I'm a pretty good listener."

"I'll bet you are. So was he..."

It felt like a jab, but Birch knew she hadn't meant it as one. He said, "Why don't you start with how it all began, how you got mixed up with him—the Overseer?"

My father, he thought.

"Okay." She dusted off her thighs, which were folded up beneath her chin, and wrapped her arms around her shins. She looked like a scared little girl. She continued, "I was married to a good man—a man named Peter. We met in college. Things were fine, except I always felt I deserved more—that I should be off having adventures, living full of excitement and, I don't know, chasing thrills. I know that must sound trivial, but it's how I felt.

"So I went to a friend's party—she was rich, worked as an art dealer, and had this giant house up in the mountains where we lived, in Arizona. He was there—the Overseer. He told me his name was Luke. He was just as ugly then as he is today, but there was something about him that attracted me. He was smart, he had an accent, and he'd been all over the world. When he looks at you, there's this kind of intensity that sticks with you. At the time, I thought it was charm. Now I know it was just another one of his tricks."

She paused, checking to see if Birch was still listening. He nodded, urging her on.

"I don't know how it goes for the other women he ensnares, but my entrapment came pretty quick. He swept me off my feet—so to speak. Took me out, buttered me up. All the while, I lied to my husband about where I was going and what I was doing—said I was out seeing movies with friends, or having dinner, girls' nights, something.

"The first time we slept together, it was fairly normal. The only thing that stood out to me as odd was how I woke up feeling groggy, and I hadn't even had that much to drink—maybe a few glasses of wine."

Birch was a little embarrassed at this, but he did his best to mask it.

She picked up on it.

"Sorry," she said. "I know this must seem like too much information, but it's important to what happened next. You see, things got progressively hazy from there. I'd wake up in motel rooms by myself, feeling as though I'd been beaten up, but I'd have no visible bruises. There's no way to know for sure, but I'm almost certain he was performing some enchantment, to numb my mind against whatever tortures he put me through." She stopped to collect her thoughts and seemed to remember something. "Speaking of tortures, are *you* okay?"

"Huh?" Birch nodded. "Yeah, I'm fine."

"Are you sure? You're adjusting surprisingly well to the whole sprouting wings thing. Not to mention the sinister plots and missing girls."

Birch supposed he *was* adapting unusually well, but he hadn't much thought of it. It was just another notch on his belt, another odd circumstance he'd have to wiggle his way through.

"Don't worry," he said, "I'll be fine. I guess you could say I've dealt with it all before."

She eyed him suspiciously. "Okay. Should I go on?"

He nodded.

"All right. I got pregnant. So, as you can imagine, I was in a pretty sticky situation. At the time, I wasn't even sure it was his—the Overseer's. I thought it might have been my husband's, but I still felt obligated to tell Peter about what I'd done, even though I knew he wouldn't take it well; I didn't expect to be treated with kindness. So I told him about the affair I was having and let him deal with it as he saw fit.

"We stuck together, but it wasn't easy. We did our best to move on with our lives together, but things weren't the same after that. It's easy looking back to pass the blame, to discredit my indiscretions to mortal weakness, to paint a picture of myself as a victim to the whims of that sadistic fuck—" Spittle flew from her mouth at that, and she stopped to get her bearings, to ground herself once more. "I couldn't have known back then what the Overseer had done, or what it would mean for the rest of my life, and hers."

Meredith started to cry, wailing through the catharsis she underwent.

"It's okay," Birch said, doing his best to console her. Something about her story touched him—perhaps because it was his half-sister whom Meredith spoke of, and because they shared so much in common, such extreme loss. In spite of himself, he teared up too.

"Sorry," she said, wiping her nose clean, rubbing the snot on her robe and letting her hand linger there, staring reproachfully at her own chest.

"That's a lot to hold in," Birch said. "I'm surprised you've kept it to yourself for so long."

"There was no one else to tell. My only family left is my mother, and she pretty much disowned me when she found out what I'd done."

"My mother was disowned by her family, too."

"I wonder if I ever met her," Meredith said. "If she stayed on, living at the compound." She stared back up at the stars. With tears coating her scars, they almost disappeared, revealing a younger woman, perhaps the woman she described of years long past. "I don't think many of the others liaisoned with him outside the walls, like I did. In fact, I don't believe many of the people living there know he leaves at all, nor how much sway he has outside the compound."

Birch remembered the tall and short men, hiding in the brush by the boardwalk and creeping by the intersection near Aunt Greta's house. He said, "I believe it. I'm pretty certain he had me followed, for years."

"It's more than possible." She nodded. "I don't doubt it for a second. He'd have taken a vested interest in you, especially if your mother betrayed him."

"I wonder why he didn't come for me sooner."

"Perhaps it wasn't the right time. Aren't you glad you got to live your life, before you had to deal with all this craziness?"

He shrugged.

"Still," Meredith said. "If I were you, I'd count my blessings. He doesn't take kindly to dissenters. The only reason he let me go on living was because of Jezebel. That and the fact that I hadn't disobeyed him outright—because I didn't know who he was at the time."

"How did you come to live at the compound? Did he drag you there, like me, once he found out you were pregnant?"

"No, not exactly." She stood up and shook out her legs, rubbing her shoulders against the chill breath of night which had crowded them. "I came willfully."

"What do you mean?"

Meredith wandered back into the cave, gesturing for him to follow. It was only slightly warmer by the fire—the solid rock walls seemed to hold onto the cold.

"What do you mean?" Birch asked again.

"He must have known all along. Much like you, they followed me. His two worst cronies—thugs in suits with greasy hair and dark sunglasses—"

peeking out from their tinted windows

peeking out from the cover of tall grass

"—stalking me 'til I was good and plump. They waited until the baby was *just* grown enough to take it from me. We were on vacation, my husband and I, and they did something—something to my husband. A demon, a Taker, overtook him—"

the old black man with his bible

DEMONS! he'd said.

"—and I killed him, or whatever shred was left of him. I had no choice. I drove away as fast as I could, but they followed me, ran me off the road. I woke up in a hospital and they'd taken her away."

Birch had already slid most of the puzzle pieces into place and figured out that Meredith's husband was the man he watched die on the boardwalk. And that the same crouched figures, who'd watched him watching the man—whose name he now knew to be Peter—were the same cronies who had followed her, who'd taken Jezebel from her.

"I said I went willfully," Meredith said, "but what choice did I really have? Run back to my mother? Face the consequences of what I'd done to Peter? It might sound cowardly, but I didn't want to rot in jail for something I *had* to do. And I wanted to watch her grow up, to at least be able to see her mature into a woman…"

Birch grasped something he hadn't before: "Wait, you're saying your daughter—Jezebel—she doesn't even know you're her mother?"

Meredith lowered her head shamefully.

"They silenced me," she said. "They left me a letter with instructions. It told me how to get to the compound, how to break free from the rest of society and leave no traces behind. And it forbade me from speaking a word of my story to our daughter. They even chose her name—that horrible, horrible name."

Birch wrestled with whether or not to tell her, to reveal the truth of what he'd seen—to reveal the additional link they shared, back on the beach where the Taker had first entered Peter—but she interrupted his thoughts.

"—I watched her grow up for years, wondering if I'd done the right thing, thinking that maybe I'd have been better off behind bars. I waited for the right moment to turn the tides, to sneak her clues about the outside world, about her origin. The link we share—a kind of extra sense—allows me to feed her signals, words, little puffs of meaning."

"You're the one who freed her," Birch realized, smiling. "Bravo!"

"Yes, except now he's brought you into the mix. And Touched you, too." She hugged him suddenly, firmly. "I'm so sorry."

"It's okay," Birch said. He thought, *I'm sorry, too*. "What does he want with her?"

"Jezebel's special; his prize. She was Touched without the direct intervention of a Taker, blessed from birth. They gave her a test, which she might otherwise have died from. Of course, she passed."

"So what does that mean, exactly?"

"It means—at least in the Overseer's mind—that she can be doubly Touched, without being Taken. If he performs the right invocation, she could be his key."

"His key to what?" It all sounded like mumbo-jumbo to Birch, a lot of droll soothsaying that wasn't ever quite clear.

"I'm not entirely sure, to be honest." She swallowed hard. "I know he wants power—more than he already has. He hasn't told the rest of the compound about what he's done—in San Francisco, or elsewhere—about how much he's already accomplished. To him, they're all just pawns in his game, stepping stones along the way to what he craves."

"How do you know about San Francisco?"

"I told you." She smiled. "I make it my business to know."

Meredith stoked the fire while Birch considered her tale, wondering how he'd have handled things, and imagining whether or not he could have done the same—if he'd been thrown in her shoes.

"So what do we do?" he asked.

"I'm tired of lying." Meredith kicked sand over the fire. It sputtered and dwindled, leaving them standing in the dark. "It's time to bring her in, to let her know what's what."

Birch searched blindly through the dark for the stone upon which he'd sat, and settled back against it, waiting to hear her plan.

"It's too late to follow her. She's already too far. I can feel that she's almost there."

"Where?"

"I sent her a message—to go to Tucson, to my mother's."

"I thought you said your mother disowned you."

"Yes, but she'll protect her. She'll be expecting her."

Birch heard her settle down alongside him in the dark, seated at her stone.

"Isn't there some way to catch up?" he asked.

"Maybe," she said. "But something tells me she's almost there. Perhaps I can call her, back to us."

Birch shrugged, though he was certain Meredith couldn't have seen his shoulders move.

"I'm going to tell her to come," Meredith said. "To return to us, here. And then we'll make our stand. Together. It's our only chance."

Even though everything was new to him—wings and demons, Takers and Touched—Birch believed Meredith, and he also knew that somehow he might be able to help them. That he might have been waiting to help them all along, for all his life.

As Meredith reached out for Jezebel—intuiting her, coaxing her, pleading for her to come—Birch lay back and rested his eyes, picturing little Isabella somewhere safe, alive and happy. But that was just a dream, and perhaps the only pleasant one he'd had since the whole mess had begun. While he'd failed to help Isabella, he would not make the same mistake. Not with his own kin—his real flesh and blood.

Jezebel, he thought, weighing her name in his mind. *The sister I never knew.*

CHAPTER XXV

Orson woke up feeling a bit like Goliath had pummeled him hard in the gut—and head, and legs, and sides. They were still in the truck en route for Tucson, unless something had changed since Jezebel granted him permission to rest his head.

Jezebel was wide awake beside him—the bisque glow of sunrise bouncing off her high-domed cheeks—and she looked as though a colossal weight had been suspended over her head. She shifted her hunched gaze, leaning squinty-eyed, back and forth between the passenger side window and the front windshield, struggling to make out their surroundings, or worried they might pass by some crucial detail.

"How much farther?" Orson asked. He patted Tom the trucker on the top of his head, but the bashful fellow didn't respond.

"We're already here," Jezebel said. "I mean, we're technically *in* Tucson already. I'm just trying to figure out..." Her voice trailed off, fading behind the ever-present rumbling of the truck. She stuck her fingertips into her mouth, simultaneously nibbling at the nails of her index and middle fingers.

"Figure out *what*, Jezebel?" Orson asked. It still felt weird calling her that, and he couldn't shake the feeling that he'd been teleported through the silver screen, right into a movie full of larger-than-life characters (the girl with psychic powers, the dead giant, the mysterious cult leader). He shook the fancy and knew—even without a pinch—that this was his life. His real, and wonderfully fucked-up, life.

"How to stop," she said. "And where to."

Jezebel was grasping at straws. She didn't at all seem to understand the gravity of their predicament; she didn't realize how life-threateningly dangerous it was for them to be coasting along I-10 southbound at a generous clip, led by a half-conscious or half-dreaming man, just as commuters flooded the highway like a swarming colony of termites. She looked like a skinny hummingbird, flitting its wings nervously, at a rate too rapid for the common eye to see—except in her case it was her gaze, instead of wings, darting from SUV to sedan to compact, scrutinizing and analyzing every passerby.

"Shit, Jezebel! Just take us anywhere. Ignore what's going on outside your window for a minute and figure out how to stop the goddamn truck." He gritted his teeth and shook her by the shoulders. "Can't you wake him up?"

"Wake who up?" she asked dreamily.

"Tom, the truck driver!" Orson yelled. "Who the fuck else would I mean? Seriously, *get-it-together.*"

"Sorry," she said, pointing at the traffic flying by outside. "They just seem so fast."

"Yes, very fast. But so are we. *And* this truck's huge, so we don't want to crash, do we?" He looked out and saw that the other cars were blazing past them. Apparently she hadn't programmed Tom to drive any faster than 70 miles per hour. "On second thought, can you make him go faster?"

"I thought you wanted to stop?"

"Yes, we want to stop, but not in the middle of the highway. Just pick an exit!"

"I'm not sure how—"

"Yes, I know! You already said that. Just *try*, please…"

Her mouth curled inward, hurt, her lips flattening out into a thin line of misery.

"I'm sorry," he said again. "But we need to get out of here before we have an accident, and before he wakes up."

Jezebel nodded and closed her eyes, tugging at the bunched hem of her robe with both of her white-knuckled fists. Her brow grew clammy, dripping with the strain of her inward focus. As her head tilted over against her right shoulder, Tom's hands rotated the wheel in the same direction, guiding them toward the rightmost lane. They merged across traffic, cars skidding out of the way in a symphony of honks and screams, flipping them off and cursing them. Miraculously, they made it onto an exit lane. Sliding easily off the highway, they settled onto a suburban thoroughfare—an eight-lane mainstay lined with parking lots and strip malls, a middle school, and a whole lot of dirt.

With her eyes still squinted, Jezebel tilted her head to the left. Tom promptly followed suit. They swung onto a winding road named River (but there wasn't one to be seen: only more of the same dirt-crusted, sloping road, fast food restaurants, a budget-minded national retail chain, and the occasional cluster of desert broom).

As they neared a park, Jezebel tilted her head down against the pit of her clavicles, guiding them toward its entrance. They picked up speed—Tom's foot flattening the gas—and shot through the closed iron gates. The truck slowed to a roll, up the main through road, settling just before a small wooden hut. Whoever was meant to man the ticket booth hadn't arrived to work yet, and the parking lot lay vacant.

When Jezebel opened her eyes again, Orson's settled gently closed in an expression of divine peace, relieved that they made it alive.

"I did it!" Jezebel shouted, her mouth curving up into a proud smile.

"Yeah, I'll say. But where are we?"

"Don't know." She kicked the door out and jumped down, covering her face against the light of the rising sun. She stuck her hand back in for Orson and said, "Let's find out."

"What about Tom-boy here?"

Jezebel shrugged, settling a grip on Orson's wrist.

He put up little resistance when she pulled him down from the truck; he was ready to be done with it. They both looked up at the rig, listening to its engine grumbling and admiring Jezebel's handiwork.

"Don't worry," she said. "What's he going to do, call the cops? *They hypnotized me, officer!* That'll go over *real* well."

"I guess you're right," Orson said, and thought, *She doesn't talk like she's been locked up her whole life.*

Jezebel dragged him away from the park entrance (and his thoughts). They started down River Road, walking east, facing the sunrise without another glance back toward the idling truck. Her hand felt soft, unscathed against his calloused palms.

"Now where're we going?" Orson asked.

"That way—" She pointed off toward the deep-sloping Catalinas, in the direction of the foothills. "Feels right to me."

Even though her inkling smelled curiously like crap, Orson followed along, apprehensions in tow, buried under his guise of serenity. Her intuitions hadn't failed them yet, so he'd just have to humor her and bite his tongue. For every possible objection he could raise, there'd be another off-world response. He was getting to understand that Jezebel was more a *feeling* sort of girl than a *thinking* one—not to say that she was dumb, just that she followed her hunches and that they were generally correct. Hell, he'd gotten to where he'd follow her right off the edge of a cliffside, if that's where she decided they should go.

There was something about the way she carried herself—so lightly, so carelessly, in spite of the fact that she'd recently faced such maudlin, comic-bookish adversity—that inspired him. It reminded him of his own adolescence, of days less worrisome: when he'd seen the world as a place full of wonder, not full of dread and death. There'd been drugs, and sex aplenty. They were his escape, his (not-so-guilty) indulgences. They were an ignorance-is-bliss flight from reality, and those few years of his life had been—in a word—paradise. Get high, fuck around—easy breezy. 'Til the debauchery caught up with him and he no longer knew who he was; he no longer recognized his slack-skinned face. There was something about it—burying his dick in any pussy or ass whose form and owner were loose-moraled or drunk enough not to object—that started to drain him, and not just in the euphemistic sense of the word. Like a heavy weight, strapped to his bits and thrown down a dumbwaiter chute, he was lost, falling down an abyssal path of purposeless viscera. All his interests lost their flavor. He mistook his apathy for freedom. There was a great negligence of spirit growing at the center of his heart, like a metastasized, bloated tumor. All that overindulgence hindered his ability to succeed, to interact with other humans in a positive way. He only interfaced with other people for selfish reasons, for gratification. Whereupon that part was done, so was he; he'd gather his jeans against his crotch, move to the stranger's bathroom, slovenly dress, and slip back out the front door. He'd seemingly lost the ability to form meaningful, long-term relationships—platonic or otherwise.

Orson shook his head, breathing in the mountain air—dusty yet cleansing. It evoked a feeling of rootedness, as though he couldn't have been anywhere but standing right there, and with Jezebel. Just as she had her hunches, he had his own inexplicable feeling of *right*-ness, as though every detail of their adventure was perfectly crafted, cut from a cloth of deep and wonderful meaning, just for them.

Perhaps it had just been her questions that brought him back there, to those darker days. After all, he'd blushed for the first time in ages—*she's just so young*—when she asked him about sex. But her naiveté was nothing at all like his blind lechery. Hers was a well-intentioned, if not hapless, exploration—not one sullied with ulterior motives. His deeming it otherwise only vitiated the purity of her plight.

She didn't flinch when she asked me, either. Totally unrepentant.

And why should she be anything else? It wasn't as though she'd been *hitting* on him.

Was she? he wondered. *Get a grip, Orson.*

She was just trying to help him—to unlock the mystery of what the shaman had done to him.

They rounded another bend of River Road, the mountains rising ever-higher above them—looking like a utopian Bob Ross painting, all spectral clouds lilting over mountain peaks—and approached the entrance to a run-of-the-mill, suburban community. Its name was proudly emblazoned across a high-arched wooden sign:

FERN VALLEY FOOTHILLS

It was a one-lane entrance, matched by a one-lane exit (the two were bisected by a sliver of dried-up, dying grass and a cluster of agave). Row upon row of hard-paved street opened up before them. They moved onto the sidewalk, riddled with cracks, lined with brown grass. A variety of succulents framed the walkways leading to the redundantly Pueblo-inspired homes, built there in morose rows. From house to house, it was largely the same motif: adobe-style exterior painted in ruddy earth tones, stuccoed walls with rounded corners, and wood beams projecting here and there from the sides of the houses—and serving no apparent structural purpose. Most of the homes had American flags waving proudly on their front lawns, as though that sense of patriotism made up in character what the sparse, ill-groomed landscaping lacked. One of the benefits of desert gardening was apparently its lack of upkeep, not outweighed by how goddamn ugly it can start to look: all vomitous greens and excrement browns.

They came upon a house that had beaten all the odds, that stood out against its neighbors—with vibrant pea bushes dotting its well-watered green lawn, like the playing pieces of a checker board, and flowers in full purple bloom. Glowing chincherinchees were interspersed amongst the landscape, painting a basket-weave pattern of yellow and periwinkle. A long driveway, lined with fragrant lemon trees, swirled its way up to a two-car port that was swung wide open to reveal its own ill-lit, sepulchral innards. Terra cotta pots bristled with wild hyacinth and kumquat, standing as guardians on either side of the gaping garage.

The house number was 40.

40 Agave Lane.

Until they reached that dwelling, Jezebel had been treading quietly, leading him along with the quick, purposeful gait of someone from 'round these parts, as though she knew exactly where they were headed, as though she was ready to get home already—to kick her feet up, watch a movie, and snack on some popcorn once they finally made it. But in front of that single-story, well-manicured home, she stopped, jaw slack.

"You okay, Jezebel?" He walked in front of her, blocking her view of the home.

"This is it," she said, gazing straight through him, as though he was comprised of air. "This is where we need to be."

He turned and regarded the idyllic residence, sliding his gaze left and right to compare it to its neighbors—those sorry excuses for homes, shanties masquerading as mansions. The top of 40 Agave Lane was not flattened like the rest; instead, it had a conventional, angled roof. The property had a much wider frontage than its neighbors, and the house had been erected on the crest of the neighborhood's highest hill.

Orson hadn't noticed they'd been walking at an incline, entranced as he'd been with his inward conflict, which was perhaps enhanced by the pervading scent of mesquite—smoky and bewitching, hanging thick in the air.

"Are you sure?" Orson asked.

"Yes, absolutely. That was easy." Her eyes glowed, bursting with urgency. She pushed him out of the way with one hand as she said, "I'm going in."

He nearly tumbled down the hill, back to the main thoroughfare where Tom might still be waiting, having followed them from the park to the 'burbs, ready for their next command.

"Are you coming?" she asked. Her question felt more like an order.

"Are you sure you want me to?"

"What—why? Of course… Why would you even say that?"

Seriously? he wondered. He considered mentioning her brush-off, how she had bounded right past him, but ended up deciding it wasn't worth discussion; she was still just a kid. He followed her to the front door.

Jezebel paused at the head of the driveway, staring into the darkness of the garage, completely stunned by the presence of a ramshackle truck, too beat up to drive. Its front end was smashed in and its tires were stripped. Simultaneously wondering why someone—especially someone who could afford such a nice place—would hold onto such a clunker and why Jezebel was so entranced by it, Orson scratched his own raised eyebrow. Tapping her on the shoulder, he asked, "Shall we?" and pointed toward the front door, half-obscured by a giant jojoba bush planted in the ground beside the threshold, at the edge of the lawn.

As the color drained from her face, Jezebel gulped and drew near to him, wrapping one arm inside his. Side by side, they approached the front door, like high school sweethearts entering the streamer-lined doors to their Homecoming dance. Orson looked down at her, waiting for her to knock on one of the windows set in the double doors, but she only shook her head.

He did it instead.

knock knock, subtle and gentle at first.

No response.

KNOCK KNOCK.

The door slid back from its frame and swung inward, revealing the hokishly decorated dwelling within. Oak furniture adorned with various knick-knacks— porcelain cats, praying children. Hand-painted ceramics on every shelf; plates mounted in rows across the tops of every wall like three-dimensional wallpaper trim. Verdigris carpet, mottled and stained, covering every square inch of the floor.

They moved through the foyer, into a narrow hallway that opened into a T shape at its far end. On the left, the living room: more of the green floor coverings, gaudy gold spray-painted frames ensconcing landscape prints, ochre-orange La-Z-Boy recliners with incriminating brown spots across the armrests, and a pair of mimosa-patterned love seats, turned to face a television so old Orson didn't know how to use it. At the other end of the intersection were two closed doors. One—the one on the left—was illuminated from within by an artificial, fluorescent glow. The other door frame—on the right—was dark, unlit.

"I think we should leave," Orson said. "I've got a bad feeling." He felt clammy and agitated. A gastrointestinal disturbance blossomed from the base of his gut, clawing up his throat with a burning sting.

She raised an index finger to her lips—*shhhhhh*—and opened the door on the right.

A bedroom. The curtains were drawn, but the thin light filtering through the centerfolds of the pilled purple window coverings revealed the outline of a modest bed, barely large enough for two, only full-sized at best. It was, however, lavish in decorum, raised high off the ground by a frame whose four-post corners pointed proudly toward the crumbling popcorn ceiling. The bedclothes were a horrendous, vomitous green-and-pink gingham. The walls were wood-paneled. A white, plasticine ceiling fan teetered in place, clanging back and forth with each of its clunky circumvolutions.

The far wall across from the bed was completely covered up by the variously-sized crosses hanging from it—brass, celtic, silver, budded, Canterbury, crucifix, Papal, and Mariner's, to name a few. A chipped, white-painted lowboy dresser sat perfectly centered below them, complete with a matching white-painted stool, its cushion upholstered in the same fabric as the bed's duvet, so whoever lived there could move from sleeping under pink-and-green at night to sitting on pink-and-green in the morning. The seat was pulled out from beneath the dressing table, as though its owner had only just completed her morning-time ritual.

The house reminded him of so many church ladies from his youth, of back when his parents used to dump him off on Sundays, at similarly gaudy homes where he was forced to endure hours-long Bible Studies with kids named Beau or Bo or Bobby-Jo, who smelled like their parents' cigarettes and also faintly of urine. At all the other baptist kids' houses—with their parents hiding hangovers behind concealer and sunglasses—Orson stuck out like a sore thumb. He didn't ululate and prostrate at the mention of Christ, and so they shunned him.

Orson was more interested in getting away from his folks than in fighting against the church trips, so he put up with whatever those slovenly pastors had to say, zoning out as often as he could without their noticing his doodles, his naps. Much of what they preached about started to sound the same, so he figured he wasn't missing much.

One summer they forced him to go to church camp—three long, hard weeks of torture: rowing boats, lifting weights, hours of prayer time. When allowed, the kids took breaks and nibbled on drab sack lunches (ham sandwiches, cheese crackers). Orson liked to slip away by himself on the field trips, especially when they visited churches that had cemeteries (*this is where God lays us to rest*); he'd laugh at the names carved onto the tombstones. He tried his best to enjoy their visits to the zoo (*these are all the animals Noah fit onto his ark, by the grace of God*), or baseball games (*God wanted them to lose, to teach us a lesson about pride and striving*), but the chaperones made it damn hard.

He got pretty good at zoning out the not-so-subliminal messages they forced down all the kids' throats.

Nod and smile.

Could be worse. Could be he had to sit at home and endure the harsher hell of his parents, or the feel of his father's cold hands against his thigh, the budding hate as he turned to look away—and his mother, lying on the sofa, not watching.

But then one day at camp, he met a boy. Isaiah, a kid who smelled like clean laundry and spun sugar, and whose parents were just as unhinged as his own—just as dismissive to the needs of their son. They bonded over their shared hate for all things church- and home-related, and they'd sneak away from the group to look at the lions, or to sit facing each other behind a cluster of the graves. He still remembered the feel of Isaiah staring at him—a sensation akin to dipping his hot, sand-crusted feet in the cold ocean; refreshing, chilling, shock and awe.

One day, without a word, Isaiah reached fearlessly down the front of Orson's pants, tugging on his penis until (alight, aflame, abuzz) it lifted up with pleasure. It was a feeling Orson had never experienced, and it felt right to have it with Isaiah, even though he was a boy.

It wasn't like the other touch—his father's—the one that hurt him and filled him with hate. This one was right, and whoever said otherwise was a *dickshit*.

He reciprocated, and they grew closer with each meeting, bonding over their well-kept secret. None of the chaperones noticed when they were gone—hell, most of them were barely adults, and used church as an excuse to meet good, Christian girls they could brag to their friends about kissing.

Even though a lot of the young men supervising them were probably gay themselves (closeted, and hiding behind the excuse of the modest Christian girls they chased), it didn't change the fact that when one of them found Orson and Isaiah—their mouths just barely touching, lips opened a bit too wide, tongues apprehensively poking out at one another like a pair of snakes raised up in threatening displays—they were both thrown into the back of the field trip van and labeled the world's worst heathens. The boy who found them was Michael, an orange-haired kid with too-full lips and high cheekbones, which made him look effeminate. Michael was often the brunt end of his peers' callous teasing.

Michael told them the pastor would be by to see them.

Orson still remembered the thought he had back then, as his cheeks throbbed with fire and worry: it was a grave concern that the pastor would *tell on them*, that his parents would beat him; or worse, he feared he'd be left with the church group forever—in the cultish hands of those leery-eyed, judgmental people.

Suffice it to say, the pastor hadn't told, and when Orson got home and his mother asked why he was limping, why he was crying, and why he wouldn't open his door, Orson had been dumb enough to believe that he could confide in her. When he told her what happened, what the pastor had done—to Isaiah first, while he stood by watching helplessly; and then to him, in dreadful, agonizing slow-motion—his mother had tightened her lips into a thin line. Then she said, "I didn't raise a faggot," and sent him back to his room.

Orson had thought, *But you married one*, and wanted to punch his mom in the face, to beat her brains in and then his father's, too. Especially his father's.

After that, it had been lots of church houses for him—more than ever before. Women convinced they could cure him, though he wasn't sure curing was what he needed. Besides which, he wasn't even sure he was gay—and if he had been, he wasn't concerned with changing it. Nothing he'd done with Isaiah deserved the torture they put him through.

His father absconded further from his life than even before the news, drinking more heavily and only showing up when punishments were due. Even though he never brought it up with Orson, his actions spoke louder than any words he could have shared. Belts and welts aplenty, Orson quickly grew used to regular beatings, and stopped asking questions like *why*. He quit begging his father to stop beating him, and focused instead on a single unexpected blessing: ever since the pastor had done to him what his father used to, Orson's dad hadn't touched him—not in *that way*.

"Orson!" Jezebel poked the tender flesh beneath his shoulder blade. "Did you hear me?"

"Sorry," he said. "What'd you say?"

"I heard a noise. Over there." She pointed past him, back toward the door of the bedroom they stood in. The light surrounding the door on the opposite end of the hallway was eclipsed by two narrow shadows, casting the aspect of legs.

Jezebel's mouth was smeared with a generous, cakey coating of pink lipstick, and her eyes were encircled with a whorish application of blue-silver eyeshadow which hadn't been there before. She stood under the harsh-glaring light of a multi-bulbed wall sconce, in the bathroom attached to the bedroom. He hadn't even heard her move into the washroom, but she had somehow managed to dabble with creams and cosmetics galore, and had sprayed something that smelled dense and cloying, powdery yet resinous, with the animalic, mossy undertone of moldering dung. It was the distinct, matronly smell of old ladies, and she'd doused herself with it.

"Orson, there's someone in there. In the other room."

The figure moved away, its shadow receding from the sliver of light which escaped under the doorway.

"Not anymore," Orson said.

Jezebel wiped away the lipstick, smearing it with the back of her hand, and quickly screwed all the tinctures and balms back up, sealing them tight. Begrudgingly, she put the bottle of perfume back on its glass riser, a little shelf set alongside the bathroom sink, and came to stand beside him.

"Who do you think it is?" she asked.

Her hand on his shoulder felt nice, a solid grounding in reality.

"I don't know," he whispered, eyeing the far door suspiciously, awaiting the stranger's return. "Probably whoever lives here. Odds are against an intruder. Besides us, of course. Two break-ins on the same day: unlikely."

Orson had begun to notice something unsettling about the home. It had a distinct absence of personage. It wasn't as though the place lacked character—there was plenty of charm built into its compulsive ambience, from the wood paneling, which evoked a Calvin Klein underwear ad circa 1994, to the white cotton doilies hanging off the edges of all the furniture. Even the overdone display of religiosity, the conclave of crosses, added a certain quaint allure, but none of those artifacts gave a hint at who lived there—neither individually nor by the sum of their parts—proudly-hung crucifixes included. Surely there was something more to the woman who made this house her home—more than a collection of painted plates and outdated furniture. Where were the photographs? The souvenirs?

Religion can't define you, he thought. *At least, it shouldn't.*

If anyone knew that to be true, it was Orson. The highly "religious" people he'd known growing up had all held dark secrets. No matter how hard those fanatics tried to hide their demons, they always came out.

Things don't make a person, Orson always said.

When people later asked him how he endured the hell of his home life with a pedophile and a fraud, he answered them simply. He would say, "I didn't have a choice or know any better. So I just lived."

Here was a woman who must have dark secrets, too. Brooding, hellbent ones.

Even Orson, who lived his life mostly clutter-free, had photos of his parents hanging in his bedroom (if not as a souvenir of love, then as a reminder of how much he'd overcome). But here, there was nothing of the sort. His realizing this cast the bedroom in a haunting, spectral light, and sent a trill down his spine. Prickling ticklishly against the inside of his jeans, his leg hairs stood on end.

Before either of them could make a move, the stranger across the hall drew open the door.

"You can come out. I know you're in there," she said, through labored breaths. "Hard not to hear the ruckus you drew, stampeding around in there, likely tracking dirt across my carpets. Treating my things with disrespect. Vandals. If I weren't an ill, old woman I'd draw a knife on you."

Orson pinched Jezebel by the elbow and started to drag her out of the room, but she pulled back and stared across the hallway, rooted to the spot with her eyes bulging. She peered out toward the source of the voice, into a kitchen as hideous as the rest of the house: rotted, unfinished wood cabinetry; brown-and-yellow tiled walls with the odd pepper- or beet-painted accent tile interspersed at random, just for good measure. The floor was done in a very obvious fake-wood laminate which bubbled at the corners of the room and dipped at its center, where the woman sat, with blue-tinted hair spun up into rollers. She pecked at her cup of tea once, and then she stood to greet them.

"She told me you'd come someday," the old bird said, her voice cracking inside her rattled throat. "But I didn't think she meant it."

Whatever anger had just been steeped in the old woman's tone instantly disappeared, replaced instead with a reverent, loving smile which showed off her set of too-straight, gleaming dentures. Her lips were painted up with the same pink lipstick Jezebel had loved, and they receded to meet with her gums against the force of her grin. Chalky, cakey whale blubber rolled into balls at the wells of her mouth's corners, into the folds of her marionette lines.

Jezebel stared back at the woman with her palms outstretched, warding off the insinuation. "Who told you I'd come?"

"You don't know, dear?" There was an icy familiarity in the woman's translucent eyes. "Your mother."

After a pause, Jezebel said, "I don't have a mother. She died a long time ago. Sorry, ma'am, but I don't know you."

The old woman sighed, reaching out to touch the side of Jezebel's face, but her gesture was rebuffed; Jezebel swatted her away. Pursing her lips, the homeowner turned toward her fridge, a hulking archaic thing, and gestured toward it with the puckered point of her mouth. She said, "You dears must be hungry."

Orson touched the pit of his torso, as though he'd forgotten all about food, but at its mention his belly swelled with cravings. Soup, sandwich, steak, chicken, rice, pasta, salad—anything would do. Before he could express his heartfelt gratitude and reply in earnest, Jezebel cut him short, holding him back with the same stern, flat-palmed hand she'd just used to swat away the woman, and she repeated:

"I don't know you, ma'am. And I don't have a mother. You must be mistaking me for someone else."

From behind the opened door of the fridge, the woman replied, "Is that what they told you?" As the cooler swung shut, the woman's kindly (if not lonesome) face came back into view—her hair undulating in place like gelatin atop her made-up head. She held a casserole dish in each hand. One brimmed with fried onion crisps, concealing whatever foodstuffs had been baked beneath those oily golden rings. The other dish was a kind of cake and, though it had just been removed from the chiller, it steamed with freshness, dispersing an aromatic blend of lavender and lemon zest through the air.

Orson was tempted to dive across the table, to grab both platters and gorge himself on them, gulping down every last bite for himself. But a hunch prevented his doing so—somehow vague, yet sharply punctuated through the center of both his temples. It was the opaque sensation of a word—*NO!*—solidified, forming itself into Jezebel's voice, bouncing through his mind like an echo through a cave.

No! Don't trust her.

It was undeniably, impossibly Jezebel, and her statement rendered him immobile, bound to the ground, rooted to the spot.

Let me handle this.

He tried to punctuate a response, to *think* one toward her, but the shock of having another person speaking in his mind prevented his doing so effectively, and he only managed the consonant sound *K*, wobbling dumbly in place while their host's look of concern grew graver by the second.

"Is your friend okay?" the woman asked.

"He's fine." Jezebel stepped between them, blocking out Orson's view of the woman and the woman's view of him.

"Are you sure?" the old woman asked.

"Yes. Now, who do you think I am?"

"Why, you're my granddaughter, of course."

Orson couldn't see the exact reaction that spread across Jezebel's face, but he felt her shifting from lioness to purring cub in a blink. Her hold on him lapsed in the whir of her excitement, at the possibilities the revelation offered.

"I told you, I don't have a mother." This time, it was more question than statement. "So I definitely don't have a grandmother either."

"She told me you'd be confused. That you'd be flustered, starved, and scared. Darling, I don't know where they've kept you all these years, and I'm sorry for whatever it is they've done to you out there, but I'm telling you the truth. I'm your grandmother—your momma's mother."

Jezebel choked on her words, feeling blindly for a solid grip on the edge of the dining table, and slid into a chair. Her head hung low, with her hair draped around her face to hide the consternation forming there. Orson moved to sit beside her, but the woman beat him to the punch, sliding closer to Jezebel and wrapping an arm around her.

"Wh-when did you last see her?" Jezebel asked, her voice muffled by the curtain of her mane and the feeling crackling inside of her throat. "When did you last see my mother? The woman you think is my mother..."

Orson wondered about his own mother, envisioning her at the lap of some man, begging for money.

The old woman spoke:

"Meredith—that's your mother—she's been gone a long while. She brought the truck back here years ago, probably not long after you were born. She was always on the run, tramping it up with some new group of assholes, pardon my French. Sneaking around behind her husband's back. Peter, your father. We never much liked him. He was sort of a simpleton, but at least he was good to your mother—in the sense that he really helped her to settle down, for a while. But in the end, it wasn't enough for Meredith. It never was. Except she was pregnant, with you.

"I noticed when she dropped the truck off how badly it was bashed up, nearly totaled. It was amazing she even made it down to Tucson from wherever she'd been. I haven't been able to start the thing since, but somehow I can't convince myself to trash it either. Anyway, another thing I noticed when she came around was that she wasn't pregnant anymore—mind you, it was far too soon for her to have had you yet. And she was alone. No Peter in sight."

While her grandma spoke, Jezebel's link to Orson held on strong. Every so often, in the middle of her grandma's speech, Orson would catch a snippet of something Jezebel thought or felt. A *bullshit*, or a long, pained *why?*, or sometimes just a dull, throbbing ache.

"That truck outside, in the garage—it's the one she brought to you?" Jezebel asked.

"The very same, yes."

Jezebel's eyes brimmed with knowing, with impossible realization. Orson knew she was starting to believe, and that she felt she'd been drawn there—not by chance, but by the intentional grace of her mother, or her grandmother.

"What did she tell you—when she dropped it off? Besides that I'd come here someday, that I'd find you?"

"She told me your name, and I remember thinking how crazy it was that she could call you that. She promised you were safe, and that she only had you early— that everything went okay in the delivery, and that you were in a good way, fattening up and the like. I asked about Peter, your father, but she locked up at the first mention of his name. She wouldn't say a word about him, about where he was. And then she got all panicky, like a dog hearin' a whistle outside of a human's range, and she told me you'd come here. She said I'd get to meet you someday and that, when you finally did arrive, I should welcome you and shelter you. That I should take care of you like you were my own."

A silence passed between them, a very palpable thing, hanging in the air like an ominous raven—its black, pointed beak aimed straight for Jezebel as it opened a sliver, whispering the single word *but*. The old woman turned away, wiping her teary eyes dry with the back of a cloth napkin. She faced Jezebel again, smiling fearlessly, and patted her granddaughter's rosy cheek.

"But you can't, can you?" Jezebel asked. They stared at each other, neither of them saying a word, not needing to. Jezebel continued, "It's okay. You needn't explain. I know nothing about you—not even your name—and we'll keep it that way. We'll eat your food—thank you for it—and then the two of us will be on our way."

"Jezebel, wait," Orson said, breaking the long silence he'd maintained. He couldn't help feeling that this was her place. Her family, her freedom. A new start. Her home. "Don't be so harsh. She hasn't told us to leave outright."

"No, she's right," the old woman said. "It's better this way. You eat your food, take a rest, and be on your way. I don't want any of the trouble your mother's caught up in following you here. I've got enough problems of my own to handle, and I don't need any of yours sprinkled on top."

Jezebel's eyes were damp and her nostrils flared, but not a single tear mounted the crests of her lower lids. None rolled down her cheek, because that was the ultimatum of her life: keep quiet, hold it in, and move on. Or else. In that way, she and Orson were very different. Whereas he welcomed new hardships for the sense of striving each required, she saw the unknown as another piece of her captors' will against her, planted there to torture her and weaken her to shreds.

Orson stared off, wondering at Jezebel's fatalistic stance. Though prone to histrionics, she wasn't the sort to grow resigned so quickly—especially not when it came to a clue about her lineage.

The far wall of the kitchen was entirely mirrored, save for the doorway set in its center. Orson looked at their reflected figures in the glass, all lined up like a miserable funeral procession, sobbing and disgruntled. The door's window overlooked a comely garden, brimming with six-foot tomato plants and rows of fine lavender, but the plants were untended, overgrown, their leaves mottled and browning.

She's afraid of something, Jezebel's voice interrupted. *They got to her first.*

The *they* she referred to probably meant Jezebel believed that—even there, in her grandmother's kitchen—she hadn't quite escaped the clutches of her Overseer. Not fully, not yet. Orson wondered at the possibilities of what it meant that they'd even made it to Jezebel's grandmother, and so quickly. Part of him expected the woman's eyes to fall out—replaced by hot red coals burning through her skull— and her tongue to split into that of a serpent's, pronged and hiding venomous fangs. But no such thing happened.

They ate their green bean casserole and finished the meal off with thick slices of the savory-sweet lavender-lemon bread. Satiated, full to the point of bursting (he almost drew a comparison to Violet Beauregarde, but doubted very much that his doe-eyed friend had seen, read, or heard of Wonka's magical factory), the two of them settled into the living room, careful to step over three surly, gray-haired cats neither of them had noticed there before. The recliners provided a welcome respite, despite their time-worn, sagging cushions.

Orson locked eyes with Jezebel, forcing all of his concentration into projecting his thoughts her way—*What should we do what should we do what should we do*—but she showed no sign of having received his telepathic message. Perhaps it only worked one way.

"Jezebel," he whispered aloud. "What should we do?"

She ignored his question, fascinated by the fat cats, who were licking their paws greedily, producing a surprisingly loud slurping sound with each pleasured lap.

"Hello?" he pried. "Are you okay?"

"Yes." She continued to stare at the cats, absorbed with their silent prowess, their calm reservedness. "I'm thinking."

He let her be for a while, taking up his own survey of the property, in case they'd missed some crucial detail. But no matter how long he dwelled on any particular corner of the room, its sheer drabness failed to disclose new secrets. Only pilled fabric under thigh, mottled and bubbling wallpaper, dander-covered carpet. There was nothing that would help them unlock an answer to their query— which was quickly losing substance. His blind trust in Jezebel was waning with each moment of their wayward quest.

"We have to find a sign," Jezebel said. "A sign that they were here."

"Okay. How do we do that?"

"I'm going to influence her." She leaned closer, across the gap between their La-Z-Boys, and lowered her voice. "Like I did before, with the trucker. And then we'll search the house, until we find its source."

"Its source?"

"Yeah." She finished her sentence soundlessly, inside his head:

The sign. A sigil. They usually leave behind a mark. We'll find it and destroy it.

"What good will that do?" Orson asked.

Jezebel raised a finger to her lips.

Whatever influence they've exerted over her will dissipate, dissolve away. She'll be safe again.

"Okay, but for how long? These don't seem like the sort of people who give up that easily... They knew you'd come here, and they beat you to the punch. Who's to say they'll give up here, Jezebel?"

Before she could respond, either verbally or psychically, the old woman poked her head around the corner, appearing as a ghost on the threshold, half her face obscured by the darkness of the hall.

"Everything okay in here?" she asked.

"We're fine," Jezebel said, and looked back toward Orson. "Aren't we?"

"Yeah, just fine." A gulp thick with grit slid down his throat. "Thanks very much."

"We'll be on our way soon," Jezebel said. "Out of your hair."

"Good," the old woman replied, patting her own skulltop, and its swirl of blue-gray, at the mention of hair. "I'm sorry you have to be going so soon." She turned to head back to her kitchen, her fortress, but something gave her pause. She leaned against the wall, her sweater-covered back turned to them and her head bowed, her shoulders hunched, as if conflicted between the drudgery of her subjugator and a budding love for her long-lost granddaughter. She turned back toward them, a corner of her face illuminated by the mid-afternoon light streaming through the house's front window. "How exactly *did* you find me, Jezebel?"

Orson had been wondering that himself, but hadn't thought to question it. They'd been pulled along their course, as if led by thin string, or by a magnetic current. Looking for an explanation amidst the extraordinary just didn't seemed proper in Jezebel's company, so he hadn't mentioned it. As long as old woman was asking, he was happy to listen to Jezebel's response.

"I don't know," she said. "But here I am—"

"Hmmm," the old woman mused, but her face shifted suddenly from inquisitive to pained. A throaty clucking began in her throat. She clutched her neck as if choking and clawed at the loose skin there, scratching and drawing thin lines of blood.

Orson rose to his feet, stepping toward her to help, but Jezebel drew him back, shaking her head, wide-eyed. They watched.

The old woman fell to her knees, her nails bending back and snapping off as she dragged them in pain down the wall beside her. Writhing against the ground, she continued to rip at her neck, tearing the skin open at the apex of her upturned chin. Her eyes rolled into the back of her head and her dentures slid free from the adhesive binding them to her gums, plopping wetly against the carpet, alongside her spasming body. In the groove of her neck, a mass of tenebrous shapes emerged. At first, they looked like worms—like the thing Orson had seen shorn from inside the man's skull, back with the shaman, the warden, the Wolf, the Turtle, and all the rest—but her Taker proved elseways. Cartilaginous tubing puckered outward, like plastic pipes bulging up from beneath her skin, growing between the folds of her fat and tissue, hardening into a frill of osseous spikes emerging from the base of her neck and angled upward, pointing toward her face. Those hardened, hollow ducts sprouted fibers like skinny hairs, which spiraled outward from the tunnels of their casings, unfurling into plumes, forming a feathered collar ensconcing her neck. The rest of her frame split open—following the fault line at her neck as it cracked its way farther down her chest—and produced more of the same stuff, rachises and plumage encasing her body in a suit of pinnas, making her into a kind of inverse Horus—her body coated in birdstuff, but her head remaining intact.

As the change continued, her hands transformed next. Those of her nails that were still intact were pushed out; falling away, they were replaced by the curved black talons of a vicious buzzard.

Jezebel moved, swooping in on her mutating kin with all the speed of a falcon. She hovered over her grandmother, hands primed for action, though clawless herself. Her fingers—curled, undulating, able—awaited the best moment for action: the climax of her grandma's change.

It was nothing like the man by the fire. It was something worse, defying the laws of corporeality, stretching her figure into something subhuman, made of mythos, until the woman was no longer a shred of herself. Orson turned to look away, squinting shut his eyes and covering his ears to blot out the savage noise of her wailing. Before he'd turned away, he saw her lips split open, bisected by the emergence of a hard-billed, black and pointy beak protruding from the hollow of her gutted throat.

And then it was over.

The cries abated, squelched by Jezebel's lethal touch. He turned to look again, to see what had transpired, and was revolted by the scene: Jezebel's hands brimmed with gore, murky globules of flesh and feather clinging to her palms; the woman who'd been her grandmother lay pinned beneath Jezebel's weight, her half-changed face split open by the bill and by the wresting of Jezebel's hands. If the woman were an egg, her head was its shell, and the pulp spilt between those two halves of her—what had once been her mind, her insides—was its yolk, splattered all about.

He fought an impulse to vomit, doubling over the recliner, crawling to jam open a window and shoving his face against the insect screen, imbibing the outside air for a glimmer of serenity.

"I had to do it," Jezebel said. "She was changing. She was Taken."

"I can see that—" he started, but before he could finish his statement (it would have ended, *but did you have to do* that?), Jezebel was up and through the hallway, back to the bedroom full of crosses.

She flipped the mattress purposefully over, but peeking through the innards of the frame was difficult. She ushered Orson near, thinking but not saying, *C'mere.* Together they lifted up the bed frame, up onto its side, sliding it over and out of the way, against the far wall. The wall with the crosses, the vanity—her grandmother's place of prayer and peace.

Jezebel returned to the spot at which the bed had lain. She combed the carpet, on all fours.

"What are you doing?" Orson asked.

"I told you, they draw a sigil somewhere near the person—the one to be Taken. It lends power to those who summon, and to the Taker—"

"Why not just call them demons, Jezebel?" The question had been nagging at him from the start. "Isn't that what they are? Looks like a demon, acts like a demon. It's a demon." The whole summoning, sigilization bit was aligned with the folklore, but felt somehow heavy, old, encrusted with cobwebs.

Jezebel stopped her frantic search and, looking up at him like a disappointed professor, she said: "To give them a name grants them power. There's too much stigma around that term, Orson. It's what they are, sure, but in calling them *that* we give them authority, power to defy our will. Sometimes we call them that anyway…"

"Sounds like a load of bullshit. The politics of witchcraft, huh?"

"It's not witchcraft," she said, leering up at him.

"Then what is it?"

"I…" she trailed off, staring into space. "I don't really know. Maybe it is, but I never participated in the more…*lurid* ceremonies. I don't agree with the policies of the Order—the ones involving what you'd call possession; the Taking."

Orson realized then how hard it was for Jezebel to think for herself. She'd been raised and immersed in the propaganda of her community, from birth. Its tenets would not be easy for her to shake.

"Jezebel, listen, I don't think it's there," Orson pleaded. He dragged her away by her elbow, like a pup by its scruff. "Let's try the kitchen again, Jez."

She looked up at him, shocked at the familiar tone he adopted in abridging her name to that—to *Jez*—but not altogether hating it either. At least, she didn't object. It actually made her smile (if only a little, at the corners of her eyes, her lips barely moving, stuck as they were in her focused, frenzied search for the thing she called the sigil).

She followed him back into the kitchen, stopping for a moment before she crossed back over the threshold of the bedroom and into the hall, looking over her shoulder at the space that had once been her grandmother's most private dwelling, at the living quarters of the only family member she'd ever met.

Orson knew how she felt. Although he'd never killed a member of his own family, he'd often thought of doing it, and he might as well have. He'd cursed them to their separate lives—in jail, and on the streets. His father was finally the weakling, in the company of convicts, and his mother was just an unshrouded version of her former self, the pretense stripped away. In some ways, their separation had been as painful as though he'd killed them outright. He'd always felt like a part of him had been cut away when they were gone, and that sensation coalesced into a disembodied, apathetic attitude that later furthered his masochistic drive to fuck and drink and smoke to death.

In the end, Orson was just like his parents—selfish. Except he hadn't been hurting anyone but himself.

Jezebel (now *Jez*) found it—she found the sigil. It was hidden under the table where they'd first met her grandma. Its aspect was complex, and it amazed Orson that someone had drawn it without the now-dead woman noticing their intrusion.

A perfect circle, three feet in diameter (as wide as the length of the square dining table), drawn in shiny, dark ink. Within its circumference, the word *SANDRA* had been written in small, serifed letters. Another smaller circle was traced inside the larger one—only about a quarter foot smaller. It served as the main casing for the symbol drawn within: a complex series of curving lines and dots set upon a perfect triangle, and it separated the word from the rest of the symbol, sandwiched perfectly between the two concentric shapes. The wiry drawing that filled the inmost circle looked quite like an ornate wedding centerpiece, with minute details encased in its body—two small crosses at the crest of the shape, set just within the form of what looked a bit like a candelabra; a capital, serifed I on either end; the bottommost curved lines, which slanted down toward the base of the shape and hooked abruptly back upward, ended in matching pincered points, as of twin devils' tails.

Orson read it aloud, "Sandra," lilting the name, entranced by it. After all, its power—as Jezebel had suggested—was *in* its name.

"No, you're reading it wrong. You start reading here—" She pointed to the A resting at the top of the sigil, centered below the outer circle and above the inner circle. "—not there." She pointed to 10 o'clock, where the S was. "If you read it from the top, moving clockwise, it says the name of the Taker."

"The *demon*," Orson corrected.

"Sure." She shrugged. "Whatever."

"*Andras*," he read, correctly this time, Jezebel nodding beside him. "I know this one. A prince of hell, or a marquis, depending on who you ask. Body of a winged man, oftentimes mistaken for an angel. Head of a black hawk—but it looks more like the head of an owl to me. He carries a sharp-pointed sword that glows brightly, and rides a wolf like a horse; no saddle. His hands and feet are sharpened like razors. And he rules, what is it, forty legions?"

"Thirty," Jezebel corrected. "Close enough. Good to know what we're up against."

"I know this may come as a shock, but I never pictured a possession—a *Taking*, whatever you call it—looking like this. Isn't the demon supposed to just, I don't know, inhabit the body of its victim? Make them float, roll their eyes into the back of their head, speak in a booming, deep voice or something?"

"Sometimes, maybe. I don't know, Orson. I'm learning along with you." She traced the ornate shape at the center of the inner circle with the tip of her index finger, tentatively, delicately.

"Why not just try and kill *you*?" Orson asked. "Why target your grandmother?"

Jezebel raised an eyebrow.

"It just seems a little dramatic," Orson said. "If he really wanted you dead—this Overseer guy—it seems like he'd come here himself."

Jezebel rose to her feet and lumbered back into the hallway. She stared at the half-human corpse resting there, quickly growing cold. A show of emotion overtook Jezebel: the crest of her back curved, her head lowered in a posture of great mourning. She wept heartily and deeply, with great regret and a spittle-spraying, rattled breath.

Orson crept up behind her and scooped an arm around her shoulder, cradling her in the pit of his scrawny chest, doing his best to comfort her. He said, "It seems like he wanted to strike at you, to hurt you, but not to kill you." He listened for a response—a whispered reply cutting through the body-rocking shivers that shot through her core—but she remained silent, dealing with the situation as best as she knew how. He imagined she'd soon move past her lamenting state and into one of action, where the next stage of her contemporaneous plan would be hatched.

"You're right," she said, rubbing her temples irritably.

Orson almost thought he saw them pulsating, as though a creature was lodged there, prying its way out of her flesh.

She continued massaging, swatting away tears, and continued, "That's exactly what he'd do—to try and lure me back. Strike for the heart. He figures, this way I'll see how alone I really am. How lonely the outside world is for me. He thinks I'll say that *they're* my family, back at the compound, but he's wrong. I have no family—never have and never will. But that doesn't mean I'll stoop to his level, or that I'll help them bring these horrors into our world."

These horrors, Orson reflected. He'd been wondering about the place she called the compound—about their objective, their goal, their endgame. For a while now, he'd avoided the question (along with many others: about her upbringing, what they'd done to her, how she'd escaped) and since Jezebel had finally hinted at it, he decided to go ahead and ask her: "What exactly is it they're after? What do they do at the compound?"

"We aren't supposed to know," she said, her eyes glazing over, "but I gathered enough over the years to stitch it together. Well enough to know it's nothing good."

"End of the world, huh?" Orson was only partly joking, so he wasn't surprised by her response.

"Something like that, yeah. Less the end and more the reducing of it."

"Reducing it to what?"

"Trust me, you don't want to know." She lifted a hand toward him and, squeezing her eyes shut, continued, "Would you be quiet for a moment?"

"Uh, sure," he said.

Orson was getting tired of being led like a blind dog with no leash, sputtering to tread water on choppy sea. If Jezebel didn't open up—at least a little—about what the Overseer and his cronies were up to, he'd have to consider heading back to New York after all. He wasn't ready to give his life over to this strange little girl, even if she was one of the more exciting people he'd ever met, and had guided him safely through the most dangerous circumstances of his life.

"Nothing there," she said, opening her eyes again.

There, Orson surmised, was supposed to mean some kind of intuition, a feeling, like when she'd spoken in his head.

"Follow me," she said.

He did, out the front door and onto the lawn, around to the driveway and into the dimmed light of the garage, where Jezebel leaned against the crushed hood of the beat-up truck hiding there. She touched the fractured glass of the windshield and traced its outline, where the window met the frame of the car—the merging of glass and metal. Her eyes were shut, but Orson could feel her focus, the energy pouring off of her, damp and stinking like sweat, although she wasn't perspiring. Even over the buzz of the cicadas' songs filling the dusty air, the sound of her throaty breath reached his ears, as though every inhalation was a labored one, her last dying breath—full of purpose and intent.

"Jezebel," Orson said, scared to get too close or to touch her, afraid he might break her focus and trap her in that place between worlds—the unspoken, preternatural place to which she so often slipped away, in search of hidden clues. "What are you doing?"

She ignored him, still tracing the length of the truck, caressing its sides, walking heel-to-toe around the vehicle like she was seducing a lover—chin to chest, eyelids fluttering, fingertips tracing the curve of the panel below the tailgate.

And then she was done. As suddenly as stubbing one's toe, and with the same expression, she drew back from whatever hidden landscape she had occupied, flung back to full cognizance with such force as to knock her to her knees.

Anxiously, he asked her, "What did you see?"

"Two men, tailing her—" *Her* meant *her mother*, he knew without asking. "They were in an old car. A big one. They almost killed her, and then they took me away from her."

"How did the truck end up here, with your grandmother?"

"She drove it here. Meredith did. My mother." Jezebel squinted again, confused by the vision, or pained. "It doesn't make sense though."

"You're right, it doesn't. There's no way anyone drove this clunker after the wreck it must've seen."

"I know." Jezebel nodded. "All the same, she did. She drove it here, somehow. And she told that woman—" She pointed back toward the house, roughly toward the living room hallway where her grandmother lay growing cold. "My mother told her about me, about what happened. How they took me. What's unclear is how they found her, and why they chose her—why they chose me."

Neither of them said anything for a while. Even though Orson wasn't completely following Jezebel's train of thought, he was careful not to push her, already knowing she had a way of locking up and shutting down when faced with too much emotion. Growing up in a cold, cultish world must have that effect.

When she broke the silence, Jezebel seemed to have intuited more, or at least processed more of what she'd seen. She said, "There was a man. It must have been Peter, my father. She loved him, but she killed him anyway. And it's the Overseer's fault."

"How do you know all this?" Orson asked.

"Things—things have memories, just like people." She bit her lip, scratched her head, and hooked her thumb back over her shoulder, pointing at the truck.

"I don't envy you your gifts, Jez."

She opened the driver side door, slid in, and felt the curve of the leather-wrapped wheel.

"We have to go back there," she said, staring at him though the shattered window. "To the compound."

"Are you crazy? There's no way! They'll probably kill you, and they'll *definitely* kill me."

"I'm sorry, Orson, but we have to." She grew silent again, as if her insistence alone would convince him. When that didn't work, she finished, "*I* have to go back. My mother—I think she's still there."

"Now why would your mother—" Orson started, but cut himself short. Before he even finished the question, he knew she'd have no clear answer to it— just another hunch, a foggy vision of the distant past, or near future, to rely upon. He thought about it for a moment, about what it might be like—crossing the desert together, perhaps eating bugs, sharing stories by firelight.

Orson decided he'd follow her, back through the extremes of heat and cold, the inconstant climes of the drylands, and into the pit of darkness from which she'd just barely escaped. The compound.

"Well?" Jezebel asked.

"Fine." He exhaled sharply, cheeks puffed out.

"You'll come, then?"

"Yes, I'll come. I'll go all the way. Because I don't have anything else but this."

She jumped down from the truck, almost tripping as she stepped onto the running board to reach him, falling into his lap for the second time in not very long. Yet again, a totaled car had brought them together.

With her arms wrapped around him, Orson savored the warmth of her skin against his, and felt a flare in the quietened energy at the bottom of a dark well in his gut. It was an innocent flutter—mostly.

"Thank you," she said, smiling at him from ear to ear, facing him nose to nose.

"Don't sweat it." He was tempted to pinch her cheek, but didn't. "So, Jez, you got another plan?"

"Funny you should ask..."

How does she pick these up? he wondered. *These idioms?* and said, "I'll take that as a yes, then?"

"Roughly, I do. We'll find the compound first—and that part shouldn't be too hard. It pulsates with energy. I could find it blindfolded from halfway across the world."

"Okay," Birch said. "Then what?"

"Well, then we'll find my mother, and we'll rescue her."

"You're never long-winded, I'll give you that much. It sounds too easy. What about the Overseer?"

"If we can, we'll take care of him, too."

She didn't seem concerned with the *how*, focused as she was on the outcome and not the actions necessary to see her quote-unquote plan through to fruition.

"Any idea how we'll get there?" Orson asked.

She smiled, nodding her head. "Yes, I think I have an idea."

"Oh, no…No, no no! Not a trucker again. Jezebel, that was scary." He thought back to how uncertain she'd been, when she influenced Tom the trucker into bringing them down to Tucson. But it worked out in the end, even if there'd been a few moments of uncertainty, and he had grown to trust her a little bit more.

"Actually, I have a better idea," Jezebel said.

"What's that?"

For a moment, he thought she might mean the truck, but he soon dismissed that notion. Even the fantastical world she'd opened up to him had its limits, and there was no way driving that truck could exist within the boundaries of that realm.

"I'll tell you up front this time: I've never tried it, not for real. But I think I can do it."

"Out with it, then!"

"There's a way of moving that bends time."

"How very cryptic of you, as always. Sounds like what you did to Tom in the semi, then. It's fair to say time bent for him, right?"

"Yes and no. Let me explain." She perused the garage's cluttered shelves, crammed with portable storage units and filing cabinets, until she found an old plastic bucket full of chalk. Orson wondered what memories it held—a container of half-used pastel chalks in the garage of a woman with no real family (a dead woman, at that)—but Jezebel didn't flinch or falter when she handled it. She rifled through the mix 'til she found a nice shade of blue, and then she began to draw.

"This should be interesting," Orson joked, bending down for a better look at her illustration.

It was a line, with an arrow at its far right end. Simple enough.

"Most people," Jezebel said, pointing right at Orson, accusatorially. "They see time this way."

"Time," Orson repeated. "Yeah, I guess that's right. If the endpoint, the one without the arrow, is meant to be the beginning of time as one remembers it, and the arrow-end is how one sees it, moving outward, away from him—or from her— then that's correct."

"Perhaps that's true—that time moves away from us. In fact, most would say it *is* how time moves, but humor me: what if time as a concept actually looked like this?" She added another arrow to the far left end, and Orson was reminded of a number line. Elementary school stuff, but he kept his judgments to himself.

"Okay, I get it." He grabbed the chalk from her hand and drew his own symbol, the sideways 8 of infinity. "Like this, too?"

"Some would say they're the same, *yes*. Both images suggest that if we move forward in time, we might also move backward through it."

"Wait, wait, wait. Hold on a minute—so now we're talking time travel?" Orson was genuinely distressed, almost annoyed.

"No, not really. Just hold on a minute…" Her head flitted across the corners of the room, searching for another impromptu tool for her demonstration. She skittered toward a pile of old printer paper gathered atop a crate of records in the corner of the garage. Disregarding whatever treasure trove of collectibles might be crammed in there, she grabbed a handful of sheets from the stack and tore out the shape of a long, squat rectangle. "Here's another analogy. If we're arguing against the notion of one-directional temporality, let's dive deeper and say this: we actually exist at all times, at once. Here, here, and here." She pointed at the end, middle, and beginning of the small scrap of paper.

"But that sheet of paper is finite," he argued. "It has an end, a beginning, and a middle. So it's different than the other two, the ones that mean infinity."

"Not necessarily—" Jezebel started.

"I think I know," Orson interrupted, "*exactly* where this is headed. Hand me that tape."

Jezebel glanced over her shoulder and rose to grab the adhesive from a far shelf. She returned to plop it down in his hand. A smug grin spread across her face, like she, too, knew where this was headed.

Psychic know-it-all, Orson thought.

He formed the strip of paper into a loop, but flipped one of its ends around 180 degrees before connecting the edges with the tape. Holding it aloft, toward her, he smiled, bearing his token of time as a gift to her.

"Explain what you've done," she said, eyeing him skeptically.

"All right, all right. So here—" Orson traced his finger along the inside of the elliptical shape. "If I always exist from beginning to end—from birth to death, all at once and such—what happens before and after the endpoints of this strip of paper? What happens to your concept of infinite time before I was born and after I die?"

"You've connected them, so you must be implying that it happens all over again? Over and over, on a loop? *Ad infintum.*"

"I guess." He tossed the piece of paper down.

"That's a little different than the arrows on my diagram, though—and from all the others, too. Here, you're always repeating the same pathway, following the same course. It's also interesting that you flipped one end of the strip before attaching it to the other side. Why'd you do that, Orson?"

"I'm not sure," he said. Come to think of it, he didn't at all know why he'd done that. It was a kind of impulse, like one of her very own hunches. He could just as easily have taped the loop together *without* rotating one of its ends at all and produced a similar effect. If anything, the resulting shape he'd created looked slightly warped, bent down by the quick flip he'd made of its end, and it strained him slightly to figure out its aspect. One part of it was forever twisting, disappearing from view by its thinness and movement, like the disappearing dots of an optical illusion.

"My turn," she said. Her tone was neither smug nor gracious—it was simply matter-of-fact. She snatched the shape up from off the floor and pinched down at it with two fingers, at a seemingly random point on the loop of paper. "What looks like a shape with two sides actually has just one."

"If that were true, it would mean the pressure you're feeling right now is impossible. It's caused by the meeting of your two fingers—your thumb and your index finger are pressing down on one another, against one another, from opposite sides of the paper."

"You're right, but you're also wrong. My fingers are opposed to one another, but also resting along*side* one another, concurrently."

"Okay, now you've lost me, Jez. Sorry."

"It's okay." Her eyes flitted back across the room, off to the spot by the old vinyls. She grabbed a pair of scissors, which she'd far too easily intuited from the murk of blackness in that corner, and returned to their spot on the concrete floor of the garage. "Let me show you something else—"

"Um," he interrupted. "Shouldn't we get going? I mean, what if someone comes by? Sees what happened here?"

"Just a minute!" Jezebel took the scissors and pricked one of its blades through the center of the loop Orson had formed, cutting her way carefully, in a perfect line down the center of the one-or-two-sided shape. Miraculously, as she completed the circle of her cut around its boundary, the form of the thing folded outward into a single longer, but narrower, loop. Any normal swatch of looped paper should have separated into two smaller shapes, but this one did not.

"You see?" she asked.

"Not really. Is it more illusion?"

"There's nothing magic happening here, Orson." She picked up another shade of chalk—this time, red—and placed its tip at the center of her new, narrower but longer loop of paper. Pressing down against the ground, she carefully traced the boundary and completed the circle by rotating the paper beneath the chalk. Afterward, she held the thing up to the light and revealed that, surprisingly, the line traversed the entirety of what looked like both its sides. "One side and one boundary. That's what your little flip did."

It all felt a lot less magical, as though the answer had been there all along.

"So what's all this got to do with time, and with how the hell we're getting all the way across Arizona in a pinch?" Orson asked.

"You'll see." She grabbed her scissors and cut the loop again. This time, she sliced it not across its center, but divided it by a ratio of approximately 33 and 67 percent. When the circumferential cut was complete, she pulled the thin strands apart, and what appeared was a surprise.

Instead of what Orson expected—*another* even narrower loop—there were two, and connected together. One was slightly larger than the other.

"I don't know whether you're a scientist," he said, "or a magician."

"Sometimes they're the same thing." She smiled. "So you see, you knew all along—or at least you had a hunch—that time is multi-dimensional, moving freely around us, and we're embodied at all points, at all times, on its track. Just like the line I traced earlier, around the strip's single boundary, our lives may seem many-sided, but our trek through time is like the Möbius strip you created: we, the line, are the product of all our places in time, all at once. Most people just can't feel it, or know it to be true. Once you realize it, it becomes so clear."

"And the second bit, with the two loops?" Orson asked. "What's it mean?"

"That's where it gets a little tricky. Most of the time, I can see forward, backward—wherever I want through time. Mostly I catch glimpses, but sometimes they're throbbing, clear visions. Once in a while, a temporal master comes along who can easily bridge the gap between past, present, and future—blend them, jump between them freely. It's not so easy for me.

"Even though we saw the shape separated into two, it was still connected. The two sides were bound; it was the same temporal loop—just different versions of the same story, like choosing between divergent paths. One leads west, the other east. For the person whose life we've just illustrated, the cycle is a part of the same loop, but separates into many possible outcomes, all of which connect right back to the original timeline."

"So, right here is the place where I decided to follow you, back to the compound—" Orson pointed to where the two shapes loosely connected, like lopsided hoola hoops stuck together. "One version of me went back to New York and the other one carried on with you, but both are cyclical, bending at my touch and pressing against one another."

"You got it. So if we want to make it back to the compound without breaking a sweat, and without aggravating the Overseer, all we have to do is find one of those points—a temporal link, like that one." She pressed her finger down on top of Orson's, indicating the spot of the link, and the moment that had passed between them, when she and Orson had met.

"What happens then? When we find a link? Or do we make one?"

"We simply jump from here—" She picked a spot on the larger paper loop, holding her finger there and rotating it counter-clockwise until it met with the other loop. "—to here."

"Seems to me that requires more than manipulation of time. What about space?" He considered her suggestion. "All this strikes me as fuzzy logic."

"You're right," she said, rising to her feet, dusting bits of chalk off her robe. "I told you, I've never done it before. A lot of it's as mysterious to me as it is to you. But I can try, at least."

Orson wondered simultaneously how she'd look in a pair of jeans and a t-shirt—in *normal* clothes, with her hair pulled back and her eyebrows tweezed—and what would happen if her latest experiment with magic failed. He didn't waste time figuring out a way to convince her not to do it, though, because she'd only shake her head and *do it*, anyway. Better to follow along and trust in her wondrous powers, like a fool hanging joyfully by one foot from a tree's high limb, ignorant to his own folly—but blissful, all the same.

"All right, then," he said. "So what do we do?"

She hesitated, arms crossed, tapping both her elbows with her middle fingers.

"You don't know, do you?" Orson asked, already knowing the answer.

"There's a few ways we could do it, but I'm not sure about *any* of them."

"Take your time," Orson said. "Pun intended. As long as you need. I know how you have your hunches." He was trying hard not to sound sardonic.

"Okay, give me a bit."

Orson snuck into the truck and, leaning the passenger seat back as far as it would go, reclined to rest his eyes while Jezebel tinkered with space and time. Her explanation still didn't make much sense, but if she could figure out a way to get them there *without* hitchhiking, he'd be happy, all the same.

He felt his eyes grow weary, almost too quickly.

He drifted into a dream.

Emotionless cinderblock walls scraped against his skin. The chill, dry air of night leaked through the iron bars filling holes in the walls—windows—and lifted goosebumps up across his arms. A trail of burning rosemary hung upon the air, herbal and intoxicating. Something dragged him, an invisible tether coaxing him through the abandoned, shadowy halls of their cloisters. A coven's muted whispers tapped against his ticklish ribs, their maniacal laughter subdued by the distance between them, but gradually swelling with each of his reflexive steps in their direction, toward an arched entryway, through the port cased in sumac (its leaves flourishing as he passed by underneath, spinning on their vines like bracted fingers, straining to scratch at his skin). The port opened outward, onto a quadrangle between the buildings that formed the ring-shaped compound. That sliver of open air, cast from the center of the structure, was used for their deepest, darkest, inmost conniving sorcery—dredging up their Takers, their demons, *with age-old words of conjuring.*

A platform was raised at the center of the grounds and hooded figures surrounded it, arms raised in supplication toward their leader, standing at his throne, at court before them. His robe was specially designed, with a separate golden hood—a detachable swatch of fabric that was tied around his neck and obscuring much of his face; only his sharp-pointed bird's nose and harsh-cleft chin peeked out. Unlike his attendants, who all wore traditional burlap cowls with wide open sleeves, the Overseer's arms were only covered up to the middle of his forearms. Veins curved and collided across his pasty skin. He was whispering something in Latin, which Orson couldn't quite decipher. It rose in pitch.

As the last of his incantation was spoken, the Overseer began to cough uncontrollably, quavering from his bird-chested core to each of his jagged-nailed fingertips. He keeled over against the planks of his stage, yet no one rose to help him. They only hummed, swaying from side to side in unison, hypnotically—like a cluster of seaweed bent by the ocean's current. While their wordless hymn surged, the Overseer struggled on, his face bloated out with breathlessness, his lips puffed out like a fish out of water, puckering for breath. He choked on whatever force they'd succeeded in extracting from the conflagrant pits of Hell. Its influence over him grew, and lifted him up, comically—high into the air by his unconscious, limp wrists—like a marionette at dance, by the guidance of his master's unseen directions. Flick of the wrist here, toppling head-over-heels; genuflect there and he was soaring up-up-up. His head rolled about, flaccid on the stem of his neck as he soared above his followers (their hands reaching up toward their Rock Star ruler, copping a feel of his bare, drooping ankles). He completed a wide showman's circle above them before the Taker—the demon—placed his senseless figure back at rest again. He lay against the hard wood platform of the stage, his breath returning to him, a string of Latin sputtering unintelligibly from his mouth.

(UT CONFESTIM ALLATA)

Blood trickled from the corners of his mouth, and he shook himself up on one elbow, reaching out with his other hand toward the frenzied crowd of followers.

(ET CIRCULO DISCEDAS)

The presence consuming him, rising like internal combustion, melting together his innards.

(AD LOCUM A JUSTISSIMO)

His ears were popping—in the dream—Orson's ears.

How can ears pop in a dream? he wondered.

(DEPUTATUM IN MOMENTO)

Jezebel's voice punctured through the dream. It woke him up, rising through a din of wind and screeching.

She shouted, *"ICTU OCULI ABEAS"* from the center of a circle—one traced in plain red chalk against the concrete floor of the garage, and without the fancy ornamentation of the sigil that had been drawn under the kitchen table. A pair of aberrations flicked in and out of view, like the appearance and disappearance of shadow under a hem and haw floodlight, there and then gone. They circled her like predatory kites—tall, fierce beasts with the backward-pointing lower limbs of birds and the protruding, feathered chests of half-ton buzzards. Their wings were leathery, more akin to bat than bird, and were spotted with warts, knotted and hardened like skin that's been pock-marked with battle scars. Their embodiment solidified, streaking into full view as though by teleportation.

One of them made for the truck, where Orson skittered backward against the front seats, sliding for the driver side as he pressed his heels against the fragile pane of glass separating him from the creature—*the Taker*, Orson realized—struggling to keep the fractured shards from caving in altogether. It pecked at the broken window curiously before it realized the frailty of the glass. Then, lifting up one pincered claw, it rose to kick in the window.

Just as it broke through, Orson bashed his foot into its giant-eyed face. The thing stumbled backward, momentarily flapping its wings like a tightrope walker batting his arms for composure, only to jump back through the window head-first. It reached for him with arms that were by most means human in form, except for the coating of tar-black feathers that covered them. Its torso was so squat and wide that it couldn't pull itself completely through the space, and it was too dumb to use the handle. So instead of tearing Orson open, the Taker only swatted foolishly at thin air, struggling to reach him—a stone's throw out of reach, but close enough for Orson to fully absorb the haunting semblance of humanity still left in its face: under its domed golden eyes the size of dinner plates, dark circles drooped with fallible ennui; its hardened beak had somehow not fully replaced the nose that once lay centered on its face, so the hooked and bisected flesh-and-cartilage aspect of it still flopped about with all its thrashings, half-connected like a pair of adenoid skin tags, framing its beak.

It was straining, getting closer. Orson couldn't ball up much tighter, and he feared what might happen if he opened the driver side door. He could roll out, crawl under the truck, and dive for the circle that seemed to protect Jezebel. But to do any of that, he'd have to move quickly. The Taker moved spastically, erratically, and at the slightest impetus; Orson wasn't sure he could outrun it. Even if he did, the other one was out there somewhere, struggling to get at Jezebel. It might see Orson's presence as an easy kill and abandon its pursuit of her—good for Jezebel, not for him.

Before he could make a decision, the severity of the situation lessened. A grating, inhuman chirp of pain came from Jezebel's direction, and was followed by the swift removal of his ferreter. Subhuman, feathered arms flailed as the thing was drawn from the truck window and thrown far, out of the garage's open door and into the middle of Agave Lane.

Orson crawled on his elbows toward the shattered opening in the passenger side door and craned his neck to see what was happening outside.

Jezebel sat straddled atop the Taker, much as she had mounted her Taken grandmother. But instead of ripping open its face, she muttered words unknown to Orson—likely more Latin, judging by their harsh sound, their hard phonemes. The thing wriggled powerlessly beneath her like a contorted quadriplegic, craning its neck left and right, avoiding the searing touch of Jezebel's open palms, which she held close to its face. While Orson feared it might peck off her fingers, the words she spoke instilled enough fear that it didn't take the chance. It strove instead, by all its fading means, to keep Jezebel's hands *off*, going so far as to bash its head harshly against the pavement of the road beneath it, flattening the back of its skull. Its eyes rolled up and its tongue lolled out from the side of its beak-slash-mouth, pink and hemmed in by only a few milky teeth of varying sizes, ones that somehow hadn't fallen in its change.

As its subjugator—the girl who could—continued to mumble in a foreign language, the feathers coating its body drew back to wherever they had come from; its eyes changed, the minute specks of its avian pupils growing just as the sclera shrank down. Its beak folded back into the depths of its throat and its nose fell flat against its face, slack, never reconnecting. It changed back, into a shriveled gray corpse, and for every ounce of meat it lost to rot, Jezebel's strength grew (her arms flexing with new power; her hair furling and unfurling as it grew longer, falling to her thighs; her shoulder blades protruding, crackling with the emergence of a bony protuberance).

It was dead, expired, a breathless sack of skin with a deep cleft in the center of its face and a pathetic, sagging chest. Its limbs had the kind of worn elastic look of a rubber band that's been stretched too far. It had been a Taken, and its friend had, too.

The other one lay dead in the gloom of the garage, just as bare and cold as the first. They were humans, possessed—not demons incarnate. Hosts, changed by the will of their visitors, but human again in death. By whatever sigils and conjuring, by whatever dark magic the Overseer brewed, the pair had been transformed into those *things*, so much worse than the worm in the desert.

A crowd had formed, a little dome of onlookers that mirrored the robed ones of Orson's dream, in that they neither offered help nor word. They only hummed and murmured to themselves, shocked beyond comprehension by what they saw— almost *not* seeing it, blinded by the otherworldly things before them (a blood-soaked girl; a maniac, a murderer), ignorant to the dark, plodding current that welled and abated. Jezebel lifted her hands up from the Taken, holding them out toward the spectators. All their eyes followed her hands' careening pathways, up and down, swirling around, as she recited:

"*Ut ab omni infernalium spirituum potestate,*

"*Laqueo, deceptione nequitia.*"

One by one, they lowered their heads and, with their eyes closed, turned to walk away—to return to their carefree lives, void of evil spirits, conjurers, and the bewitching spells of Jezebel.

Orson pried at the handle and spilled out of the car, pushing himself up onto his knees and traipsing out of the garage toward her.

"What the fuck was all of that?" he screamed.

She turned to face him, revealing her face in full—a changed face, more harshly angled and flush.

"You could have helped me," she said. "Used your hot-tempered hands on 'em."

"Seems like you managed okay." He squeezed her by her shoulders, feeling her as if to check for her substance, to confirm she wasn't just a specter of his dreams. "How did I sleep through all this?" He pointed loosely back toward the circle she'd stood within, which he now saw was adorned with little bits of chicken-scratch, gibberish symbols that could have meant *tomato* or *Lucifer* for all he knew.

"I, um—" A flush of embarrassment rose to Jezebel's cheeks—as though she'd just been seen naked for the first time, or had bled all over after her first intercourse. "That was because of me."

"What do you mean?"

"I put you under, so I could concentrate."

"What? Why?" He subdued his anger. "What did you do to those people? Should we be running? They might call the cops!"

"Slow down. Everything's fine. Those people—I made them forget all about—"

"Wait!" he interrupted, realizing what she'd said before. "You put me under, like you did with that trucker?"

"Yes," she said, evenly. "Well, kind of..."

"What the fuck, Jez?" He waited for her to respond, but she only stared back at him doe-eyed, with her feet crossed out in front of her. She'd changed clothes—must have found something in her grandmother's closet. Now she wore a lime-green sun dress, its thin straps continually falling over the slope of her soft shoulders 'til she picked them back up, again and again.

"I'm sorry," she finally said.

He couldn't stay mad at her. She looked like a pageant queen on her off-day, her freckled skin beaming and dewy, her hair—which had managed to stay long, despite the end of her witchcraft—spilling over her back, but not quite covering the emergence of a set of wings, folded up, cradled against the small of her back.

"Who are these people—these Taken—and how did you get *those*?"

She craned her neck, peeking back at them, over her shoulder. It was a good thing she'd changed clothes—those fresh pennons would make her look hunchbacked, folded up under her old robe.

"I brought them here. They were his worst cronies: John and George. Not long ago, they changed—willingly. They allowed themselves to be Taken, so they could become these things. I know this because of what I saw, when I put you under."

"What did you see?" Orson asked.

"I touched the sigil again, and I found a link to them. They were the ones who drew it—the sigil. When my grandma was sleeping, or perhaps while under some of their influence—maybe even one similar to what you just woke from—they crept in and drew it under the table, where we found it. It hooked its way through her, had her awaiting their orders. The Taker was there, inside of her, just waiting to *SNAP*—waiting for the right set of words."

"They looked similar to the one that took your grandma. Can they do that? Can a Taker possess more than one host?"

She struck her tongue across the insides of her cheek, staring down at the husk that had once been John, or maybe it was George. "One," she started, pausing to wipe her face, patting away sweat and stilling her hand's tremors against the slope of her brow. "One of them can command thousands, can Take a whole city."

Jezebel disappeared into the garage and through the doorway there. He followed after her, peering back over his shoulder and eyeing the shriveled corpse of John or George, left out in the street like a shovelful of bone and ash—the unclaimed remains of a crematory, dumped on Agave Lane. Perhaps no one would notice. And those who had already witnessed the cause of the mess—well, Jezebel had taken care of them.

Back in the house, Jezebel was seated, legs crossed, against the verdigris carpet, poking at a damp patch where her grandma's blood trail ended, some few inches from her body.

"What's the plan now?" Orson asked. "Gonna flex those wings?" He found it hard not to write off her change to some fresh mania. It was getting to be too easy to change all the rules in her weird world.

"Maybe," she said, lifting her chin up to him and winking. "The whole time-space thing wasn't working out."

"I figured."

"We have to do something about *her*."

She was right. They had to get rid of the body. As tragic as it seemed, no one would come around for weeks, and by then the carcass would have rotten to hell. Orson weighed their options: burn her, chop her up and sink her, or carry her with them to the desert, to dump her down some no-man's bluff. The first option seemed the easiest, but was also sure to draw the most attention.

Jezebel rose and disappeared silently down the hall, back into the bedroom. He followed her, and found her standing on top of the bedclothes, rifling through her grandma's drawers and throwing her things all about—tossing a stack of matronly dresses onto the undressed mattress; heaving an armful of ugly, coarse blue jeans in Orson's direction.

"What are you doing?" he asked.

"Looking for something."

"I can see that. For what?"

"We need to wrap her in something." Jezebel pulled the last dresser drawer out, its contents flying as the wood-panel repository shot through the air, spilling knee-length tweed skirts (left over from decades gone by). The peeled-back paper liner of the drawer curled outward—more mimosa print, and a sprinkle of potpourri, too.

"What—why?" Orson tugged at her wrists, but she ignored him, singling out the largest of the garments from the bunch.

She balled the clothes up and dumped them on the center of the gross gingham bedspread, which she used to easily lift her bounty past Orson, through the doorway, across the hall, and into the kitchen. Avoiding the upturned table, she sidestepped the furniture and opened the farmost door, centered in the mirrored wall. She vanished into the backyard.

Orson made his way down the hall, stepping over the corpse of her grandma, and watched from the living room windows overlooking the garden as Jezebel gingerly spread the blanket out against the lawn. Then she came back in, scooped her grandma up and dragged her out onto the lawn. It was not a pretty picture: the dichotomy of those aromatics, fruits, and vegetables half-grown and half-dead, alongside the corpse of their caretaker. And Jezebel—ever the emotionless—was clenching and unclenching her jaw while she arranged bits of clothing atop her dead kin, smoothing a camisole against the bubbling cleft in her chest, wrapping the corners of the bedspread tightly around her grandma like a mummy, so that only the woman's old, malformed face peeked through the front of the fabrics swaddling her.

Orson decided to let her be for a while—to let her try her luck with guiltlessness, as he so recently had. Somehow, he guessed, hers was a battle whose outcome would be far less absolute.

Instead of helping her (she'd ask for help if she needed it), he idled himself with ransacking the house. In the den, he found an old glory box sandwiched between the recliners. Somehow, he hadn't noticed its gaudy golden lid before, nor its odd depiction of a woman, who was eating flowers and buds under the shade of an almond tree in half-bloom. Inside the box were mostly sour-smelling linens, but at the bottom of the chest—underneath the boring bits and alongside a folder labeled, plainly, DOCUMENTS—was a plastic baggie, wrinkled by constant usage, constant touch. Inside of the bag were twenty or thirty photos, all of them visibly worn—but not worn by time. No, this nameless croon had been careful to bar her keepsakes from air and light, retrieving them only when she most needed a pick-me-up. So what had aged them was something less elemental, nor more human than the sebum of her own skin—what scant oils still remained in her latter years. Touch and love had effectively worn through the photo paper at its corners, where she held them, fondly regarding her long-lost family. He set aside the bag of photographs and lifted out the manila DOCUMENTS folder. He folded back the front flap and pulled out its contents.

On a worn sheet of paper, folded into thirds:

ARIZONA DEPARTMENT OF HEALTH
CERTIFICATE OF LIVE BIRTH

The name printed at the top of the certificate was Meredith Renee Dietrich. Born on the eighth of September, during the quiet, magical hours of late night—2:11AM, to be exact—in the year 1970.

Jezebel's mom, Orson thought.

On the birth certificate, Meredith's mother was listed as Norma Renee Dietrich, and her father's information had been left blank, which might have meant anything.

Norma Renee Dietrich—that was the name of the woman whom Jezebel had killed; her own grandmother. Somehow, knowing her name made the act of killing her seem that much more distressing. Certainly, the photos he found also made it more grievous.

Orson flipped through them, admiring the high-waisted lycra leggings, the neon bangles, the rolled-up, acid wash, denim shorts. Meredith had very clearly been a teen of the '80s, an era Orson had only missed by a few years—and one whose films he knew well, and loved.

In all the photos, there was Norma—Jez's grandma—staring down at her young daughter's curly-haired crown, or patting her on the shoulder while they both smiled for the camera. There were no signs of distress, of the strained relationship Norma had suggested. Perhaps their disagreements came later—over the promiscuous tendencies Meredith had, a characteristic the fanatically religious Norma would not have put up with.

Orson peeked out at the garden and the lawn. The sun was just setting behind the Catalinas, clouds parting to make way for the full glory of that golden sinking orb.

They'd been there for almost a full day, at Norma's—meeting her, eating her food, and then killing her. Summoning Takers and slaughtering them, too. And now, outside, Jez was finishing the last of her silent observations, a funeral procession for one. Her head was bowed and she sat on her heels, knees together, palms resting open and face-up against her thighs. She lifted her chin, glided to her feet, and came through to the kitchen, to the hallway—stepping over the clotted ring of blood there—and into the living room.

"Will you help me?" she asked.

"Of course," Orson said, hiding the plastic baggie and manila envelope behind his back, shoving the linens haphazardly back into the chest.

"What have you got there?" She lifted an eyebrow up at him. "Behind your back."

"It's nothing, it's—"

She grabbed for the folder, dashing toward him and easily plucking it from his grip before he could repeat that second ill-concealed lie: *nothing*. It was something— would especially be something to her.

As her eyes drifted across the birth certificate, and then across the other documents, which Orson hadn't had time to read—certificates of achievement, diplomas, and the like—the look of cursory interest that laid there about-faced into one of wide-eyed heartache. Her lip quivered, though she quickly stilled it, slamming the file closed with a grunt.

"Norma," she whispered. "What else? I can handle it."

He handed over the bag of photos, which she opened using only her index fingers and thumbs—the rest of her digits, from pinky to ring of both hands, were lifted upward in a gesture of apprehension.

"That's my mother," Jezebel purred, less upset than intrigued. She touched the images of a teenage Meredith—whose teeth were knotted up in braces and whose hair was grossly permed—and left behind a wet trail. "We have to go find her."

Orson took the photos from Jezebel's iron-clutched grip and redeposited them in the baggie; he hid the documents and keepsakes back where they came from, at the bottom of Norma's treasured glory box. "We will," he said. "We'll find her. But, first things first: what can I help you with?"

Jezebel nodded and took him by the wrist, back down the hall—both of them less afraid of the crusted puddle of blood than before—through the kitchen, and through the door set centered in its mirrored wall.

They both looked down at Norma, side by side, and Orson felt a tinge of remorse for the loss of her life. Even if she *had* been a loner in the world, she didn't deserve to die, not in *that* way. He only hoped she had slipped so far from her former self that any pain Jezebel imparted was delivered to the Taker, and not to her.

"Do *you* feel guilt?" Orson asked.

"No," Jezebel said. "Not really."

He wanted to pry deeper, to figure out this phenomenon they shared—the absence of guilt, where it should most definitely have been. He wondered, also, if the experience of guilt (and of disgrace, and of shame) was an inborn one, like a predator's burning urge to hunt, or if it was something that was learned. Clearly, Jezebel hadn't been programmed like him—hell, she'd been cut from an altogether separate cloth, as was evidenced by her frankness in bringing up sex, where any other girl her age would have blushed, if not run for cover.

"That's okay," he said, as if her response warranted some of his forgiveness.

"Will you do the honors?" She indicated the sheathed remains of Norma, her grandma, by nodding her head in the vicinity of the makeshift fabric tomb.

"What?" he asked. "How?" But before her response, he knew what she meant.

Orson lifted his right hand up before him, high and straight out from his chest. With one eye squinted, he stared down the length of his forearm, across his lifted thumb like a sight, and over the tip of his extended index finger, the barrel of his otherworldly gun. That weapon of his—made from his own flesh, but powered by something not intrinsic to humankind—shot blanks that night. No matter how he tried to gather the shock of white lightning through his palms again, it wouldn't come and it wouldn't shoot.

"Sorry, Jez."

"It's okay." She drew near, circling up behind him, and cradled his fist in her hands, rubbing them together to shake out the cold. "Try it now."

Something had changed, right away. Whether sleight of hand or true magic, he did not know, but Jezebel had somehow replenished the wellspring of his power. Like a shift in his aura, there was a new lightness of being in his joints. He saw the dusky yard with greater clarity—the worms crawling, tunneling through the ground beneath their feet; the blood pulsating through the long ears of Spotted and Townsend's bats flying by overhead—and he felt the resurgence of that unhallowed urge to shoot, to release the balled-up prism of light engulfing his soul. A figure made of shadows stood attached to Orson's hip, invisible to the world yet fully manifest to him. It was that culpable fiend who loosed the blow, a crisp gash of white light sparking across the lawn; it lit the target—a pile of clothes, of sheets, of Norma—in a twisting tower of flames.

Violent sputtering tendrils of fire ate first through Norma's downy cocoon and then, once they'd burned all the lingering symbolic swatches of her material world, they devoured her, too. The acrid fumes of her burning flesh stuffed up Orson's nostrils with a smell that combined melting plastic and charred chicken. He circled around the blazing corpse to stand opposite Jezebel, and to give her time to process whatever raw emotions the grisly scene might have unmasked.

Her head hung high on her shoulders, and her lips did not quaver. She looked like a fresco—Saint Nicholas by Dionisius—the way the flames illuminated her face. She was almost all cheekbones in that lighting, taut skin like a still bowl of milk, and as agleam as one. And how the burning disc of autumn sunset crowned her head, its upper curve just visible (more crescent than circle, eclipsed by her figure). That downturned gaze of hers, so oblivious to his analysis of it, reminded him of the enigma that she was.

She came around to his side of the flames, which were just dying down, leaving only charred, indistinguishable remains—a bone protruding here or there amongst the ashes. Her hand encircled his and she led him back inside.

"We'll sleep here tonight," she said. "In the morning, we'll leave."

"You still haven't told me *how* we'll get there, Jez."

The nickname had stuck—he already used it involuntarily—but his use of it had an altogether unexpected effect on her then. She tightened her jaws together, narrowing her eyelids to slits, as though the familiarity of *Jez* were a curse, a poison—or one of the names of power, used sparingly and, even then, with a dash of unease.

"Let it be a surprise," she said.

"I hate surprises, though." Orson followed her into the bedroom.

She lay across the bare mattress, her winged back exposed, flexing her feathered appendages.

He nudged her. "Show off."

"I didn't get these to not use them. Let's get some rest. No one will bother us here, I promise."

He resisted the urge to ask the expected questions—the *what, how, why* (mostly the *why*)—knowing full that, if he did, she'd just ignore him anyway. Instead, he settled into bed alongside her and turned onto his side, to face away from her.

"I can sleep on the couch," he said, "if you want."

"Don't be silly."

He could feel that there was more there, the way he could tell when his roommates were hiding something—they'd stolen money from his wallet, or one of them had sex with his ex-girlfriend. Their silence was always *too* silent then, a quiet as of bated breath, expectation.

"I'm not tired. Like, at all," Orson said.

"Just close your eyes," she replied and—before he knew what she was doing—she turned and wrapped her arms around him. "What do they say, count lambs?"

"Sheep," he corrected, chuckling.

"Right, sheep."

"Sorry you had to do that. To Norma, your grandma."

"I'm done talking about that." She lifted her arms away for a moment, but not long enough for him to respond, before cradling him again. "Is this okay? I've never slept beside someone before."

"It's okay. Can you turn around, though? Face the other way?"

They both turned in the bed. Orson adjusted her arms so they lay out in front of her. He could feel the slopes of her winding body, adjusting against the contours of his stringy form.

Lulled by their closeness, she eased into a respite. Her dozing, heavy breath—punctuated by the occasional throaty snore—told him she'd fallen asleep. The tension he'd felt emanating from her subsided as she drifted deeper into dreams, rustling and mumbling under her breath.

No matter how Orson wriggled and writhed for the perfect spot, he couldn't get comfortable. Instead he lay awake, feeling the contours of Jezebel's recent acquisition—her aerial accoutrement. The back muscle surrounding those unfamiliar limbs was hardened like the knotted brawn of an athlete, rippling with the scar tissue that had formed on the fly to support the burden of a forty-pound pair of wings. That was a lot of weight to carry around, especially for a girl untrained in the art of heavy lifting.

Black-skinned stalks erupted from the center of her smooth back like lightning rods shooting from both shoulder blades. Where the charcoal flesh melted into feathers, about six inches from the base of the wings, cowlicks of fuzz like baby hair began to emerge. They were feathers, sprouting in clusters, growing in density and length as he traced his fingers outward along the curve of the tendons running across the top of each wing. They unfolded at his touch, as if permitting him to explore, but he soon realized it was Jezebel herself who acquiesced.

Her head was lifted over the rest of her still form. Smiling back at him, she said, "Having fun?"

"Sorry!" He dropped her feathered fins. "I'm just...curious."

"I don't blame you."

"Are they permanent?"

She smiled, considering his question for a moment before responding. "I don't know. Maybe not. What ever is?"

"Deep," he joked, and sniggered. He realized her answer contradicted what she'd told him in the truck—that he would be like that forever, Touched—but didn't feel like pushing the issue.

Tired of talking and ready for bed, he patted her shoulders gently and rolled away.

It wasn't long before she was snoring again.

As Orson closed his eyes and started counting sheep, wondering how Jezebel would carry them across the desert—*would he ride on her back? in her arms? dangling from her feet, like a couple of cartoon characters?*—he realized something. Orson realized Jezebel accepted him, without bias, for exactly who he was. And without knowing much about him—at least, without his having directly disclosed much. She already knew enough: enough to make an informed decision about sleeping with her back (and wings) turned to him; enough to entrust him with her secrets; enough to show him her weaknesses. Perhaps that was why he trusted her so fully, why he was willing to follow her through the desert on a madwoman's journey. If, for the first time, someone had truly accepted him—flaws and giant, hanging question marks, and all—he would follow her to the ends of the earth.

Appropriately enough, that was just where they were headed.

On that note—one of equal parts appreciation and musing—he finally subdued the roar of his waking anxieties, zoning out on the drone of the insects crying just outside the window, and finally fell asleep. Their hymn stayed with him as he left the real world behind for one of specters and smoke. It dragged him by the ankles through a surreal dreamscape:

Abalone. Mollusks, giant ones. Their million-legged strides prickled across his bare, immobile figure. Their shells radiated, pearly and iridescent, inlaid with great Delphic mystery, symbols, and striated with alternating bands of creamy pink and foggy gray. The way they ambled across his belly and chest, tickling him to death, was torturous. If he could move, he'd tear them off and bash them to bits against the sides of the damp stone walls of the ossuary.

The ossuary, that's where he was. Skulls lined up in rows, resting on shelves made of shells, all staring at him—their eye sockets empty, but staring all the same. Staring not at him, but into him, mocking his still figure on the muddy, earthen floor. Berating him, calling him pathetic, the skulls' teeth almost chattering in ridicule.

The earthen floor was ill-lit by a single port-way set in the dull, domed ceiling—a concrete- or cinderblock-ceiling, lifeless and sterile gray. The port-way was made of wood, a wooden door set in the floor of the ground up above, and was the only way in or out. The center of the door had a little window carved into it, which was barred by metal rods. Up there, above ground, it was night and the moon hung low, and above the moon hung Saturn. Its many-banded figure drooped and swayed in diffuse neon brush strokes, and the penumbra cast across its face evoked the sentiment of a smile.

The slugs left a trail of sludge across his skin that chilled through the meat of him and into the bone, yet he couldn't shiver. He could feel, but he couldn't move—not even in response to the suffocating, frozen air. The air down there, it smelled like rotting plant matter and tasted like chicory.

A tinny sound of metal on metal. Coins scattered then gushed through the slice in the door overhead, pouring across him, burying him—nickels and pennies, but no dimes, nor quarters.

The abalones drifted away, seeking cover from the metal rain. They settled into the mossy corners of the buried crypt.

All the skulls directed their attention elsewhere, toward the door overhead as it was hauled open, but only for an instant. A peek and a piss—the liquid warm, acrid, and briny—splashing into his face and seeping through the coat of coins covering him, neutralizing the chill of the gel left behind by the abalones.

The stranger who'd pissed on him lowered a transparent tube, dangling it down by a few feet, into the depths toward Orson's inert face. It hovered overhead, like a still predator waiting to strike, before it finally did its thing: first a few drops of ruddy thick blood and then a constant stream of it. In an instant the coins were washed away and his body was coated. Its flow did not abate, but only seemed to gain intensity, puddling around him, pooling and then drowning him, flooding the room. A room that had once seemed abyssal was now only a pint-sized nook.

The blood rose and rose, up to his neck and then to his chin, yet still he could not move. When it overcame the mount of his nose and pooled in his wide-gaping eyes, he finally awoke.

Jezebel stirred him softly, fully clothed in an all-new getup: navy platform Mary Janes and knee-high purple socks, with high-waisted blue jean cutoffs, a strappy white tank top, and a knitted violet scarf. She must have found a stockpile of her mother's old clothes. She looked like a sloppy, kinderwhore-schoolmarm mess.

"You were having a bad dream," she said.

"No kidding."

Orson rolled out of bed and staggered to the bathroom, knocking over the bottle of Norma's granny scent in the process. The potent draught spilled across the counter, letting loose its fragrance of wilted white blossoms, baby powder, and caskets. He wiped it up with scraps of toilet paper and splashed his face with water, but the smell had latched itself onto him, like a fly caught in his nose hairs. It followed him, even once he left the bathroom and crossed the bedroom to rejoin Jezebel in the kitchen.

But she wasn't there anymore. She was outside, on the lawn, staring at Norma's remains.

He opened the door and, poking his head outside, said, "I don't want to bug you, but you're the one who woke me up. Do you need me out here?"

"I'll only be a minute."

He took this to mean, *Leave me the fuck alone*, and left her alone, occupying his time with a search for a suitable breakfast. By the look of Norma's kitchen, she'd sunk all she had left of her food into their welcome meal. All that remained in the pantry was a bag of cornmeal, a tin of baking soda, and a can of sardines. The fridge was no better: an open pitcher of still water, a jar of pickles, and a bag of moldy shredded cheese.

His stomach growled. *Pickles it is.*

He ate two, and left four for Jezebel.

Leaning against the closed door of the fridge, he surveyed the room. It was still in shambles, so he righted the table, centering it and sliding the chairs back under it. He was hesitant to sit down, worried the sigil might impart some of its last bits of dark magic on him.

No, thank you, he thought. *Once Touched, never Taken.*

Jezebel entered, the door slamming behind her, and sighed.

"Everything okay out there?" Orson asked.

"Fit as a fiddle and ready to fly. Thanks for cleaning up in here." She moved toward him and sat down at the kitchen table, fearlessly. "Whatcha got there— food?"

He handed over the jar of pickles, which she quickly finished off, crunching away at the spears with her mouth wide open, managing to mumble between bites,

"You kept me up kicking." She even drank the juice.

"Sorry."

"It's okay," she said. "I had a dream of my own. Although it wasn't as crazy as yours—" She winked. "In mine, I saw my mother. She was camped away, in a sliver of a cave carved into the earth, into the side of a bluff, a cliffside. She was there with someone else—a man. I couldn't see him clearly, but I know it was a *him*, and that he was friendly. They were calling out to me, saying *Jezebel, Jezebel, Jezebel.* Repeating my name, over and over like some monotonous ghosts. As though they wanted me to hear them and answer their call, by coming."

"You saw all that, so clearly? Are you sure it was a dream?"

"No, I'm not sure. Do you think it's worth looking into?"

He wondered if she really wanted his opinion or if she just wanted him to be the one to make the choice, as if his saying they should *look into it* meant she was freed of implication. Should their plan fail, she'd get off scot-free.

"Sure," he said.

"So we'll detour." A hint of smile crept across her face—a hint of hope.

"How will you find it?"

"Oh, I'll know."

"Okay," he said, but what he really wanted to ask, as always, was *How?* Some unspoken, psychic daughter-mother bond of the Touched that he'd never understand? Or perhaps, along with the wings, she'd acquired some extrasensory prowess—the ability to see through the dark, for miles and miles. He knew Jez would only change the subject if he pried, so instead he sighed and prepared for their departure as best as someone who's never flown on the back (or in the arms? or on the shoulders?) of a winged girl before *can* prepare himself for such a thing: scrubbing his hands at the sink, lathering up to his elbows, savoring the forgotten aroma of cleanliness and finally splashing his face with water, rubbing it through the fast-forming bristles of his beard. "I'm ready."

"You know how this goes by now, I'm sure: I've never actually done this, but I've already got the basics down. I practiced a little while you were still sleeping. Wind makes it tricky, but it's a pretty still day. Most of the gusts that came I could handle okay, but with you hanging on, I'm not so sure."

"Hanging on? How exactly *do* we do this, Jezebel?"

341

"There's a few options, none of them great. We can tie you to the front of me, strap you across my chest with your legs wrapped around back. Or we could tie your wrists to my ankles—"

"I'll pass on that one."

"Didn't think so—sounds risky. One slip and you're gone."

"Any other options?"

"I'd suggest my shoulders, but that could get tricky, too. You might get caught up in my wings or throw off my balance."

"Strapped to your chest, then."

She was prepared for this, swathes of ripped fabric piled up outside, next to the cindery pile of what had once been Norma. Orson recognized many of the fabrics as those he'd found in the hope chest, burying Norma's secrets—her photos and files. Jezebel had managed to rip long, foot-wide strips of fabric from the bedding, and tied them together with knots he recognized from the month-long stint he had as a boy scout (another activity his parents had thought might keep him out of sight, out of their hair long enough to fix up and booze on), the figure-eight.

Little girl knows her stuff.

"So, this cave," Orson said. "You're sure you'll recognize it?"

"Nothing's for sure. We'll see."

"Do you at least know where we're headed? I mean, in which direction, roughly?"

"That way." She pointed in a northwesterly direction, back toward where they met.

"Think we can pick up my rental on the way?" he joked.

She laughed, finally catching his humor.

"Come here," she said. "Let's get started."

Flexing her wings outward to make room for the straps, she wrapped the fabric around her torso twice and then—eyebrow raised, chin lifted—gestured for Orson to approach her. She slipped each end of the makeshift harness over his head, crossing it around his back and then across her own, switching the bands in her hands to complete the circle. He was swaddled, wrapped up in gray Egyptian cotton—decent thread-count, too, by the feel of it. He could only hope it would hold out for the duration of their trip.

Ladies and gentlemen, please fasten your seat belts. We anticipate some turbulence on today's flight.

Orson wrapped his arms around her, looping his fingers together just under the curve of her back, where those foreign appendages emerged. Their wonder, in a world so full of crazy, fucked-up shit, was already starting to dull.

Jezebel finished tying him up, looping his thighs in the bedclothes and crowning her creation with another sturdy knot. The effect was one that evoked an adult baby, bound up in its mama's forward-facing baby carrier. Nevertheless, he tugged on the knots and admired their resilience.

"I'm impressed," he said. "Where'd you learn to tie knots like this?"

"I read a lot, back at the compound. Plenty of time for it when you spend most of your life locked away."

He was thankful he hadn't shared much about his past, knowing for certain she'd read what she needed from him already. At least he'd been able to have friends, to interact with people outside of his screwy family circle. Even if most of them *were* loony Jesus Freaks, it was still something; better than nothing. Sure, he had also been forced to endure his father's endless beatings, but there was enough distraction going on in his life to keep him going. Here was a girl who'd been blessed with none of the niceties of human life: social interaction, flirtation, texting, sex; traveling, school, shitty bus rides. None of that. Orson wouldn't have changed it—he would rather have endured the abuse than trade in all the rest. A holding cell, a robe, and a stack of encyclopedias were not enough for him.

"We should get going," she said, more to screw up her own courage than anything else. She glanced across the lawn for a final peek at the riddle of Norma—now just flashes of white in an ashen mound. "I don't know how fast we'll be moving, but I hope to get us there by sundown."

"That's a lot of miles to travel in one day," Orson said. "Are you sure? You don't even know how straining it'll be. Take it easy when you're up there, please. The last thing we need is to crash."

"I'll be fine."

"If you say so. So now what?"

"Now we go," she said, wide-eyed.

343

Surprisingly, she kissed him on the mouth. Her lips felt cold and dry.

Even though the peck lasted only a moment, Orson felt the aspect of her young, fleshy chops against his for what must have been aeons, as though the thread of time had been ruptured and had left him imprisoned in that instant, to forever endure Jezebel's awkward, ill-timed display of affection. Their surroundings blurred in an explosion of minutiae. In his periphery, he saw millions of swirling flecks of dust, flicks of minerals gleaming like diamonds, and the fickle up- down- and side-drafts of a monumental wind, a storm that threatened to devour them— yet somehow the billows just missed them, as though a forcefield protected them from harm.

They were up, airborne, aloft on the sky, Orson's legs drooping, the weight of his body tugging against the harness, testing the strength of Jezebel's handiwork. He did his best to keep his hands interlocked against the curve of her back, though they were already clammy and even slick with the perspiration that dripped from the fleshy stalks of bone and brawn erupting from her back.

She flapped and flapped, yet not an ounce of strain showed on her face; that creamy complexion of hers was lit from within, in an expression of delight as she relished in the wonder of flight. Were it not for Orson, he thought, she'd be flipping through the sky in painless pirouettes. But she wasn't alone, and so she steeled herself against his weight, set on a course for the somewhere cave, the place she hoped they'd finally meet her mother, Meredith, and another nameless (though hopefully helpful) stranger.

Just as they shot upward through a mist of cloud, the sun completed its morning ascent over the Catalinas. Orson let his arms drop, leaning back into the invisible, gauze-wrapped daggers of wind, which stabbed against his legs, sending them whipping in his seat, and flailed through his hippie hair.

It was true: he'd follow her wherever she went—forever, from now on— because she was his savior, a miracle who'd swooped in to rescue him, not just from death, but also from boredom, from normalcy. Now winged, she fit the profile even better. His soaring wonder, Jezebel.

What he experienced then—wrapped up against her, feeling her heart beat steady and watching her eyes scan for direction, swerving easily into the flow of what might have been a jet stream—was the closest thing to love he'd known. It wasn't that his endless plowing through lovers hadn't given him a spark; it was just that theirs was a short-lived feeling, a fleeting buzz like all the other drugs he used to do. But hers was a weightlessness, no doubt enhanced by their aerial funambulism—a love more akin to winter with family, holed up in a cabin under blankets, sipping cocoa by a blazing fire.

He wanted to touch her again, on the wings and the neck and the mouth, but in a pure, exploratory way.

When we find it, Orson thought. *Once we're there, at the cave, things will only get better.*

His hopes were imposing ones, considering the fact that it was her mother who awaited them—a mother who hadn't seen or held her child since its birth. He'd just have to hope that, unlike his own mother, she'd be one who welcomed new friends, who lived by the adage *The More, The Merrier*, especially since they needed all the help they could get. After all, there was the stranger—the male figure. If mother Meredith was allowed a plus one in their little entourage, he only assumed it would be the case for Jezebel, too. It really was the least that she could do.

He put his worries aside—left them there in Tucson, to melt away in the heat of the sun—and forced himself to imagine a better outcome (one halcyon, if not a bit fantastical): of Jezebel, her mother, and him, living together in peace, somewhere quiet, free to run or fly wherever they pleased, disentangled from the worries of the mortal world. No taxes, no grocery stores. Instead, they would live off the grid, grow their own vegetables.

A sensation of pinpricks, where the sun touched his dreamy eyelids, brought him out of his waking dream.

First things first, he reminded himself. *To the Overseer.*

They flew on, drawing nearer and nearer to the somewhere cave, a place Orson wholly trusted Jezebel could find—just as much as he trusted her with his life, dangling from her by some decades-old thread.

—

They arrived on time, just before sunset.

Orson had slumbered through much of the trip, and awakened feeling rested, optimistic, and sunburned. The entrance to the cliffside cavern was barely discernible upon their descent. Jezebel roused him, with a cyclical stirring of her thighs against his hips, and pointed in the vicinity of a downward sloping trail, a zigzagging pathway between a smattering of desert broom; it started at the apex of the cliffside and curved downward, at an angle Orson wasn't sure he'd have been able to stomach on foot, and evened out on a little precipice before the entrance to the cave. With its eastward-facing opening shadowed by the sun, nearing its final dip off toward the west, the little hole serving as its entrance dissolved into the gray-and-dusty figure of the sand-coated escarpment. Like an abstract figure only some can discern, it effectively concealed their pebbly porch.

Jezebel set them down, skidding against rocks, guarded by the rubber-soled heels of her Mary Janes, and ground to a halt that ended in a topple forward against the momentum they'd so long sustained.

She scraped her knees a little, but Orson took the brunt of the fall, his back grating along the runway lined with jagged stones and flowering, pincered vines. He already felt the dull, throbbing pain of infection settling in as he absorbed God-knows-what plant-borne poison into his bloodstream.

Jezebel dragged him into the shade of the cave, whose walls were surprisingly slick with dampness, and untied the harness that bound them together, bending over him and cooing into his ear, "Sorry, Orson. Sorry. Sorry. Sorry."

It was music to his ears, but no cure-all. The alien backdrop of the cave bent in and out of focus around him. At one moment it was a barren, hollowed chink in the side of the cliff; at the next, it was a resplendent grotto, teeming with fruit-bearing trees and a genial, cool-watered brook.

"Sorry," she said again, and her face blurred into the taut-skinned face of one of the other winged things, the ones Jezebel had slain. But redress for his injuries ducked away, secondary to the approach of two blurred figures, approaching over Jezebel's shoulders.

One was a woman, whose resemblance to Jezebel was undeniable, even to Orson's bleak constitution. The other was—as Jezebel had predicted—a man. His face was soft, young, divergent from the character his expression conveyed—one of utmost acerbity (his arms crossed, jaw clenching-unclenching-clenching) and care. He was the one who spoke first, and he said, "She's here!"

"So it seems," Meredith added. "And with company, too."

PART THREE: THE OUROBOROS
THREE MONTHS LATER

A serpent is entwined by a serpent. The male serpent is bitten by the female serpent; the female serpent is bitten by the male serpent. Like the cyclic nature of the Universe, the Ouroboros represents creation coming out of destruction. Heaven is enchanted, as is the Earth.

—Pyramid of Unas

The tail-devourer holds the key to eternity and the soul of the world.

—*Pistis Sophia*

turn and face the strange! ch-ch-changes!

—David Bowie, "Changes"

CHAPTER XXVI

Cezar sat, face buried in his hands, wondering how to clean up the mess he'd made, and questioning whether he should ever have let Birch leave.

No, he reassured himself. *Sheep may wander, but they always return to the flock.*

John and George hadn't come through. He knew for sure they'd failed—and not long after they'd left, either. The link between them, like the coal of a cigarette ember shining through the dark, had at first diminished and then fizzled out altogether. So the Overseer sat, scratching under the hood of his robe, picking at the dry scalp hidden beneath it.

Although the meaning of Cezar's own name was "head of hair," he had few locks left of which to speak. Thankfully, few knew this about him. The Overseer most always kept his skull (and much of his face) obscured by the shadows of his great, draped cowl. After all, it wouldn't befit a leader to show his shiny-skinned, bald-scalped head to his followers. It dissolved the mystery, and it would create fresh dissent. The last thing he needed was more dissension.

Since the girl had slipped through his fingers, people were beginning to question his ability to see their dreams to fruition (a dream *he* had drawn *for* them, when he single-handedly recruited them to *his* Order—*damned, near-sighted bastards*). Their ceremonies had become mere procession, routine and vapid; gone were their spittle-flying shrieks of revelry. They were going through the motions because they hoped he'd sort things out, but their doubt showed in their slant-eyed glances, and in the placid tone of their orisons. Anymore, they humbly bowed at his feet, singing his praises through clenched teeth, only to turn the corner and slander his name with baseless, sideways chitchat.

He had it under control, though. He always did.

As with everything in Cezar's life, he needed only to find the right moment for action and all the pieces would fall back into place. He had his army and he had a plan. Roughly. It wouldn't be long before Jezebel—and her whoring slut of a mother—would come waltzing back into his primed clutches, through the gates of the compound and back to their assigned fates. Then, he would *finally* win. All the testing, waiting, hiding in shadows would be over—finally over. That moment of the Order's history—their constant, arduous striving—would end, and their long-overdue days of triumph would begin.

But still, a thread of doubt lingered, hidden like a spider's first weak-spun thread, stretching across a daunting, Herculean chasm—the last void separating them from their ultimate goal. At the back of Cezar's mind, a hope hid; a wish, a prayer was buried there.

He slapped himself. Those were not the words nor thoughts of a fearless leader—the bringer of change, the usurper for their new world. *Hope* was not a concept intrinsic to action. But no matter how he pleaded with himself, there was still that flicker of doubt, a dread that—in Jezebel—he had created a thing whose power even *he* could not control. For as much as the Order had their doubts, he matched their concerns in privacy, with his own uneasiness—with the fidgety, nail-biting fretfulness of a pathetic greenhorn (a *new-robe*, as they called them). But he wasn't a new-robe; he was their chief and guardian, their dark beacon toward escape from the travesties of a damaged world, one already half-dead. So he needed to start acting like one, again. He needed to start acting his office, and to start putting his age-wearied brain back to work; to pull all the stops and kick their metaphorical brooms into high gear.

Seated in the privacy of his chambers, in the ataraxic confines of what he oft reminded himself was the Best Room of the House, he scratched at his scalp again. Guiltlessly, heartily, he scratched.

One of the downsides to prolonged life was the onset of age. It came slowly, with the creeping agony of dragging a dead chain gang through heavy mud. The way weight accumulates over time—sneaking into the haunches and hips, little love handles blossoming into a full-blown gut—but gradually enough that its onset is hidden in plain sight; that was how his aging came on.

He lay in thought across a duvet at the center of his room—which was resplendent, a far cry from the compound's other cinderblock cells with padlocked doors. His was a bedchamber befitting a sultan, set with Indian rugs and lit by gilded candelabras holding tall black candles, evoking all the decadence of a Huysmans novel.

Cezar, the Overseer, rose to his bookcases. The three sets of shelves were made of a rare scarlet oak, trees grown on the acid-soiled grounds of an ancient coven and stained by the blood of virgins. Cezar only placed his most prized possessions on those shelves. He lifted back the topmost glass enclosure and retrieved his journals; he fingered each cover longingly, with closed eyes, feeling for the gumption and bloodshed buried beneath the soft-bound spines.

It was a thing he seldom did, dwell in the past, but the circumstances called for a quick stay there. A brief appointment to those fledgling years was just what he needed; they would be a reminder of his climb to reach his great seat—one he'd earned and was entitled to. His place at the head of their Order was one he'd beaten his way to—the way a true artist sculpts with his innards, feeling outward from nerve to fingertip, carving the perfect image of his subject. He had created the Order in like manner, of his own flesh and blood and bone. A reminder of that history would squelch the speck of doubt that crept unnecessarily across his spine, against all his better wishes.

Like any indulgence, lavishing in one's past achievements intoxicates. As sure as imbibing floods the head with drunkenness, reverence of the past threatens to drown out the battle cry in front of one's own face. He knew this, yet he needed it.

He opened the volumes of his history and looked backward, beginning with the beginning. All the things indicative of a proper black magician were there: pages of violence, bloodshed, trickery, fornication, and lust. But before the onslaught, something else had occurred. Something more personal. Hidden on the top shelf, shoved far behind all the other volumes, was another past, a history he oft dismissed as nothing more than a faulted memory—a blip of weakness predating his ascendancy. He returned to the bookshelf and, feeling blindly around its deepest, highest corner, touched the unmistakably weathered cover of that most ancient of biographies.

He opened the book and skimmed the pages, feeling the thin, yellowed parchment. Their texture was that of dried corpse skin, crinkling at his touch, as though the words—and his memory of the events inspiring them—might suddenly disappear. But they didn't. Despite the temptation to curtail his trip through the crowded avenues of his own far-fading memory, the story of his birth retained its mark across the first pages of the journal. It began in a script that wasn't his own: it was his father's dainty, thin, and curling handwriting, telling the story of his son's birth—the story of Cezar's creation.

June 10, 1920

Our son was born today.

At first, he was just a vague lump of flesh, shrouded in Katjaa's meat and pus and blood. My initial fear had been that he was demon-born but, now that they've cleaned him, he looks to be human.

Blessings to Baal above!

Katjaa bled too much but pulled through in the end, thanks to the doctor. Still, watching all those wet, red towels pile up in the hall was enough to send my pulse climbing. I've never been one to feel with my heart—I was raised to intuit with the mind first and foremost—but I did experience a flash or two of fear for my wife's well-being. When it was over, the uncanny sound of neonatal squealing rose to my ears. I was finally permitted to see her, and to hold our newborn son.

Somehow, I've always been averse to the prospect of fatherhood, perhaps afraid I could never live up to the expectations of my own pa—as though he might descend from parted clouds, returned to ridicule the choices I make with our boy. A part of me also worried about the kind of life I would be bringing him into. We aren't a wealthy people and, although we are a happy family, our gates seldom part for newcomers.

Letting a child come into the fold was a choice made my many, not just myself. When all the others agreed it was time, that rearing a child in the traditions of our group would be essential to our long-term goals, I allowed myself to plant the seed of child inside Katjaa's slender, young belly.

It had taken a toll on her, carrying the burden of the growing life within her. Whereas the myth of pregnancy leans toward an expecting mother's fresh, mystifying dew—a lit-from-within glow—the harsh truth of it was just the opposite, at least for Katjaa. Her limbs seemed to sag, at odds with her growing paunch (the babe must be huge in there, I remember thinking), and she took on an aubergine, deathly pallor.

I was almost tempted to call it off, to bring in the doctor to force termination of the child. But she had pleaded against it, and took to locking herself up at even my most subtle hint of concern.

Finally, though, it has ended—with birth.

I wonder how things between us, Katjaa and me, would have turned out differently if Cezar hadn't been born. There are seers among us, but I have stopped myself from seeking their counsel, in the fear that I would see something better through their rounded crystal; I worry I'd grow to hate the child, too.

Nevertheless, seeing her (at long last) holding little Cezar—already with a full head of hair atop his mushy skull—made this old man feel something again. He's a miracle. Our miracle. We will find a place for him in the fold, and carve out his potential to match the esteem of the seat he'll inherit upon my death. I'll do my best to impart the same great knowledge to him; we will share in the arcane wisdom my father bestowed upon me, and that which his forefathers instilled in him.

Now I must go and sit at Katjaa's side, consoling her while her birthing wounds are tended to.

June 20, 1920

Already, my wife is up and moving. The doctor has discouraged her from vigorous activity, but she's a stubborn one (always was) and so she ignores his prescription. Instead, she waltzes about, hovering between bragging out the bedroom window to the ladies of our group, trading French novels hauled in on our last import, and clinging to the crib of our son.

When she looks down at Cezar, it's with a kind of love I'll never know: the sort only a mother can have for her child. Her irises swell with light, and I fight to hold in an insensible feeling of jealousy. He's my son, I remind myself, and yet it is there: that itch through the fingertips, as though my mind compels my body to latch at the babe's throat. She pays me attention no more—attention I seldom appreciated before, and yet now it's her touch that I crave.

My bond with him is, apparently, slow to form. If anything, my interest in Cezar has already dwindled to nearly nothing.

The initial revulsion I felt when regarding his bloody, alien form has returned, twofold. It swelled to replace the fleeting bit of pride I felt when I held him after birth. Although he is no longer coated in gore, there is something dwelling there, as though a deep-seated mania lingers in his skull, under the forward folds of his brain. His eyes: they are inhuman, vacant and apathetic. They are not the eyes of a civil man; their dullness concerns me. Katjaa only calls me stupid for worrying so much, and she tells me Cezar will "do great things." It remains to be seen.

I can see the bond between them growing, just as whatever shred of filial care I may have briefly exhibited vanishes.

He loves her, too. Very much. Though he's not yet two weeks old, a flicker of delight runs through the boy's face whenever his mother draws near. Yet when I approach his bed, he begins a tone-deaf squeal that does not cease until I've parted, until I've drawn far from him, even out the foremost habitations. It's only once I'm clear onto our modest dirt plaza, in the company of our denizens (who look back and forth, accusatorily: toward me, and toward the tremulous cries of Cezar), that his threats finally abate.

From now on, perhaps I'll leave Katjaa to tend to little Cezar. The baby was more hers than mine to begin with—she bore and birthed it, against my insistence to discontinue his life.

Anyway, I've a community to care for. Let them have their fun.

August 15, 1920

Today a group of dissidents threatened to revolt. Hayforks lifted up in protest, they wished to quit our walls, and to spread news of our great secrets to ears unready for the truth. Thankfully, the community (though small) is comprised of enough good and honest folk that the rebels were quickly quietened, and peacefully.

Katjaa watched through the open windows of their loft (hers and Cezar's; I've taken to sleeping on the hay-covered floor of the cupola, where I can see all that occurs below me—today they slaughter our hens, the diviners tell their tales by appointment, and one of the old ones turned a century). Her eyebrows were raised in the way I know so well, arcing into a vexed hook. As soon as the troubles were resolved, she disappeared again, her figure replaced by the curtains. It's a real hassle getting her out of the house anymore. She'd rather care for that infant of hers than socialize; though she used to love interacting with the other women of our group, she now avoids them. I've begun to worry if she isn't too attached to the child, but the doctor insists it's all normal, just a part of the psychological healing process.

I wonder what he means by that, and what there is to heal. Mostly, she's recovered: fully mobile, able, and alert.

I'll trust the doctor's word, for now.

October 30, 1920

More trouble last week, but the outcome was less favorable than before.

Whereas our more learned of acolytes would usually step up to placate the protestors, this time they were nowhere to be found.

I was left to single-handedly wean the trio of rebels from the bitter teat they'd fixed their mouths upon—repudiating our oaths, asking for permission to wander from the grounds, to see the way the world has changed since our beginnings here. When one of them moved against my permission to unlatch the gates, I had to cut him down. I threw a sharp-edged sickle at him; it lost its head in the stump of his neck and killed him. There was no other choice. His departure would have set a precedent I cannot afford to let live—not here, at this most hallowed of sites. My brethren and forebears shed blood and gave their lives to protect our investments, and an ill-tempered scamp won't sully it. His co-conspirators promised to stamp shut their bleeding mouths, for good. The dead man will have no funeral.

When I finally found the elders of the camp, they were gathered under the shade of a tree at the center of camp—the oldest ironwood with the lowest-hanging branches—sipping drunkenly on bits of roasted agave stalk around a fresh-stoked fire. They saw my bloodied face, but none rose to inquire after my safety.

I take their fresh ineptitude, their complacence, as a sign of our end days drawing near. It approaches faster and sooner than I have feared.

Something must be done here. These are not the people they once were, as though some clandestine creature—perhaps an invisible succubus—has single-handedly drained them of their once great capacity for action, and meaningful study. They neglect the rigors of our pact, eschewing their research in favor of an uncanny indolence. Something must be done.

Katjaa reminds me that our son is only eighteen weeks old. This is her way of saying not to act foolishly, as though I should look out for him and consider our family's best interests. But I no longer know my family—neither my immediate fleshy kin, so freshly born, nor the brotherhood to whom I've dedicated my entire being. They are strangers in my house.

Is it foolish for a wolf to bite a snake, when the serpent has set hold across its neck?

January 10, 1921

A two-month spell of quiet, which I welcomed on tenterhooks, was finally interrupted last night.

Just as the child grows larger, fatter and longer, so too does the sense of foreboding swell within me. A sneaking suspicion that all of them conspire against me has flattened against the membranous skin that covers my eyes, bloating my seeing bits with unrest. Perhaps, in some inexplicable way, bringing new life into this world was the beginning of this curse—as though the child's sinister presence was my punishment, for dabbling in these arcane arts. But no, I have not crossed that line; our cabal has stayed just below the line of sight, skirting with danger but never threatening the devil outright.

There must be some other explanation for what occurred—a reason for how the clouds gathered, and for the unholy downpour they released.

When the sky opened, I'd been lying out on a thin cot, seeking inspiration from the afternoon sun, praising its warmth. Admittedly, I'd moved past gnosis and simply fallen into sleep, but not much time could have passed before I was awakened by the feel of unexpected dampness plodding against my cheeks, dripping into my mouth and filling it with a horrible, metallic burn. What the sky threw down at us was not water, but blood. Red gouts of it streamed upon us, puddling in the sand; it beat so fiercely as to loosen the foundations of our threadbare tenements. One of the apartments now sits slanted, its outer walls bent outward, as though punched from within by a hulking golem. I fear it may collapse, yet none of the others offer help to reinforce the structure.

Whereas I took the event as an omen—a hint of what might still be waiting down the line for us, should whatever force threatening our peace be left to linger, to grow and fester—others among us rejoiced in the happening. They called it The Requital. It's unclear who coined this impious term, but no one seems to fight it worse than me. The camps are abuzz with talk of it, as though everyone here has been charged by its stark force. Like psychotics feeding off the raw, inborn energy of their collective madness, the sense of an impending schism has become palpable here.

At this, our ancient land—a site bequeathed unto me by my father and his before him— these heathens, whose sloppy recruitment to our band I rightly admit guilt over, stormed the depot and looted our cache of precious decoctions. The blubbering bastards imbibed until they were near the point of regurgitating all the spoils of their loathsome attack. Wasters. Pathetic, indolent slobs.

My initial thought was to kill them all, in the name of our cause and the names of my dead kin, but I'm only one man and they were twenty- or thirty-some, and incensed by the dark spirit of their bloodlust. I could not have taken them alone. So I retired to my chamber, where I sat thinking deeply—through the night, and the dawn of this day, the 10th of January, 1921—on what course of action I should take. If there's one thing I understand, it's this: those miscreants won't be the death of me. Even if it takes employing the devices of my most dastardly potential, they'll be fixed—and in short time.

Let it be known and here recorded that on this day I, Nikolai Lagunov, do will and declare my unending hatred for all those set against me, barring my path to good and righteous learning.

Any among our cabal who prohibit the harmonious pursuit of unknown wisdoms—or who seek to rush their way down a path meant for careful, precise plodding, or to access those secrets by devious, violent means—shall be banned from this, our great Order of Baal, forever.

Cezar, the Overseer, closed his father's journal, perking his ears toward the distant sound of footsteps; hushed, like fingers grazing cotton. Too hushed. Someone was creeping by outside his chamber door. He awaited their knock, but none came.

Standing to replace the old tome back on his prized oak shelf, the Overseer was struck by the similarity of their predicaments. Although he had no son of whom to be suspicious, Cezar was growing increasingly skeptical about the trustworthiness of his attendants.

The situation was still within his grasp, though.

Unlike his father, he had no male heir to whom he could surrender his seat— at least, none worthy. There was no one on the premises powerful enough to overtake him, either—besides which, they all still feared him. Cry as they may, slandering his name, no one at the compound would lift a finger in reproach of his failure to find the girl: their hope, their future.

Jezebel wasn't ready for what was to come, yet she had to be. They'd delayed long enough. The time was already upon them—perhaps even past them. Still, she had much to learn before she could lead alongside him.

Although born of his own flesh, she had no knowledge of their kinship— unless by some invisible, pulsating feeling in her bones. She always seemed to hate him, just as much as Cezar's father had seemingly hated him. But the difference between them—between Nikolai and Cezar—was this: the Overseer did not hate his kin, even though she ran away. No, he did not harbor any malice toward Jezebel in his heart. Just the opposite, in fact. When he thought of her, his mind soared with the possibilities of their reign. Together, they could do anything. They could command the forces of older, greater ones than his father's pathetic Baal.

Four Takers were already theirs to command, and more would join their ranks—soon, if only Jezebel returned.

When she returns, he reminded himself.

The footsteps receded. Whoever endeavored to spy upon him would receive no answers that day. His was a conscience immune to the judgment of others, settled and prepped for reaping, ready to sow the seeds of their century-long labor.

CHAPTER XXVII

Jezebel awoke across from her mother, whose high cheekbones and ringlety hair were undeniable proof of the blood they shared. She reached out to touch Meredith's soft-skinned face, not quite believing it was real, tracing the winding path of the scar running from her mother's jawline to her gnarled ear.

Meredith's eyes opened—a clear and bright blue which exactly mirrored the color of Jezebel's left iris—and smiled.

At first glance, when her mother had crept up on them after their crash landing—Orson bleeding on the sand, crying out for help—Jezebel had blanked; she was completely overwhelmed with emotions so mixed that she didn't know how to act. First it was with hatred, pushing Meredith away, but then it was coupled with an almost nirvanic exultation at the sight of her. Her mom, alive—and anticipating her, no less. Their acquaintance was delayed by the pressing matter of Orson's injuries, and when the first hug finally happened it was bathetic, not at all worth the build-up, the longing. Meredith was just another human, like Jezebel—except maybe not as powerful.

Meredith's gifts barely included the art of divining (more prediction than prophecy, as was the case; she could guess at a series of possible outcomes), and an extra-sensory touch of clairvoyance that allowed her to funnel her thoughts and dreams into the minds of others (just as she'd done to Jezebel way back when, at the onset of her journey, in the challenge-that-wasn't-a-challenge).

Her mom's moods had been inconstant since they arrived, flittering back and forth between caring matriarch and stern lecturer—with all the capriciousness of a toddler at Christmas. She had prepped them for an advance on the compound, where they hoped to raze the grounds and destroy the Overseer, but it had taken slow progress.

At first, Jezebel was tempted to ignore her call to arms, pleading with her mother to reconsider an advance on the Order ("Let's just take off," and "We'll forget the bastard ever messed with our lives"), but something in her mother's injured gaze—a hint of what he might have done to her while she was living there—told Jezebel to still her defector's dream and screw up all her courage for the fight ahead. So she dug in, even if the sense of camaraderie between them was still only frail.

The other one, the stranger, had a crazy story to tell: about mass chaos in a town called San Francisco. It was a fantastical tale, but plausible; she did not discount the Overseer's prowess, even his capacity for guiltless destruction on such a large scale (and Orson confirmed that he'd heard something on the radio about it, just before he and Jezebel had so chaotically met). He was Touched, too. In his case, its byproduct was also the gift of flight—only, he was slower at mastering his skills.

His name was Birch—

"A trio of odd-named kids," Meredith kept saying.

Jezebel, Orson, and Birch.

Birch only shared as much of his life's story with the group as was necessary to keep things moving, yet he was less careful in his manner of dealing with Meredith—as if they shared some secret, earnest bond.

One thing he didn't tell them was that his mother had been harmed by the Overseer, perhaps even killed, a long time ago. It was a detail Jezebel intuited on their first night at the cave, simply by touching Birch's arm, in a gesture disguised as salutary. She saw flashes of his life with a moody, religious woman not unlike Norma; and she caught a glimpse of his conversations with Meredith, discussing how hard life at the compound had been for her.

This revelation must have been the glue that had bonded Meredith and him together. They shared a common goal: retribution in the final, mortal ruination of the Overseer.

Jezebel's link to Meredith continued to fluctuate to and fro, between loving and cautious. A trip toward the former occurred when her mother brushed out her hair late one night; it was a dive toward remorse in reflecting upon the time they'd lost.

Jezebel's relationship with Orson was also strained. She couldn't help wondering why he decided to continue helping her. Sure, she'd rescued him, and by some odd circumstance they'd been brought together (and *just* after his having been Touched), but that didn't account for the odd way he stared at her from his spot across the cave (they were divided into pairs: the girls on one side of the cave, boys on the other). He even occasionally looked like he was crying, unabashedly, with his legs drawn up against his chest, crunching his body together into a pathetic fetal position. She didn't need someone to take care of. Things would be *much* easier if he just went his own way. But he was obligated to her by some idealistic blood contract, a crazy notion he'd dreamed up—an idea that, because she "saved his life," he would follow her forever, to the depths of the Overseer's depraved hell and back.

Perhaps she was being too hard on him. At one point, back at Norma's house, Jezebel *had* felt a connection to him (once, as strong as opposite sides of a magnet being drawn together), and she'd even considered him the closest thing she ever had to a friend. But now that she'd found her mother, things were different. Or *should be* different. She didn't need a friend anymore; this was all she ever wanted but had denied herself the luxury of wishing for: a family. None of the other bits mattered any longer, nor crossed her mind. She had to tell herself that—to push those concerns out of the way—so she could focus on the objective at hand, and on the promise of the future.

But there was something else, buried underneath all that hard resolve. A bit of sadness still, where there should be none; and on top of that, a plodding drip of dread, as though some part of the picture was still shrouded from her, lying just out of sight.

What are you afraid of? Jezebel wondered. The answer, no matter how she strived, would not reveal itself.

Jezebel, Orson, and Birch decided they should formulate their plan; it had been long enough, and they were much better trained, more prepared. If they waited any longer, the Overseer would find them, corner and nip them out like rats trapped in a hole.

But Meredith kept saying they weren't ready—not yet.

"Then what do we need to do, to be ready?" Jezebel asked. "It's been three months already."

Meredith stared at her feet, ignoring her daughter's valid question while the boys stared at their leader too, arms crossed, waiting for answers. She had aged a lot in three months—crow's-feet deepened—and was still dressed in the compound's customary robe. The poor quality of lighting in their cave didn't do her wrinkles any favors either.

"I've gotten better," Birch chimed in, licking his lips like a greedy, starved cur. "At flying, I mean. So let's get the fucker already!"

Jezebel flinched at his curse, not because of the word he chose, but because of his inflection: he sounded as vehement as the Overseer standing at his rostrum, inciting fear in his people, shoving them into action. Both of them had that distinctly masculine quality, too: a vehement, vindictive excitement for violence. Looking at Birch in passing, Jezebel wouldn't have actually guessed that he *was* that sort of man (he looked soft, the way his long, slightly-wavy hair hung just to his shoulders and how he swung his hips, ever so slightly—not quite effeminately, but in a distinctly nonvirile manner).

"Not yet," Meredith pleaded, in the same irrevocable tone.

She's trying to be a mother, Jezebel thought. *To all of us. But it's not working. She's never been one before and she's not cut out for it. Someone else needs to step up.*

"I disagree with you, mother." It still felt weird calling her that, erasing the fact that she'd wondered her whole life about her origins while the woman who birthed her sat idly by, perhaps no more than a stone's throw away. "I think it's already past the time to make our move."

A silence drew out the tension between them—on one side, the three little orphans (one reunited to her ma, but still feeling lost) cried out for war, while at the other end of the battlements Meredith pleaded for patience.

"What do you think, Birch?" Jezebel asked. She was increasingly curious about his motives. He often spoke about wanting to slice the bastard—or fucker, or any other number of slurs—but he never offered strategy, nor elucidated further on his

362

motivations. But none of them had a calculated, exacting plan with which to execute their grandiose notions of conquest. It was all talk—of victory, vengeance, retribution—and no game.

"Since you asked," Birch said. "I think we're a little short-handed. Four of us, mostly newbies, against a pack of them. Not to mention whatever demons they might throw our way." Jezebel stared at him, long and hard. He corrected himself, "Sorry, *Takers*. Regardless, we have to do something, and *soon*. Like, now!"

"Two of us *aren't* newbies," Meredith corrected. "Jezebel and I both know their ways. That's an advantage, of sorts. I was once very close to the Overseer myself, and Jezebel was his most promising student. Resistant, but promising." She reached for Jezebel, showing surprising affection, rubbing her shoulders, caressing her hair while she smiled ear-to-ear—the displays of a proud parent whose license plate might be encased with a cover that read, *My child is a First Degree Necromancer.*

"That's true," Jezebel said. "And we aren't giving the boys enough credit. Orson knows how to channel his energy with better control. Birch has almost mastered the art of aeronautics, while I've mostly plateaued. I don't think there's much more training we can do. We just need a thorough plan."

"We just charge in, guns blazing—metaphorically speaking," Birch said.

"That won't work." Meredith sighed heavily and glowered at him. Her eyes said, *Calm down, cowboy.* "Even if we make it through the gates—which will be hard enough, as heavily guarded as they'll be—we'd still have to take out the whole lot of them. He'll be locked up tight in his room, not waiting for us out in the open with his arms spread wide 'n' welcome."

"I remember you once told us something," Orson chimed in. "You told us that if we took him out, all the others would be useless. Like stamping out the queen of a massive hive: the rest of the Order would be senseless, powerless to fight back."

"Hate to admit it," Birch said, "but he's right. You did say that." He pinched his hair together, drawing it back into a knot at the crown of his head. He only did that when he was thoroughly irritated, or had been bested. "Seems like our best option's to target him directly."

"So how do we get in?" Jezebel asked. "And how do we distract all the others?"

They directed their collective gaze back at Meredith, as though she was sure to have the answer, as though—just as Jezebel predicted—there was still some detail she withheld, a small but crucial key to the success of their invasion.

Meredith turned away from them, toward the entrance of the cave. The moon was out in full, outlining her silhouette in silver flecks of light; she looked like a cloud of smoke, billowing truculently on the entryway. "There's one option we haven't considered. I was hoping it wouldn't come to it…"

"What is it?" Jezebel asked, even though she already knew what Meredith would say. She'd been catching flickers of her mother's musings lately—more than usual. They weren't blurbs that Meredith voluntarily surrendered; they were her deepest secrets and most private thoughts. Like her mother, Jezebel was learning to dive headfirst, to swim deeper.

"Jezebel surrenders—" Meredith started.

"No way!" Orson interrupted, jumping in front of Jezebel like a spellbound Prince Charming. "He'll kill her on sight."

"Hear me out," Meredith urged. "The Overseer wants her more than anything, and *alive*—"

"Yeah, we know that already, but you still haven't told us *why* he wants her!"

"She's right," Jezebel said. "Let's hear what she has to say. If it'll get us in, I'm willing to try it."

"Thanks, dear." Meredith cringed immediately after speaking the endearment, as though she hadn't even fooled herself with it. "He wants her more than anything and *yes*, he will kill her if given the chance—but not right away. He would need her alive for some time, to prepare the invocation."

"What kind of invocation?" Jezebel asked. She crossed her arms over her chest, instinctually guarding her breasts and thorax at the thought of his long-robed approach, his spindly hands touching her, the feel of his cold breath, drawing her down and into the web of his spells. "A summoning?"

"Yes, and a Taking." Meredith turned to face them again and approached Jezebel. She scooped her daughter's hands into her own, warming them, pulling her close, and cradling her the way she never could before. "He wants to put the devil in you, Jezebel. The devil himself: Azazel, Baphomet, Abaddon, Iblis. The One with Many Names."

Jezebel squeezed out of her mother's grasp and collapsed against the floor, scraping her legs on the gravel underfoot. She didn't even feel the collision, she was so numb and frightened. Still, she knew Meredith was right—it was their only chance. She also knew that if he planned to raise *The* Devil himself, things weren't looking good—not for them, and not for the rest of the world. If the Overseer succeeded, and roused that most indomitable evil to Take her, she wouldn't be able to fight it.

"Why me?" Jezebel asked. She immediately felt silly and selfish for asking the question: a very human concern.

Meredith hesitated for only a moment, letting a trickle of thought pass between them. She filled Jezebel's mind with words that stung with sharp penitence: *Just tell her*. Finally, her mother said, "You're his daughter, Jezebel. And raised behind those walls, primed for the unfortunate purpose he saw fit." She pointed outward, through the cavern's opening to the north, toward the badlands, toward the sward of dead grass, the fractured husks of trees lined like skeletons marching toward the gates of hell, toward the compound. Her eyes were damp with sadness and regret—it was sorrow insurmountable, for the undertaking she had dumped against her daughter in that gruesome revelation.

It hit Jezebel like a ton of boiling tar, burning her resolve with an acid that penetrated through to her soul. She knew immediately that her mother had kept it from her, and that she could have shared it at any point prior. She'd been able enough to set her free, to guide her to Norma and back again—yet she never found the time to share this urgent message.

You're his daughter. It echoed through her skull like knives on springs, repeatedly stabbing her with the same pang of repugnance and nausea.

"He's my father," Jezebel said slowly, processing, "and you're my mother. But what about Peter?"

Meredith didn't respond, only whimpered pathetically, lip-quaveringly.

Jezebel continued her reproach of Meredith: "Norma warned me about you. She called you a whore. She wasn't proud of you, and now I know why. You gave up everything for that bastard, but when he threw you to the curb you came crawling back to Peter, didn't you?"

"No, Jezebel. That's not it." Meredith eyed the boys as though warning them of Jezebel's fast-approaching explosion of rage, which was gaining momentum every second. They moved away, back to their grass cots. "I loved Peter very much, and we intended to fix things, but I made some mistakes along the way. Peter forgave me in the end. He offered me a second chance. I took it, hoping I'd spend the rest of my life with you both. He would have loved you as his own, dear, regardless of *my* mistakes."

Jezebel slowed her breathing, promising herself she could deal with it, she could move past it, she could somehow ignore the searing truth of her ancestry: that she was made of a diabolical pedigree. It explained her great aptitudes, and the oft-discharged longing for normalcy she experienced, then quickly forgot. Others her age would have imploded in the solitude, the quiet introspection, the torturous examinations and constant mind-games—but in the face of such wicked experiments, Jezebel had thrived. Perhaps it *was* her birthright to be compelled to that final rite, to be consumed by and transformed into a harbinger of doom.

"Are you okay?" Meredith asked pathetically, side-stepping closer, dragging her leaden feet, raising her trembling hands uncertainly toward her daughter's neck.

Jezebel batted her away and said, "I just need time to think."

"It doesn't change anything, dear…" That awful expression again, peculiar as an elephant setting table for tea—a forced sentiment that didn't fit falling from her mother's mouth.

"Stop calling me that." Jezebel gritted her teeth, staring down at her shriveled-up, downcast ma, and projected thoughts toward her:

If you're listening, pay attention. If you can hear me, know that I hate you more than anything I've ever known—though, considering I don't know a lot about anything outside our Order's ways, that's not saying much, is it? You did a good job making sure of that, keeping me there when you could have done this a long, long time ago. You could have set me free.

"Don't do that!" Meredith screamed, smashing her hands against her ears, squinting as though invisible needles pierced through her eardrums. "You're hurting me!"

If you want me to stop, you're going to have to make me. I know you have the power. Before I knew I could do this, you were butting into my head, invading my dreams, spying on my private thoughts. Even when you didn't speak, I always felt you there. All those years, wondering if I was going crazy. But you don't need to go crazy when you're already born that way.

"ST-STO-STOP!" Meredith shrieked, collapsing to the floor and gripping her stomach. Blood trickled from her nostrils, and down from one corner of her snarling mouth.

Orson and Birch ran to her side, pushing Jezebel away.

"What did you do, Jezebel?" Orson asked, his brows lowered.

"Nothing," she peeped.

"Grab her arms!" Birch commanded, having already latched onto both of Meredith's ankles himself.

He and Orson dragged Meredith's spasming body toward the far corner of the cave, pushing together their balled-up mossy beds and setting her down slowly. Birch lowered himself to sit alongside her, wrapping an arm around her waist to pull her close beside him. He lowered an ear to the side of her mouth.

"Her breathing's shallow," he told the others, eyes wide with focus, lips barely quavering for fear of interrupting the sound of Meredith's subtle intake of breath. Satisfied, he pursed his lips and rose to face Jezebel directly. "What the *fuck* did you do to her? She's your mother, goddamn it!"

"I- I- I only wanted to…" Jezebel trailed off, her eyes brimming with moisture and an unfamiliar tightness that pinched through the center of her chest, as though all her mass had gathered into a sharp point at her sternum. "I just wanted her to know how I feel."

"Help her," Orson pleaded, shuffling to stand between them, facing Jezebel and glowing with as much wholehearted sympathy for Jezebel as Birch had exhibited for Meredith. He touched Jezebel's knotted hands, ensconcing them in his own and said, "I know you didn't mean it."

Jezebel nodded, pulled free of her only friend's grip, and wobbled toward her mom. She straddled Meredith while carefully avoiding her slow-rising, slow-falling upper chest; with her breath already ragged, Jezebel needn't apply further strain. She balanced on the top of her mother's pubis, legs splayed outward along either side of her pelvis as though looking for access to re-enter the womb. Gently, she bent forward and pressed her unmoving, puckered lips to Meredith's cheek; it felt cold, smooth and waxy (the way she imagined a department store mannequin's plastic flesh might feel) and Jezebel's dry mouth adhered to the skin for a moment as she pulled away, like a tongue against hard-frozen ice.

From coccyx to the tip of her skull, Jezebel stretched upward, as though an unseen force pulled her by a knot of hair atop her head (not unlike the fashion Birch so loved to sport). Drawing the cumulative force of an unseen eye from the throbbing reverb at the tip of her brow, she connected to the deepest living part of Meredith, caressing the piece that had dragged her from the scene. Finding that spot—where her mother had withdrawn—was like swimming through a briny, clouded pond (one teeming with sentient, sharp-toothed creatures; the kind that disguise themselves in the murk until, a breath away, they strike in a momentary shimmer of scale, and with a thrashing of flesh-shredding jaws). Impossibly, she found she could easily maneuver toward the ball of light, still dully throbbing at the bottom of that dark pool: it was her mother, ashamed and ragged, but alive. With an intuitive bewitchment, and a little sleight of mind, Jezebel enticed Meredith out of her nestled spot, lifted her up to the surface, and dragged her out of the pit of gloom into which she'd been cast.

Jezebel opened her eyes and saw that her mother's had unlatched, too. Staring at one another, Jezebel felt a fondness akin to symmetry, like being lifted to float on the edge of a seesaw by a perfect counterweight. A balance had been struck, an equanimity that spread thin the knot of tension dragging at her gut, flattening it out into even-tempered, clear-minded focus.

"I'm sorry," Meredith whispered.

"Me, too." Jezebel pried Meredith off the cot and dragged her across the cave, arms wrapped around her shoulders in support, with daughterly benevolence.

"That was a quick one-eighty," Birch quipped, more to Orson than the girls.

"You guys okay?" Orson asked, ignoring Birch.

"I'm fine," Meredith said, craning her neck to see Jezebel's face, positioned close at her elbow.

"Me?" Jezebel asked. "Yeah, don't worry—I'll be okay. I just want to get this over with. The more we wait, the more confused and scared I'll get. If we act now, soon, I might be able to ignore the implications…"

Meredith gained her footing and cleared her head of the hot-tempered torrent which had engulfed her; she unwrapped her arms from Jezebel's trunk and wiped the half-dried streaks of blood from her face. It left ruddy marks around her lips and cheeks, like the streaked-lipstick smear on a prostitute's mouth after she's finished servicing her client. It was an image Jezebel quickly pushed from her mind—and one she wasn't sure how she'd acquired.

"Here's what we'll do," Meredith started. She placed a hand on her daughter's head and addressed the group: "Jezebel will fly in from overhead, right into the center courtyard, where the Order convenes. That'll draw most of them out from the far corners of the compound, leaving us—hopefully—free to break clear through the front."

"Shouldn't someone back Jezebel up?" Orson asked.

Meredith gnawed her lip and said, "No. Birch can get away quick if she needs us. I'll be able to tell, to hear if she's in trouble. Our connection will let me intuit her distress. Jezebel's made that especially clear today."

"I'm fine with that," Birch said, flexing his wings, patting them gingerly, an immodest smirk spreading across his face. "I'm happy to stretch these puppies out, if need be."

Meredith nodded and continued, "The Overseer's strongest comrades were killed back in Tucson. As far as we know, that leaves us at an advantage: no one else at the compound can fly. Unless something has changed over the last few months, they'll only be able to trap us if we remain grounded. So Jezebel, try to keep to the air once you've drawn them out. They won't be able to hurt you if you keep moving. Same goes for you, Birch: keep them distracted, draw their focus, and Orson and I can go for—"

"*Him*," Jezebel finished. "You can say it. Go ahead."

Meredith cracked her neck, her lips drawn inward. "Yes, the Overseer. He'll be locked away in the safety of his quarters, no doubt schmucking about while his lackeys do all of his dirty work. But if we can get to him before they seize you—"

"They won't!" Jezebel interrupted.

"Yes, well, of course they *won't*, but if they *did*..." Meredith's thoughts dissolved into unclear mumbling. "It won't matter either way. We'll take him out long before anything like that can happen."

"Yeah," Birch said dispiritedly, with a knowing, vacant look—his eyes bulged, his lower teeth bared in a garish underbite. "Hope so."

After a stretch of quiet indecision—the air so taut, so discomfiting, that the rise and fall of dust stood out as brash, brutal clutter—Jezebel finally dispelled their uncertainties with an upward flourish of her arms, where both her hands met in a resounding *CLAP*.

"So then, it's settled," she said. "We leave first thing tomorrow, with the sunrise. We've wasted this day, and besides which could do with some sleep."

Meredith patted a clump of Jezebel's flaxen-oreish mane and stilled whatever lingering doubt might have persisted from the tip of her tongue. She kissed her daughter's crown, where her hair split into a center part, a little peek of pale scalp, and she said, "Good idea, dear. We could all use the rest."

Somehow, the sentimentality of that excessively spoken word—*dear*—had quickly grown on Jezebel. Its meaning had segued from placating, edgy, and awkward to just sweet enough, without the despotic condescension of a domineering Mommie-Knows-Best. Like it or not, Jezebel had begun to accept Meredith, to let her in, and to believe in the potential for a demonstrative, feeling— perhaps even loving—mother-daughter relationship. It was still floundering (neither of them quite knowing how to act, relying on impressions of what they thought it *meant* to be a mother or a daughter, as though there was a secret formula to which they must aspire) but the consanguineous bond between them was there, beating along, just out of sight, as instinctual and ever-present as a vein floating beneath the surface of the skin, its aspect just visible but its route unknown.

They retired to their respective sooty spots, sprinkled around the perimeter of the cave, separating their beds again and reclining to wait for reprieve in erratic sleep, curled into little balls against the floor: Birch, dreaming of revenge (*I'll get you, you bastard!*); Orson not far away, smiling, imagining what wonder awaited them tomorrow, with an inkling of longing there, too (*We'll make it, we have to…*); Meredith, within arm's reach, lying to face Jezebel with a sedate grin, eyes twinkling. Her mother's thoughts were well-guarded after what she'd done.

Closing her own eyes, doing her best not to imagine a gloomy outcome of their fatal plan, Jezebel drowned out the boys' thoughts with a sturdy, steady hum. The cloud behind her eyelids was translucent gray—like swimming through fog— and it led to the private, infernal regions of her restive, thrashing mind, where the Overseer—her father—glared at her from across his chambers with inhuman eyes, orange-rimmed cinders, gaping holes where his urbane orbs had once been; where she sliced his neck herself, and the others all bowed to her—their new leader, the

370

new Overseer of the Order. In another version of that uneasy haze, they bound her to a stake, watching her slowly sink into a bubbling pit of mud at the nucleus of their quad; writhing maggots and fist-sized flies swarmed from the coughing slop, swarming around her and shimmying up her thighs, disappearing into her maiden folds.

Jezebel awoke the next morning as agitated as the night before, but ready to pull all the stops. Her crusade had been a foundling one that turned into a fledgling one (of self-exploration and preservation), only to transmute further to the doom-laden endgame of the day.

She stretched her spine and slipped on her favorite dress (one of only three she owned, including the Order's robe).

A month earlier, Meredith and Birch had scouted an abandoned motel off the nearest highway, and brought back the cream-colored piece she so loved—along with some jeans, a few t-shirts for all of them, and some expired vending machine snacks they'd eaten tentatively, much to their stomachs' collective regret later on.

It was a modest cut, its hem reaching just above her knees, with pleated details that made it sway without wind; its jewel neck accentuated the long curve of her throat and proudly displayed her collar bones, lofty and full of grace.

The others gathered around her at the edge of the cave, looking like a ragtag troop of dullards: Orson blowing his nose, Birch combing knots from his unkempt coif, and Meredith rubbing her temples. Jezebel picked up on their need for direction, the way they stared, waiting for orders.

Where was their leader, the fearless Meredith, now? She'd absolved herself of the secret she withheld, and seemed to have passed the baton in doing so. Reluctantly, Jezebel accepted her role, sliding to the center of their haphazard ring to address them en masse.

"Today's the day," she said, her throat crackling with the morning's first toils, and admitted: "I really don't know what to say."

"It's okay," Meredith said, setting a hand on the crook of Jezebel's back, below her indrawn wings.

It tickled a bit, and Jezebel stretched them to full span. An expression of wonderment spread over the rest of the group, as though they gazed upon a great deity, their god.

"Do what you need to prepare," Jezebel said. "We leave in twenty."

The sun slowed its mount toward morning in respect for the perilous outing before them. Time seemed to creep by, as though awaiting their first move, expectant and frightened by the multitudinous outcomes that might result from their march on the compound.

For the first time since she and Orson had made it to the cave (and not many times before it), Jezebel did a reckless thing: she hoped.

CHAPTER XXVIII

Cezar returned once more to his father's journals, his decanter of red half-empty and his head swilling with insobriety. He was filled with expectation—excitement for the passages, perusal of which never grew old—a rush at the onset of majesty: the complete logging of his ascent to the seat of Overseer, from his father's pathetic perspective. He skimmed to reach the parts of Nikolai's memoirs he adored most: diabolical moments of bloodshed, evil, and frenzy.

June 10, 1930

The boy is ten years old now, and just as spritely as ever. Katjaa insists he'll hit a spell—a growth spell, or maybe she called it a growth spurt. I never needed one of those; I was born long, and only got longer. Either way, she adamantly defends his shrimpish physique. More importantly, she has taken to decrying the redundancy of my seat, as though she's already settled on the boy as my successor, mouthing off about the wonders he'll bring and the power he'll absorb into the fold. Baal willing, I'd let him sit as head of our group, even within my lifetime, but not until he's grown and has demonstrated he's ready for the task.

Katjaa planned all the festivities for Cezar on his birthday, today. He's soft-spoken and, since there aren't other children around for him to play with, he mostly sat by himself all day, quietly counting out sparse blades of grass, picking them out of the sand and holding them to his mouth as makeshift instruments. The sound he produced in that display was like grating metal on metal, a sharp-pitched whine which only seemed to amplify with each puff of air he exhaled. I rose from my spot under the great ironwood, mid-discussion (I'd been reminding the Old Ones of our

Order's principles of peace, a topic that's seemed to grow in popularity with every passing day, as our group continues to question the efficacy of our pacificity) to pluck the boy from the strip of lawn. When Katjaa saw me handling him, she rushed to me at once and ordered me to set him down, in front of all who'd gathered on the lawn.

What was I to do? Tell her no?

She is my spouse and is the boy's mother—though I may at times detest her for it. This gives her final say in matters of the brat's upbringing.

She scooped him away, no doubt to lock him up inside what's further become—exclusively— their chambers. I haven't shared a bed with her more than twice in the last year, and only then at her insistence.

I've given up on the both of them. If the boy grows to fit the name of Overseer, so be it. Until then, I'll do my very best to continually avert these little crises, which continue to pop up and which all share a common theme: Cezar.

Mayhap there's need for a Purging someday soon.

June 10, 1932

Another birthday, bringing Cezar closer to the Reaping age. Now he's twelve, and in just two years' time, he'll crouch below me and plead his case for the seat of Overseer. I appeal to Baal daily for some miracle, drawing his name in the sands at my seat, under our dried-up tree, perhaps blinded in part by my duty to him as his father.

What I've come away with is a grave sensation of dread, an ominous foreboding that points me toward inciting the actions I've avoided for too long.

It's years in the making, though.

There's no other choice, really.

July 18, 1932

The hellion has done it. He's broken our pact.

I found the rat bastard skulking the halls, late last night, and followed him to the moon-lit center of the grounds, where he and five others lay out in the pattern of a star's limbs—a pentagram, formed by their prostrate bodies. Cezar traced their figures with the rough circumference of a circle, pouring a dark liquid onto the sand that sizzled while it hit the ground.

I know this—I heard it! I saw it!

This is undeniable proof of his scheming, yet I fear my approach at reckoning his misdeeds was ill-timed. I'd been ready to begin the Purging next month, set to nudge into action what would be his downfall; but with this latest bit of evidence, there's no denying the need for immediate action. He must be Purged from us, forever.

Tomorrow I'll approach him, and be done with his child's antics for good (even if it means wrenching his breath away, sending him off to forever sleep). So be it.

July 20, 1932

I'm done for. There's no saving me to the cause of my forebears. I'm abandoned to their quest, and set loose to the mortal world.

It remains to be seen whether this is just some perverse form of justice (for an evil deed whose verity eludes me), or if my situation is just a result of the morbid workings of time. Maybe I was overdue for an upheaval, an usurper as conniving as he. All great eras do, after all, eventually come to an end—and often fall to the flags of false, alluring prophets. I only wish I could have spared those of the Order still loyal to its founding ideals.

How a boy of only twelve—a babe, truly—achieved such a swift and absolute upheaval, a complete transformation of our group's mindset, is beyond me. The things I saw over the last two days are of such a grotesque, abominable nature that I daren't even write them here.

I've wandered across the desert for hours and hours—thrown from our encampments as I was, with only the clothes on my back to act in my support—finding solace in the night. By cover of darkness, I've flicked my way through the desolation of these badlands. Until I find the most appropriate, safe enclosure in these spartan lands, I'll close this volume, though my eventual aim is to return to it, to recount the deeds of my besting.

Until then, steer clear of the Order of Baal, of where it once lay. It is Baal's circle no longer.

Cezar turned that last faded page, looking for more words in his father's jagged script, even though he knew they weren't there; that was the last of Nikolai's transcription. Of all people, Cezar knew this best, because *he* was the one who'd bested his father—and *he* was the one who kept the secrets of that sanguinary night, locked away in the invisible box of his heart. He was the one who followed his father through the desert, across the dunes like a sly, cloaked predator, waiting for the perfect moment to strike a final, fatal blow—waiting until Nikolai collapsed, wracked with dehydration and the swill of hallucinatory rage it brings. It had been easy, too, to slice his father's neck. To the consummate young Overseer, the spout of blood spurting out of Nikolai's fractured neck looked delectable, and he bathed his face in it, savoring that patch of warmth in the midst of the desert's bitter, gusting winds. Upon his return (with sand sticking to his soaked face), no one at the Order noticed the way Cezar dripped fresh with blood, how he swilled his mouth at the public tap, spitting copper across the square. Red-handed, he went to his mother's bed, and sat alongside her, gripping her by the wrist, whispering, "It's done."

He'd done it for her, after all: for Katjaa, his mother. The dumb, quixotic bastard had been so completely blindsided by the threat of Cezar's new regime that he neglected the care of his wife, and hadn't noticed her swift slip to infirmity.

Since he'd been born, Cezar had been glued to his mother's hip and so, when she first began to show signs of an unknown ailment, he was the first one to point them out to her: a peek of scalp where there'd once been buoyant curls; splotchy skin; a rancid undertone to her breath that grew into a stench like fetid, rotting onion. Her hair became gray, limp, and brittle; it broke easily when he ran his fingers through it.

Whatever the cankerous disease afflicting her was—in its most injurious moments, splitting her lips with whitish pus and drying out her milky skin, splotching it with smatterings of sores—would, if Cezar could help it, soon be put to bay.

Nikolai's neglect of Katjaa redoubled Cezar's hatred for his father, and was the cause for his initial dabblings with the forbidden texts—old tomes locked away, brimming with unholy pacts, strange sigils, forbidden spells. Instructions for the reanimation of corpses; poisonous decoctions of recherché plants; philters designed to dampen lovers' loins; and worse. Those dastardly branches of magic (ones foreign to the kindly, tranquil members of their compound) held the key to his assured success, to his ascendancy. It had been easy to pick the most volatile bits out amongst the withered pages of those arcana. Once he'd stolen them all from Nikolai's study, he could freely peruse those rumpled folios and wood-stamped leaflets, tearing out and circling the stanzas of greatest elegiac profundity. His fingers were naturally drawn to those lines, and his flesh seared pleasurably against the pages, like they were on supernal fire.

The first line of text balled up at the back of his throat; he couldn't quite get the words out. In time, though, it became easier, and whatever suspicions he had toward the nature of the texts were replaced by enjoyment of the budding powers they instilled—and the benefaction of vitality he observed flooding back to his mother.

At first, Katjaa had shown only slight signs of improvement—she was mobile, smiling, and regained much of her bird-like disposition, flitting about the room, cleaning or changing her shoes again and again, moving to the window and shouting down at passersby, more for attention than for any real reason. But the effects of his witchcraft were short-lived, and he soon realized the charms he selected were more novice enchantment than thaumaturgical whammy. She still showed the telltale signs of age, of illness, of approaching death: dark circles, loose skin, rotten breath. He revisited the words with a fastidious, formidable eye, and with an ache for more of their combustive force.

One day, not a week before the onset of what would become the event of his father's fatal displacement, Cezar stumbled across a grimoire whose tenants— bound behind the alluring, intricate cages of their sigils—promised him a real, permanent, and complete renovation of his lifestyle: the way he lived, and how he projected forward with the rest of his mortal years. The prospect of such a change (brimming with luxury, power, and the enduring love of his mother) was enough to convince him to dabble further. A trio of demons lived there, buried in those pages, and Cezar would come to rely upon them for the remainder of his adolescence (his so-called *growth spurt*). They would be his confidants, his directors, and the Takers he'd turn to when he needed them most.

With Katjaa growing ever weaker, he called upon them. The first proceedings were floundering ones, conducted in the privacy of Katjaa's room, drawing odd shapes beneath her bed, using his unfamiliar, fumbling hands. With a flicker at the wick of his candles and a sudden drop in temperature, the room would suddenly change—from the denuded light of his burning white tapers to a gauzy, dingy haze. The ambience had shifted noticeably to one bursting with wicked energy, as though a horned goat might appear at the threshold and, craning its neck, would bray before speaking: *Who summons me?* But nothing like that happened. The vague mist cleared and the obscure sensation—pinpricks along his spine, goosebumps on his flesh—absconded from the room, leaving Cezar and Katjaa enduringly alone.

That didn't stop him, though. Just as his father erringly vied for the continued support of his brethren, Cezar found success in the names of the darkest, unilluminated shadows of those he worshipped. He gave all of himself, willingly, and in turn found that things took a strong swing in his favor. The others ran to Cezar, even the Old Ones (the supposedly wise, loyal ones), mesmerized by the glow of power emanating from him like a just-visible aura. Drawn like flies to carrion, they smelled the brooding spirits he conjured to his aid, the ones whose names he dare not say aloud—except in seclusion, in the dark privacy of his bedchambers, where he had *almost* cured his ma (*a flash of color returning to her cheeks as she gripped his chalk-stained hands; a quaver across her mouth; a droplet of blood falling from each nostril; the curl of a smile, of gratitude for her son's endless endeavoring to help*).

Katjaa had long been aware of his plans, since well before the full conjuring occurred, and yet she did nothing to stop him. She was more than satisfied with the changes she noticed: the return of pliability to her skin, the unaccounted-for disappearance of her liver spots; and, perhaps most importantly, whatever had threatened her life—had shackled her to her bed like a paralytic—flew from her. So she kept her mouth shut.

Finally freed of the ailment, she became her son's biggest advocate, whispering words of encouragement into his ear and slipping to the doorways of those most influential among their company. She was Cezar's shameless solicitor, his Pied Piper, gathering up the troops for a great rebellion. Though she wasn't sure exactly what she sold them—and they knew not what they bought, nor with what currency—the fold took the bait, and turned against Nikolai with unforetold ease. Having quickly forgotten their once-great leader, Cezar was free to do with them (and with his father) as he saw fit.

What happened next—the *incident* Nikolai deemed too disgusting for a place in the annals of his written history—wasn't something Cezar had wholly planned. Feeding off the intuition of the fiends he summoned, the young Cezar brought about the destruction of those still unwilling to change their ways, to bend to the new reign of his will. Like a conduit for their demons' cunning, Cezar singled out the acolytes among them who he knew would stay forever loyal to the Order's former causes (of passive, placid exploration; of the white arts, healing magics and alchemy; of a demon whose real name, whose Goetic ties to darkness, they didn't even know: pathetic ol' Baal).

The harbinger of their schism was the fire. It started at the ironwood, a tree that wholly symbolized Nikolai's long reign as Overseer. Its destruction was a fitting call to arms. Cezar didn't even need to strike a match; it lit up with ease at the command of his will, and it drew them all from their far corners of the compound, out to its center court to observe the rising conflagration. The way it illumined their eyes in the night, with voltaic sparks, cast the crew in a somnambulant light: Cezar's little automatons, to do with as he saw fit. When his father finally emerged, last among them to do so (besides his mother, who only sat watching at her window with a single, pensive hand raised up to her mouth), Nikolai rushed beneath its lanky, flaming limbs, skidding to a halt against the ground, writhing on the sand, beating his chest, as though anger alone could reverse the tree's ruination.

Cezar walked up behind him and, placing a hand against each of his father's broad-but-bent shoulders, whispered an imprecation:

"*Vale ad vitam.*"

Nikolai turned knowing eyes upward—filled with a mixture of fright and resignation, pupils dilated—seeing, in a moment, all the possibilities of what might come to pass, all the events leading to his banishment from the fold.

Those who followed Cezar's new way dragged their departing leader Nikolai by the hackles, down into the depths of their most sanctified grounds, beneath the ruins of the compound's former edifice, into the untraversed tombs of the once-great sorcerers who lived there before them. Passing down through dank passageways (ones which hadn't seen the light of day for decades), lighting the stubs of candles left set in the crevices of the moldering walls, they descended deeper and deeper, through the impossibly cavernous bowels of the grounds, to a place no man but the Overseer himself was usually allowed. They tied Nikolai up in chains, fettered with all his limbs splayed outward, stretched to their breaking points. They raised up their hoods, obscuring their faces. Their recumbent figures blended together as they lay out in a circle below the slab of rotten wood Nikolai was bound against, suspended from.

Cezar brought out a knife, curved and glimmering in the twinkle of their candlelit mass. He waved it about in Nikolai's face, in a proud, aggressive display, delighting in the way his father squirmed like a pig at slaughter. But it wasn't his father whom he'd kill—that would be too easy.

A finer torture was in store for Nikolai: the pain of watching all of those still loyal to his ideals suffer to death before him. Cezar would turn his father's misgivings, about his son's ability to lead, into the impetus for their punishment.

The first acolyte was dragged down—wallowing, screaming, eyes cast up to meet his prophet's gaze, mouth imploring their Order's collective pity—kicked to the ground under Nikolai's shackled figure. Cezar offered no time for supplication, only for purgation; knife to the gut, driven deep and then twisted with a forceful pull, across the width of his belly. All the man's guts spilled out in an almost-comic display of abundant gore, but the dampness spreading across the grounds of their hallowed circle served as very real proof of the man's mortal suffering. He went out like a light—no, faster—and the next was dragged down to replace him.

The second supplicant was a woman, and she received a special treatment. Cezar dragged a sharp-edged whittling blade against her scalp, pruning the skin of the woman's head back to reveal the skull underneath; then he cracked it open with the handle of his blade and stabbed its narrow point through the aperture, into the flesh of the woman's brain, wiggling it around while she spasmed—perhaps from the pain, or perhaps involuntarily, while the blade pureed her cerebrum.

They threw her away like trash, to rest atop the former victim.

This carried on for some hours, the lot of them prostrated, moaning to themselves in pleasure while their newly appointed Overseer slaughtered those last resistant parasites—loyal to the end; to their very, very end. When a pile of them had been stacked, some twenty of their peers already stinking of death, the circle sat up to observe the results of Cezar's grave methods. Many grinned, intoxicated by the devilish proceedings, imbibed on the bloodletting. With their feet wet with gore, and hands dripping with it, the group devolved quickly to a baseless, orgiastic mass of crazed maniacs.

They tore off their robes and, stark naked, rubbed themselves against one another or against the flagellated, flayed bodies of the heaped-up corpses. The necrophilial horror of their mindless show segued into an anthropophagist's wet dream as they tore their victims' limbs free from their sockets—endowed with the superhuman strength of their Overseer's Takers: those bold, novel demons whose names they still did not know. They gorged themselves on the fat-dripping, blood-slick flesh of their brethren.

Cezar stood by, enamored by the nightmarish display, by the palpable frenzy of loyalty his people arrayed just for him. All the while, Nikolai hung—stripped naked—from the plank of his seat, his gonads dangling pitiably, limply from his body, shriveling up for some solace inside his stomach. He vomited out the sparse contents of his starved gut, and an older man (whom Nikolai had once harangued for sleeping too late; Peter was his name) lapped it up, slurping away at those regurgitated chunks of unknown food swimming in bilious sputum.

By the end of it all, the tall, cylindrical chamber buzzed with their delirium. Their cries echoed up toward the far-off, high ceilings of that hellish borehole, and Nikolai finally collapsed from exhaustion and fright. He dangled slack on his board above them.

Cezar himself had to fight off a growing urge to disrobe—to squat, shit, and smear his excrement across the walls. Whatever primeval force his Takers commanded had quickly grown strong enough to threaten his self-possession, and to usurp his hold over the assembly. Not knowing what else to do, he drew out their symbols, which he'd committed to memory, in a neat little row. Upon their completion, all three of the renderings glowed with infernal inborn light, and then with incendiary flames, not unlike the blaze that had started it all, way up above them at the ironwood tree. Again, all the acolytes' eyes lit up, reflecting the flames, their gazes drawn to the signs on the floor: those flame-bound forms rising into pillars of combustion taller than the most gigantic among them. Some of the collective abandoned their feast, dropping their slabs of thigh to stare in wonder, gristle still hanging from their teeth; others withdrew from or paused in their tensile, carnal poses of debauched, mindless pleasure, enamored by the strange glow and the emergence of those alien figures.

He'd succeeded in drawing them out, up into the world as physical, form-bound beasts. They were there, his Takers:

Andras leapt from the spot of his summoning, with a bird-like head set against thick, brawny shoulders. He stood naked, wielding his sliver-thin claws like rapiers primed for attack.

Beelzebub surfaced, a bobbing mound of scaly fat, a blob emoting the mannerisms of a bee—with the wings, but without the customary stripes. More than an insect, he was the idea of one, all shiny bean-shaped glaring eyes and pus-dripping mandibles; his antennae were made of a strident, metallic substance; and his wings—hanging like wet cheesecloth from his hairless, fattened body—barely kept him aloft. Yet he flew nonetheless, buzzing toward them, skewering some through the abdomen, lifting them up on his course.

The last to emerge was Astaroth, at a slovenly, bored pace. His anthropomorphic head was bloated to comic effect; it hovered like a bobble head atop his pinky-thin neck and above his bony, scant figure (ribs protruding, back hunched). He wore a golden crown, which shone with the fierce white light of irradiated, volatile metals. He carried a serpent; its skin appeared grafted to the flesh of his keeper's hand, as though it were a physical extension of Astaroth's body, an extra digit to his own five fine-pointed fingers.

A great beast, hairy and nimble, slithered up from that hell-trench, too; its pointed, dripping coal-black rhinarium and clawed, blocky paws hinted at his pedigree, but (unlike a wolf) his hairless flesh was marked instead by the occasional advent of long, palatial feathers. He skulked alongside his master, lowering himself to offer a seat.

Astaroth consented, and when his dangling, bare protuberance settled against the beast's side, it flattened out like a deflated bockwurst, swinging against the curve of the hound's back 'til it found a comfy spot.

The three Takers fanned out against the congregation, pushing them back toward the pile of corpses they'd amassed until there was no room left to move.

Beelzebub bumbled to and fro, dropping the cadavers he'd snatched, dripping neon sputum from the tips of his lacerated, bloodied mandibles.

Andras barely blinked his all-seeing, effusive eyes and whirled his head all about his neck, in jerky unfeasible patterns.

Astaroth, riding his beast, yawned as he approached, cutting a line between his two brothers to face them all, unabridged. He addressed them from atop his varmint's throne. In a wiry, thin voice (akin to an ice scraper creaking achingly against glass), he said: "*Salve, vermis.*"

Not knowing what to do, the acolytes turned to their leader—Cezar—for guidance. But his help came delayed and, before he could interject, the demons had their hold on his flock. Across the room, their eyes rolled back to reveal the whites, and their mouths lolled open. In only an instant, they had all become the obsequious servants to the Prince of Hell, Astaroth.

Cezar knew it wasn't his end, yet. They had come under his instruction, and would soon be made to bow before him.

"Stop it!" Cezar commanded. "Stop what you're doing this instant!"

Astaroth turned, his giant head slanted, curious; Beelzebub dipped and rose above Cezar, dripping pungent, acidic spittle onto the top of his head; the lithe and nimble Andras cooed in response to the instructions, his beaked mouth parting in a demonstrative show of acquiescence. It seemed they would obey. Despite their propensity for brute force, they abandoned their assault on his people and, turning to face Cezar, bowed to his bidding.

"It is you," Astaroth began, his crown shifting forward along his scalp to reveal a peek of scaly head under ringlet curls of hair. "You *are* the one who summoned us, are you not?"

Uncertainly, Cezar stepped toward them, wiping Beelzebub's rancid spittle off his robe. He said, "That's correct. I am the one."

"What do you wish of us?" Astaroth asked. It seemed he was the only one of the trio capable of human speech. The others only cooed and buzzed in tenebrous falsettos.

"I called on you because…" Before finishing his statement, Cezar considered the question for a moment longer, scanning the room (his attendants' barbarous fingertips writhing in anticipation, Nikolai coming to). "I yearn for the death of this man, and for his eternal, painful imprisonment at a sore seat in Hell."

All of the acolytes cheered, raising up their voices in a vulgar, animalistic display, like wolves howling before a hunt.

Unmoved, Astaroth lifted up his chin and stared at Cezar—no, *through* Cezar, into the deepest recesses of his volition.

"Are you not willing?" Cezar asked. "This is the purpose for which you've been loosed from your pit—from your damned captivity—"

"You fool!" Astaroth interrupted, raising his head and a finger-pointing hand (along with the macabre, curving serpent it contained). "Surely someone with powers as great as yours—strong enough to summon us—can himself handle the disposal of one *fragile* old man? Leave your pathetic, mortal squabbles for another day. What is it you *really* wish of us, Cezar?" The way the demon held out the *s* sound of Cezar's name, like a *sssssnake*, sent a shudder down his backbone.

Cezar knew how he felt, and what he wanted, but (because he'd never voiced his boldest longing) he didn't know how to say it. He'd always known he was destined for greater things than the Order of Baal could offer, and here was his chance to seize the opportunity being offered by those dark specters. He composed himself, formed his words, and spoke:

"Power—greater than any man before me—to command as I see fit. To quell any dissenters who pass through our gates, and to reach out to others for aid in support of our cause."

In response to Cezar's declaration, Beelzebub buzzed happily and Andras swayed on his hackles, tittering like a hyena.

"Power's what they say," Astaroth said. "Always what they say. Cezar, *how* do you wish to acquire such power? We are but three, and cannot command the deference of your whole, entire world."

"Grant me the strength to influence others and, insodoing, I'll be granted the means necessary to fulfill my wish. I'll soon command great legions." Cezar trembled, overcome with the pervading stench of the Takers' ghostly juju; it percolated in the air, bringing with it the feeling of drowning, as though the cloying dampness and rise in temperature might suffocate them all on the spot.

"Now *that*—" Astaroth nodded, humming to himself before his lips cracked apart, revealing a wide, gummy smile inlaid with rows of giant, umber teeth. "That is something we can do."

Cezar stepped closer and extended both his hands toward them, with the palms facing upward. He said, "I am ready."

"Pray!" Astaroth screamed. "Pray to the impious gods below us that you *are* ready, feeble human." He gripped Cezar by his wrists and pulled him closer. Cezar was forced downward, tumbling to lay in a reclined position across the barbed spine of Astaroth's pet. Astaroth hummed above him, cackling between wordless syllables of a demon's psalm.

A floaty feeling appeared at Cezar's extremities, rising through his limbs to the pit of his chest, where the sensation coalesced at his solar plexus. He drifted toward a drowsy, druggish haze, as though encased with cotton, only vaguely sensing the presence of those around him anymore.

Without warning, Astaroth lifted Cezar's face up and planted an open-mouthed kiss against his conjurer's lips.

"A kiss, for good luck," the Prince of Hell said.

The feel of that reptilian cache—of Astaroth's scaly mouth surrounding his lower head, drowning his outward breath and coating his chops in smut—was enough to lift Cezar out of the delirium that tugged against him. Just as a fish leaps out of its pond when its home has been envenomed, Cezar roused and batted against his benefactor, striving to break free.

What are you doing? he tried to scream, but in vain.

The serpent attached to Astaroth's palm cinched more tightly 'round Cezar's thumb.

"A token of our gratitude," the Taker said. "For the vessel you present." Astaroth wrapped his arms around Cezar, swaddling him tightly. "A symbol of my unerring devotion to your cause." Astaroth's jaw unhinged and a creature emerged from the black, puckered sphincter at the back of his throat—a forked serpent's tongue. The demon's ophidian organ dove into Cezar's mouth, pitching against the back of his jaw with such force as to bruise his palate and tear his uvula. Where the sharp-edged tips of the demon's tongue struck, a numb stinging impression blossomed in Cezar's mouth.

As fast as it had begun, it ended. Astaroth withdrew his barbed *lingua*, his head flapped shut, and he set Cezar down. Then he spoke: "A dash of conniving, with which to lure in your prey." He lifted his jeweled crown up from his head in a salutary gesture and, tilting it forward, bowed low. "Now, Beelzebub's turn."

Cezar lifted his sore, numb head up in time to see the pustuled pest land alongside him, smashing its fatty proboscis against the ground while its salivary glands oozed a noxious substance in gouts. With his head still swimming, mouth still tingling with whatever unhallowed decoction Astaroth had affected by his potent kiss, Cezar lay helpless to resist the advance of the Lord of Flying Things. Beelzebub simply and easily lowered his bits, stuffing the end of his labial tube into Cezar's already-throbbing maw. His mouth was flooded with a tar-like goop, a congealed, molten venom which felt like sulfuric acid dissolving through his flesh.

Yet he had the composure to lift a hand, to feel the substance of cheek still covering his face, and to trace the wiry-haired barrel of the giant insect's mouth.

Once it drained enough of its gift into him, Beelzebub extracted its member and flitted away, its bulging abdomen just a little less plump than before.

The last to approach was the gaunt, creeping figure of Andras. Dragging his claws low against the ground, he shimmied toward Cezar like a bird-headed ape, his beak fractured to reveal a tongue that was surely too squat and short to do much kissing. Counting his blessings, though they were few, Cezar lay back and closed his eyes, passively awaiting whatever fresh torture the avian fiend might impart. Yet all the odious one did (as was fitting of the most silent—perhaps even the most respectful—of his company) was drag a pincered claw across the width of his own wrist and, lifting Cezar's head up toward the rising dribble of inky claret, deliver a sip of his ownmost to the sore mouth of his ward.

It was almost sweet, and coated Cezar's inner cheeks, numbing the pain of the others' attacks; it fueled him, coaxing him out of injury and into the single-greatest moment of his life: where he saw with crisper clarity, with a different mindset, from a paradigm befitting the world-ruler he aimed to become.

So it was that Cezar, the Overseer, was Touched—not by one, but by three—and given the emblematic gifts of the demons he assembled:

From Astaroth, power with words, sleight of tongue—to convoke and mesmerize followers from far across the world;

From Beelzebub, an aptitude for poisoning the well, and a death-giving, pestilent touch;

From Andras, the cunning to cut deep, and a slight reconfiguration of his anatomy—elongated fingers, a high neck, durable bones, thicker skin.

"Our gifts are now yours to handle, as you see fit." Astaroth mumbled something, an unintelligible throat sound that called the others back, toward the three symbols scrawled on the ground. "Should you need our assistance further, I ask only one thing: question first the principles of your creed."

Still reeling, Cezar did his best to push himself up from the floor and, gripping his knees for support, also lifted his head. He rubbed his sore jaw to confirm its corporeality and urged them: "Wait! Just a second, please! What does it mean— question the *principles* of my creed? Is there some price to pay for your aid? A comeuppance for the forces you convey?"

The smile Astaroth fashioned, so recognizably his, told Cezar more than any words could (though his wide-mouthed grin now seemed to hold far pointier teeth than before). But the Prince of Hell did, finally, speak. Before he and his cohorts dissolved away into clouds of wine-colored fumes and moorish gas, he said, "Perhaps, and perhaps not. That's up to you. May your grandiose plans bring us closer." He winked and was gone; he, his beast, and his brothers vanished completely, without a trace.

The sigils that bound them sizzled once more and then, for a spell, all was calm.

Cezar already felt the fresh energy of their gifts coursing through him, and the modicum changes his body had undergone—he gripped his robe more firmly, almost tearing through the fabric with a finger's touch; he felt every hair on top of his head, and could probably count them in a single breath, should he wish to.

It wasn't long before the congregation roused from their mesmeric daze, their bloodlust returned. They kneeled at the base of Cezar's stage, lifting up their chins—supplicants ready for their leader's New Order—waiting for him to irrevocably settle their first order of business: Nikolai.

Nikolai had fully awakened while the Takers smeared their vitriolic poisons across the mouth of his own son. He watched, helplessly bound to the board suspending him—hovering above the crowd of sadists, his former herd—awaiting whatever cruel punishment they had in store for him. His eyes were spread open in wonderment and fright.

Cezar lowered his father, unshackled his aching wrists, and threw him toward the crowd. They took turns punching Nikolai in the ribs, nibbling at his skin, tearing out clumps of his hair. Watching them turn on their erstwhile chief filled Cezar with a euphoric tingle, beginning at his groin and rising up toward the crown of his head—perhaps a lingering effect of the demons, fermenting their oral decoction inside his jowls.

The throng threatened to completely drown Nikolai, to cudgel him to death with their blows, so—not wanting to miss out on any of the fun—Cezar addressed them:

"Wait! Stave your torments for scarcely a while! I—your leader—should have a turn, too."

Obligingly, if not a little aggrieved, they shoved Nikolai back up to the lectern, hoisting him onto the stage where he lay sprawled out moaning, sputtering vermilion spittle across the floor.

"Stand up, father," Cezar ordered, but Nikolai ignored him. "I command you to rise!"

Cezar's veins popped out in bass relief across his forehead as he screamed; yet, despite his blaring commandment, the impeached one wouldn't stand, or couldn't.

A pair of the Old Ones (though they no longer bore that name, having betrayed their Nikolai) rose to assist Cezar, swayed by the urgency in their commander's tone. They strapped Nikolai back to the board and hoisted him up, where he dangled like a solitary Christmas ornament on proud display. The two Overseers faced one another: the ousted one, with fresh trickles of garnet leaking from the sides of his eyes, and his usurper.

"Hear me," Cezar began, slapping his father repeatedly across the cheek, 'til his eyes finally lit with some slight trace of recognition. "Hear me well when I say this: I hereby banish you from these grounds, and from all affiliation with our newly hallowed Order. If you ever set foot in the compound again, I'll be the first to drive one of our many, fine-tuned knives straight into your gut."

He pinched his father's face between his palms, squeezing together his cheeks, and planted a kiss square against his mouth.

Nikolai groaned, twitching in his pendulous prison and sending it rocking. Its wayward path humored Cezar, who encouraged it on its course, pushing him high above the heads of his satiated subjects. Screaming to them, Cezar said:

"Take a last look at your old Overseer! It's the last you'll ever see of him!"

And he turned to leave, silently dismissing the *hoi polloi* back to their regular duties (wash the walls, study their books) until the day he'd need to rouse them again, under their proud banner of influence: of mastery, of dominion. Gesturing toward the duo of bearded attendants who'd just helped him—with a curled finger that said, *Come closer*—he told them, "See to it that he's not killed. Have him dumped far from here. Give him only enough water to last a day, and nothing more; no common fabrics with which he might disguise himself, no food. He is homeless, a wanderer. Not even shoes should house his feet. Do you understand?"

They nodded their assent to the plan, and lowered Cezar's disgraced predecessor—the blight, the detestable, the already forgotten.

Cezar stole a backward glance, just before turning the corner toward the private stairs (ones that led straight to his father's library—no, to *his* library, and what would become his chamber), and recognized something familiar concealed in Nikolai's wounded face: an inkling of eminence, like the last stubborn coal on a grill, fighting even as it loses its battle to hold on to existence. There was at once a sly nod there—to kismet, to the inevitability of Cezar's own downfall someday far into the future—and an unpresuming bow.

—

Thus, Cezar became the Overseer—informally, having never received a proper procession or initiation. Since no one before him had claimed their right to the seat of his title using such brute force, such conniving violence, the Order never knew quite how to handle the shift of power. Instead of celebrating the events of his appointment, they avoided it altogether, speaking only of what had occurred in the dark privacy of their berths, as though they hadn't also played their own parts (as though they hadn't eaten their fill of their own comrades' flesh, beaten the wounded figure of their former leader, and coupled with partners whose faces were hidden behind the disfigurement of their mid-coitus, which turned them into wild beasts in heat). In due course, mentions of the Incident dwindled to idle gossip between only the ladies, and eventually (finally) the episode vanished from their minds as completely as though it had never happened at all. Its only surviving impressions were in the spatters of blood still staining the wooden boards of the stage beneath the ground, deep in the bowels of their blessed compound. And none of them could see that, tucked away as it was; only Cezar had the key.

He buttered them up to the changes he offered, slowly. As goddess Freya, in the old Norse, transformed her protégé Óttar into a swine (and herself into a falcon), Cezar transmogrified his people from pacifistic purists and dovish idealists into the army he needed—an infantry of the Touched. They let themselves change, willfully, and under his guidance were subjected to the Trials, to the Takings and Touchings, as he—the great Overseer—saw fit.

389

Just as the demons had promised, followers swarmed to his calling. While beacons conventionally warn those approaching of imminent danger, his signal did the opposite: it was an imperceptible yet irresistible glow, a buzz of energy that drew many toward the walls of his mighty covenant. The strangers came often, and arrived seeking knowledge, power, dominance, vengeance; they came to the gates of the compound, sometimes emaciated by their penniless odyssey across the desert, having abandoned their jobs and their families for the unknown—for the assurance of renown. Whether it was, indeed, the blessing of Astaroth that brought them—those doe-eyed, hungry, malleable prey, primed for the picking, ripe and ready—straight to his doorstep, or it was perhaps something more (word of mouth; a mole in the system telling others to come, to flee their homes for the safety of the Order, to follow the wise word of the Overseer before the Earth's end) mattered little to Cezar, just so long as they came, and followed him to the letter.

Cezar had lived through many decades since then, watching the world change, hidden in the shadows. Since his inception as Overseer, he heard all (and experienced much) of the Earth's great atrocities, and learned more about the nature of humans: that man is a cruel and unforgiving beast, no more civilized than wolves when it comes to mortal qualms of land, or of sex, or of money.

Yet the puzzle pieces never quite fit together, still. He wasn't ready to uproot them, to bring about the end. While the vagaries of generations swept him by (tempestuous shifts in government, World Wars), the Overseer laughed, because he could and because he had the time. He aged more slowly than most, so he felt life more deeply (and yet, also more peaceably), without the inching advance of death and the sense of doom it brings to most. Instead of dread, the Overseer felt optimism, a sense of *striving* toward death.

It hadn't been in the bargain, though: eternal life, the fountain of youth, the great and rarefied key to immortality. He knew he wouldn't live forever—the creeping advance of crow's feet and the thinning of his hair told him as much. Still, they'd at least given him tannins of that elusive gift, enough to keep him ticking for more than three quarters of a century since his having been Touched.

And now, sitting at his desk and reflecting on his belligerent beginnings as Overseer (reflecting on the place in time when he'd been a young man staring— abhorrently glaring—up at the old man his father had become, and wishing him dead), Cezar came headlong to face the great carelessness of his policies. At once, he wished he hadn't let Jezebel slip away. He wanted to drag her down to the abyss below him, to drive stakes through her hands and to do the thing he hadn't done before, which he should have done before.

The thing he should have done to his mother, but couldn't.

The action that might have completed his upward clambering toward the crown of the world: a Taking greater than the rest.

What he hadn't written—what wasn't transcribed in his or his father's journals—was this:

Cezar went back to his mother's bedside that night—after the conjuring of the three Takers, after his having been Touched by them—to find Katjaa unwell. Whatever interlude of peace she'd enjoyed, whatever chimeric pretense of health she had feigned, was gone. Instead of rosy cheeks and puckish japes, she was laid out, unconscious against the floor with the sheets tangled in her feet. His mother teetered on the brink of her final quietus, with her gown half-opened and her chest heaving—with the grueling labor of respiration, despite the barely audible row of her breath.

Cursing the devils who'd deceived him, the Overseer lifted his mother back up to her cot and spent the night with her, incessantly bathing her sweating bust and neck, using a bucket of chilly water and a sponge to cool her—gripping the latter with fingers that felt strangely foreign, fidgets growing ever-longer as the moon sloped by.

In the morning, she was barely there, her complexion devolved to pellucid ash. He wrapped her body in a tight cocoon of her linens and dragged her down easily—blessed as he was with fresh, alien strength—to the far side of the stairwells, to the deep-most place, to where he lately met his hellish contributors. He lit candles, spoke their names, and drew their symbols; yet the beast-bestriding prince and his companions concealed themselves, stashed away in whatever hallways of hell they made their homes.

Wondering at the meaning of Astaroth's censurial departing words, Cezar hoisted up his mother and strapped her to the board, still fresh with her late husband's blood. Again, Cezar beseeched them:

"Astaroth, I summon thee!

"Beelzebub, come hither!

"Andras, show yourself!"

But none of them arrived, and he was left to contend with her mortality by himself. He kissed her, perhaps hoping to impart some of their demons' gifts, to transfer his powers to her by his display of affection. That didn't work either; she only smiled at the sensation of his touch before drifting back to senselessness.

"Mother, come back," he implored. "Please don't leave me. I need you! All this was for us, for you. I don't know what I'll do without you. Father's dead. I killed him. I thought everything would be perfect with him gone, that we'd be together forever and no one would stand in the way of our Order. But it's not working. None of it's working."

Inflamed, blood boiling, Cezar pried at the tips of his tapered nails, plucking them off his fingers one by one. They weren't his any longer; they belonged to some*thing* else, something that had lengthened them and sharpened them to tapers. His was a being damned to the biddings of the Takers, forever.

"They won't have you!" he shouted, beating his fists against Kajtaa's silent chest.

He chastised himself for his own recklessness, and caressed his mother's cheek, which quickly grew cold.

Headstrong child, he called himself. *Imbecile. Pitiful ass.*

In his self-absorbed ranting, Cezar distracted himself from Katjaa's pain—and from her side, from her last abating breath. It was a whisper whose meaning would forever haunt him, like a stargazer who dozes at the precise moment of his hours-long enterprise, when his subject finally ascends the sky, mounts the horizon, and leaves its glittering trail. He missed it.

For Cezar, her corpse held special meaning: it was the culmination of all his years of self-denial, his temperance for sensuality (abstinence, really), and it was a symbol for the curtains on his most essential yearning.

He lowered the board and unstrapped her, fingers trembling, fumbling with the leather clasps and pricking his finger on the prong of the buckle. A droplet of blood surfaced, budding but not falling; he smoothed the seeping claret over her lips, a macabre *maquillage*, which made her appear more ribald than saccharine. Cezar lowered himself toward her, crushing her lifeless chest into the ground, and let the full weight of his body intuit the contours of hers; like an infant who perceives with his hands, the Overseer stroked every inch of her until he was certain he'd never forget the shape of her outline.

Into her ear, he whispered, "I'll never find love like ours again," and kissed her cheeks, bathing them with tears.

Cezar rolled off of her onto his back and, lying beside her, weighed his options.

Bury her.

Burn her.

Eat her.

Go to bed with her.

No bolt of shame shot through his mind; to the Overseer, nothing was prohibited, even fleshly acts of Oedipal love or cannibalism. It would be his first, in either case, but the blessings of either would outweigh any sense of shame he might (ashamedly) experience—for an Overseer, shame itself was deserving of disgrace.

In the privacy of that low hall, that chamber of tortures—with the anguished cries of his father still hanging on the walls—Cezar yearned to comply with his cravings, but stopped himself. Instead, he hauled up the banned arcana and, rifling through its tattered pages, sought the spell that would raise her up from death.

He toiled through hours of pain—his body still stretching, reeling, growing, changing with the gifts of the Takers—and anguish, 'til he realized the spell. With a flourish of his nailless hands, he scrawled the symbol required and shouted the prescribed words:

"*Mortuos suos fugit*

"*Do hoc ultimo depraehendo*

"*Auctore Deo*

"*In via decedere*

"*Animae in manu.*"

There was no preternatural gust of wind, no flicker at the candlesticks. Instead, Cezar felt a pang of presentiment, an inexplicable knowing that he'd done something wrong. His fears escalated with the protracted drag at his gut; he worried after the bitter return of Astaroth, Beelzebub, and Andras. Cezar brushed aside the pattern he'd composed on the floor and quickly moved to his mother's side, lowering himself to check for a breath, a murmur, a telling rise and fall of the bust.

She roused, coughing up a miasma of rancid gut's nectar that sent him falling back against his palms. He helped to lift her up, and searched her face for a thread of knowing, a human cognizance. At first, she showed hints of humanity—the return of that familiar grin, and a flutter across her eyelids—but both withered when she spoke. It wasn't so much speech as a wordless grunt, an unintelligible soughing like autumn's wind through the old ironwood. She blabbered and slavered and gnashed at his face, clamping her jaws open and closed with such force as to shatter her teeth (though she showed no sign of physical suffering in her ferocious countenance).

He had no choice but to do what he did. It was better than waiting to see what had Taken her—which of the many faceless monsters, hauled up from below, was eating its way through her body and soul. So he killed her again. The second time was worse, by far. This time, he had to effect her end by his own hands. Using a small, jagged rock, he slammed her skull at the temple, repeatedly bashing there until her face was reduced to a barely-recognizable pulp of bone and drooping flesh.

With her passing, something also died in him, as though the keenly hidden shred of optimism, still buried within him, was finally demolished—turned to vapor, never to return.

He almost convinced himself to try it again, to call on another, since the others had so fully abandoned him. But she was too far gone, and he was too afraid of what she might become, of what the Taker might do, of how it might render her changed—into the Devil's concubine. As he cradled her distorted face in his hands, Cezar realized he had no other choice: he must dispose of her.

Slicing through her was a laborious job; he channeled his frustration, anger, sadness, and mourning into the stopgap cure of that undertaking, hacking away at her corpse until he'd successfully severed her head and limbs, then bifurcated her trunk clean between the breasts. He crosscut and quadrisected the largest chunks of her, all the while struggling against a burgeoning compulsion to sample of her flesh.

Stave off the itch, for just a little while, he told himself, and hauled her pieces away.

Later, Cezar—with the aid of fifteen cooks—prepared a regal feast for his disciples: steamed wild grape leaves stuffed with amaranth, beans, and agave rosettes; corn coated in jojoba oil and roasted over open flames for a crunchy-sweet taste; a platter of fine-carved meat, beaten soft and slow-cooked for the occasion.

He considered explaining the darker origins of their uncommon bounty, but too greatly savored the engorged expressions plastered across their grease-smeared faces to interrupt the meal. It would be an enduring, confidential amusement of his, one he'd reflect on that night in the privacy of his bedroom while he quietly nibbled on the last mealy links, made of her chitlins. Even though her body would soon pass through them, a little bit of her would osmose its way into them all— silently, as a microscopic parasite invades the brain, bequeathing only a notion of its madness, and only over time (a pill-rolling tic, a stammering of words).

Her sickness would be the first of many tests, of the Trials that would determine who among them was strong enough to stand by his side, to lift their Order—and their Overseer—up to greatest heights. In the weeks that followed, half the Old Ones fell ill, succumbing to death in a matter of days, declining from their once-sagacious, cross-legged seats of power to bungling, frustrated convalescents, shut away in their homes 'til their stench or absence drew them out as corpses stacked on a handcart. Their passing made way for the younger, brighter, more ambitious ones just arriving at the gates. In them, he planted the seeds of the Touched, and even (on occasion) of the Taken, that they might carry out his fiery-skied dream, for the Order.

And he drank, and he fucked, and he sliced his way through them, until only the most impressive of his clan remained. They were tokens of the power Astaroth had promised.

In time, Cezar learned to live without his mother, and to find other ways of venting his great sense of longing—though they were temporary reprieves from a deeper anguish.

Something was undoubtedly missing: he needed a son.

No one but his own flesh could be *completely* trusted with the gifts he possessed; the rest were peons, fit only for the most basic, mindless tasks of their commune: wipe the floors, water the garden, cook the meals. Even those who demonstrated a keen aptitude for their arts were prone to erratic spells of recklessness (flying free of their walls while celebrating their new wings, or destroying a section of the compound in a flurry of flames). When this happened, he killed them all, and the compound ate well again.

A new trial came—one they didn't even know they traversed. It was a test reserved exclusively for the women of their group, a test designed to single out those most apt, who might also bear a child worthy of his name and seat.

For every hundredth fecund lackey, only a few would pass. He planted his seed in them all, though, in an attempt to boost his odds, dismissing those who miscarried and banishing those who produced, because all they birthed were girls. He privately blamed himself for the sequence of failings, but he publicly denounced the girls, calling them abortive whores and ejecting them out of their gates, banished, never to return.

As the century turned, Cezar redoubled his efforts, certain he'd found the perfect candidate: a woman whose eagerness to debase herself under him, and whose zeal for intercourse with him, more than impressed. She birthed him a son—*At last, a son!* he'd rejoiced—but the child was powerless, a weakling from birth who could neither lift objects nor bend time, nor anything else. That wouldn't do—would not work with the plans he had in store—so he moved on to the next one, the next woman, hoping she might bring greater success.

For a period, the Overseer lost all hope. The other potentials continued to miscarry, many deserting their company by cover of night, perhaps afraid of their leader's wrath. A woman infertile was a useless one, to him.

Then, a most unexpected thing occurred: one of the women who wasn't their own—one of the women he met when he occasioned to secretly leave their walls—showed promise. A glimmer of a possibility: charming, beautiful, and conniving enough to cheat on her spouse. Cezar lauded her, pampering and spoiling the woman in ways he hadn't before.

When Meredith became pregnant, she severed their ties. But that didn't matter; he carried on, had her followed—all the while doing his best to stave the sense of jealousy that choked across his throat. His best men tracked her to a ramshackle motel, where they tried to Take her husband. Things got complicated.

In the end, John and George—though they may have misfired a bit—managed to sort out the mess and Jezebel was born.

A girl.

When his lackeys brought her back to the compound with news that she had passed a test—the passing of which proved she was endowed with certain special gifts—Cezar was unmoved. He made to quieten her cries, to stamp out her life, as was growing so customary. But in his frustration, he was lax on the girl; her little fingers gripped for the top of his hand and, with a crackle against his knuckles, she broke several bones there, freeing herself of his grip.

Jezebel. Most promising indeed.

The mother was offered a stay, on the grounds that she might participate in her child's rearing, even if from afar. And they'd grown, both of them: Jezebel showing greater promise than any of those before her; and Meredith, honing her skills as diviner and mentalist.

But now they were both gone, a fact that made the Overseer's blood boil—so much so that he'd been prompted to question his own prowess, to revisit those ancient tomes of his upbringing, and to rekindle a flame of longing he'd effectively cast aside. That pain—the sensation of loss, the remembrance of his mother—was the mainspring that would either whet or stamp out his bold grit as Overseer. In the face of those lesser demons—ones whose names were more private even than Astaroth, Beelzebub, or Andras—Cezar wept. He wept for the beasts named Grief, Perfidy, and Matricide.

His old spine ached, and his heart sank with the memory of his greater years— a lifespan of atrophied probabilities dissolving before him, just as a cloudy haze of disunity settled, like a viper's poisonous fangs, into his ranks. As his father's dying expression had told him: his time would come, but not tonight, not if he could help it. He sensed the moment growing near, when a new Reaping would occur—one that would once more set the worst of them away from the loyal, the faithful, the true. Those who were ready would stretch to the limits of their preternatural Touch, and the ones disloyal would be set right, would be Taken and *made* to follow his commands.

The time was nigh.

CHAPTER XXIX

"I need to tell you about what happened," Jezebel said, leaning close to whisper in Meredith's ear.

"What's that? Tell me about what?"

"With your mother—"

"There's no need, Jezebel. Really, it's fine."

"But, don't you want to know—"

"No," Meredith interrupted again. "I don't. I could venture a guess, but it wouldn't be anything pretty. I'd rather turn a blind eye. As you said yourself: you don't want to know anything more about your father. Same for me. I'm done thinking about my mother; that part of my life's over now."

A long pause passed between them while Jezebel flexed open her wings.

They made their way toward the edge of the bluff and overlooked the dry plateau, gazing across the barrens separating them from their destination—the compound, the Order, the Overseer.

"We have each other now," Jezebel offered listlessly, touching her mother's cheek.

"Yeah, I guess we do. You came to me. You followed my call."

Jezebel wondered why it had taken so long for her to open up, for Meredith to show some trace of affection since they arrived. Her mother knew they needed to train for the forthcoming fight, but a little tenderness couldn't have hurt. Just looking at one another—with that intensity of knowing, which Jezebel had never felt before—was enough to make up for all the years of missed moments.

—

Orson was uneasy. An admixture of doubt and presentiment ate at him. It stemmed largely from how outnumbered they would be, but also partly from the fact that his gifts were a lot less *compelling* than the others' were.

Theirs were many. Foretelling the future, even if in snippets, seemed greater than the guessing he could otherwise do

Soaring across the sky, while he could only walk, tripping in the sand and falling to his knees, an easy target.

Orson couldn't do much—what, channel a little sprout of lightning through his fingertips? Shoot a gust of wind? Those were the makings of superheroes—fairy tales, make believe—and he didn't feel very super. Instead, he wondered if his being there was right at all. It didn't feel good; he didn't fit in amongst them.

Jezebel had shied away from him since they arrived at the cave, although he couldn't blame her—he'd be feeling overwhelmed, if he'd just met his mother for the very first time, after having (unknowingly) lived alongside her for all of his life. Too, he wondered how he'd have handled realizing his father was the very man who'd imprisoned him for all those lonesome years. The Overseer robbed Jezebel of any shot at normalcy she might have had, and stole her adolescence. She grew up too fast, and was spoiled for it.

Orson wouldn't leave her, though, even if she *was* acting unkind lately. The experiences they shared were the most moving he'd ever had—more so than the drugs and sex, by far. Jezebel showed him how he could be great someday, that he might finally overcome the cruel burden his parents had left balancing on his shoulders—of addiction, abuse, and neglect.

Someday. That was enough reason for him to stick by her side—that and the unmatched feeling of artifice that had crept into their camp, a feeling he simply couldn't shake.

He felt as though Meredith was hiding something—and perhaps Birch, too (with his creepy, slightly hunched back and effeminate, sculpted cheeks). He could see it in their eyes when they looked at one another. Neither of them had felt compelled to explain the latter's origins, nor how they'd come to meet. Despite that, Jezebel was unperturbed, wholly trusting them both.

Knowing she hadn't picked up on their hushed communion gave Orson a feeling of pride, and helped him carry on at the camp. If nothing else, he knew he had to keep an eye out, in case Jez was blinded by allegiance to her mother.

There they were: Jezebel and Meredith, out on the cliffside, staring into space, holding hands and whispering encouragements.

Birch was far off in the corner of the camp, bashing apart their earthen cots and stomping the fire pit to smithereens, hiding the signs of their stay.

Orson crept closer to the girls, hiding behind the pretense of sweeping the bush-covered cliffside that served as their cavern's vestibule.

"You can come away from those weeds, Orson," Meredith said, pursing her lips.

He approached them, wiping his brow clear of the spreading sweat (though the sun had only just risen).

"Are we almost ready?" he asked.

"Yes—we'll be leaving soon," Meredith said. "Did you need something?"

"No…" Orson pursed his lips and wrinkled his brow. He'd never been much of a liar. "I only wanted to help. Birch is clearing the cave, mussing things up so's anyone passing through won't know we were here." He spoke in vibrato, barely stopping to breathe.

Jezebel giggled, covering her mouth.

Meredith only nodded, smiling back at him. She turned to face Jezebel, petting her wings, and nodded before she turned and walked wordlessly away.

He watched Meredith depart, waiting until he was sure she was gone from earshot before he sidestepped closer to Jezebel.

"Everything okay?" he asked.

Jezebel turned her back to him, gazing off in the direction of the compound, her former home and the subject of all their fermenting angst. "I'm fine," she said. "What do you want?"

"I told you, I was—"

"Cut the crap! I know you were *spying* on us. You might as well spit it out."

"Oh…" He scratched the tip of his nose, as though the words he couldn't form might flake off and fall onto his lips.

"What *is it?*"

He blurted it out: "I don't trust them."

"Seriously?" Jezebel raised an eyebrow at Orson, gazing over his shoulder toward Meredith and Birch.

"I know it sounds crazy, but they're definitely hiding something. I can tell. I grew up in the company of liars and thieves."

Jezebel scoffed, stepping away to move back through the entrance of the cave toward her mother, but Orson grabbed her by the bicep and held her to the spot.

She shook free of his grip and said, "Now's not the time for paranoia. We're about to leave. You'll just have to trust us. All of us."

With no room left to argue, Orson let her go, admiring the way each of her sundry feathers glistened in the budding daylight. He sighed and settled into a defeated slouch against the sandy, rock-flecked ground, lifting his eyes hopelessly toward the sun. By his estimation, the day would soon be nearing its shift out of early morning and into daytime proper. They needed to get a move on, and he still had things of his own to put in order before they left.

Perhaps they should *go alone*, he thought.

He nodded an inward acknowledgment of his plan to decamp. Just as he rose to tell them the news, a flicker ran through his palms, and a stirring against the periphery of his mind—as of mice in an attic, scuttling by just overhead, out of reach.

Don't be ridiculous—you're not leaving. It was Jezebel's voice inside his head. *I sense it, too. Calm down and trust me, okay?*

He gulped back the urge to gasp at the arrival of her placating, omniscient voice; it had arrived so suddenly and reverberated through his mind long after she finished speaking—no, *thinking*. Venturing a response, he thought back, as best he could:

I trust you.

Casually lifting his eyes toward Jezebel, he caught a wink—and a simper, too.

She replied without speaking, within him:

Good. Now, get ready to leave.

—

Birch had changed a lot since childhood: from an awkward, gangly kid (obsessed with outer space and aliens, card tricks, levitation, and spontaneous combustion) to this latest boastful version of himself, winged and stern. It wasn't that he didn't *like* Orson or his own half-sister, Jezebel. In fact, he wanted to like them both, if not also to *love* his half-sibling; but, as Meredith asserted, it was *too much, too soon*. The revelation of their shared blood might send her over the edge. So he bided his time and promised to do his best, to protect them without giving too much away. If that meant being flinty, so be it. Later, there'd be lots of time for palaver with Jezebel, bridging the gaps between their respective narratives over long draughts of moonshine, learning from one another, sharing their gifts.

Assuming they survived. Assuming also that they succeeded in uprooting their father from the last leg of his wicked plan: his scheme to rattle the world to its core, to send every land across the globe up in conflagration, to His name. The demoniacal extermination of the world.

The apocalypse. It was a concept that made Birch laugh, but not because he didn't believe it was possible. He laughed because this was the life he'd always wanted to live—to face danger, to explore the unknown. Now that he was there, face to face with the potential of his total ruination (and the world's complete destruction), it was all suddenly a lot less glamorous. He wondered how things might have ended up differently, if he hadn't been on that boardwalk all those years ago (it was a fact he still hadn't shared with Meredith; somehow he knew it would disrupt their solid kinship). Instead of his current predicament—readying himself for a kamikaze dive through the desert—he might have been married already, with children of his own.

No, he mused. *Some things just aren't possible...*

Perhaps he'd be a plumber, then; or an electrician, living a simple but happy life in a suburb whose main attraction was its most recently constructed fast food restaurant.

No, that wasn't possible either. He would never be *normal*, at least not by the standard definition. His mother had made sure of that by settling in with the Order, and by sleeping with its Overseer.

What's normal, anyway? Have a wife, go to church, make a bunch of kids? Not for me.

Still, it had felt so nice to care for someone—someone more vulnerable than himself—back in San Francisco, with Isabella. But things hadn't ended well for her. Maybe he wasn't cut out to care for another person—be it a lover, a spouse, or a child.

Even if he hadn't been on the boardwalk to watch Peter die, it wouldn't have changed the inborn compulsion he'd always possessed for things dark, gloomy, or otherwise taboo. While some parts of his life might have ended up differently, Birch warmed to the thought that much of his path would have stayed the same. He was, after all, born of the Overseer.

Birch breathed deeply, forcing out any concerns he had that didn't relate to their undertaking. He entered that final stretch of quiet with mental composure, feeling primed, but another of Meredith's protracted speeches disrupted his concentration and had him second guessing the potency of their plan.

She was severely overcompensating:

"This is the fatal moment. We'll pull back the curtains on his scheming and expose him for the monster he truly is. If we can publicly oust him, in front of his followers, they'll tear him limb from limb; they'll do all the dirty work for us."

Birch stood up, tied back his hair, and advanced on Meredith from behind. Grabbing her by the wrist, he pulled her rigid, finger-pointing limb down into a relaxed position, at rest against her hip. He rubbed her shoulders, cooing in her ear: "You're right, we'll do it. But calm down. You're scaring them."

The others were staring up at her, wide-eyed, perhaps afraid Meredith had cracked under the pressure.

"It's a lot for anyone to take in," Birch told them. "We just need to get down there and do it. Standing up here and grasping at straws won't do us any good."

"You're right," Jezebel said, rising from her seat. "Let's go."

Birch could *feel* her readiness: her long, braided hair pulled back from her face to expose her tense-locked jaw, narrowed gaze, and tensile neck.

He turned to Orson, nodding a silent affirmation: *You'll do great.*

They left behind the cave (each of them full of apprehensions they wouldn't admit outright; stomachs in knots, minds painting pictures of all possible outcomes). Pushing out toward the lip of their desert's headland, they gazed across those badlands and imagined the opening moments of their war.

But first they had to fly.

CHAPTER XXX

Orson was enraptured, soaring through the clouds, feeling the stir of wind against his grimy-whiskered face. He held on tight, trusting Jezebel with his life. She was his friend, after all, and perhaps the only real confidante he'd ever had. If anyone could be trusted so much, it was her. He cherished those last moments of quiet, savoring their closeness (feeling the murmur of her heart against his cheek, warm and thrumming), wishing it could last forever though he knew it wouldn't. They'd arrive soon, and unsnarl the threads that bound them.

Off to the right—through a blanket of cloud cover—Birch flew alongside them carrying Meredith. He struggled to maintain pace with Jezebel. There was an uncommon playfulness in their traversal of those skyward grounds, as though the clear air of the firmament had been the missing puzzle piece to unlock Birch's acid heart, to warm him to their company. Although Orson was still skeptical about the angle-backed stranger, he did his best to share in the enjoyment of their game, humoring himself by wondering how far ahead Jezebel and he would finish. If Orson could speak over the roaring gales, he'd have told her how well she was doing; he'd have encouraged and cajoled her toward the gates. Perhaps their game was just the distraction they needed, to get their minds off the fiendish grounds they traveled toward.

Past the second hour of their route and with no sign of slowing, Orson began to notice a dip in Jezebel's shoulders, a shift from their customarily smooth, horizontal plane, toward something closer to a curving hillock; too, her eyes showed signs of fatigue, fluctuating between closed and open with more uncertainty than an incontinent's bladder.

Orson hoped they could keep up their rate of flight. The sun, having just surpassed the apex of its curve, would shortly begin its denouement for a downward, setting path. They needed to get there before nightfall, before additional questions would be raised, before doubts and terrors they hadn't fully accounted for would come into play. Absence of light meant the surging influence of beasts whose beady, blind eyes would do them better service than by day. The group's entrance past sunset meant they'd be in the full sway of His domain, in the Overseer's service.

To combat Jezebel's exhaustion, Orson took up a childish but effective method of rousing her: he periodically poked her in the ribs. Just when she appeared to be dozing, he'd rouse her with a sudden, sharp jab. She'd squawk like a bruised bird, pushing his hands away from her chest and nodding, as if to say, *Okay! Okay!*

Birch and Meredith closed the gap separating them, drawing alongside them again and proving true the adage *Slow and Steady Wins the Race*. As they pulled up, Birch waved his arms maniacally, pointing down, toward the ground far below. Meredith kicked her legs like an infant suspended over water, panicking. They were clearly finished with recreation, and their expressions delivered a terse message:

STOP! DOWN!

Jezebel nodded her understanding and commenced a steep dive toward the ground below, plunging parallel to Birch. Cutting through the billows like butter— using Orson as her knife—they chopped through the sky's silken stratum 'til the clouds fully parted, revealing the scenery beneath them.

They were at the site, floating just above the ever-feared locus of their labors: the compound. From high above, it looked rather unthreatening—its tedious stone-built edifice was shrunken from monolithic to minuscule, held up by walls that could have been those of any insipid government hangar or an old, abandoned prison. But the closer they drew toward it, the less sterile the compound appeared, and the more volatile, brooding. It mutated from barren ghost town into a menacing megalith, which shot grotesquely up from the earth, with a circle of sand carved from its center.

The mood of the group shifted abruptly, from play to the point of convergence.

Jezebel's heart beat against Orson's face and told him all he needed to know about how she felt. She slowed their descent and paused, flapping mid-air as she looked around for Birch and his passenger, Meredith. Finally, they came into view several hundred feet away, just surfacing from the base of a pallid, grayish cotton mist. Jezebel approached and flew right past them—toward the west, the sunset, and a forest of dead trees: hulking skeletal masses stripped of their leaves, reaching their charred limbs up to the sky with the intensity of an evangelist at pulpit.

Jezebel landed gracefully, this time without injury to Orson or herself. She seemed familiar, comfortable, as though she'd been there before.

A whoosh out of earshot told them their friends had also touched down. Disembarked from the safety of Birch's mount, Meredith rushed through the first cluster of tall, alien trees, flitting about between them (hiding behind each broad trunk as though evading some phantom which was veiled to the rest of them). The group reconvened.

"Which way do we go?" Meredith asked, breathing heavily, breaking a sweat.

"I don't know," Jezebel said. She admired the peculiar patterns created by the outlines of the trees' limbs, tracing their flesh with her fingertips. "It's hard to say."

The woodland was populated primarily by a host of impoverished-looking yucca trees, their surreal shoots bending at angles that baffled the mind, like some long-lost H. R. Giger drawings. Fifteen-foot tall mastics were sprinkled here and there and, though their snarling branches were largely leafless, they managed to blot out the sun. The trees cast shadows that bewitched, and the atmosphere amidst them was approximately nasty. The way the quiet air hung with apprehension, it could have been any time, and they might have been anywhere.

"Hold on," Birch said, and alighted, vanishing up through the straggly canopy overhead and knocking loose a few needle-sharp twigs, which showered down upon their heads.

Jezebel lifted up her wings to blot them out and she shouted after Birch, "What are you *doing*?" She sighed, shaking her head.

Meanwhile, Meredith carried on with her nervous fit, gritting her teeth and tapping her elbows, arms crossed, with increased intensity. Thankfully, before her bout turned into an outburst, Birch reappeared with a smile and pointed confidently in a direction that could have been any way. He assured the group:

"The compound's straight through there." He indicated a path, cutting across the most densely packed part of those dead woods. "There's a plume of smoke rising from the center of the compound. That wasn't there before."

No one responded to the ominous news; it did little to put them at ease. Instead of bounding, freshly inspirited, they trudged silently along, not speaking to one another, listening for any startling sounds—an approaching Taken, ready to tear them apart with its bare hands, or the telltale racket of broad-spanned, flapping wings. Birch continually stopped to pucker his lips and scrunch his brow before he assured them that the path they squeezed their way along was the correct one. They scuttled slowly past the tensile, horny thorns of other nameless trees, all of whose limbs did their best to prick the group with the honed tips of their boughs, perhaps to deliver a drop of death-dealing poison, but none succeeded.

Meredith was still on edge, holding her breath 'til she couldn't hold it anymore—until she sucked at the air with the sound of a vacuum cleaner. It reminded them to stay alert, to steer clear of the most tightly-packed thickets.

As the density of the unlovely plant life finally thinned—and the wayward light of the sun rejoined them on their course—they emerged, safe and sound, to find a warm but fading remainder of the day, and a respite before the final leg of their race.

It lay just ahead of them, across a quarter mile's stretch of rolling dune—uncluttered and barren, free of obstructions—

The compound.

"Now what?" Orson asked, covering his mouth and nose, blocking the sting of the airborne sand flying in his face.

"We stick to the plan," Birch said, and drew in a lung-bursting breath. Taking the first brave step, he withdrew from the cover of those unknown woods (at once menacing and safe, guarded) for an even greater uncertainty: a vulnerable stroll across those drifts of deceptively dulcet sand. He ushered them out, "Come on."

Surprisingly, Meredith was the first to follow, abandoning her neuroticism for the cold determination she had once displayed—a reserve which had, in the first place, seen them there. She paused mid-way out to Birch and stood fixed, right at the margin between procedure and action. Turning to face the stragglers, Meredith nodded a wordless affirmation.

Orson grabbed Jezebel by an attenuated wrist, dragging her after the others, but she slipped from his grasp and took wing. He jumped up after her—reaching for her ankles, looking like a dog barking up the wrong tree—and fell flat on his ass. He screamed after her—"Come back! What the fuck!"—until Meredith tackled him around the waist and rose to cover his mouth, *shoosh*ing him, her mouth pursed together into a finger-sealed O.

Jezebel left them without a passing backward glance.

While Meredith did her best to calm Orson down, Birch kept on marching, heading up their hike without regret. He waltzed ever forward, unrepentant and unsurprised.

Orson suddenly remembered what Birch had said earlier, in response to his questions about the way ahead.

We stick to the plan.

And the plan they'd agreed upon meant Jezebel would eventually go it alone, in an attempt to distract the Order, for the greater good and ease of the group; for them, she would wholly and singlehandedly unlock a clear path to the Overseer.

Orson watched her go, ignoring Meredith's persistent tugging at his waist.

Jezebel shrank, rising ever upward until, at the pinnacle of her incline, she finally veered off to the left, heading for the compound's center court—the communal grounds at which the group hoped she might succeed in drawing all of the Order's attention.

The three of them—Orson and the other two, whom he still didn't fully trust—neared the stoop of the unwieldy camp with less fortitude than Orson would have liked. It was a colossus whose imposing design carried through to its gateway: an archway thrice their height had been cut into the structure's stone skin and was inset by a portcullis, whose latticed metallic grille was rusted and smeared with a dismal, viscous clot.

Birch was the first to approach it and, wrapping his fingers through the square eyelets of the gate, he leaned in for a peek through the barrier. What he saw frightened him; he stumbled backward, releasing an unruly, revelatory gasp like the mewl of a sniveling cur.

Behind the barricade, a swarm of anesthetic, gaping eyes stared out at them. An unhappy horde of their enemy lay in wait, ready to welcome them with portent. There were hundreds of them: ready and anxious, unsurprised by the group's arrival to the gates. Broad grins glowed with hunger on the women's salacious faces. Likewise, the carnal longing of their men was displayed by the appearance of their prominent poking rods, pushing stiffly against the coarse fabric covering of their robes. The lot of them appeared somehow lifeless, yet were animate, like zombies roused to the biddings of their—still absent—master.

It was clear: they were Taken, not Touched. The lot of them had been completely overwhelmed by some demon's influence over them, their apprehensions upturned and their cognizance quelled. It was apparent in the way they advanced toward the gate, unfaltering even as they sliced their cheeks upon its sharpened grating, and in the collective meaninglessness of their moaning, interspersed with a high-pitch clicking, which Orson was already all too familiar with.

So this was the fallacy of certainty. Their failure to think of how they might best a hundred, or a thousand—all the raving pawns of the Order's Apollyon leader, now degenerated to the playthings of beasts—while the very cipher himself absconds with the girl, with Jezebel, to do as he sees fit.

As the gate started to rise, the three of them dug in, sturdying themselves for the onslaught at hand, and Orson questioned how they'd do it—how they would make it through this layer of Hell and into the next of its many blazing circles. And he wished—nay, prayed, by whatever thread of piety he had (or didn't know he had)—for Jezebel's safe-keeping.

The Taken slithered out from beneath the half-raised gate, writhing and rising to properly greet them, to meet them by bunting blindly, charging headlong at the trio of warriors threatening to enter. The whites of their eyes were unseeing orbs set in the frames of their frenetic faces, and their teeth (fractured and grated to nubs by the constant clacking of their jaws) hung like razors, ready to cut.

Meredith drew a clip-pointed bowing knife from the side of her belt. Its small blade was no longer than her own palm, yet she hoisted it with the determination of a swordsman, ready to jab it up the first assailant's nostrils to the brain. Instead, it found its home in the warm seat of a young woman's neck, all gaunt skin and bones, whom Meredith beheaded with a flick of the wrist. The girl's wild eyes carried on roving across the inside of her own skull, and her gnashing mouth kept gnashing, clamping wide open and then shut like a grotesque clamshell whose pearl was her dampened uvula, swimming in blood at the back of her throat.

Birch put an end to her, flattening her skull to pulp with one smash from the flat end of his boot, brains and bone flying like biological shrapnel. He beat his wings, casting a furious gale-force wind toward the oncoming horde. Many of them toppled under the duress of his pinions' breath, but some overcame their force, or avoided it altogether by fanning out onto the dunes outside, spreading out beyond the gates. The strongest of the mob approached first, toppling over the weakest of their group, and they corralled the trio in.

Orson, Meredith, and Birch were locked at the center of that tightly-cinching circle. They were surrounded, yet all Orson could do was stammer, gawk, and pray (besides which, to someone or -thing he'd never much believed in). He wished for the restoration of a gift he'd left to rankle, down at the pit of his loathing. Squinting, hoping for its return, Orson felt with all his being for the electrified thread of that power, that he might help his company to beat them all away. But that familiar tingle didn't come. His fingers were as plain as they had ever been before, and his palms didn't spark with Baal's supernal gifts. Whatever hold he had on nature—of its thunder and its sparks—was kept from him.

Yet something stopped the Taken from crushing them. Though the incensed masses could have already torn them apart—and easily—there was an unseen force retaining possession of their urges, keeping them at bay.

Orson glanced around. Though still helpless to fight, he seemed to be the only one feeling that pulse of energy. Meredith carried on hacking away at their heads, and Birch tossed away whoever drew too near, throwing them back to the outer ring of the ever-encroaching band (or against the walls of the compound with an audible *SNAP* of their necks, spines, and skulls).

Jezebel? Orson thought.

It was less than a stab in the dark, but he figured it was worth a shot. If anyone was capable of holding them off—even from afar—it was her. At first, there was no response. Orson resigned himself to the advancing horde, ready for what would most assuredly be a rather painful death. He did his best to block out any notions of that pain, busying himself instead with his hands, massaging them in an attempt to bring back their electric vitality while evading the swinging clutches of the Taken at the inmost point of the ring.

Just when the aperture of the Taken around them shrank to the point of no return—the savages drawing too near—a familiar buzz shot across Orson's lowermost vertebrae, as though a pin had been stuck to the base of his spine. That dull, thudding pain was replaced by a floating sensation. As the mindless masses closed in on all sides, Orson rubbed his palms together again. A current leapt between them—like some behemoth's feet drawing static over carpet—and he heard an inward voice that wasn't his own:

You can do it, Orson. But now you're on your own.

He couldn't be sure—he couldn't hear well over the humming of the monumental pulse he produced, bristling within him, drowning out the rest of the world—but it seemed like Jezebel. It *felt* like her there, inside his head again. If it was her, the utterance of those vanishing words also meant the end of her influence over the Taken; now they were free to pummel, pound, and kill as they wished.

His companions' blood-spattered faces grew heavy with fatigue—hacking, slicing, throwing their way through arterial gouts of gore. In a moment, it would all be over. But not if he could help it.

He smashed his palms together, loosing a wide kinetic pulse. In response to the expanding dome of blue-white light which he projected, every strand of hair rose up across his body, instantaneously sizzled and singed as the force which he projected from within blossomed into a field of highly-charged sparks around him. Its unwieldy load lit the muscles through his arms, legs, and chest on fire, as though they might melt clear off the bone.

The sphere of energy unfurled quickly, growing from a small dome—just wide and tall enough to surround Orson—into a vast arc that spiraled outward, swallowing the dunes and the compound gates, leaping through and against the front walls of the edifice and tearing them wide open. All the players on that battlefield were engulfed by its meat-licking white heat, scorched by its intensity and reduced to a pile of twitching barbecue meat, strewn carelessly across the sands. As it grew farther, swallowing up the first hall of the compound on its course, the dome cast the air thick with haze. Orson's vision faded against the budding mist of its effulgence. All was colorless, reduced to bleached textures, impressions of what once had been life.

For however exponentially his power had bloomed, it was equally quick to depart. In a moment, the ether cleared and Orson saw the effects of his electric blast. They were gone, all of them. Dead. Every last Taken, set alight with white flames and reduced to melted pulp, half-charred bones, and ash. But among the wreckage, the ruined dead, he could not find Meredith, nor Birch. Overturning those nameless, charred remains on his search, Orson chanced upon a few whose guts had been preserved by the cage of their ribs and spines; they released a stench like overcooked pig and fecund, moist earth. He wondered if his friends had been hit, too, and killed by the radius of whatever nameless force he emitted.

Orson grew tense with fear. He was, at once, the Orson of before: keyed up, hapless, and plodding.

"Meredith!" he screamed. "Birch! Please tell me you're okay—tell me you're *fucking okay!*"

No response.

He moved toward the felled front gate, now a gaping orifice in the side of their ghastly fort—its innards scarcely lit, revealing no trace of whatever dangers might still lurk past its outer walls. Kneeling in the shadows of the heaped rubble, Orson closed his eyes and willed the voice to return, begging it to help.

Please help, Jezebel. I don't know what to do.

Superstitiously, he crossed his fingers, though it didn't do much good. There was no response.

Please, he begged again. *Tell me you're okay. Should I carry on alone?*

He waited, listening for anything—for a wordless sensation, a nod of assent, something. But no response came.

She'd told him, *now you're on your own*, through an unspoken augury, and she couldn't have been more right. Jez was gone, perhaps just now begging for her life at the hands of her twisted father. Meredith and Birch were missing, and he might have mistakenly killed them.

Lowering his head into his hands, Orson waited, coaxing himself out of commiseration, avoiding that conclusion until it proved itself absolutely. He lifted up his own trembling hands; every fingertip was blackened like overcooked toast, coated in the afterbirth of his deathly detonation; and his forearms were greased from wrist to elbow, with the smutty viscera of the corpses he'd upset on his search for Birch and Meredith.

He said, "I can't do this…"

"You can, Orson," someone said, behind him, in a voice of strong conviction, with assurance and pride. It was in Birch's prominent tone, and it reached Orson's ears as a welcome recess from the well of misery into which he'd so quickly sunk.

"I thought you were dead," Orson said. "That I killed you."

"You didn't." Birch spoke from the side of his mouth; his lips were cracked, charred at the corners from exposure to the current, and leaked a trickle of blood. He raised his fingers to pat away the dribble.

"Sorry about that."

"Right, about *that*." Birch chanced a grin, one perhaps a bit too broad; it loosed a fresh spill of red. "What the hell *was* that, Orson? Where did that come from?"

"Baal, I think." Orson chuckled. "I guess I'm slow to blossom." He felt himself blushing, genuinely.

"Well, whatever it was, it worked." Birch flourished his free hand around them, admiring Orson's handiwork.

They sat quietly for a moment, avoiding a greater question.

"Where's Meredith?" Orson finally asked.

"Not with you?" Birch raised an eyebrow.

A flash of panic shot through Orson as he grasped for the gist of her absence, but dearth of evidence kept him from drawing a real conclusion.

"No," Orson said.

"I'm just messing with you, pal!"

Orson could have slapped him. He thought, *What a time for jokes*, and said, "Well then, where *is* she?"

"Pushed ahead to scout the area."

"Inside?"

"Yeah. Don't forget, she lived here for years. Knows the place like the back of her hand."

Orson didn't know what to say. He only stared at Birch, waiting for some directive.

"Don't worry," Birch said, grinning idiotically. "We'll head after her if she's not back soon. Catch up quick, too. Lickety-split."

"All right."

What Orson really wanted to say was,

fuck you asshole i got us out of that mess and you're still acting all high n mighty get your head out of your own ass for a second and put it back in the game quit joking around now's not the time let's get this show on the road rescue Jez kill the chief call it quits,

but instead he only sighed, and they tuckered in against the blackened debris.

It wasn't long before Meredith rejoined them. She, like Birch, was a little overcooked by the impact of the blast. Nevertheless, she walked calmly, almost in a trance, as though their quest had little urgency. The light that normally shone behind her eyes—one of either steel composure or of panic, depending on the hour of the day—had dimmed. Something wasn't right.

They moved toward her, each taking an arm, and barraged her with questions.

"What is it?" Orson asked.

"Something happened!" Birch howled.

"Is it Jezebel?"

"Where is everyone?"

"You okay?"

"Say something!"

"Anything!"

"Speak!"

She seemed to notice them both suddenly, like ghosts just shimmering into her periphery. She turned her head to survey them for some long moments and shook free of their grip. They let her go, and she slid slowly against the floor, her back grating audibly along the rough-hewn walls, one of the few left standing in their vicinity. She left a trail of black and red along her course down its vertical plane.

"Meredith," Birch said, lowering himself to squat down beside her. "If you don't tell us what's going on, we can't help."

They waited a moment. When she offered no response, Birch huffed and moved to walk away, grabbing Orson's shoulder and mumbling something (*uselessbullshitdoitmyself*). They approached the hallway from which Meredith had emerged.

"Wait…" A voice, weak but full of import. It was Meredith.

They stood rooted to the spot, waiting to hear more. Orson could have sworn every cell of his body was frozen, mid-function, in anticipation of whatever news Meredith might share.

"It's Jezebel," she said. "He has her." The Overseer. "Our plan backfired." She spoke weakly, with her mouth half-parted, through her throat. "He foresaw our approach, and sent the lot of them to distract us while he snatched her away. I saw them heading into the depths of the compound, a place I've never been." She turned her gaze downward and started to sob, rocking forward and banging her head demonstratively, back against the wall.

"Stop it!" Birch yelled, moving toward her and dragging her up from the floor. He lifted a hand up to slap her across the face but caught himself before he loosed the blow. Ashamed, he smoothed his palms against her shoulders and sighed. "So—what you're saying is that Orson single-handedly took them out? All of them? The whole compound, except for the beast himself?"

Orson felt a pang of what wasn't regret—*I killed them; I killed them all.* All those bodies, all those souls. He reminded himself that they weren't themselves, that perhaps their spirits had long-vacated their bodies, replaced by those devils, the Takers.

"Yeah, I guess he did." Meredith smiled at Orson, an owing gesture which eased some of the queasiness in his stomach. "Well done."

"Thanks?" Orson wasn't sure what to say, and he was surprised by their inaction. Jezebel was being dragged toward the pits of the compound, and they needed to set out after her. Filled with resolve, he said, "So then, there's still a chance—a good chance. Can you show us the way?"

"I think so, yes. But the vision was weak."

"Meredith," Birch said. "Use your gifts. Surely you haven't already forgotten them. You drew them to us at the cave—Jezebel and Orson—just by calling out to her. She's your daughter. You'll intuit a path."

Her eyes scanned both of their faces, looking for the further assurance of Orson.

He nodded, smiling with camaraderie as best he could.

"Down the hall," Meredith said, rising onto wobbly feet.

She led them through darkened, labyrinthine passages, past the occasionally opened portals of abandoned rooms, some still illumined by quavering flicker-flames of white tapered candles—a reminder of, an homage to, the man or woman who'd once attended to their Order's needs, slaving away over thick-bound, deep volumes for some necessary magic. They traversed the communal lawn, a broad but barren open-skied niche carved from the center of the structure. At its epicenter was the fossilized husk of a once-great tree, its lifeless limbs gray and black, hardened to rock by time or some strange sorcery. As they passed it by, Orson pressed lightly against a low-hanging branch and was filled with a sensation of suffering, a brief yet intense fluttering through his whole body, a fibromyalgic tremor against all of his nerves. But it left his body as quickly as it had come, burning impressions of a great rupture that had once occurred at the selfsame spot: the tree ablaze; hundreds stampeding through the grounds; a cannibalistic feast; the masses copulating, switching partners with mercury.

The others didn't notice him lagging behind; they were already nearing the far end of the yard, past a raised platform of black-painted wood. A podium rest at the fore of the stage with a black, leather-bound volume laid opened. Orson scuttled to catch up with them and turned to glance back once more.

The moon was out early; it hung low and full, a misty green tinge hovering 'round it, softening its glow.

Trepidation padded through Orson, its whetted pincers fastening into him.

"It's just here," Meredith said. "I think. These are the stairs that lead to his room. I've only been there once, a long time ago." The usually full slope of her mouth flattened out into a line of distant reflection, and her eyes squinted painfully.

"Why should we go to his room?" Birch asked. "You said he took her down, below."

"Yes, but the entrance must be there somewhere."

Her assertion kindled fond memories within Orson, of mystery tropes:

False bookshelves. Switches built into the eyes of a sculpture. A cane on its stand that, when lifted, pushes back the fireplace to reveal a cobweb-covered crypt.

They set foot immediately upon a winding staircase and began their ascent. Orson wondered silently if there wasn't something else—perhaps a loose stone which would reveal an alternate, downward path—but he held his comments and followed them on the rise, Meredith leading the way and Birch's giant wings directly in front of him, blocking his view of their course.

When their pace slowed—and then finally stopped altogether—Orson peeked around them. A gnarled wooden door greeted them at the top of the stairs. It was sturdy, made of thick-cut lumber, and tightly sealed the entryway to the Overseer's room.

Meredith fiddled with the handle for a while, pushing against the door with all her might, but to no avail.

Birch tried his luck for only a moment before he declared, "Shut up tighter'n Fort Knox. Orson, give it a go with your wham-bang-pop." He winked, in a gesture that felt sarcastic to Orson.

Ignoring the flush he felt rising through his cheeks, Orson squeezed to the front of the line and felt for the handle. It barely moved from its stubborn spot— not much more than a wiggle. Touching his way across the outline of the doorframe, he hunted for any sign of weakness he might make good use of. Fruitlessly. He rubbed his palms together, feeling for their customary spark, and curbed a sudden rush of nausea at its arrival. He held his breath, his fingertips igniting with vigor and light, illuminating the steps of the stairway's cylindrical enclosure, and of the room's threshold. Before the queasiness could overtake him, Orson connected his hand to the doorknob and pushed. Its metal form melted to his designs. The out-facing end of it liquefied and dripped against the floor. From the other side of the doorway, a subdued thud reached them. The door stirred within its frame, freed of whatever lock had once held it shut.

Orson stumbled into the chamber, flopping immediately across a settee shoved against one of its walls. He slowed his breath, wiggling his fingertips to shake them of the burn until he calmed himself enough to lift his gaze upward. It was a high- and dome-ceilinged circular apartment, with no flat walls to be seen; its ever-curving aspect of smooth arching surfaces disoriented Orson as he followed them round and round: the walls hanging with golden artifacts, *fleurs-de-lis* sconces holding still-burning candles, scenting the room with malodor. Cloves, anise, rosemary, and an undertone of sweet, rotten decay.

The others joined him in the room—Birch with a sense of wonder, and a dose of pluckish surveillance, picking up artifacts here and there like a detective on speed; Meredith with less attentiveness, with a kind of sad fascination that had her supporting herself across the belly with both hands, wandering toward the bed, feeling its four high posts with bittersweet remembrance (though mostly—close to wholly—bitter).

"I *have* been here before," Meredith said drowsily, rubbing her temples. "But it's all…a blur. I don't remember how—how I got here, but I was here once before."

Birch rushed to her side, simultaneously the knight gallant—there to save her from fainting—and the hard-boiled detective, grilling her while supporting her by the elbow: "Think hard, Meredith. Do you remember *anything* that might help us get to Jezebel?"

She squinted, thinking deeply, as Birch had instructed. Whatever horrors flashed through her mind—across the insides of her eyelids—were enough to dislodge any notion of aid to their investigation. Instead, Meredith became wholly engulfed by her visions, screaming and lashing out at Birch with her nails, digging fresh rivers of blood into the side of his face.

He gripped his cheeks and pushed her away, involuntarily. She fell against the high bed, flailing paroxysmally.

Orson rushed to her side, grabbing her by the wrists, pinning her down to the mattress and hoping her fit would abate. Spittle flew upward into his face as she screamed monosyllabic curses—they sounded like the kind of banter spurted out on evangelical TV sermons. Amidst the blather, a few intelligible words came forth:

"Hurting" was one, and roused Birch from his wounded state. He rushed to aid Orson—cheek already healed—wrenching one of Meredith's wrists into his own grip that they might, together, do her better service.

"What did you say?" Birch asked.

Her eyes opened with sudden understanding, full awareness. She calmed momentarily as she said, matter of factly, "He's hurting her."

Then, as if she'd used up all her strength and sanity—to fight up from the bubbling abyss of madness, to share that pithy phrase, only to be re-consumed in the process—Meredith devolved back into a convulsive state.

Her hands turned white, and her face was nicely coated in a thin layer of mucous. Yet still she persisted, thrashing under their grip, kicking out and upward, upsetting the bedside table and its oil-burning lamp, which rolled across the room to settle upon a fine-woven Persian rug depicting open-mouthed birds in flight, caterwauling as they shot through the air, their turquoise feathers lifted. The oil spilled out and lit the textile aflame.

Orson let go of her wrist, leaving Birch to tend to Meredith alone while he sorted out the rug. He beat against it with his foot, careful to retract the stump of his leg from the quickly rising flames, to avoid them catching fire. The rug burned on, so he grabbed it by one of its still-preserved edges and flipped it nimbly over, so the flames faced the floor. It worked, trampling the fire and leaving a ghost of smoke hovering around him on the air. He looked through the haze, back toward Meredith and Birch.

They stared at him, amazed, Meredith finally shaken from her outburst. Birch was clearly relieved, and slowly let his manacled grip on Meredith relax and settle against his lap.

"Is everyone okay?" Orson asked.

"Yeah, I'm fine," Birch replied.

Meredith didn't respond; she only continued her stare, dead-eyed, her eyes bulging larger with every passing moment.

"What is it?" Orson asked. "Meredith. What now?"

By way of response, she lifted up a lone, scarcely bent finger and pointed toward the rug.

"There," she said. "They're down there."

Orson sidestepped to follow her gaze and the direction of her finger, tracing its scrutiny to a thin crack along the floorboards where the rug had been disrupted. He moved the floor covering off to the side, unveiling a hatch whose aspect was revealed by an inset handle, a metal ring which lifted up and shifted the doorway open. Underneath the trap door were stairs leading steeply downward, into a dark unlike any they'd traversed—denser, sturdier by far than their brief stay in the weird woods; damper and mealier air hung on the walls than in their high home in the desert cave; seedier than the odd coven of natives who'd given Orson his gift. This was the path toward the Overseer and Jezebel below—toward their final conflict. It had to be.

They hesitated on the threshold, glancing back and forth at one another as if waiting to see who would make the first step.

Though he dreaded the moment they'd face their menace, Orson was flooded with fresh resolve for the sake of his Jez, and steeped himself in the courage which that focus brought, braving the cobweb-lined spiral descent and leading the pack downward, into the abyss. As they crept (silently, on eggshells), the stench rising from below grew to nauseating heights: a putrescence of death and decay, it burned with each inhalation. More than the smell, there was a sense of mass expiry pervading the air—it nauseated them all and had them gagging, to the edge of being sick.

They pushed through it, carrying on and continuing round—and round, and round—and downward, past critters uprooted from their sleep, crawling over the rotting walls as silently as though cotton encased their feet. Yet none of them screamed. They were entranced, pushed forward by equal parts compulsion and bewitchment.

The quiet of their voyage afforded them ample warning of danger on their approach. As the first din of the Overseer's voice rose to greet them, a shiver ran down Orson's spine. He paused on the trail, clenching his jaw, raising his shoulders, and lowering his skull like a turtle retracting for the safety of its shell.

"Awaiting" was the word he thought he discerned, but they were still too far off for him to be certain. It might have been, more simply, "waiting."

He turned to his partners with searching eyes, hoping they'd heard it, too— hoping he hadn't succumbed to the madness of the stairwell's dark claustrophobia. They nodded.

Finally, they reached the base of the stairwell, but the hall it dumped them upon was no better lit. Feeling his way forward with arms outstretched, tracing the aspect of the walls entombing them, Orson staggered forward. In the distance, at the far end of the corridor, an impression of light glimmered in and out of view. It was a sense of light and yet not absolute, because of its quavering aspect. Still, it was enough to propel them forward, to drive them toward its source with a fatal pull.

Closer, and it became clear: the hall ended and opened immediately upon a giant earth-floored room. It was almost an amphitheater, the way it was constructed: walls too high to measure; an open ceiling showing starlit night; and a stage at dead-center, upon which stood two figures. Although their aspect was largely concealed by long, thick shadows—cast by the flickering flames of tall black candles set along the walls—Orson knew who they were.

The next word spoken was still whispered, but because they were closer—or perhaps because he *wanted* them to hear—Orson made it out: "Here."

The Overseer said, "They're here," and Jezebel let out a soft whimper, crumbling under his touch.

CHAPTER XXXI

Jezebel was strapped to a board, her legs bound together by thick silver chains, her flesh poking out between each tight-wound link. Her arms stretched out like the Christ figure (sans the stigmata), held aloft by another set of chains curving up toward the far walls of the room. These chains ran through metal rings attached to the walls and looped back to the spot of her confinement on the stage, where they ended up attached to the wheel of an ancient device—a three-foot-tall wooden box, with a metal crank attached to it its side.

Her head bobbed against her chest and a trail of blood oozed steadily from her fractured lower lip, dripping against the stage beneath her with a repeated, audible smack.

The Overseer turned, leering at them over his shoulder as, with one hand, he gripped Jezebel's lower jaw. He wrenched open her mouth, stuffed in a gag, and addressed them, screaming:

"You've arrived at last! And just in time, before the fun begins."

Deep, gut-bubbling loathing burned through Birch. He felt his eyes might burst. He wanted to fly to her aid, to tear her down from the grotesque fetters binding her, and to rip their father's head off.

Bastard, he thought, unclenching and clenching his fists.

Birch, Orson, and Meredith stood in place, helpless to act out their half-boiled plan. They cringed while the Overseer finished stuffing the loam-smeared, dirty cloth down Jezebel's throat. Once he finished, the Overseer mounted the stair-top and descended toward them, the air growing thicker with each step of his approach. He grew from the far-off fiend, squawking on the stage, into the towering animate carcass Birch remembered—reeking breath, cold touch.

Birch's joints tightened and his knuckles grew heavy, as though they might drag him to the floor if his father came another step closer.

"Ah," the Overseer said. "And who do we have here? The bitch's lover, perhaps?" His upturned nose peeked out from the shadow of his cowl, pointing like a woodpecker's beak; his long, thin nostrils dilated with each puff of air as he circled around Birch, sniffing his neck and tracing the aspect of his wings with bony fingers, settling on the subtle curve of his hump. "I see your little bump has straightened out a bit since we last met." He clapped sarcastically and then continued, "Thanks for bringing her back to me, but the entourage? Was all this really necessary?"

The Overseer spun around, as if to show the aspect of his own curved back, his spine rippling against the fabric of his robe.

Birch wanted to shout, to turn and spit in his progenitor's deathly face.

"No, no, that's not quite right," the Overseer said. "I got it all wrong, didn't I? You couldn't be her paramour. That's not it at all, because the love *you* have for her is somehow more generous than that of a lover's. The *inamorato* takes, selfishly at times. But your love is selfless; it's that of a comrade at battle. No, perhaps greater still." He lowered his voice, whispering: "Yours is the love of a sib, is it not? And what's this?" He turned to Orson, expanding his reach, arms outstretched between them, to touch the boys simultaneously—looking like a man made of soft, gray putty draped in yards of cloth too large for his rake-thin frame.

Orson's eyes burned with a fury that matched Birch's inward storm, yet neither of them found the impetus to move.

"You're stuck between feelings of tenderness and lechery, aren't you?" the Overseer asked, cackling right into Orson's face. Those crumbling teeth, spaced far apart along the track of his gangrenous gums, reeked even from where Birch stood. He couldn't imagine how Orson endured it, breathing in those noxious puffs of the Overseer's breath, faced up close with those rapacious, stinking sniggers. The Overseer continued, "And my most favorite of all...she's *returned to me*!"

He spun in a coquettish whirl toward Meredith, where he bowed impossibly low to the ground, under her full scrutiny and downward gaze. Though she couldn't bash his lowered skull, she at least managed a grunt of dissent.

"Fair enough," he said. "No need to reciprocate the sentiment. I'm a man of exceptional graces, and I can take a hint, *bitch*. Life's lonely at the top, but lonelier still in death." He paused to let that last bit of wisdom simmer, but it brought no significance to Birch's moral sense. He couldn't speak for the others, but they generally seemed nonplussed. The Overseer continued: "Isn't this just the loveliest little family reunion, though? Mother, father, daughter...and *son*—though borne by a different bitch, that one!" The last phrase of his statement—*that one*—was an indictment hurled at Birch, index finger primed, trembling joyfully. His teeth seemed to glow with phosphorescent heat, a limey yellow-green.

Jezebel tossed a glance of silent knowing down toward Birch, and her habitually stolid eyes welled with impossible tears.

"You know, I always wished for a son. An heir to uphold my name. I even prayed, to many dark and wondrous Lords. Because that's the thing all leaders need, right? A *son* to uphold their name, to carry on the legacy of their namesake— just as the Christ did for his Lord. That should have been *you*, mister—" he pointed toward the stage, toward Jezebel's slackened spot of subjugation and screamed, "But you'll never be so great, will you?"

The Overseer loosed a fresh bout of laughter—a spell of delight that devolved into sorrowful groans, as though whatever saccharine pleasures were left in taunting them might finally have abated. He turned toward his daughter and lifted up her chin, speaking to them all as he faced her: "Jezebel. *She* holds the key to uprooting our Earth. Even though she won't serve that purpose *will*fully, she's better off than you. Her name will be recorded in the annals of a new world history—ours, the Great Usurpers' story. We'll undo the years of waste and frittering. In time, the world's pitiless survivors will praise the great rupture brought about by her sacrifice.

"The way things are going, there might be a place for all of you there. Birch, the Winged One, who broke her heart and helped to seal the deal. Meredith, who brought her into the world and ushered her back out of it. And this new stranger, whose name I've yet to learn...what role will you play? Perhaps, at least, you'll make the footnotes.

"You're the ones who strolled along to exonerate her of all her past sins: of piety, of righteousness, and all things thoughtlessly benevolent—for those are the values of the weak, the crutch-bound, the short-lived. You came with promises of family, of normalcy—the brother and the bitch and the lover over there—and you riled her up real nice, just so she could do the job *that* much more swimmingly. You're packing a nice punch, yet you needn't say a word.

"I've got news for you, son, and bitch, and nameless one—I've got news for all of you. There is no happiness, not alongside others—not in the normalcy each of you craves. Both those ideas are abstractions, concepts created in the mind. You make your own happiness, and you do so through striving." As he wrapped up his soliloquizing, the Overseer trailed off, distracted by the pull of some dark heartstring, a hole in his ticker that he just couldn't slight.

His contentions were jumbled, like the ramblings of an odd bum Birch knew back in San Francisco, who hung out at the waterfront, and whom he occasionally brought sandwiches (except on that last day, on his run, he'd neglected to even say *Hello!* to the poor old fellow). Somehow there, at the edge of the end of the world, the image of that man's face was what loomed over Birch's conscience, drowning out all other things—even the Overseer's longwinded sermon—with shame.

"—listening to me? I need you to see it happen, so you can bear the burden of your irresponsibility. You'll remember the moment, when she died right before you, and you'll know that you *could* have run. You *could* have turned and walked away before it got so deep, and perhaps she would have lived. But you didn't. You followed the orders of the trollop and the lover. Smooth move, sweet brother Birch."

You would have come after us, Birch thought. *Until we both were dead. 'Til we were all dead.*

Even gagged and bleeding, Jezebel looked resolute. Whatever blip of emotion she'd experienced, at the revelation of her growing family tree, left and was replaced by undying resolve, so terribly characteristic of Jezebel. She was resigned as Joan of Arc, bound to her post and ready for whatever came next.

Jez, Birch thought. *I never got to call you that. Only Orson did.*

"You're all so quiet," the Overseer said. He snapped his fingers at them. "Wake up! The party's just begun."

Leaping back off the stage, down to the dusty ground, he dashed in a circle around them, completing a capering bolt around the circumference of the room, lighting more candles set in sconces along the walls as he passed them by, with some invisible coal. Diffuse heat welled up through the bowels in which they were trapped, walling them in with an imposing, heady steam that—combined with the Overseer's frenzied sprint—created a heightened sense of claustrophobia. The fresh light of the glims brought more than warmth; they also dragged in dread.

"Will none of you have at me?" the Overseer asked. "We haven't got all day. Let's see what you've brought. Meredith, perhaps you can read my mind when I think this, but I'll say it anyway: I expected more out of you.

"Birch, maybe I can't remember which whore was your mother—they all blend together over time—but I'd expect you to man up by now.

"And you, the lover—" Before the Overseer could finish his judgments, he was knocked off his feet.

Barreling headlong into their adversary's chest, Orson had charged the Overseer, launching clear off the back of the platform, and was skidding across the sand-streaked humus. Their tussle was cut short by the Overseer, who set his hands on Orson's neck and, strangling him, shouted the words,

"VI DAEMONIS

"SUSPENDET."

A tremor shot through Orson before he settled on the ground in a comatose heap. The Overseer kicked him hard in the side and dusted off his robe, climbing back onto the stage and glowering down at Birch and Meredith.

Meredith succumbed next, prey to the Overseer's dark energy, falling abruptly alongside Birch and leaving him to fend for them all by himself—to save Jezebel by himself.

Birch dug his heels in deep for lift off.

"What now, son of mine?" the Overseer asked. "Do you fall to the same fate as these weak-minded, sniveling Touched, or do you rise to a greater cause?"

After a hesitation, Birch replied, "What are you saying?"

"I'm offering you a chance to escape from your mortal constraints, to rise above the limitations of your grounded, physical body. Wings are one thing, Birch. But here's another…"

The Overseer lifted off the ground, feet dangling below him as he floated up and up, spiraling as he shot toward the ceiling, out of sight. He plowed through the air, back down, and completed a dramatic backward flip just before settling gently on the ground.

"You won't need wings to fly," the Overseer said. "Not with the Touch I can offer."

Selfishly—momentarily—Birch considered it, wondering if, after so many years of yearning, of searching for contact with the nether realms, this was finally his calling.

But he remembered the dull impression he still had of his mother: her injured, pained expression, beaten and bruised. And he thought of his aunt, sweet Greta, who cared for him selflessly and enduringly, through all his years of awkward self-searching. Even though he barely knew Meredith, he already felt a connection with her; an almost maternal warmth emanated from her. And the others: although only one of them was his blood kin, he had grown to view both Jezebel *and* Orson as his adoptive siblings, whom he'd privately sworn to protect.

"You're walking a very thin line," Birch said. "Between Taken and Touched."

"What ever do you mean?" the Overseer asked, placing one spindly finger against his lipless mouth.

"A thin red line, between king and pawn. Is this truly your cause? Do you even know what you want? Do you remember what it was to be human, once?"

By way of response, the Overseer laughed again, a throaty cackle that held no trace of sorrow. He lifted his robes up, over his shoulders and head. They dropped to the floor alongside him.

"I am still very much a man," he said, and lifted up his arms. Loose skin dangled from flimsy, thewless bones. "Whatever that may mean."

With the inch-long blade of his fingernail, the Overseer sliced a nick in his own wrist and knelt to the deck of the wooden stage. Daubing at the blood that flowed, he traced the aspect of a circle, like some morbid child's finger-painting, and completed the sigil with a smattering of arcane, abstract shapes. Its full aspect was shadowed as the Overseer rose, gangly knees bent inward, spine curved down in an unpleasant reminder of Birch's own deformity.

The Overseer's body was pock-marked with lesions dripping pus; flaps of skin sagged from his chest, punctuated by a set of dark-brown, puffy nipples hemmed in by countless wiry black hairs, like innumerable spider legs writhing against his chest, in stark contrast against his gangrenous, rotted skin. The long-fingered hand he held aloft—wrist ever-spurting blood down the slope of his forearm and dripping off the tip of his elbow—was like an angular, knobbed scrap of wood, gnarled and knotted by years of dry desert air.

He turned to face the bound Jezebel and—with the same cadmium yellow nail—cut across her wrist, massaging the yawning sliver of his own stigmatic wound against hers, blending together their blood. She roused, moaning against the gag shoved deep in her mouth, and wriggling her fettered limbs against the chains that bound them.

Birch dashed for the stage, but the Overseer swiveled to face him and lifted his bleeding arm, screaming again,

"*VI DAEMONIS*

"*SUSPENDET.*"

Birch stopped dead in his tracks, as if rooted by some enlivened vines writhing tight across his ankles. Nothing physically bound him to the spot, and yet he could not move. A white, light feeling of lethargy besieged him and he fell to one knee, battling the swelling urge to close his eyes, to rest his head in sleep.

Above him, the Overseer moved to the ancient wooden box and wound its crank, pulling tight the chains that held Jezebel aloft. She rose higher into the air, above the monster's head, and he clasped the soles of her feet, slicing them both along their arches. He lifted his face up to bask in the falling flow of blood, letting it douse his face, dribble down his neck, and spill across his shoulders, racing all the way down his bowed back. Some of it splashed across the sigil he had drawn, feeding it.

The symbol began to pulse with strange light, like the faint glow emitted by a lightning bug. The glimmer grew in intensity, shifting by gradient from golden to cardinal, and then cruddy red. Finally, it alighted in flames, licking high toward Jezebel hanging eight feet above.

The smell of scorching flesh which soon filled the air had the apposite effect of disgusting Birch, and the unexpected upshot of faintly rousing him from his torpid, spellbound state. He lifted himself up on one elbow and began to crawl toward the stage.

Draped behind the smoldering flames, which acted as a translucent dressing screen, the Overseer stretched his spine. With a series of appreciable clicks, the hump of his back straightened out. He cackled, savoring the fresh strength coursing through him at his daughter's constrained torture. He pushed out his chest, and the once-lax skin drooping there was stretched taut. His shoulders rippled with wiry resurgence. Using his newfound strength, the Overseer reached up for Jezebel and, gripping her by the shoulders of her restrained wings, tore them right off her back, in a single cruel pull. They easily snapped clean, and left behind a pair of bony, protuberant bumps—useless excrescences where once were august things.

Summoned by Jezebel's suffering and blood, a tubular, veined projection emerged from the flames, sending spikes of an inferno flying outward all around it. The extension slammed downward, crashing against the stage. It leveraged itself farther from the confinement of its nether cage, prying itself up from the symbol on the ground and the hellmouth to which it was linked, stretching the opening wider as it struggled to break free. The Overseer threw Jezebel's wings toward it— peaceably, in offering—and the florid-skinned beast caught them with ease (though there was no immediately apparent organ by which it might have seen them hurled toward it). It squeezed the gift tightly in its anthropomorphous grip—if burning translucent flesh could be described as such—until it dissolved completely, as if absorbed by osmosis or diffusion.

Hungry for more, the demon's limb searched the space immediately around its issuance, purposefully swatting at Jezebel's swinging form, still wobbling aloft— above hand, as it were. It grasped for her—once, twice, missing both times and clasping only air—until it finally steadied a blind stare toward her, flexing all of its human-sized fingers toward her, readying for the kill.

The Overseer clapped in delight, hopping in place with a juvenile sneer on his face.

Birch closed his eyes, gritted his teeth, and (with all the will he could muster, bounding against the Takers' forces binding him) rose, quivering, onto his feet. He flew, soaring into action and pummeling blindly against the flame-wreathed arm of the beast, disrupting the Taker's pursuit of Jezebel.

Instead of attacking her, the demon's hand found a new prey in Birch—an easy prey, too. It swiveled its wrist and plucked Birch aloft, burning immediately through his clothing and flesh like butter on a skillet, crackling and searing its way through him to the bone. His entire midsection was engulfed with white-hot pain, which in seconds deliquesced his skin into senseless, numb pulp.

It hoisted him higher as the rest of it emerged, slithering, from the symbol that bound it below. First came its head, a skinless skull with down-sloped, thorned horns emerging from its temples. It had no eyes—only a pair of nostrils set low on its face, above a toothless, sphincteral mouth from which five serpents' tongues loomed, wriggling fast and recoiling back for the dark cavity of its hollow *embouchement*. Something like skin began in a ring around its neck—like a morbid turtleneck—but the scraps of parchment-like membrane draped here and sheathed tightly there, hanging down toward its distended gonads, were vellum-thin and only half-obscured its sinewy form underneath. It had no nipples on its breast and it was (despite the slouched sack swinging between its fawn-like, hoofed lower limbs) distinctly agender, as it also lacked a penis. Only that fatty sack, greased and swinging, hinted at any semblance of sexuality which may once have existed, in some earlier iteration of the fiend.

Freed from its prison, the Taker craned its neck to survey its new realm, and loosed its grip on Birch. The flames surrounding its body faltered, quavering and then abating as the Taker succumbed to corporeality.

The Overseer delighted in the beast's arrival, continuing his happy dance along the edge of the stage until the Taker noticed him. It lowered itself down to face him, sniffing the air around the Overseer before it suddenly shifted back on its haunches, like a mutt at a pile of dung he finds just a bit too revolting.

When Birch made to quit the stage, rolling fast toward its edge, the Taker scooped him back up with ease.

"Not him, fiend!" the Overseer screamed, jumping up, waving his arms pleadingly toward the invoked. "Take the girl instead—it's *her* death that's essential."

In a sonic booming voice which shook the foundations of the compound and ruffled the boards of the stage with its bass, the Taker said, "You've summoned me for her?" It turned to regard Jezebel, who drooped unconscious from the board.

"She's yours," the Overseer said. "You'll find her body a worthy seat."

"You wish it also that I should possess her, to live alongside you on the Earth?"

"Yes, yes! That's what I wish! Together, with the blood of your brothers coursing through me, we'll conquer the world. Take back what was once yours— that which was stolen from you by a selfish god." The Overseer rubbed his hands together, unashamed of his ardor.

"My brothers? The demons who came before me are *not* my brothers." The Taker tossed Birch asunder, flinging him like the last nub of a used-up cigarette (and Birch felt like one, too, though he somehow still clung to consciousness).

"Forgive me, great Prince of Darkness. Your majesty precedes you, and my excitation blinds me. I know that yours is a name all below must revere. And I, by that token, also worship you."

"That's better, mortal. I feared you might have underestimated my esteem. The louts you summoned, those many moons ago, have fallen from my graces— Astaroth especially, the bumbling fool. Their aiding your conquest was not granted my permission."

The Overseer's smile melted into an even, expectant grimace. He asked the Taker, "What do you mean?"

"They're conniving, just as you are. That's a quality I often admire in mortals, but an attribute I don't welcome among those serving my ambitions."

"I understand, and I wasn't aware of their treachery. I swear it."

"Still, they've granted you much, and you've repaid them little. Why should I not squash you along with all the other mortals gathered here? You've shed blood in my name. I am satiated, and might just as easily abscond, and fly back to my own domain."

The burns across Birch's body pulsated with fresh, blistering pain, yet he commanded himself to hold on. His wings were crushed, as useless as though he no longer had them. Jezebel still hung overhead, out of his reach. Meredith lay impossibly still, as she had since their arrival; Birch only hoped she was still alive. And Orson lay far away, behind the wooded platform of the stage; his comfort was unassured, the state of his well-being impossible to detect.

"Then humor me, please," the Overseer said. "Listen to what I have to say, for at least a while. I've waited a long time for this moment. Many moons, as you've said yourself."

"Don't take for granted your impunity, summoner. Even he who beckons may live to see the wrath of his own invoked."

"I don't underestimate your bulk, nor your power, Great One."

"Lay quiet your flatteries, goose. I've many names. It's clear you know this. Yet your knowledge of them loses weight with every passing moment. Impress me further."

The Overseer thought a moment before he spoke again. "You've lived through many eras—perhaps all of them—lying in the shadows, quietly awaiting moments at which you might surface unnoticed, to show the world brief glimmers of your wonder. But why should you have to hide?"

The Taker stared down at him for a quiet second before it cackled acerbically, gripping its hips as the goitered sack of flesh between its legs swayed all about. It said, "You think this lofty offer of yours to be an unfamiliar one? You are dumber than you look. It's no wonder you found such close company with the likes of Beelzebub. Might as well you should turn into a fly as well, and live the rest of your days out noiselessly, feeding on shit."

Red crept through the Overseer's cheeks, yet he held his tongue, lowering his chin to demonstrate his servility. "As host to your fancy, I accede. I may be dumb, but I can also be loyal—"

"Loyal!" The Taker interrupted, pausing with a look of disgust on his face before he toppled over himself with a fresh round of laughter. "You feign to something you are not. Ambitious you may be, but loyal? No, I think not. Try again."

All their snooty rhetoric afforded Birch the chance to wobble around the perimeter of the stage, toward its far side and closer to Orson's slouched figure. His friend's absolute stillness held little promise, but Birch carried on nevertheless. A fist-sized stone found its way into Birch's hand; he threw it at Orson, and it smacked him on the back.

Nothing happened.

The Overseer was speaking:

"—together, I'm sure you can be greater than your one combatant. If we tear

433

out the ground beneath them, they'll have no choice but to perish. The ones left behind will have been yours all along, protected as they are by their devil's contrivances—their spells, and their self-serving pride. Those are the people who'll see to the final and total death of God, and they'll help us bring about the resurgence of a pure, unbridled vigor for sensation, for life, for power."

The Taker seemed to consider his offer, twirling away at the many forked tongues hanging from his mouth—like a tic, as though they were strands of idle hair.

Birch steadied his breath and wrenched up another stone. It was larger, and capable of causing a concussion if he didn't toss it well. He hurled it over at Orson. It smacked him on the back again, this time a clean bulls-eye between the shoulder blades.

Orson writhed slightly, emitting a whimper of consciousness, of awareness to pain.

"And if I Take the girl," the beast was saying, "then what would we do?"

"I have some ideas. I think you should try her on for size. See for yourself what she's capable of."

"What about the bitch makes her a vessel befitting my talents?"

"She was borne of a Touched."

Without pause, the Taker said, "She's your daughter. So what? There are many Touched. It's no surprise they're stronger than any ordinary mortal, but that doesn't make her better suited to bear a burden as strapping as *mine*."

Birch grunted, tossing grains of dirt and sand at Orson to rouse him, hoping he didn't draw the attention of the Overseer and Taker looming above them on the stage.

Orson lifted his chin, coughed once—though softly, and the pair overhead didn't notice—and turned to face Birch. His face was besmirched with grit, but was otherwise unharmed.

Freed of the restless spell that arrested him, Orson immediately took in the scene, his eyes narrowing as he absorbed all that had come to pass—Jezebel swaying higher above them, beaten and bleeding; the Overseer stripped bare, bristling with vitality, revived by his magics; Meredith unconscious, perhaps swimming through an abyss of nameless worries, guilt and forbearance; and the great beast, fully realized, brought into the waking, walking world of their Earth, primed for an attack, ready for a Taking. Lips narrowed, Orson pointed to the flames, toward the symbol that had conveyed the beast into their world.

Birch knew what Orson meant to do, but he wasn't sure how to help. He wracked his mind for solutions, watching helplessly as Orson launched off the ground, leapt onto the stage, and—with a disc of blinding light budding in his palms—staggered toward the beast.

The Taker turned on its loins in time to see its advancing foe, and lifted up its fist in self-defense. It crashed down onto Orson's head, but not before the powers Orson harnessed sprung from the well of his grip, shot up at the Taker, and carved a hole through its trunk. The beast lowered its head, peering down and through the crater cut from its chest, back toward the Overseer, whose jaw had come unhinged.

The demon slapped haphazardly toward Orson, skimming its knuckles against him.

Wobbling, Orson rose and addressed the Taker:

"This world's seen enough of hell. Go back below, and leave us all alone."

Shocked by Orson's declaration, the Taker (who was lowered to one knee, massaging its insides 'til they materialized again, as though nothing had happened at all) lifted up its fist, readying for another attack which was sure to hit its mark.

Orson ducked, covering his head, and waited for the inevitable, fatal bashing that was coming to him. But it never came. Instead, a snippet of Latin, screamed from far across the room, interrupted his pained grimace and drew his attention to its source.

Meredith. She had roused, and was lifting up one hand, screaming at the top of her lungs toward the Taker, shouting:

"DAEMONI

"HAEC SUNT MALA

"IN FUGAM

"RUMPE ANIMAM SUAM, IN NIHILUM

"PER TEMPUS ET SPATIUM."

The sigil began to glow with diffuse pink light, and a cloudy mist emerged which spiraled toward the demon, wrapping cottony tendrils of smoke tightly around its ankles, wrists, and neck, pulling it back toward the hellmouth from which it crawled. The flames which had abated lit up once more.

Though Birch was fading, he could feel the warmth of that fire against his face, and could see the great beast writhing against the pink smoke's touch, pulling back with all its might.

Jezebel rocked overhead, the chains holding her loosening as the Overseer wrenched at the handle that held her aloft, struggling to set her down before the Many-Named One disappeared. Perhaps he hoped their pact could still hold up— that the essence of Azazel, Satan, or Baphomet would not be dragged back to hell—if only its spirit could make its way quickly into Jezebel, to fill her with its vitriol. But the Overseer struggled in vain, and the first of the demon's legs disappeared into the porthole.

"No! No! No no no!" the Overseer screamed, abandoning his plight with the chains and running toward the beast, jumping onto its arm, latching against its bicep.

As the rest of it was pulled down through the hole, the beast swung up for Jezebel once more, but she was just beyond its reach. It dragged its palm angrily across the sand just beside the stage, and lifted up Orson instead.

The force of its grip squashed him, threatening to drag him under, into a gauze-lined hallway of tunnel vision and distorted hearing, where he could barely discern the pain he felt from the ambient sounds of the fire toward which he descended. All became one giant blend of suffering, a hellish nightmare from which he could not escape. But something dredged him back out of that muck, and saved him from resignation to a fate worse than death, where he'd have been damned to live in hell 'til his mortal passing, at which point he'd *still* go on with a pained, torturous, unliving existence—forever.

It was a force as turbulent as the beast's, but was also its antithesis. Whereas the leathery grip that bound Orson had a balmy, sinister power by its lightest touch—and an effluent stench hanging from every fold of its rotten skin—the beacon of light that summoned him back from the brink was cooling, sweet-scented, and soft. It was welcome; it was Jezebel.

Cut me down, it said. *Cut me free.*

As if propelled by the force of a geyser, Orson wriggled loose from the demon's grip, flapping his arms with all the strength he could muster. Just as the beast caught hold of one of his legs and threatened to drag him down, Orson screamed to Meredith, "Your blade! Throw me your blade!"

She did. It whizzed through the air and smacked against the stage, just out of Orson's reach.

Birch alighted, revived by the danger his ally faced, and aimed straight for the blade.

He lifted it up. It felt firm against his palm, snug and right. He hoisted it high and, without delay, drove the knife down against the demon's wrist. The Taker roared in pain, tongues falling from its mouth. Again, Birch lifted the tool and cut, hacking downward as though aiming at a stubbornly thick block of wood. Again and again, he lifted and crashed, wrecking the wrist of the vexed Taker, whose body had mostly been tugged below, up to the middle of its chest. With every blow, an arterial spray of impossibly frozen blood rained down from the wound, until finally all that remained of the spirit's tangible paw was a dangling, lurid mush.

Coated in the demon's carnage, Birch and Orson fell back against the stage, pushing themselves up on their elbows to crawl toward the far edge of the platform. They fell off and smacked against the sand, a welcome reprieve from the infernal torture they nearly endured.

Birch cackled, throwing sand into the air, savoring the feel of it as it stuck against his slick, wet skin. The last of the fiend was vanishing—a ridge of bone and the tip of one horn still glinting above the flames—along with something else. There too, pinned beneath its weight, was the Overseer, being flayed, torn apart, and ripped below. At the rim of the inferno, his human hands pried, fighting for a grip on the sawlogs of the stage, the skin dissolving away to display a skeletal, twitching hook, thinly coated with the last remnants of his muscles, of half-cooked meat dripping from the bone. As the ring of the gateway closed for good, cinching up in the blink of an eye, the Overseer was expelled from the Earth, leaving only the tips of two fingers behind; they rolled a foot across the stage, leaving behind a thin trail of mortal carnage.

The hand of the Taker, which Birch had severed, exploded into ash and smoke, but the pained, writhing fingertips of the Overseer did not abscond. They remained, a fresh reminder of their shared mortality, and a reassurance that they had succeeded in assuaging that great evil, which had so nearly threatened to destroy the world—or, at least, their beloved Jezebel.

Meredith lowered her daughter down, who was barely conscious and badly beaten, her face swollen with the lashings she'd been dealt, and yet smiling through her suffering—a hopeful, gummy grin, because she knew what her rescue meant.

Orson helped to untie the chains, which were stubbornly jammed (the links seemingly melded together by the extreme heat that the damned one had produced). He gathered a bundle of white energy through the tips of his fingers and—lovingly, gently—coated the length of the chains with it. The diffuse burn of his touch did the trick, bending and melting the metal to nil, lickety-split.

Jezebel lifted her wrists up to her face, glaring at them through her puffy eyelids like a myopic rambler—the old fool, whose wanderings under the abiding sun stripped him of his sight—and rubbing them in succession with her palms. Meredith coated her shoulders with caresses 'til her daughter acknowledged her being there, and they embraced in a heartfelt hug: a long, forceful embrace which Birch and Orson admired.

Birch, in fact, felt tears rising hot through his face. His cheeks burned with something new—half embarrassment, half excitation. It was an exotic sensation, sweet as a first kiss, but perhaps most like the feeling he had when he first saw the man—Meredith's husband, Peter—lying pained against the boardwalk, dying: it was a sense of knowing, of foreshadowing, of changes 'round the bend. But those changes would be for the best; he knew that much for sure.

He approached Jezebel, who'd settled against the sand and was rubbing her ankles to bring back the flow of blood.

"I'm sorry," Birch said.

She looked up, her lips half-parted in what might have been assent (but could just as easily have been a demurral). Something in her raised eyebrows hinted at optimism, as opposed to anger.

He waited a moment to see if she would speak, *if* she could speak. When she didn't, he said, "You don't have to say anything right now. But I mean it. I'm so, so sorry. We shouldn't have left you alone."

That's not what you're really apologizing for, is it? It jumped into his head with such brevity and force as to shock him from his stance.

"No, there's a lot more that I'm sorry for, too. Things I haven't admitted to any of you, yet."

You don't have to explain it to me.

"But I think you should know. Probably, it would be important to you."

I know all I need to know. You saved me in the end.

"Yes, but…" Birch gazed back over his shoulder. Orson was regarding them, but took Birch's gaze as a hint and walked away, to confer with Meredith.

You didn't ever have to tell me, Jezebel said. *I could feel it in you from the moment we met. You're something special, and so am I. We are connected.*

"For a moment there, I considered breaking faith, turning against the group. I mean, I wouldn't have—not ever. But I thought about it."

To this, she didn't respond. She seemed to stare up at him with empathy, a knowing grin spreading wider on her face to reveal her blood-encircled teeth.

"The only thing I don't understand is why he didn't call me sooner. I might have already saved you from this hell, a long time ago." Birch sighed heavily.

"Perhaps," Jezebel said, her actual voice much more solid than it should have been, more resolved that the voice of a young woman who'd just been badly tortured, chained to a board. "But it doesn't matter. It doesn't—" Her voice quavered momentarily. She stood up as best she could, leaning against the remaining splinters of the crumbled stage. "It doesn't matter what might have been. We have each other now."

Birch's lips quavered with feeling. He took her in his arms, savoring the feel of her breath against his chest, warm and alive. He considered mentioning the beach all those years ago, where their fates first intertwined, but settled against it. The notion that another dispiriting revelation might sever their cozy bond was enough to quell his pangs of compunction.

Later, he promised himself, and then wondered if she'd heard, perhaps even hoping that she had. Somehow, partly, he knew that she already knew, and that all would be okay.

Orson and Meredith approached them. She looked saddish, even though they'd survived, as if awaiting some dreadful news. Orson was equally discomfited, his arms crossed and mouth pursed.

"So," Orson said, biting his lower lip. "What do we do now?"

They glanced back and forth at one another. No one said a word until Jezebel broke the silence. It was, after all, her call; it was her word that would determine how they made their next move.

"Now we leave," she said. "We move on."

Birch nodded and added, "Orson met some people who were Touched, too. They might be due some reckoning yet."

"That's true," Orson said. "But first we should look through the compound. There might be some things worth knowing, buried deep in all the books."

"I already know most of them by heart," Jezebel said. The pained expression she'd borne earlier, when speaking to Birch, had mostly dissolved. Now she spoke with calm resolve: purposefully, determinedly. "Except for the ones the Overseer kept locked away—the ones that inspired all *this*."

"The ones he used to kill all those people back in San Francisco," Birch added.

"And give you those wings," Orson said.

"That, too." Birch lowered his gaze.

Something kept them from action—some unspoken knowing which they all shared, yet none of them could articulate it.

"We should burn them," Meredith said. Her sadness was replaced with smoldering conviction, almost madness. "Burn them all. Every book, every last scrap. And level the walls 'til there's nothing left but rubble on the sand."

"Now hold on," Birch said. "What if there are other Overseers out there, administering their own crazed plans? There might be knowledge here that would help us to stop another crisis—"

"For as much good as might come from looting this place, at least twice as much bad would come of it. Can't you feel the evil still burnt into these halls? Another fiasco like this and we're done for." Meredith pointed back at the stage. Her finger slowly drifted back against her side. She stared into space for a long while, until she finally came to a resolution. "I'll tell you what, I'm done with it."

"What do you mean?" Orson asked.

Meredith turned to her daughter, ignoring Orson's question. She smiled, sadly, and tears rose up.

"You don't have to worry," Jezebel said. "I'll be fine."

"Can't you come with me?" Meredith asked.

"You know I can't, mom." The last word was spoken with emphasis, crowded with import.

They hugged, and Meredith turned to address them again:

"I still say we burn it all. And then we go our separate ways."

"But you're family!" Birch screamed. "You can't just walk away."

"That's true. But we'll never *really* be apart. Jezebel and I are linked, joined in a way that few mothers are lucky enough to be. If she needs me, I'll come."

Jezebel nodded.

"Besides," Meredith added. "She's got a new family with you."

Birch smiled, and turned to face his sister. Her eyes were equal parts his and her mother's—the right was gray, yet not unkind, full of warmth and deep as a cloud-rimmed sky; the left was soaring, azure blue.

Orson stood by wordlessly, looking less than enthusiastic.

"I meant both of you," Meredith said, nodding to Orson. "Family has many meanings. The three of you can come up with your own definition of what it means for you."

Jezebel folded Orson's hand up in her own.

—

They burned it down, leveled the whole thing. The ash off the books they set alight was dark, bubbling green, auguring the fates they might have met, should they have read the words scrawled there. The walls fell easily and, though Jezebel could no longer fly, she did her own part, flattening hallways with a single touch, stoking the fire that finally finished off the compound.

All of them stood in a line atop the highest dune outside the crumbling, dwindling grounds, watching as the final whispers of smoke sizzled off the sand, rising to meet a moonless sky—a beginning.

All the desert's wolves howled up at once, greeting the promise of the unsullied sky; and the scorpions lifted up their backs, pincers primed, stingers pointed forward, steeled in a proud display of their strength; and the spiders spun fine-threaded homes with which to catch any who might threaten their small, spirited resolve; and the snakes hissed; and the beetles shook together their fine-molded wings with an aggregate hum like a thousand shakers full of rice; and the turtles stuck their heads out of their shells to raise a silent psalm. Every animal delighted in the spirit of the night, and then lay haste for future days, turning back to the contrivances of their quotidian stratagems—burrowing holes, hunting their quarry, building their nests, or simply aiming to remain alive 'til the next hollow moon.

Meredith's journey would draw her westward, toward personal absolution.

For the others, it would be a different kind of wandering, of striving for significance, of building their own definitions for love and kindness; it meant finding a niche, building a community, their own compound. At first, it would be a tribe of three, a triad. In time, they might find others who shared their gifts— people who'd been blessed by birth or circumstance, and who needed their guidance. On the other hand, there might be those like the ones who'd Touched Orson—or worse, like the Overseer himself. Should they meet anyone like that, it would mean new battles, to mete out any threat. Until then, though, they'd be one another's succor, reveling in a closeness none of them had felt before—fulfilled and sustained by turns.

CHAPTER XXXII

Window down, wind in her hair. Meredith cruised. Westward, like before.

She'd returned to see her old neighborhood first. It left her feeling numb, beat up, with a kind of regret akin to when she'd given Jezebel up. None of the old neighbors remained. Perhaps they'd moved away because of all the trouble she and her mom had caused, shouting and such. Or perhaps they'd been freaked out by her mother's sudden disappearance, a phenomenon none of them could explain (none of them remembered a struggle; they only found ashes on the yard, strange burn marks scattered around the garage, and a few seemingly mislaid giant feathers). There were still a couple of **FOR SALE** signs around, but none on the lots of people whose names she could remember.

The Robertsons were gone, as were their church mates the Smiths. It was probably for the best. As far as Meredith was concerned, nothing good came of that town. Better to be out and wandering, living free.

A vagabond. A troubadour, whose song was her story.

A scavenger—that's what some might call her. She didn't care, though. Begging didn't bring her down. She'd been conditioned to beg before, and these circumstances were a lot less dismal than the ones in which she'd previously pleaded.

With a rental (a beet-red truck, no less) and enough gas to *just* make it, she'd set out from Tucson, across the highway's dry and dusty veins, as a lone cell of brooding life looking for answers, or at least a bit of peace. All the little details she had somehow absorbed back then, even in her half-groggy sleep, had hit her in turns—like the invisible bite of some hidden insect who'd crawled up her dress. The campgrounds. The border. The radio.

A song came on, a rock 'n' roll classic. Its lyrics filled her with optimism, yet also served as caution against the unknown: against whatever spoor drew her further on by its scent. The sound of the music devolved to a blur, smudged behind the gauze of her reminiscence, but its message still came through, clearly enough.

Just like all those years ago, she traced the last of that hushed pathway through the witching hour, with dead and dusty rocks sleeping by the roadside as her only speechless company.

The fading sounds of the radio crooner dissolved into a more mournful ballad, something about cats aspiring after their own fathers' ambitions—and about the moon. She looked up at it, a waxing half-quarter whose subtle indentations and shaded crannies brought burnt toast to mind (perhaps she was just hungry—and a little burnt, herself); it was nearing its descent toward the western horizon.

To the east, the crumbling landscape was beginning to show signs of the sun's rising gaiety: tendrils of quiet violet dissolving by gradient into blaring yellow at the edge of the far earth. It warmed against her sleepless cheeks, and she rejoiced in its significance:

Almost there.

The highway traffic picked up and Meredith tuckered in, gauging her mileage to estimate if she'd make it, if she got stuck in rush hour. Thankfully, it wasn't a problem. She pulled off the expressway and onto a narrow stretch of freeway; it ran parallel to the west coast's most mundane few miles, and its crowning glory was the wheel.

Above all the gray, standing tall over the condos which hadn't changed— except that they perhaps were a little grimier, a little more in need of some high pressure cleaning—was the ferris wheel, the commander of the boardwalk and the emblem of the horrors she once faced.

A wheel spinning over itself, over and over, 'til it finally came crashing down, tumbling walls, ripping the door off its hinges.

Her foot weighed a bit heavier on the gas pedal as she moved past the boardwalk, where she'd once seen a gaggle of mindless officers tending to a geek-faced teenager who'd seen it all, who foretold the inception and conclusion of her journey. No one stood there today; only a couple of jalopies sat idly by, one a rusted gray and the other a telling, vibrant pink.

As she continued along that uneasy road, The Peach Pacific closed in on her, rising like a revolting neon tidal wave and filling her with disquietude. A montage of horrific images pulsated through her mind: blood dripping off the tip of a kitchen knife; Peter's face, sunken in, a mass of gnarled bone and gray roughage; a group of old men, their distended guts pressing against her and their peters poking her. Some of that had happened. Most of it. The rest was as impactful *as* the real, and equally dissuaded her against continuing on her path. But she wouldn't turn around. She couldn't. She promised herself she'd come here, to retrace her steps—to relive those moments, and to put to rest any culpable thoughts she still held onto from back in those days. Like a rotting corpse, which she kept locked away in her closet, it was too important—to her legacy, her historicity—to bury without closure. She needed to be free of it, to expunge its memory by facing it completely and truly. Only then could she see herself as a realized, responsible woman, free of errancy and its burden.

She parked the truck in the same spot as before and sat, thinking. Inside, she could see an equally oafish attendant was working the desk. He had a shaved head, with a ring of fuzz overgrown around the perimeter of his skull like a bird's nest; his clothes were too tight, his belly pushing out against the sheath of his t-shirt, bubbling over the waistline of his board shorts.

As she left the truck and walked toward the office, the gravel already felt hot against her soles, even through the inch-thick foam of her sandals. The sky was incalculably clear, idyllic, the apotheosis of summer.

"Is Room 210 available?" she asked, startling the porter, who nodded and smiled a gummy smile, scratching the top of his head and sending flakes drifting through the air, across the counter.

All the vases were still there, clumsy giant ceramics painted by an awkward, untrained hand. She wandered to the concessions and took a free donut and a sip of orange juice—

After all, she told herself, *beggars can't be choosers*.

445

The man—whose name tag dubbed him Omar—ushered her out the double doors, up the stairs, and to the same derelict room as before. She wondered about his conscientiousness and care in handling her only bag. No one had offered to carry their load on her last visit.

"Thank you," she said. "I'm wondering, do you know what time the boardwalk opens?"

He nodded, pursing his lips like a bashful child, afraid to speak.

"Well, what time?" she asked, not unkindly, pushing her bag back with her foot, into the darkness of the room behind her.

"Tane o'cloak," Omar said. His speech was thick, and impeded by a cleft palate and lip which she hadn't noticed before—because he was careful to angle his face away from her, to show himself only in three-quarter profile, where the disfigurement could barely be seen.

She smiled warmly at him, unfazed, and stuck out her hand.

"Thank you," she said, again.

He extended his arm slowly, cautiously, and limply shook her hand. When the moment had passed and he was freed, the porter curled inward and walked off, head sloped down under the forward arch of his spine.

In the quiet of the room, Meredith unpacked her belongings: well-worn camisoles and tattered brassieres; a little change purse which was stuffed to capacity (it currently held twenty-six dollars and thirty-three cents in ones, quarters, nickels, and pennies); a photo of Peter, which she'd printed from the video of their drive across the state—toward The Peach Pacific and his final restless night. It was a little blurry, distorted by the motion of her clumsy hand, but it served its purpose. It reminded her of his deep affection, and was perhaps the last thread of physical evidence that still implored her further—backward, as it were—on her quest.

The carpet had long been replaced. Nevertheless, she traced the aspect of its shape, searching for a feeling of the moments that had passed: when she bludgeoned his skull, when she smashed in his face. Finding none, she moved into the kitchenette and crawled across the cramped tiles, on the hunt for a speckle of lingering blood—under the mini-fridge, at the seam where carpet and kitchen met, and even on the tips of all the knives.

Nothing, she thought, and reminded herself why she was there: *To forgive yourself.*

To move on.

She took a quick shower, her first in over a week, reveling in the feeling of purity it brought as she squeegeed the water from her squeaky-clean hair. She sniffed her own armpits, smiling at the absence of odor, a simple delight.

With a tank top, shorts—though these were less holey than the ones from before, and more modest by far—and her trusty flip flops on, Meredith set out the front door. She checked for her room key (dangling from the same chipped, laser-etched diamond of plastic) and bounded across the nearly vacant parking lot, across the highway, and off toward the boardwalk. It was a long stroll, and provided her the respite she needed before she faced the unknown. Sterile remnants of humanity flickered by in her periphery—plastic bags winding on the wind, plastic bottle caps settled against the dirt. Cigarette butts and mascara wands. Waste and vanity.

Every step closer to the boardwalk meant a greater sense of dread, a tighter knot in the pit of her stomach. The ferris wheel grew taller above her, threatening to topple with every subtle wind, as though it had saved itself for her, waiting quietly for the moment of her return, when it could finally take her down with it in a suicidal collapse. A kamikaze big wheel. She laughed, in spite of herself, and part of the tautness within her dissipated, the collywobbles set straight.

At the boardwalk, it felt as though all the creeps of the coast had gathered to rest off their late night buzz, and they'd just risen to face the burgeoning hangover of living. A threesome of punks, decked out in leather and spikes, stumbled in her direction, reeking of booze and sex; they brushed against her shoulder. She was inclined to thoughts of bathing again, but reproached herself. *You're just the same.* Wandering, searching, finding herself.

Meredith drew in a heavy breath and pushed forward, past derelict shops lit with half-ruined neon lights, whose messages were no longer clear:

WE COME: OSCAR'S ODD ES, OBS UR   & ABERR   ;

THE MAJE   MARI   SEE AL ;

DINAH ALL-YOU-   EAT DO   ONE FRE RID TICK .

She managed to find one open vendor, a cotton candy stand. Even though it was her only choice, she felt somehow fortunate, as though her purchase of the pimply kid's goods was bound to kismet. The sweetness was fortuitous indeed, and did much to soothe her boundless anxieties, to quieten her questions, to be satisfied to live.

So far there were no answers there. Anything might have happened to Peter, and it mightn't have even happened there.

She wandered along the uneven planks of the walkway, toward the outthrust of the pier, and settled against its damp surface to let her legs dangle below her; she appreciated the gentle burn of the salted mist against her bare legs and face, and the caw of the ravenous gulls overhead. She threw the last puff of her sweets to them and watched them battle over it, wondering simultaneously if they should eat it, and if it would mean the difference between life and death for one or some of them. The runt of the group had already lost an eye before, and walked with a subtle limp—like a pathetic but lovable orphan. Its bark was more muted cough than battle cry, and she suddenly wished (by the deepest traces of her maternal instinct) that she had another stick of the air-spun sugar she'd so carelessly tossed.

The kid was watching her from up the coast, a white stick standing out against the blue of the sky—holding his dorky paper hat in place against the wind, pinning it to his orange-haired head with one hand. She waved up to him, but he ignored her salute and turned away, to stare off into space.

Meredith thought of Jezebel. She settled onto a bench, wracked and wondering after the well-being of her only kin. She stamped shut her eyes and mouth, clenching a marble-shaped gobbet down her dry throat as she turned and pointed her focus inward, to the place at the tip of her interior, but also just beyond her corporal being (a kind of ill-defined schema—equal parts tactile and abstract feeling). It was a realm she seldom visited anymore, and a part of her being which she hated to call upon: full of raving gales that weren't easily traversed. She pushed aside the thoughts clouding her prescience and drew into focus an image of her child, though she was no longer that. Jezebel had become a woman.

There they were—Jezebel, Birch, and Orson—living much as Meredith was: by the skin of their teeth, in ramshackle tenements with cold, concrete floors, squatting and wandering, questing.

Birch's wings were bound up with masking tape and strapped tightly to his back; he wore a thick canvas jacket to soften its shape. He'd also grown a beard, which served to offset his more feminine features, lending him a far less androgynous look than he'd sported before, but his long hair was still bound up in a knot on the top of his skull.

Orson had filled out with brawn, and was doing his best to keep himself groomed. Whereas Birch was sporting a Vandyke, Orson maintained what appeared to be only a day or two's worth of stubble. There was something new, something special and bristling, about the way he held himself. Before, he'd been little more than a maladroit clod, scurrying with his tail wagging behind him, struggling to keep up with Jezebel. Now he was sanguine, glowing with self-assurance; his shoulders were raised in horizontal decisiveness. He could very well have grown to become their leader.

And then there was Jezebel. All Meredith could say for sure was that she was sheltered, in good company, and happier than she'd ever been. In all the years Meredith had spent spying from the shadows—during which time she'd observed her daughter grow from pliant disciple to dissatisfied dissident to brave deserter—she had never seen her display so much joy. It was there in the nuance of her mouth, the way it curved upward and affected her eyes with a slight pinch—of genuine contentedness. It was there also in the physical gestures of her body, holding hands with the boys, tilting easily back in her chair, occasionally lifting a palm to twirl at a strand of her hair.

Meredith withdrew from the vision, back to the scene of the starving seagulls, and was left with a feeling of vacancy, with the realization that her daughter didn't need her anymore (in fact, had seldom needed her, if at all). She only hoped that she'd done the best she could by Jezebel: by setting her free, by calling her back, by meting out the Overseer's harsh punishment.

The one-eyed gray-mantled runt wobbled to her feet, staring up at her imploringly, almost judgmentally.

"I'm sorry," she told the gull, uncertain whether it was tears or sea mist that burned in her eyes.

It squawked up at her, but its forlorn cry dissolved into a throaty rasp before it could complete any more judgments.

Overcome with unexpected rage, Meredith swatted the bird away with her foot. It drove its open-mouthed, heavy bill for her flesh, but missed by an inch. She shouted at it, "Go away!" and retreated for the boardwalk, stamping a fitful pace back up the stairs, over weed-covered dunes, past the kid spinning sugar for his second customer of the day, and across the now-teeming freeway.

Safe in the company of man, away from that vacuum of murk and shadow, Meredith slowed her breath. She rotated on her heels to survey the scene once more: the crumbling timber; the weary, untamed jetty bobbing on the tide; the towering rounded erection of the ferris wheel—at once a symbol of the puerile, careless joys of youth and the inescapable, recurrent seasons of life.

She was somewhere in the middle of all that, teetering mindlessly between having been born and plummeting headlong toward the abyss of death. But Meredith's was a path not limited by others—especially not now, in the cold desolation of that place, and in the realizations which revisiting it had brought her.

She was free to go and do as she pleased. In the clarity of that knowing, she resolved to leave that place—the bathetic sea, The Peach Pacific, the forced remembrance of days gone by—for good. Perhaps for somewhere quiet, away from all the sound and tumult. A silent wood, an isolated cottage, where the company of deer was welcome and that of man was not. She envisioned it, smiling with fondness at the image she convoked: a coven of one, to learn and to live. She'd never been much for fellowship and, besides which, could always call out to Jezebel, if the need for human interaction arose.

Perhaps happiness wasn't an idyll found in others, not for Meredith.

Maybe she'd find it in the quiet whisper of wind between trees, and in the lapping of a small brook's tongue against smooth stones lined neatly beneath its surface, and in the wisdom of introspection, of grounded reflection. Some day, that might change again—she might suddenly feel the need for sex, for passion, for love. If that day came, she'd reconsider her choice to leave the world behind. But until then, she would resolve to decamp from society and live off the land—using the survival tools she'd acquired from her long stay with the Order, perhaps their greatest gift to her.

Meredith checked out early from The Peach Pacific, after she took a quick nap and one last shower.

She drove the truck back to the nearest rental office, walked far to the bus station, and booked a ticket to the most remote, quiet state she could think of. On the ride there, on a bus she had all to herself, she dreamed peaceably—of lying in the shade on soft grass, with her hair sprinkled throughout it, grown long and wild as a horse's mane.

That would be her peace. It would be her happiness.

CHAPTER XXXIII

Days drew into weeks, into months, and then into years—a comfortable blur of wandering and learning, together. Jezebel blossomed into a full-bosomed woman— one whom Orson couldn't keep his eyes off of. It was only a matter of time before they commenced their shy relationship—privately plodding through the motions, courting her in the dark, caressing her inner thigh, and finally taking her virginity with a sweet-scented moan of pleasure parting damp across her lips. They carried on in that vein, happy for one another's company, not feeling the need to name what they were up to.

Birch began to notice, though: Orson sneaking a touch of her neck from behind, when he thought Birch wasn't looking; the way they sometimes fell into fits of groundless laughter, at jokes Birch never understood. He felt excluded, but was happy to see his sister getting the fair attention of Orson, a deserving suitor.

Jezebel started to notice a bump swelling under her shirts, and all the telltale signs that came along with it—ones she'd read about, but never imagined she might experience herself.

Craving odd foods. *Almond butter smeared across waffles, with sugary-sweet cereal sprinkled on top.* Check.

Mood swings unlike any she ever had before. The end of her monthly cycle. A sharp spike in her sex drive, as though she couldn't get enough of Orson's hands and face down there. Check. Check. Check.

She imagined herself burping her child—hopefully a baby boy with fat, rosy cheeks and ringlets of soft, orange hair—and smiled. Still, she couldn't find the courage to broach the topic with Orson. She feared what he might say.

It's not safe for a child.

We can't afford to feed another mouth.

What if something happens to it? I couldn't live with myself.

She knew him well enough—even without the extra dose of prescience she seemed to have gained with the onset of pregnancy—to know he would say all that. And he'd be right, too.

She weighed her options. Find the means for an abortion, give the child away, or have it. Choosing any one of the three would be a start, a fully accountable start. But instead, she hid her belly, invading the boys' wardrobes for frumpy t-shirts emblazoned with the logos of brands she'd never heard of. They did the trick, for a while.

As her stomach swelled, Jezebel did her best to ward off Orson's advances (they increased in frequency, as though he could smell the bond of parenthood growing quietly between them, and in response craved more comfort, more romance, within her). Strangely, when she rebuffed him, he surrendered straight away—always the gentlemen, he was. Still, a little persistence might have paid off. His submission pained her with guilt over the announcement she withheld, and so she decided she'd have to say something—and soon.

The night she settled on spilling the beans was a quiet one. They'd been squatting in the same place for a month—a three-story brick tenement whose walls smelled faintly of mold, and whose floors were persistently damp, to the point that they could never remove their shoes, unless they wanted to risk damp socks and feet (or worse, ringworm). Jezebel stoked a fire at the center of their open-roofed room on the top floor of the building. It was quiet there, no one harassed them, and they were free to do their own thing; writing in their journals, intuiting the mood of their surroundings.

Orson sat alongside Jez and—because Birch was nowhere to be found—freely stroked her thighs, surveying the feel of their flexed mass as she squatted, rotating the cans labeled *Frijoles Negros* which they'd tied to a stick and propped above the flames. They were almost ready to palaver, a nightly tradition of sharing stories, dreams, aspirations, and any intuitions they might have had about their next move.

As was the case with most of their long talks, Birch was running late. He was never a huge fan of beans, but—if he didn't arrive soon—he might be left with nothing at all to eat.

On cue, Birch fell through the hollow doorframe, just in time for the doling of the first bowl. He was laughing, and mumbling something under his breath. Before Jezebel could ask what he was on about, she saw the answer to her question. Following in tow were two people—kids, really—a young girl, covered in dirt, and an older boy whose sparsely prickled face suggested he was in his late teens. They were undoubtedly related, as was evident by the wide, knowing eyes they shared— deep wells of white set on their grimy mugs, punctuated by identical primrose irises, at once soft and harsh. They also shared the same deeply jarring, furry brows which lent an expression of careful reflection to their eyes.

Ushered on by Birch, they entered and gaped at Jezebel and Orson, as though in fear of predatory animals who might attack without warning.

"Hello," Jezebel said, struggling to stand against the growing weight of her paunch. "I'm Jezebel." She smiled forcibly, fighting off the voice of Orson in her head, reminding her of what she already knew (*more mouths to feed, more danger in numbers*), pushing him out of her mind so the kids could feel a genuine, warm welcome.

The moment her hand interlocked with the boy's, she knew he was something special. Yet she couldn't quite decipher the nature of his skills. Whatever gifts he possessed, and how he'd acquired them, were barred from her knowing.

He nodded and smirked, as if he felt Jezebel prying in his mind.

"I'm Adam. That's Diana." His voice crackled when he said his sister's name, betraying the trace of hesitancy he tried to bury under his cordial smile. This was a young man who'd grown up too fast—much as Jezebel had—and whose sole mission in life was to protect his sister. Against whatever force had rendered them this way, Touched and abandoned.

Maybe they weren't abandoned, Orson thought, at the center of Jezebel's mind. She regarded him and he continued, lips arced downward in a doubtful frown: *They might be bad news. They might be a trap.*

"That's Orson," Jezebel said. "He's a little suspicious, but don't mind him."

Orson lurched backward at her imprecation and moved to speak, but stammered through his words. He ended up doing little more than stuttering: "I-I-I'm sorry."

"It's okay," Adam said, "I understand your suspicions. I'd be worried if you weren't at least a little skeptical. We're homeless. People like us have to do everything we can to survive."

Jezebel gnawed at her lower lip and regarded her own brother across the room, standing behind the newcomers. He was beaming, hands on his hips, proudly regarding his find. They were, after all, the first Touched they'd met since they left the desert some four years ago. Up until the point that Birch had walked them through the door, Jezebel had been growing increasingly doubtful of the existence of any others like them. Still, at the deepest parts of her, she had always hoped for this. More than wishing, she had also always kept an open mind, prodding through the muck of other peoples' thoughts on the highways they traversed—crawling across the country, awaiting the familiar glow of someone like them, Touched.

But she hadn't picked up on these kids at all. At no point during their stay in the ruins of that old, dusty town—a stay which had already been longer than their usual day-long stopover—had she detected the presence of other Touched. But here they were, young and sprouting power.

"I found them under the highway," Birch said. "About a mile back. They were curled up under a ratty old blanket leaning face-first into a fire pit taller than it should have been. Cold night like this, I knew right away there was something going on."

Jezebel nodded, approving of what Birch had done in bringing them home to their fold.

"You mentioned survival," Jezebel said, nodding at the boy, Adam. "With us, you won't have to worry about that. We get by."

Adam's little sister tugged on his tattered shirt sleeve. He leaned low so she could whisper in his ear.

Jezebel caught every word:

How do we know we can trust them?

"You can," Jezebel said. "Trust us, I mean."

The girl looked shocked, but the blow quickly settled into further speculation as she drew up toward Jezebel, sauntering with all the startling scrutiny of a proper banshee, lip snarled and giant eyes squinted.

"Diana, right?" Jezebel asked, lowering herself onto her heels to face the little girl. Up close, the dirt smeared across her face revealed itself to be ashes. "How'd you get covered in this stuff?" She smeared her finger across the girl's brow and uncovered the milky, soft complexion buried underneath—a streak of white which stood out as starkly as the gleaming sclera of her eyes.

"Adam makes fires," the little girl said. It was a simple statement, but it meant a lot. The sound of her voice was like springtime sprinklers spraying against skin. The tone of it was all cotton, soft and guiltless, without lies.

"Can you show us?" Orson asked, moving closer.

Diana looked up at her brother and nodded.

He sighed.

"It's okay, you can trust us," Jezebel repeated.

Adam drew in a heavy breath, held it, and lifted up his arms. Speckles of soot drifted off of them. He reached down to hug Diana, and he whispered something into her ear that Jezebel couldn't pick up.

Diana took a broad step back from her brother and stood to face him. She kept her hands locked securely against her sides, where the denim of her dirty jeans blended into the flesh of her palms. Dirt on dirt, skin on cloth, one indiscernible from the next.

Suddenly Adam was floating, suspended in the air above them and twirling in place, his legs locked solid as a board below him. As he gained height, arms raised higher, his fingertips trembled with the burden of his task and blood rushed to his cheeks, staining them pink even through the grunge guarding them. Relaxed as a napping kitten, Diana closed her eyes while Adam soared—weightless, turning by the mechanisms of his sister's influence.

She set him down lightly and opened up her eyes, turning to face Jezebel, Orson, and Birch with those bushy-eyed brows of hers raised upward in expectation.

Birch and Orson stared, jaws hanging slack.

Jezebel broke the silence with a genuine round of applause.

"Bravo!" she shrieked.

Diana jumped in place, delighted by the ovation she received.

Her brother smiled, beside himself, and scooped her into his arms. He planted a wet kiss on her cheek which broke apart the ghosts of cinders gathered there. Slowly, the quiet girl became human again, a child, freed of the mask that guarded her.

Birch clapped his hand against Adam's back and said, "Now show them *your* shtick."

The boy smiled, snapped his fingers, and a single, flickering flame bounced up from the tip of his index finger. His eyes burned like orange coals as he quietly admired his own pyrotechnics. The flame rose higher than the tops of their heads, up toward the torn-open roof and the eddying clouds above.

It must have risen four feet above them before Diana had enough. She collapsed to the ground sobbing, and a trickle of blood escaped from her nostrils, dripping across her lips. She wiped away the blood and stumbled back to her feet, pulling up alongside Adam to tug at his shirtsleeves again.

Adam looked down and was quietened by his sister's pitiful state; the infernal wink in his eyes diminished, replaced by the pacific hue they'd held before. He quelled the flame, smashing his finger against the center of his palm; it sizzled out like spit on a grill.

Jezebel helped pat Diana's face dry with a rag from her pack and lifted the girl's face to tell her, "You're okay."

Diana squirmed away and ran to hide behind her brother's trunk. Gone was the ball-breaker they'd just met; she was wet behind the ears and bashful to boot.

"She gets this way sometimes," Adam said. "When I use the flame. It reminds her of our father."

Jezebel reflected then on her own dad—the Overseer, whose true name she never came to know—and wondered if they harbored the same contradictory feelings for theirs as she did for hers. Hating him, missing him, wishing she'd known him sooner. Wishing she could have changed him. Saved him.

She didn't pry. Still, she could sense there was something the girl was holding back.

"What is it?" Jezebel asked, and the girl peeked out from behind the cover of her brother's legs. "Is there something else, Diana?"

457

Pensively, she came out of hiding, and her melon-sized eyes appraised Jezebel timidly, feeling for her character and checking for signs of spoilage, of violence, or any other evils. Diana seemed to settle again on trust toward her new companions, and sighed.

"What is it?" Jezebel asked again, gently touching Diana's chin. "You can tell me."

Diana wrenched her own palms against the front of her shirt, drawing the fabric up into a ball which she twisted left and right. She lowered her eyebrows in dismay and whispered, "Don't wanna say."

"It's okay, you can tell us."

Diana blurted it out, a child whose secrets can no longer be kept: "You're having a baby. And *your* brother likes *mine*."

Jezebel clenched up—teeth grinding, elbows and knees locking—at the girl's shrewd, or perhaps extrasensory, awareness.

Orson's mouth shot open, and he moved from consideration (eyes floating around the room, not settling on any one person or specific minutiae of their setting) to unrestrained joy (jumping up and down, leaping across the space to scoop Jezebel into his arms and shower her with kisses).

"Is it true? Tell me it's true!" Orson begged. He set her down and crouched to one knee, lifting his hands up in a prayer-like salute, toward his patron saint of adoration, Jezebel.

"Yes," Jezebel confirmed. Then, nervously, she said, "If you're okay with it."

"Are you kidding? Of course I am! A baby! We're going to have a baby." His gaze drew inward. "There's so much to do—a name, a proper home. No more of this wandering around. We need to settle down, white-picket fence style."

The triumph of the news deflated, like a popped balloon dying with a hiss, careening out of control.

"We can't do that," Jezebel said. "Especially not now."

"Can't do what?" Orson asked. "What do you mean?"

Jezebel responded by pointing toward the group: toward her brother Birch, and the newcomers, Adam and Diana.

Orson's slaphappy grin melted as he realized what she meant.

"There's still a lot to do," Jezebel said. "Now more than ever."

Orson nodded.

"We'll figure it out," Jezebel continued. "Besides, you don't really want the white-picket dream, do you? You're better than that cliché, and more interesting, too. Just because we never had that, it doesn't mean we have to give it to our child. We don't even know how it'll be born. Touched, or—I won't say *normal*— *Un*touched."

The heat of the other three staring at them weighed on Jezebel. She'd never been one for embarrassment, but the situation was thorny enough to inspire a trickle of doubt. After all, they were catching a very private discussion. Knowing the little one, Diana, might also intuit their deepest emotions—their most personal thoughts—had Jezebel further abashed, red cheeks and all.

"Enough of this," Jezebel said. "The secret's spilt, so let's move on to another unexpected announcement."

Orson sniggered and threw up a jocular wave. He and Jezebel stared at Birch, awaiting some response from him, an explanation or an admission.

Adam, meanwhile, busied himself with the backs of his own hands, brushing particles of dirt loose from the ridges of his knuckles, aloof and oblivious to their inquiry. It looked as though he might be hiding a dash of unease, though; he shuffled his feet, peeking up at intervals to check for Birch's response.

Diana—ever stoical—only stared, straight-faced, as the events unfurled.

Birch tightened and loosened his wings. It was a tic he'd picked up in recent months, and it always let the group know when he disagreed, was uneasy, or was hiding something (before, it had been a scrap of jerky he'd found on the trail; or a bit of whiskey he kept hidden for himself, left over in the flask at the bottom of his pack). He blushed through his scraggly stubble and adjusted the knot of bedraggled hair at the top of his head.

Adam, perhaps assured by Birch's silence (an almost cinched admission), approached his admirer and smiled at him, face to face. Despite the gap in their ages, they were almost exactly the same height; so, when Adam leaned in for a kiss, Birch had little room for retreat. It was a wet, full-mouthed smack, and Birch fell backward in response, wobbling comically in place for a second, arms flailing through the air 'til he hit the ground.

Jezebel rushed to her brother's side and, clenching his arm, helped hoist him back up. She whispered into his ear, "It's okay."

Birch sighed, and breathed with the unsteady breeze of someone trembling in fear.

Adam—all lithe and handsome—gripped Birch's other arm to help right him on the ground, but this did little to assuage the fright spreading over the winged one's face.

"I, uh—" Birch struggled for words. "I don't know what to say."

"You don't have to say anything," Orson said, and smiled. He approached Birch and gave him a hug.

They all settled down by the fire. Together, they feasted on scraps of food— savoring the few chunks of bacon buried in all the bean, sucking on the fat. They pretended they were kings and queens, reveling in one another's company.

Jezebel patted her belly, relieved she no longer needed to hide the child's existence from anyone, thinking, *Shame and secrets can't have helped you, little one.*

Orson retrieved the last can of beans from the stoke they were tied to, hands wrapped in soiled cloth to keep them from burning, thinking, *A child, a child, a baby boy or girl.* After their meal, he felt the baby kick against the inside of Jezebel's tummy and, for the first time, shed tears of joy.

Birch did his best to calm his nerves, breathing with focus as Jezebel had once taught them, *The Singular Method or something,* and though he hadn't spoken a peep since the little girl's exclamation, he was satisfied with his tacit admission and thought, *Glad they know, glad it's out.*

Adam reached out to hold Birch's hand, a clammy reminder of their fallible, mortal states. Even the Touched, the feathered, and the supermen were prone to fits of human feeling, to anxiety, to fear.

Diana was contented to watch, fulfilled by the great, open displays of affection occurring around her—by emotions she'd been conditioned to disbelieve existed anymore.

"How were you Touched?" Orson asked.

Adam and Diana looked at one another, hunching their shoulders in unison.

Jezebel added, "He means, how did you get your—special gifts?"

Adam was the one who answered, because Diana had withdrawn again (as she seemed so readily able to do, at the drop of a silent pin). He said, "Our father."

When Jezebel encouraged Adam to tell more, a wellspring of emotion erupted from Diana. She sobbed, chest heaving, tears streaming.

Adam calmed her down and continued, "He's like us. Gifted, or Touched, as you say. But in a bad way."

"A bad way?" Birch asked, and his hand slipped out of Adam's grip.

"Our mother took us away from him, because she said he was an evil man, that he did bad things to women. He—"Adam's voice caught in his throat.

"It's all right, tell us," Jezebel said.

"He cut people open. So he could become stronger. That's why our mother made us flee. She threw us away to fend for ourselves."

Jezebel and Birch exchanged knowing glances.

"He killed her," Diana said, punctuating the unspoken hunch. "After we escaped. I saw it happen in my head."

Adam stroked her knotted hair consolingly. He whispered something to her and she steeled herself, wiping the tears away in streaks of softened grime.

"No wonder you don't trust anyone," Orson said. "How long ago was this?"

"Just a few months. We've kept moving, running, since then. To keep safe, away from him. We hide under all the ash of the fires we burn. Birch was the first one to find us since then. Since we left our father behind."

A long hush settled on their camp as each of them contemplated the meaning of the kids' confessions.

"Where is he?" Jezebel asked.

Adam ensconced his sister, wrapping her up in his arms, and he asked, "Why?"

"Just tell us."

"North—" His eyes were prying into Jezebel, the lids soft with feeling, betraying the confidence he struggled to exude. His lips were still soft and full with youth, barely encircled by hair which was not much more than fuzz. "Northeast, near New York."

Jezebel looked toward her lover.

Orson took those two words like a punch in the gut—New York, the place of his past, where he'd faced and conquered his own demons. Most of them, but perhaps not all of them.

"If you let us, we'll take care of it," Jezebel said. "The world doesn't need another man like your father. Birch and I share a lot in common with you, and I'd love to tell you that story, tonight. Once you've heard it, I'll ask you to consider going back. Back to your father, in the Northeast. And if you agree, I can promise you—no harm will come to you."

After a spell of consideration, Diana nodded to Adam, and he nodded to Jez.

"Good," Jezebel continued. "Now settle in. No more tears—that's over. You're strong when you're with us. Always remember that. And remember that the world's not against us, if we do right by it. You won't have to live in fear, in shadows, covered in dust. Not anymore."

Jezebel smiled, a full-mouthed, face-splitting grin that her old friends thought looked a lot like Meredith's smirk. They dug back into the few scraps left of their beggarly meal, savoring each bite with daydreaming insouciance—Jezebel thinking of the fight before them, not fearing whatever might come; Birch imagining what his life might be like, now that he'd met someone like him, who could accept him and maybe even love him one day; Orson still reeling over news of the child steeping, growing inside of Jezebel.

They finished eating and Jezebel settled in, smoothing the hem of her oversized shirt against the growing aspect of her thighs. She told them the tale, as she'd promised, leaving no detail out. When she finished, she paused, looking to Adam and Diana for some word of assent.

In a way that their group would soon come to learn was so characteristic of the younger siblings, Diana and Adam stared wordlessly at one another, across the jumping blaze, their wily eyes full of hope and hazard as they held a silent communion, deciding on their course.

Adam, the spokesman of the pair, regarded Jezebel and said, "Okay. We'll go back."

www.ingramcontent.com/pod-product-compliance
Lightning Source LLC
Chambersburg PA
CBHW070857260626
47162CB00007B/2485